TEMPERATURES

TEMPERATURES

SUZANNE CRAIN MILLER

WINDING ROAD STORIES

NEW YORK   LOS ANGELES

Jacket design by Rejenne Pavon
Jacket Copyright 2023 by Winding Road Stories
Interior book design by A Raven Design
ISBN#: 978-1-960724-00-7 (pbk)
ISBN#: 978-1-960724-01-4 (ebook)

Published by Winding Road Stories
www.windingroadstories.com

*Dedicated to that little Pennsylvania girl,
laid to rest in South Caroline.
All my stories begin with you …*

"...the prevailing point of view in criminology seems to be that homicide is seasonal."

—*From Is Crime Seasonal? by Carolyn Rebecca Block, Statistical Analysis Center*

88°F

Hogue

We pull down the driveway and there it is—a bright yellow sign in the yard that tells me we're up for one hell of an afternoon. *Thank You Jesus* it reads. It's going to be a weird thing to walk by it on our way to bring her in. Seems like with what's gone on here, the sign would've been the first thing to get thrown out.

I'm already wondering if they're inside thanking Jesus right now. Are they thanking him for the early summer heat? Maybe they're thanking him that the mother's beautician had a long wait yesterday morning and that's what caused her to be in there three hours instead of two? Who needs three hours in a fucking beauty shop? Not that two wouldn't have been bad enough. We'd still be standing right here.

Don't matter. People with that kind of yard sign faith always find a way to be thankful, even when their lives are as fucked up as they can get. That's why they got the sign—a reminder. Helps them keep it uppermost in their minds that the Lord works in what they like to call *mysterious ways,* and they got no choice but to thank him.

"I hate these religious types," I remind Cobb right off before we exit the car.

He doesn't listen, just opens his door, gets out, starts walking up the sidewalk. Up on the porch, you can already hear a woman wailing and carrying on. Cobb's head hangs like a man knowing a fate he's met a hundred times without it getting any easier.

Had one of these cases last summer over in Johnston and the summer before that. Got me so I'm already dreading the end a spring every god damn year now. It's got me so I look in every backseat car window I pass on my way to go inside of just about anywhere.

Heard tell on the news of some app that's supposed to help parents remember to check in the back. Won't do no good. Ain't like anybody over this way's checking their phone for anything but TikTok or Snapchat. Downright pitiful what we need apps for now. Got to where our phone's having to help us so more people don't die. Fucking shame.

"I'll do the talkin', alright?" Cobb says.

"Hell, you ain't got to tell me twice."

After he knocks, we hear some scuffling around.

"Stop, now I mean it!" somebody shouts from the behind the door and then it opens.

A short lady peers out at us. Her face is all red, red as a Black woman's face can get, and she's got hot pink lipstick smeared to the side of her mouth.

"Mitchum," she greets Cobb, nodding to him.

"Hey Miss Florrie," he says back. "How you doin'?"

She bites her bottom lip, spreading lipstick to her front teeth.

"Well, I'm sure you know how I am. Don't mean no disrespect, but itn't nobody doin' too good if they're openin' the door to you."

Something about the way she says this makes me snicker before I can help myself. Cobb elbows me.

"This here's my partner, Cyrus Hogue." Cobb makes the introductions.

She opens the door a crack wider, eyes me.

"Afternoon, ma'am," I say real gentle like.

"Cain't say as I know him."

"Aww well, he's new. Come over from Johnston a few months back."

I wished he didn't feel the need to tell every damn soul that. Johnston County ain't got the best reputation. Seems like people get to thinking that if you come from a place like Johnston over to Lee County, you're on the bottle or a junkie of some kind. Nobody buys that I might just be going through a messy divorce, and I just might not wanna run into my ex-wife and her new boyfriend or his family everywhere I look.

We all three stand here, sweat beading on our foreheads, humidity pressing in. A small breeze flaps against that sign in the yard, but it's gone before it can help cool us at all.

"Y'all better come on in," she finally says softly, and I come close to hugging her cause I'm so damn sticky.

The entry way has still got pine paneled walls. Seems like every house I been in on this side of town has them. Creeps me out. Ain't no good reason you cain't paint those white or something.

Soon as I walk in and look up, there it is—a portrait of the good Lord himself. One of those real old-time ones with a plastic gold frame that you can just imagine Norman Bates picking out to hang in his hotel right over the rocking chair he rocks in while wearing his mama's dresses. Wonder if it ever bothers them that Jesus is always white in those pictures?

I let Cobb lead since he and this woman go back a ways. Soon as he saw the name on our dailies he like to bust out crying. Said he went to church with them and that he's known the family since he was a kid. I told him I didn't know they went to the same churches as we do. Said where I'm from, Sunday's the most segregated day of the week.

Cobb says his pastor was never much for anything racist. Believes the Lord holds everybody in the same esteem. Said the pastor's son runs services now, and he took after him. Always has made sure to go against hatred of any kind, that that's what Jesus would do. Ballsiest pastor I ever heard of. Ignorant but ballsy.

He made sure to tell me these are good people. I told him jails are full up with nothing but good people, to hear them tell it. Cell after cell of *good* people who claim they got themselves in a bad way.

We follow Miss Florrie down a long hall. Goes on forever. Feels like that endless stretch of highway between rest stops. We finally step into a kitchen. A woman's sitting up to a table with her head laid on top of her arms on it.

Wished I'd waited in the car. I could've. Sure as hell didn't sign up for all this today. Just supposed to be riding along, picking up a thing or two. My C.O.'s hell bent on my rehabilitation. Not sure why. Never has liked me much. Guess if a son of a gun like me comes back over to Johnston all reformed, it'll take some heat off him.

Miss Florrie walks over by the woman.

"Rae," Miss Florrie coos real gentle to her, rubbing her back slow. "Rae, the officers are here."

The woman shoots up, wide eyed like lightening just shot clear through the roof and jolted her awake. Odd to me she'd be asleep at a time like this. She's darker than her mama making the whites of her eyes even whiter. Her hair's done in those real tight rows that takes a long ass time. What she said about how long she was in the beauty shop is more believable now.

"Mama! You let 'em inside?" she starts hollering for all she's worth. "Why? Mama why?"

Miss Florrie don't answer. She bends over, slips her arms in around her, pulling her close, whispering. And whatever it is, Rae calms—a wild horse easing into the rope. She lets her mama help her rise to her feet. They walk over to Cobb.

"You remember Mitchum. Y'all come up together over at the church, member? An' this is his partner, Mr...Mr—"

"Hogue. Hogue ma'am," I say.

"That's right. Mr. Hogue, an' they jus' need you to come down to the station with 'em so they can get it all down an' you can tell 'em all about what happened, tha's all." Miss Florrie's coaxing. Wish we could take her with us when we gotta bring in Jed again next week after he's drunk off his ass and tearing up Merl's bar.

Cobb don't take out his cuffs, he offers Rae his arm, and I get it. Wouldn't touch her myself less it was to cuff her, but he's got his own kumbaya kind of ways. Worse comes to worse, I'll chase her down if she bolts once we get outside.

Getting tired of him expecting me to be the one to give chase when it's called for though, all on account of me being the one who actually goes to the gym. Seems like the more I work out, the more double cheeseburgers he orders.

Rae links her shaky arm in Cobb's. I trail behind, down the hallway. Miss Florrie's trailing me. I can hear her whispering prayers all along the way.

"Lord, help my child. Lord, help her."

"Now you just keep your eyes on me, Rae. Alright? Right on me," Cobb instructs in that fatherly voice he has.

Watching him walking along with this woman, small enough she looks like a scared little girl there beside him, I wonder again, as I have throughout my time with him, how he ever got himself tied up in law enforcement. His tender heart can't have long left. To hear Jolie tell it, my heart turned to stone within the first six months of me being on the job. Said my heart was already about the hardest of anyone she knows anyhow. Bullshit. Adaptation's what they'd call it if we were any other species. Since we're human, people say I'm hard hearted. In my book, it's called toughening up and growing a pair.

As Cobb helps Rae walk down the front steps with him, an irritation sets in. He's going on a decade on the job still with some kindheartedness intact. I got no earthly idea what makes one man's goodness hold out longer than another's. What gives one any goodness to start with? Way I see it, an ounce of goodness in your heart is no different than a bullseye on your chest. It's for suckers.

"I'll be right behind you, Rae. I'm just g'ttin' my purse," Miss Florrie calls, hanging back a second.

Our mournful procession makes it all the way down the

sidewalk, passing Jesus' sign, and heads towards our car. All of a sudden, Rae looks away from Cobb and out at the car parked ahead of ours. I catch sight of what she's seeing. In the back of the passenger side is a car seat. I'd like to sucker punch the paramedic who didn't just take the fucking thing with him. What use has she got for it now?

"Brandon! My Brandon!" Rae screams, flinging herself against the car, beating on the window. "My boy! Mama, I want my boy!"

Something in the way she's carrying on seems like she's starring in a play. Just don't add up a woman who was asleep at her table not five minutes ago going to pieces like this. The front door flies open an Miss Florrie rushes down the steps. Cobb moves over just in time for her to throw herself on her daughter, doing her best to calm her again.

"No, honey! No! Come on now."

Due to the vibe I'm getting about how all this is going, I walk down the driveway, pull out my phone and call dispatch. I try to talk as low as possible, giving them the details.

"Who's he callin'? Hey, who you callin'?" Rae yells, having raised up off the car just in time to catch me.

I pocket my phone and shake my head, holding my hands up like she's doing the arresting.

"Nobody," I lie.

She's too quick for Miss Florrie or Cobb, jerking away from them, she does just what I thought she was liable to do and takes off running for the back yard. I don't know why, but I give her a second, just like I used to do with the kids on my street in elementary school, a head start because I knew I was the fastest. Before she rounds the side of the garage, I take off after her.

My mind's racing, looking all around, trying to figure out where she's headed. Ain't a thing back here but some toys in the yard, a grill, a table and a field out ahead. The air's so thick, I don't know how either of us are breathing well enough to run at all. And there it is—what she's running to. The grill. I see it a split-second before she grabs it. A meat fork. A big ol' long one. She whirls around. I stop dead in my tracks.

Part of me wants to bum rush her, go on and risk getting stabbed just to get on with this fucking day, but looking her in the eyes, I feel it. That part of me that thinks I'm in enough trouble as it is trying to put me in check. I put my hands out, like I'm patting the air.

"He said I can bear it, but I cain't. I cain't!" she shouts. "My Brandon… my Brandon. It was so hot! So hot!"

"Now, see you don't know me, Rae, an' I don't know you," I tell her.

She goes quiet, just grips that big fork tight holding it out higher.

"Rae, now," I say louder. "We don't know each other, so I got no call to say anything about what you did or didn't do, you hear? Me an' Cobb, we're just the ones they send to pick people up, an' look into things."

"But tha's why!" she screams. "They sent you cause they think I did it! They think I left him in there on purpose, an' I cain't be going to jail. I cain't!"

Then quick as she was yelling, she drops her arms down by her side. The fork now next to her thigh, dangling from her hand. She stands real still, her face all confused, tears drying up.

"How long you think it took him? Hmmm? How long?" she asks.

I hear steps coming behind me in the grass, I turn slightly. I give Cobb a look letting him know I got it then turn back to her.

"How long to what, Rae?" I say.

"How long you think it took him to quit breathin'?"

I take a deep breath, having no idea how to answer. There's no good thing to say. It's a lose/lose, and I hate those because I'm the winning type. And even though I remember my own mother telling me never act in hate or frustration, and I hear that part of me not wanting more trouble shouting louder in my head, I do it anyway. I know it's wrong from the get go, but it'll get some traction one way or the other and get this damn shift over with. I take a step forward.

Soon as I do, Rae brings that fork up and uses the sharp part of its prongs to slice hard across a wrist. Then she takes the fork with the other hand and jabs into the other wrist. Cobb pushes me aside, runs over and knocks the fork out of her hand onto the ground. Rae slips down the front of him like a limp rag doll, but he catches her just before she hits the grass.

I watch as he tears his collared shirt off then his undershirt using one on each of her wrists, tying them tight. He hoists her up into his arms, carrying her through the yard, his bare gut hanging out from under her body, his pants barely staying up. She's whimpering as they go.

"What do you want me do to?" I call to him.

"I don't give a damn what you do," he barks without turning around.

By the time I walk around front, he's loaded her up in our car. Miss Florrie's in the back with Rae in her lap, and they're pulling out of the driveway. I guess I'm walking. Before I go, I look over and know I ain't making it one more step without doing what I wanted to do the minute we drove up.

I stomp over and snatch up that *Thank You Jesus* sign. I thwack it against the bushes, tearing the shit out of it. I'm thanking him. I'm thanking him alright!

"Cy!" a voice interrupts.

I turn, dropping the sign into the bushes. The ambulance had driven up without me hearing it, and here's Larry. Should've known this would be his time of day to respond.

"Hey Larry."

"You called right?"

"Yeah, yeah, we did, but Cobb took 'em on over to Beacon. It was quicker."

We shoot the shit a few minutes. He asks if I want a ride home, but I tell him I'll walk. He says I should call an Uber, but I tell him I need the exercise. What I really need is to figure out why I did what I did. Why I stepped forward when I needed to hang back. Why I have to keep piling on the trouble when the trouble I've got's about to crush me.

And if I knew the answer to that, I know I wouldn't have had to be transferred over here. I'd be back in Clayton with Jolie, still on at the department over there. If I knew the answer to just that question, my whole life would be different. I might've just turned out to be one of those people buying a god damn Jesus sign instead of beating the shit out of one.

Looking down at the s-u-s part of the sign sticking out from under my shoe, I shake my head. I could never be one of those idiots. Another question takes over my mind, pushing out any thoughts about what all just went down. *Who said she could bear it, but she cain't? Who?* Tends to be all you need to set off on a hunt— one question. I can't help but smile.

40°F

Cobb

Cousin Loel came over from Morganton last weekend. Said he knew with it being my first winter since Stacy's passed, I might need to get out, do some fishing. Seemed pretty cold to be out on the boat, but I didn't argue. You don't get to pick what people feel they have to do when it comes to helping you bear the weight of your grief.

I wondered if he remembered how he was always telling Stacy he'd take us both out there and how we never got around to it. Once I was out on the water with him, I was glad to be someplace in Sanford she'd never laid eyes on. That's been hard to come by. She's been everywhere I look.

The more that cold wind blew against the boat, the more I thought about how Stacy always loved the crisp chill of winter. She'd wear this red pea coat with brass buttons. Picked it up at a vintage store. Made her look like a country clubber. Just beautiful. Oh God, I miss my girl!

"Still fresh for ya," Loel said when I confessed missing her was getting the better of me. "Give it time. You'll find your way."

There wasn't anything to say in reply. He cast his line out. I followed his lead, casting my own line out. He'd never loved a girl like my Stacy. A girl so incredible that when she'd gone there was no way left to be found. All the light just gone. Only thing left is days to stumble around in the dark praying I don't hit anything.

She understood me the way I'd longed to be understood. In a way, I'd imagine all men need to be known even if they can't ever put words to it. There's not enough time left on this earth for me to find anyone who'll grasp and accept me the way Stacy did. My girl who looked my demons in the eye and called them angels.

Even in the fall, it wasn't so hard to keep the memories at bay. All the prep work in the yard to do in case we see any snow, whatever snow we get in the Carolinas. Used to be we'd rarely see freezing, but here lately, what with the climate changing Democrats stay in an uproar about, we get snow like clockwork in December and January. Last year, even had some in March. Bought myself a snow shovel after that. This old southern boy'd never in his life had to buy one. Never thought I'd live to see it.

I find I dread each new season since she's left us though this winter's proving to be the worst. Traps me inside with nothing but thoughts and I know it'll bring them all back to me—all my ghosts who are never far. Ones who feel they haven't gotten their due. Those from the past and the not-so-distant past, who collided into one another last summer on the bank of the river out back of the old hospital.

I've got my reasons I don't want to talk much about it. Stacy would've said it was on account of what all happened with Hogue. I know that itn't it at all. It goes back way farther than that.

Come August, it'll be a year since it all went down. No matter how much time passes, there's nothing cloudy about that day the captain told me Hogue was transferring over our way. He handed me his file. Soon as I got a glimpse of it and then him, I figured it wouldn't be long. When you meet some people, you get that feeling they been living on borrowed time, that you're sneaking in the back of the theatre getting a seat for the end of their movie, and you ain't gonna change it one way or the other. That's how it was with Cy from the get go.

Reason I don't like looking back on those months in particular is because Stacy lost her next to last one of our babies not long before then. On that fourth loss, we thought we might give up, say having any wasn't in the plans for us. You never know how many tries you have in you for that kind of thing, and four felt final.

The whole irony of it wasn't lost on me. While I was catching a case where a kid died, lost to this world, I'd also just lost another kid at home. Both of them lost by means out of my control. Both of them cut down before they had a chance.

We named each baby. Stacy said any life that made it so far as to register on an ultrasound, deserves to be named. The first was Fran, after Stacy's mama. She came early and only lived a day outside Stacy's womb. Year after her, Carl came. He never made it to the second trimester. Pearl followed him. She made it the whole nine months. Well, we think so, but cain't be sure. She came out silent, already gone. Doc couldn't say for sure how long she'd been that a way.

"White names," Stacy told me about her choices. "My Aunt Ranesha always says you give babies white names, an' when they gotta write it down on job applications, they might at least get their foot in the door."

That struck me strange seeing as how most of her family wasn't none too happy she married a white man, and a cop to boot.

"Bout time we had one on our side," was all her Daddy'd had to say about it.

I knew what he meant. I would be going over to their side by taking up with her, not the other way around. No matter how pale Stacy was, she'd never be crossing over to my side. Always the way around here. A Black marries a white, more than likely it's the Black family that's going to eventually open their doors. Rest assured it's the white's family who's going to shut their doors tight. My family did accordingly. It was alright by me. Seems I'd been aiming for a way to leave since I came home from the hospital in mama's arms. Just took meeting Stacy to admit it.

Stacy was tight lipped about the name she'd picked for the fourth. I'd tried to coax it out of her. She wasn't having it. Told me I'd know soon enough, and sadly, she'd been right. Our next to last little one only made it to the third trimester.

Stacy said she was a fighter. Felt her kicking all the time, day in day out, til she didn't, and then it was clear what had happened again. By the time I got home that night, Stacy'd packed a bag and was setting on the couch, sweating bullets from pain.

"Leave your shoes on, Mitchum," was all she said, and I knew where we had to go.

She had to have an emergency C-section. None of the others had. They'd all left on their own, "typical" miscarriages doc had called them. I couldn't get my mind around how a person does a job where dead babies are called typical.

"I got a scar now," Stacy told me when she woke up and I could go in and see her. "Should a known the minute I named her Kelly, she'd be sure to leave her mark. Now we'll always have her with us."

I swallowed back the vomit right then and there. Kelly. She was naming this one after her sister. I cleared my throat.

"I'm sure she'd have liked that," I said.

I didn't like it at all. I hated it. Stacy had no way to know I had no interest in her sister staying with us, yet somehow, knew I deserved it. I was lucky it had taken three babies to get to this. Yeah, I deserved to have her sister saddled to me the rest of my days, across her stomach, a thin line of raised flesh. Deserved to have to run my hand over it every morning. With what all that happened with Kelly, all the things Stacy never knew, and I didn't fully recall myself. I'd run my hand over her belly praying that the scar was the only physical manifestation of Kelly that we'd ever see.

Setting by Stacy's bed, I put a hand on hers. When our hands were on each other's, our age difference always caught me off guard. My tan hand, a weathered thing, while hers was soft, light brown, with hardly a line that had managed to stake a claim on it. *Black don't crack*, my grandma used to say. I tried to get a read on how Stacy felt about this souvenir she was talking about, then she lifted her gown and showed me the jagged thin line just down and to the right of her brown belly button.

"Ain't too big a stitches at all," I whispered.

"Doc did 'em his self. Said he wanted to make sure they were done right."

The stitches were neat and tiny. I marveled at how doctors can do something so tedious like that just perfect but couldn't help us keep a child in this world.

"Yeah, that'll heal right up," I assured her.

She shook her head.

"Hope not. This makes it like it really happened. The other three, sometimes it's like we just imagined 'em, you know?"

I looked at her. I didn't know. They were all real to me. Each as vivid as if they were alive and well. Stacy'd never know how often those babies were with me. I'd think about how Fran might've had tight curls like Stacy did when we first met. How Carl would've been a lineman like I was in high school, or how Pearl might've been a pageant queen like our niece across town. And baby Kelly's time would come. She'd join her namesake in haunting me in her own way.

Before long, Stacy fell back to sleep. One hand still under mine and the other across her scar. I slid my hand off slow, got up and went out in the hall, feeling a little jealous, about that scar of hers. She'd have something tangible. All I'd have were the thoughts, and torturesome memories. I've always had the opinion a scar gives you somewhere to assign things, a place for your thoughts to go instead a running like a rabid dog all through the back woods of your mind.

Doc stood down at the receiving desk chatting up the nurses. Just standing there sipping on a cup a coffee. Soon as he saw me, he put his mug down, and his face found that hangdog look he'd had the last three times he'd been through this with us. He walked towards instead of away from me. I respected him for that. Had to be one of the longest, saddest walks he'd taken.

"Mitchum, I'm just sorry as the world," he said, reaching up, gripping my shoulders with his hands. Unlike most people, I knew he meant it. I'm sure my family thanked their Lord above each miscarriage we had. They'd never been for any race mixing, but Doc hadn't ever seemed to be a typical good old southern boy. College in New York might've turned him off to it. He trickled on back down here and stayed put, though. Most of us do.

"I really am sorry," he said.

His sincerity didn't mean I didn't still want to unholster my glock and put a bullet right through his foot at least, but I stood there feeling the weight of his hands on me.

In the short time he'd known me, Hogue called it. He was always on me for being what he called *reserved*. Said it could make people think I didn't give two shits. Truth is, I always have given too many. If I even start to crack open that door and let out any feelings, I don't think I'll ever be able to wrangle them and shut the door again. And that itn't no real surprise. Only two kinds of cops. There's the ones who try to help people keep their doors shut tight, hold their shit together. Then there's the ones who're trying to prove they're still good people, locking up perps to atone for those times they didn't keep their own doors shut. Itn't any in between. Only the two and you gotta pick. No other way around it.

"Preciate all you've done, Doc. Really," I heard myself tell him, reaching a hand out, watching as he took it.

"Y'all give anymore thought to adoption, Mitchum? Y'all take a look at that brochure I gave Stacy for St. Marks? They have some beautiful children in need a homes, right over in Seven Lakes."

I slipped my hands in my pockets, felt for my keys out of habit. Felt for any words I could say while I was at it and came up with the same I'd told him before.

"Doc, you know as well as I do, they wouldn't know which kind a baby to give us, a Black one or a white one, an' they'd just turn down our application so they wouldn't even have to think about it."

Doc cleared his throat. I could tell he was readying to say one of those things people are about 95% sure they shouldn't say, yet foolishness prevails and they go with the other 5% of them that feels they have to say it anyhow.

"Most wouldn't know it to look at Stacy."

I ignored this as I knew Doc didn't mean anything by it. I switched gears.

"I'm wonderin' can I see her?"

He looked past me at Stacy's door.

"Thought tha's where you came from," he said all confused.

"Not Stacy. I'm a… I'm wantin' to see Kelly. Tha's what we named her. What Stacy named her, Kelly."

His eyes clouded up. He got all fidgety and panicky, looked down the hall behind him. No doubt he was hoping somebody would have themselves an emergency, and he'd be saved from saying yes or no. A couple orderlies came out of a room at the end, and I saw that's who he was really looking for. They were carrying white trash bags. He rushed down to them, leaned in and told them something that caused one to duck back inside the room before he turned back around to me, motioned me to join them.

"Darrell, this is Officer Cobb. Mitchum Cobb."

The orderly nodded. Another orderly was still inside behind the glass, wheeling a cart, looking all jittery with the way he kept tugging at the collar of his uniform as he came out.

"They were uh, they were preppin' for my next surgery, but they say you can go in. We got a few minutes," Doc told me as he opened the door to the room.

He lingered in the doorway. He wasn't sure he was making the right call. I wasn't sure either, but I respected that he complied anyway.

"Mitchum," he called to me as I stepped inside.

I kept my back to him.

"Sure it's the best idea?" he asked so soft it barely made it over to me.

I turned back, stared at the painting hanging on the wall behind him. Painting of an old barn. Didn't make me feel better. Don't know what they could've hung up there that would have but that sure didn't. The dark wood and gray skies lent themselves to tragedy.

"Did Stacy see her?" I asked.

His face fell even before he nodded. I knew she had.

"I'll just be right outside, sir," the orderly said.

"Thank you."

I heard the door click as he pulled it shut. The cart was across the room under a bright light. I bet that orderly had to fish Kelly out of one of those bags. Probably already got her ready for the mortuary to cremate her. Stacy had them all cremated. Never told me what she did with their ashes. To this day, I never asked her. She'd always go and pick them up on her own. For all I know, they're lined up on some shelf in the storm cellar of our house. Figured they were part of her body, she got to decide how they took up space in this world.

My feet weren't ready to move. I stood near the door, craned my neck to see what laid on the cart, and there she was. Wasn't what I'd imagined. Looked like a big old wad of tan chewing gum. I bit my bottom lip at the thought that Stacy'd seen her. Why had she needed to see her?

Thought for a minute I wouldn't get any closer, but then I made out a foot. At the bottom of the wad was a tiny foot. It was all but fully formed, but it was clear that's what it was—an honest to God foot! This doubled me over. Tears came out from behind the dam where I'd been keeping them. I'd worried how little I'd cried about the others. Kelly'd brought them crashing in.

When I could finally stand, I inched up a little closer to her, ran my finger along the toes, tiniest light brown toes, already icy cold. Never have understood how they got that cold that quick. As my fingers traced her heel, I pictured that foot alongside her other one walking around our kitchen floor in that unsteady way babies got of walking. Wobbly steps towards me and then I could picture her. I could finally see the little girl those feet belonged to taking shape.

She ran on the beach calling "Grandpa! Aunties!" to Stacy's daddy and aunts who'd meet us there every July. She was in our backyard jumping rope. I saw her on the playground of the school waving to me when I'd drive by on my lunch hour.

That was as close as I dared get, just close enough to touch her foot. Just a foot, and I thought about how Stacy'd seen so much more. All those months, she'd carried them all, felt them inside her, seen them die and what a coward I was.

"I just hope you two don't start resentin' each other," Stacy's grandma told me after Pearl came and went.

I hadn't understood what she'd meant til right then and there seeing Kelly. I knew a seed of resentment took root in my heart that day. I resented Stacy because she was so much stronger than me, and I knew she had to be resenting me cause no matter what a good husband I tried to be or how many criminals I helped bring to justice, it wasn't enough for God to see fit to let us keep a baby. Just one baby.

Not two months after that, I left Hogue behind in my rear view to drive Ms. Ellis and a bleeding Rae over to the hospital. Poor Rae. Went and slit her wrists with a meat fork. Looked all crazed in my back seat, I couldn't help but wonder how God had seen fit to give that woman a baby—one she'd gone off and left in the car to suffocate in the heat. And for the first time in my career, I knew no matter what surfaced about her, whether it was accidental or not, I'd wrap it all up quick.

Wouldn't have to do it because I was 100% sure she wasn't blameless either. I'd have to so I wouldn't have to see her or who she'd taken up with. Couldn't stand seeing either of them. Made me think one of two things. Thought about how just maybe she was proof there wasn't a God up there deciding anything. That the whole damn world was a crap shoot, if a woman like her could have a child.

The other thought was that God hadn't decided at all. I had. Way back on that night out there at the old state home with Stacy's sister, Kelly. Whatever happened to her had condemned me and my wife to a lifetime of barrenness. A trail of never ending of hurt.

Likely, I deserved every bit of it, but poor Stacy. My poor girl. She never did anything. Not one damned thing to speak of up til we'd met. Just by choosing me, she joined a long line of women in this life whose only crime is not being able to help who they love.

83°F

She pulled his briefs out of the dryer. Grey, t-shirt material, Calvin Klein briefs, similar to ones he'd worn as a boy minus the designer labeling on the waistband. As she folded them, she wondered when exactly she became a woman who'd raised a son who wore such things. His father had always worn boxers. In high school, so had he. Her little Bobby boy.

Did he pick up this preference at college? Maybe it's what his friends did, though he had never seemed impressionable. From her observations of him with his friends when they'd come over after school, she'd pegged him to be the trendsetter. That was years ago, however. He'd gone from graduating with his degree in business to living with Heather, and only came home every now and again. No, she could not say what kind of man chose these briefs. This dug into her like the ingrown toenails she was prone to getting from wearing fashionable shoes instead of comfortable ones. A small price to pay for looking her best.

Rain cascaded down the glass. The wall of windows had been one of her favorite features of the house when her husband had talked her into such a modern rebuild. It hadn't taken her long to come to love the way they invited the outside in, and their lot was big enough that neighbors couldn't see much. Not unless they stood still and really looked.

As she walked past them carrying his clothes, she felt conspicuous. She wished she'd have bought blinds. If she did that now, it would be incriminating, what with her having gone all those years with uncovered windows. She knew that no matter what she believed about her son, his oddly timed visit and horrible story, she could not draw attention.

The bathroom was gray, only the light from the skylight pouring in. Without thinking, she walked in, putting his clothes on the vanity sink.

"God damn it, Mama!" he hissed from the tub.

There he was, his reflection in the mirror, this man who'd replaced her boy. She kept her back to him instantly shutting her eyes tight.

"Sorry, honey. I just—I just thought you'd need these."

"Thanks," he muttered, laying back in, resting his head on the porcelain ledge. "Anything yet?"

"Hmm?"

"On the news? Have you seen anything?"

"I hadn't looked. Did you want me to?"

At this, she heard a thrashing sound, and the thuds of his feet against the bathmat. Eyes still shut, she reached out to her right grabbing a towel, handing it to him behind her back. The air from the door flying open alerted her that she could open her eyes. She leaned down, wiping his wet footsteps up with the bathmat, then positioning it on the side of the tub to dry, she reached in and pulled the stopper so the water would drain. He'd always been one to leave the water, no matter how many times she'd shown him how to drain it.

"Something'll come up from there an' get me!" he used to squeal when he was barely big enough to see over the side of the tub.

"Now, don't you worry. If anything ever comes up from there, I'm here. I'll keep it away from you," she'd console.

And in this second, all these years later, she questioned for the first time, why she'd said such a thing. Why hadn't she told him *Nonsense! Nothing will come up from there?*

She stood in the doorway between what was now only her master bedroom and the bathroom staring at his bare wet back as he sat on the end of her bed flipping TV channels. The towel around his waist, caught some of the drips from his body, but not all. He'd get up from her bed, and there'd undoubtedly be a large spot. Who was this man? This man who wore briefs, took her Lord's name in vain and was now ruining her silky bedspread.

"I thought there'd be something by now," he griped.

"You said you called 911 as soon as you found them?"

He didn't answer, only kept flipping from one channel to the next. He was right. There should've been something. Raleigh being only an hour away, any news from there usually found its way to their local channels and vice versa. Leaning over, his elbows rested on his knees, made the muscles in his back all the more pronounced. He had lost a lot of weight since she'd seen him. CrossFit. All he would tell her was that he was getting more and more into his CrossFit group.

"That's him," Jeanie Doyle from the Junior League had told her, holding her phone out showing a picture of him flexing alongside a couple of sports-bra-wearing young girls who were not Heather. A large CrossFit Raleigh sign over their heads on a banner in the background.

She'd passed it off, made some dismissive remark she couldn't readily remember. It had been embarrassing. She remembered that. If his father had still been living, he too would have found that kind of behavior somewhat trashy. It was not the behavior of a married man with two children.

And there it was. That very picture of him up on the screen with a news commentator's voice behind it.

"Shhhh!" he warned, swatting behind himself in her direction. She hadn't even uttered a word.

He turned up the volume. They listened as the newscaster, the one she usually liked to watch from WRAL, the one with the Sean

Connery good looks, told viewers what had happened to her daughter-in-law and her two grands. Her precious, precious grands —two girls. She wished she could shut her ears the way she'd shut her eyes a few moments ago, but she couldn't. She had to listen. She had to compare what they said with what he'd told her. Instinctively, she knew this wasn't maternal. This not believing one's own son, but her girls, oh those two beautiful girls!

When the news cut to the weather, he turned it off, flinging the remote down on the bed next to him. He stared at the blank screen of that old Magnavox she couldn't imagine upgrading. It had been one of the first things she and his father had bought when his father had been promoted to president of the company he went on to retire from. There they were, the two of them reflected in it like two freakishly disproportionate people in a funhouse mirror. She was so glad her husband was dead. It was the first time and only time she'd felt glad about it. Her glee disarmed her.

A gust outside blew the rain harder against the windows across from them. The forecast had said just light showers. You never could tell about the weather anymore. Weathermen were more gamblers than scientists it seemed. Usually, she loved rainy days. She'd sit in her overstuffed chair in the den and read, nursing a cup of tea, or rewatch episodes of *Law and Order S.V.U.*

"I thought you said you called 911 before you came here. That as soon as you found them, you called. That you walked in an—"

"Jesus, Mama! You think that would make good news? Hmmm? You think they're gonna say I called the cops?" he raged, hopping up off the bed.

She turned her eyes to the floor in case his towel didn't hold. He stalked over to the window, pacing back and forth. It was then, as she saw him bringing his hand up to his wet hair, that she realized she had not seen him with a phone since he arrived. This was not like him, especially with his job. For the last ten years, she'd seldom seen him without it in one hand or the other. Where was it now?

He stopped abruptly and, as if reading her mind, stared at her. His eyes began watering as if on command. Oh, how she wanted it to be genuine. He was their father, Heather's husband. Yes, he was grieving. Surely, he was.

"Mama, don't you see? I'm an affluent white male. I'm fuckin' done. Don't you get it? This is it for me," he told her with a conviction the likes of which she'd never seen from him.

It moved her. She stood, crossing over to him, putting a hand on his shoulder. He folded into her, leaning down to hug her and be embraced fully. It had been years since he'd hugged her so fiercely, so in need of consoling, of acceptance. Though every part of her logical mind and her gut told her this was the opposite of what she should be doing, she did it.

She comforted him, all the while pushing out the idea that these same hands, the ones holding her tightly to him, might have choked his daughters and their mother just hours before. She pushed at this notion, keeping the door shut to it as long as she could. It happened as he said. He came home from work. He found them all upstairs with a note Heather had left for him. Had he shown her the note? Did he have it with him?

The doorbell interrupted them—its ringing no less alarming than the sound of a medieval bell, tolling loudly, calling peasants to come see a beheading. He took her shoulders in his hands, moving her back from him. His eyes meeting hers, his conviction hijacked by a frenzied self-preserving nervousness. Just like that, in that one gesture, she felt not like his mother but like an accomplice. Was that so very different? Were they not one and the same?

They didn't speak as she left the room. Both knowing what needed done.

"Coming," she called to whoever it was over the sound of the rain as she descended the stairs.

She did not hurry. She'd taken a fall on those steps last year. It had nearly caused her to have to have her hip replaced. That's what had taken her husband. Well, it had been the beginning of the end anyway. He'd had to have his hip replaced. Then a blood clot formed. She'd keep her hips. She took the stairs methodically one at a time. Headlights flashed from outside readying her for who she was about to talk to. As ready as one can be in such a situation.

The bell rang once more before she could open the door to find the headlights belonged to a police car parked directly behind her Mercedes. There was only one officer and she knew him—Mitchum Cobb. Her heart lurched in her chest. Even with his mustache and beginnings of a potbelly, she'd recognize his face anywhere. Yes, they'd gone to school together, played ball and had been quite chummy til that last month senior year, he and her boy, fast friends until that night with that girl.

"Mornin', Mrs. Olsen," he greeted kindly, as if canvasing for a missing cat.

"Morning."

"You 'member me?" he asked as if that had any real bearing on anything.

"Yes. Yes, of course I do. You played football with my Bobby," she told him, being sure to smile.

Was she sweating? Oh, she felt like she was sweating bullets. Mitchum Cobb... She hadn't laid eyes on him in a dog's age. She hoped she might never have to again. Last she'd heard he'd married a Black girl from over on the west side. She remembered her heart had gone out to his mother when she'd heard. What a thing for him to have done. Especially after everything.

"I did; you're right ma'am. I sure did."

Even though he stood under the awning, the rain was pelting in on him. She knew the longer he stayed out there, the worse it looked.

"Come on in. Come out of that," she instructed, moving aside, glancing briefly upstairs, seeing no shadows on the wall. Wherever Bobby was, she hoped he could stay there quietly.

"Thank you, ma'am." He stepped inside being sure to wipe his shoes on the rug in front of the door several times.

Conscientious. He'd always been so. The type to take his plate to the sink and acknowledge her with a hello on the afternoons he and Bobby hung out at their house. The other boys had not been so mannerly. She'd hated how his friendship with her son had needed to end, so abruptly, but there'd been no other way. Protecting her own had been uppermost, back before he'd done so much that required it.

She supposed it made sense that Mitchum had become an officer of the law. It had been the only way he'd had to protect himself, what with his family coming from nothing, his mother being in the state she'd been in for most of his youth. And just maybe, after all that surrounded that Black girl they'd gone to school with, he had wanted things to be more balanced. She herself had longed for this many times; the world being what it was. Being a police officer provided Mitchum a way to make it so. She envied him that—a way to make some dent in the injustices of this chaotic life.

They stood awkwardly in her foyer. Her looking away from him and out at the rain on the windows, making them seem as if they were the wall of that fountain in the Trump Tower building she'd toured with her cousin Janine in New York City. It had looked like a wall of a cave, with water coming from a thin line in the ceiling down it, a backdrop as people sat eating in the lobby restaurant. That had been a good trip. So long ago now, but a good one. When she had a bad day, her mind often took her there.

"Hope I didn't wake you?" Mitchum asked, penetrating the quiet, as his eyes wandered to the top of the stairs just as hers had a moment prior.

"No, no. I've been awake a while," she said, still smiling.

Arms crossed? Uncrossed? She wasn't sure. What was more casual? She'd never been very casual, but he might not remember that. Her pensive ways could go against her now, and she wished she could play it cool like her husband would have. He always played it cool.

"Ever since Thom died, you know I still get up at the same time? 6:00 a.m. on the button. The body can't forget I guess," she went on, knowing full well it was too much even as she said it.

"I guess not," he said, shifting a bit from one foot to the other.

His arms were hanging in front of him, hands clasped. Water

dripped from them to her floor. If he stood there long enough there'd be a full puddle.

"I'm wonderin' if you've heard from Bobby?" he finally came out with it.

Cocking her head to the side, she did her best to look skeptical, as if she had no idea why he'd suddenly be back in her world asking about her son.

"Well, not in a few days," she lied. "He lives in Raleigh now, you know. He calls about once a week, but we spoke, I believe it was last Monday. Yes, he called last Monday. I remember because I'd just gotten home from the Junior League."

Again, she knew it was too much and yet likely not enough. Why had she said *he* and not *they? They live in Raleigh...They...* What would possess her? Had she so readily accepted their deaths to erase them like that? No, of course not! It had been a simple error, but the time for simple errors in her life was over.

Her babbling had been too much and too specific. Were her son not upstairs, she'd just be another old lady who watched too many courtroom drama reruns on TNT. But be that as it were, she was an accomplice not doing too well at the cover up. Mitchum had perfected his poker face already, though he was not a day over 35 if she remembered right. He looked at her, and she had no idea if he believed her or not. He reached in his jacket pocket, pulling out a steno pad and a pen.

"Monday," he repeated to himself, scribbling it down. "An' nothin' since?"

"Yes, that's right."

He reached in his other pocket pulling out a card, handing it to her.

Mitchum Cobb
Lee County Police Department
886-334-9087

She turned it, held it in her hand gingerly not knowing what to do with it. What did he expect her to do with it?

"I can't get into specifics, Mrs. Olsen. I imagine if you haven't seen the news, you'll know soon enough, but I really do need to talk to him. The Sheriff from over in Wake's already sent somebody our way. I asked 'em if I could come over instead seein' as how we have history an' all."

Did they? Still have history? She figured they did, but that whatever it consisted of, it couldn't be good. After that night that girl disappeared, when the police had shown up asking questions, thankfully no more officers ever returned. She'd doubted they would what with all the donations to the department that she and her husband made and the policeman's New Year's ball they sponsored annually. She'd also assumed that meant Mitchum had corroborated her Bobby's rendering of what transpired after they'd all gone to the Sonic, yet she couldn't know for sure.

What she did know was that she had a guttural suspicion that Mitchum knew a Bobby she had never been acquainted with. This had been reason enough to discourage her son to have any further dealings with Mitchum at the conclusion of their time in high school. Oh, she'd claimed it was just a precaution, and it was, yet it was more than that. She knew. It was a pulling down of the blinds, a turning away from truths she could not look in the face.

Mitchum opened her door again, instantly dousing them with dank humid air as he did.

"He's not in trouble, not yet, but if you hear from him or you see him at all, you call me, you hear? It's real important," he told her, reaching out putting a hand on her own.

Man's hands. The small hands that had helped rinse her plates, clicked buttons on gaming controllers in her living room. Now man's hands that held guns and had likely had to fire them. Hands that handcuffed criminals and may soon count her son among them. This was all she could see. Her son, being led from her house in handcuffs, ushered into the back of that car in her driveway. And though this was a horrible thought, she couldn't bring herself to be convinced beyond a shadow of a doubt that it would be wrong.

"Can't you tell me, tell me anything? I can't imagine what—"

"It's not my place, Mrs. Olsen. Not when we just need to talk. You have good friends in the League?" he wanted to know.

She nodded.

"Call one of 'em. That'd be best an' I'll tell you this. Don't go believin' for sure what any of 'em on TV say. News can be skewed; they can get it wrong," he cautioned, yet she could tell by the way he said it, it was rehearsed.

Tears came down her cheeks faster than the rain drops overhead had onto her windows, and she let them fall. There was no reason to stop them.

"If you don't get me when you call that number, call the station an' ask for me, alright? I'll get here soon as I can," he reminded as he pulled his jacket up around his head and made for his car.

She stood transfixed, watching him as he got in, sat for a minute, likely making more notes on his pad, then finally pulling away. Her body moved back. She felt it moving and her arms and hands working together to shut the door, but she was not telling them to. They were doing what they'd always done when she'd stood in that spot and someone had left. Her mind having a mind of its own.

Her feet climbed the stairs again, no laundry this time.

"Bobby?" she called with a tinge of fear she could not squelch.

The hall closet opened. He crawled out, clothed now, yet barefoot. He'd remembered. All these years later, he'd remembered this closet had a space in the bottom that went far back in under the ductwork of the air conditioning. He'd always hid there when they played hide and seek, and when he did, she'd marveled at how a child, so scared of what would come up from the drain, was not scared of what was in that crawlspace.

Still holding Mitchum's card in her hand, she watched her son put the linens that he'd upset on his exit back in place just so. She ran her fingers over the embossed letters *Mitchum Cobb* and had the sinking feeling she would call. She had to. Didn't she?

"Something'll come up from there an' get me!" those words of his played once more in her head as he stood, brushing off his pants.

And if he said those words now, right here in front of her, she could not promise that she'd keep anything away. Maybe she should have told him this when he was still malleable. That there are times even your mother won't be able to keep away whatever it is that is coming for you.

86°F

Hogue

"Kid flat out suffocated. Hot as it's been lately. She said she forgot him. That she went in to get her hair done an' he slipped her mind," I tell her. "I mean how do you do that to your kid?"

The shrink's eyes give away that she's listening too good. She's doing that thing Jolie does where she's squinting and taking in every word I'm saying, but not for the reason I want her to. She's gathering up bullets for her gun, and she ain't at all trying to figure out how not to use it.

"Our brains are on autopilot a large percentage of the day. It's a lot more common than people realize," she tells me. "They even have an app to help remind parents now."

Seems like women always stick up for each other no matter what. Some kind of bitches code.

"So I heard. Damn shame somebody had to invent such a thing if you ask me. To top it off, they got me ridin' shotgun with a blue blood lived here his whole life. Boy, he's takin' the whole *blue* part way too serious. Gone all liberal. Even married himself a Black gal an—"

I stop. Here I been jabbering on and on. I hear myself, but I'm not really thinking about what I'm saying to this head shrinker and I should be. Instead, my mind's on how I told Cobb I won't be too long with this Freud-loving moron. She clears her throat. Here we go.

"Mr. Hogue," she says.

I open my mouth to start up again. She beats me to the punch.

"Mr. Hogue, due to how our last two sessions have gone, and the nature of what it is I'm supposed to assess, I feel I should remind you we're not here to discuss your cases, your partner or your divorce."

My eyes give away that this sounds like bullshit. Thought we're here for her to shrink my head. Figured she'd need to know what's in a head before she can do that. Needs to know what to throw out and what to keep. I also just want to fill the god damn time. Worked for thirty minutes. Only got twenty to go.

"Well, your divorce on one hand, I mean we *are* and we *aren't*. It is relevant," she corrects herself.

Sitting up on the edge of my chair, I get cagey, crack my knuckles. She uncrosses her legs, crosses them back, putting the right leg over the left this time. I don't know how she keeps those pudgy legs together. The suit she's got on has got her wrapped up tight like the plastic on a Jimmy Dean sausage roll. Bet she's the best looking shrink the state's got on payroll. That ain't saying much.

Should've known the state don't have any of those hot therapists like the one Tony Soprano went to. Man, that was some good TV. Right there, episode one, a mafia dude talking to a shrink. God damn genius!

"I thought you might need a little back history's all," I explain to her. "Thought you might wanna know about Jolie an—"

"I think I've got what I need on that topic. We've covered quite a bit about her in your last four visits."

I lean forward, rest my elbows on my knees, lower my head a bit, then look up at her. Hope my hangdog face can still work its magic, even on Jimmy Dean sausage here.

"I think we'd be best served by getting more into the particulars that your former department's interested in, so they can make a decision about your reinstatement," she says.

The bookcase behind her only has a book or two. The rest's filled with pictures. Tony's shrink had a whole library in her office. Where'd this one get her degree? University of Phoenix online?

"Your department's interested in ascertaining, when your ex had a restraining order already on file against you, exactly what would bring you to be sleeping outside her house?"

"She whatin my ex yet."

"No, not at that point, but you were separated. You were not supposed to be within a hundred yards of her or her domicile and—"

"You mean *our* house."

"At that time, it was *her* house. You were not living there, Mr. Hogue. She hadn't invited you, and even if she had, with the active restraining order, it still would have been illegal for you to be there. Had she invited you?"

It's clear our last few jam sessions hadn't done me any favors. Here I been thinking I was laying groundwork, swaying her to my side. Turns out she was just waiting. Biding her time. Getting up the nerve to tell me what's what. Like most of the bitches in my life, she's made up her mind without giving me a fucking chance. It's all over her face. Sure as we're setting here, I'm fucked.

"You can see, Mr. Hogue, how anyone would take issue with you camped outside, your car parked behind shrubs at 3:00 a.m."

"How bout we talk about why he was there. Hmm? Nobody wants to talk about what that Ni—"

I stop myself before she writes that down and she will. *Get in the game, Cy.* You got to readjust your vocabulary for this kind of feminist magna cum laude asshole.

"Why was he out there at that time a night?" I blurt.

"Who?"

And I see what she's doing. Trying to connect me to the *victim*. Yeah, I see her coming a mile off. I ain't about to give her the satisfaction.

"The guy in the hospital, the—the *plaintiff*."

"Your ex-wife's boyfriend? The same one who'd been sleeping there night after night, whose only crime was going out late for cigarettes after the graveyard shift and hanging out a bit too long with his friend?"

Her hands are folded in her lap. If she's not scribbling, that's a good thing. Maybe I still got a chance. I stare up at her. Naw. It's a real bad thing. Bet she's already written her report before I came today. Me setting here's just checking a box for her.

"Is that who you mean? Your ex-wife's boyfriend?"

I don't answer. This time last year, I didn't have an *ex*-wife. I just had a wife, and she didn't have any Black fry cook boyfriend fucking her in our bed. I know there's got to be a laundry list of things that preceded me getting from there to here but for the life of me, I can't name them right now.

"I didn't know that's who he was. I'd fell asleep. The noise a him shuttin' his car door woke me up, an' all I saw was a man creepin' over to my porch."

"*Her* porch." She won't let up with that shit.

I hop up, storm over to the door. Soon as I do it, I know it's a bad call, less I want to let them have my badge for good and become a fry cook myself. I look at the chair I just left and think about getting back in it. Too late. I'm committed now. Overcorrection. Never a good idea. Gotta keep steering and pray I don't flip.

"I was watchin' out for her," I tell her, too loud to help change anything on that report. "Done it for years, cain't just quit cause she says so. That's how it is when you love somebody. You don't just quit."

She stays put, unfolds her hands, puts them on the arms of her chair like she's riding coach on an airplane that's hit a hell of a lot of turbulence.

"Please sit back down, Mr. Hogue."

I set to pacing. Over by the window. Back to the door like one of those rodeo bulls behind the holding pen gate before the cowboy spurs him, and they let him loose.

"Sit. Please." She gets stern, leaning forward, patting the chair across from her with one hand.

Her other hand reaches behind her for something. Wouldn't put it past state workers to have one of the same standard issue tasers they give us. I know I'd want one with all the nutjobs that come through here. I walk over and set back down. She brings out a notebook, putting both hands in her lap. I feel sweat gathering on the top of my lip. I don't wipe it away. Bet she keeps the thermostat set so high in here to keep all of us nuts uncomfortable. Smart tactic. You're bound to say more if you're all hot and irritable.

"I'm hearing you say you haven't been able to stop watching out for her."

"Yeah."

"While I sympathize, it leaves me to wonder what other kinds of things you haven't been able to stop doing."

Oh, I'm kicking myself for that one. Shouldn't ever tell anybody who's got to take notes on the state of your brain, that you cain't help but to do something. Shit! I cain't win for losing.

"I should a said, I just wanted to make sure she was okay. Only planned to be there a few minutes, see that she was safe an' move on, then sure enough everything whatin okay, an' a situation came up."

"The situation being Jolie's boyfriend?" She questions with this tone, the kind that says she's laying out the rope so I can do the hanging all by myself.

"Yeah, only—only I didn't have no idea he was her boyfriend. Hell, I didn't even know she had a boyfriend!"

Looking down at her lap, she thumbs through her notebook.

"But you knew he came over, correct? They'd called before when you were camped out there, hadn't they?"

"Bullshit."

"Did you stop to think that she might've called him to come over that night because she'd seen your car?"

I just look at her. I'm picturing her needing to call the boys in blue one of these days and me showing up just a minute too late for whatever the fuck might be happening to her. There's a lot that can happen to a woman like her.

"I have a note in this file I was given stating that Jolie told the officers, she'd seen you driving around the block several times throughout the course of the evening, before you finally parked."

Her gaze goes down to my feet. I realize I've been tapping my left one like a meth head overdue for a hit.

"When they talked to you about it, your claim was that you were there trying to help, to protect her," she reads from her papers.

"That's right."

"I guess what I want to help you come to see is that despite your previous role in her life, on this night, Jolie was in fact was calling someone else to protect herself from you. And, well, I've refrained from exploring this, yet since you brought up your partner's wife, I'm wondering if the night in question would've gone differently if the boyfriend was white. I can't help but wonder if he'd still have ended up in intensive care."

With that smile she's trying hard to hide peeking through, you can tell she's been storing it up, waiting to use that one for a while. Fucking cunt. Ain't nothing to say to that. Well, there is, but not a thing that won't keep me from being tazed or dragged out of here in cuffs. It's one of those times, I keep my mouth shut tight because I know if I let out one word it'll all go to hell.

Seeing I've gone quiet, she gets up and goes over to set behind her desk, put some distance between us. Good idea, bitch.

"I'll see you next week, Mr. Hogue." She dismisses me like she's my grade school teacher.

My letting her door slam behind me is my way of saying *bye*.

From the front stoop of the building, I see Cobb's got his feet propped up on the dash. Just wiped that down yesterday when we washed the car. He's leaned back catching a nap. Those two dogs with chili and slaw from Sonic are like Xanax for a big old baby like him. I click the car lock, but I didn't need to bother unlocking it. He'd left it open. He hears the beep. Pops straight up like the bride of Frankenstein.

"All done?" he asks as I pull out of the parking lot.

"Left the car wide open. Guess you oughta be glad it's me. Could a been anybody."

He laughs.

"Yeah, I reckon it wouldn't be the worst thing if somebody else took that seat for a while."

"Trust me, ain't nobody linin' up for this spot," I tell him.

He leans his head back, closing his eyes again, deciding I can handle the ride back to the station all on my own. I got a little pit stop first. Take time to wash my mind clean of the last hour. He don't have any questions about where I'm taking us. If Cobb don't have somewhere he's gotta be, he's pretty good about going with the flow.

Trusts people too easy, but he's alright. Pretty good fella to have in a jam. Does his best to stay out of them though. Sometimes, when I hear him talk, it feels like he's done all his living. Like he's coasting, his best days behind him. That for him, we're in some kind of after life. Never have asked him much about his past. I try to keep it that away. Don't really have any interest in knowing a man who'd marry one of them any better than I have to.

On one hand, you gotta be leery of people who don't ask too many questions. You know they want the same treatment. Cain't get too nosy. Never know what they got to hold back, and you might not want to look at it if they showed it to you. Good thing for him I really don't give a shit. Anything behind us ain't got nothing to do with what's in front of us.

I pull up into a driveway in front of a for sale sign. Sun's gone and faded the realtor's picture. She looks like a ghost in red lipstick. The potholes jostle us. Cobb opens his eyes, sets up taller.

"Wanna show you something," I say.

Don't really know why I want to show him. We hadn't exactly crossed over to being friends necessarily. Ain't enemies either but itn't like we go to each other's backyards for barbecues and shit. Won't have to worry about that happening. Pretty sure the first time his half Black wife were to meet me, that'd be all she wrote. Seen her come in the station once. I couldn't even tell she wasn't a hundred percent white til Buddy Roland from dispatch told me.

"Don't know how he does it," Buddy'd said about Cobb. "They ever actually manage to have a baby, that young'un could pop out blacker than my grandma's leather Bible."

I wondered why he couldn't see Cobb ain't no prize really. Probably had to go fishing, cast his line on the other side of the tracks to get any nibbles. Got a gut on him like he's about ten years older than he is, and his face ain't nothing to write home over neither. Only thing he's got going in his favor is he got himself a badge, a steady income, and he goes to church on occasion.

"The old Hill place," Cobb says as I put it in park.

It's nearly dark now. What's left of the sunlight renders the pasture to the left of the house a deep green. Across the way, there's a few kids on their bikes hightailing it home, trying to make dinner. Same kind of quaint day it was when the realtor brought me out. This is the exact kind of place Jolie'd talked about getting. Always has been her dream. It's my dream now.

We get out and walk through weeds that've taken over the sidewalk all the way up to the house.

"Whose house you say it was?" I ask.

"Hill's. Berthine an' Terrence Hill. Lived here, Lord, must a been thirty years or more. Passed on a while back within a few months a each other. Weirdest thing. She had the pancreatic cancer, but he was healthy. Whatin any reason he should a passed, but he did not long after her. His heart just stopped."

"Didn't keel over in the house, did they?" I exclaim as we get to the top of the porch steps.

"She didn't. Heard she spent some months in hospice over in Cary for she went."

He stands still for a second, catching his breath after making it up the steps.

"Guessin' he could've. Cain't say for sure. Didn't know 'em real well to tell you the truth, just a family me an' mine came up with is all."

"Were they Black?"

"Why?"

I shrug. He don't answer, and that don't set too well, but I'll find out on my own. Won't be nothing I cain't Google at the station. Cain't wait to have a real phone again! I promised the captain, though. Promised to fly under the radar, stay offline unless I'm under the station's login. I know soon as I pop up on the web at all, even check my Facebook or Tinder, that'll be it. My whereabouts'll be out there for everybody in no time. Flip phone's gotta do for now.

Soon as I barely open the front screen door, a bird swoops us from one of the porch rafters. Cobb swats at it. Nearly topples back down the stairs before I grab his shirt.

"Easy there, buddy. No tellin' how long it'd take for an ambulance to get out here."

Cobb reaches out, runs a hand along the rusted hinges of the screen door.

"Copper," he informs me. "Once you clean 'em, they'll be good as new."

I swear, he knows a little bit about everything, but not much about any one thing. I push the numbers the realtor gave me on the lockbox, take out the key, then unlock the door. Smells musty— nothing open windows and a little Lysol won't solve. We walk through looking it over like we're in a museum. Cobb takes his steps slow, feeling out if these old floorboards'll hold his ass.

"Got a good price on it. Needs some work, but it'll be nice to have somethin' to do after a shift stead a drinkin' all the Michelob's over at Jack's an' runnin' my fool head off on the treadmill at the gym. Hell, plenty a room to put my own treadmill in an' some weights out in that barn out there," I tell him pointing over at the window.

He feels along the wall, roughs up an edge of the wallpaper, peels back on it, lets it fall on the floor. Cain't take him anywhere, I swear.

"Didn't peg you for a fixer upper type," he says.

"Guess I hadn't rightly figured out which type I am. This is as good a place as any to work on it."

"Ain't too far for you to drive? Once you're back over in Johnston?"

I know what he's getting at, the temporariness of my situation. Sure, he'll be glad to see me go. Ain't never claimed to be no picnic. Truth is, place is growing on me. Might be nice to have a new start. As new as a person can get.

"Naw. Only about fifteen minutes further than I was drivin'."

No sense letting him know anything about the possibility of staying on. Too early to tell, but once I bust open this case with Rae, prove it wasn't an accident, the captain'll be asking me to stay. Cop that catches a baby killer, well, that's a hero in any county.

Cobb's hell bent on the fact that she wouldn't kill her baby. That's one of the many forks in the road where me and him part ways. See, I believe in the willful wiles of the subconscious. That you can want something so bad, it just gets done. Just because Rae says it's an accident, don't make it one. Somewhere deep inside, she wanted that kid gone.

Cobb walks ahead, looks out the window at the barn I pointed out. I come up on the other side of the window. His reflection in the glass shows his eyes ain't set even. One's a little higher than the other. Never noticed it before. Funny how you can spend so much time with somebody and never really see them.

"Thinkin' a puttin' in a offer then?" he asks.

"Already had the realtor put one in this mornin'."

His hands go in his pockets. He sideeyes me. Here comes the judgement.

"You must feel like it's goin' real good with that head shrinker, huh?"

"Got a few more sessions. Ain't worried. She'll come around. They always do," I tease, punching his flabby arm. "Gonna be just fine. I mean with that guy out roamin' where he didn't belong at 3:00 a.m., plus him havin' a convict brother. I tell you that? His brother's a honest-to-God Valentine Blood. No lie. Done all kinds a shit. Did a two-year stint up at Central. Just got out."

Cobb shakes his head.

"That's some luck," he mutters.

I'm impressed I made it through all that without calling Jolie's fella the *N-word*, but I know that'd be a fightin word for old Cobb here. All the officers over at the station made sure to tell me that too. Part of why I got paired with him from what I can tell. Captain acts like he's a white Martin Luther King or some shit. Thinks he's gonna help me see how we're all created equal.

"Yeah, that ain't gonna help Jolie's fella none," I say.

"I don't know all the ins an' outs. Captain didn't tell me much, but I'd be more worried about that head shrinker. Seems like they can sure put a spoke in a wheel. Knew a cop over in Smithfield claimed he had reason to fire when a perp was on the run. When he did, it ricocheted, clipped an ol' lady who was settin' out on her porch. His shrink made sure he's workin' at the Piggly Wiggly down in Myrtle Beach now."

Wonder what he does know about what all went down in Johnston? Thought for sure the captain would've told him.

"Total different thing, man. Mine'll write up a good report," I try to convince him and me at the same time. "Hell, I'm pretty sure she'll do it just to get my petty ass off her roster."

We head out the back door to the barn. Looking at the empty stalls and the yard next to it, ripe for gardening, I think about how it really is just like Jolie described. Always wanted to get a horse and teach kids to ride. Sure, would rather be showing it to her instead of this dough-bellied old badge.

No matter how bad I want it not to be true, I know Jolie won't ever see it. Not now. Not after everything. Some kind of satisfaction in knowing I have something she'd want but won't never be able to afford on her own. Specially not shacking up with no fry cook. I guess about the next best thing to being with somebody you cain't be with no more is knowing you're living a life they'd envy.

The grass in the pasture behind the barn's getting outta control.

About up to my thighs now. The realtor told me the people here before me had a goat. The shed where he bedded down's still standing.

"Accordin' to the realtor, a blind goat was kept out there by a animal rescue," I tell Cobb. "She went on an' on about what a nice man the former owner was to let them keep it there. Let the rescue use that pasture 'til the goat passed. You know they can live into their twenties? Damn shame to keep a fucker alive like that."

A *nice* man? More like cruel and ignorant. I'd of shot that thing. No point in it going on. Survival of the fucking fittest.

"No tellin' what kinna things went on out there," Cobb says. "Looks like a place you'd find somebody's remains."

I lift a hand, rub it over my mouth to hide where I'm simpering away. He wouldn't like to hear me say it, but this confirms we're of like mind. Yeah, every now and then we're on the same page. He tries to make like his pages are cleaner. In the end, I think he knows, you get this badge, you sign up for this life, you got some damn dark chapters in your book. Only hope you got is that nobody ever sticks around long enough to read them.

83°F

Cobb

You never know how much somebody knows about you. There's what you think they see and then what they actually see. Ideas you have about them if you grew up around them. Ways they are around people, how they act in certain places. None of it's anything but the cover of their book. That was always the problem with me and Stacy and her family. Always had to make sure they didn't get past the cover, and it got tiring. It's real tiring keeping a book closed so tight.

Stacy's Daddy, Hicks, knew Ms. Florrie for years. Seemed like he knew everybody on his side of town. Sometimes, I wonder if in small southern towns like ours, every Black person knows every other Black person. Guess there's a solidarity living in the same pressure cooker. Hicks said it was only right we all went to Rae's son, Brandon's funeral. Wasn't sure right off how that'd go with me and Hogue being assigned the case so I ran it by the captain. He figured it couldn't hurt since we'd all but closed it up anyhow.

"Leave Hogue home," he'd added after giving his permission.

I understood. I'd tell Hogue about it after the fact, if I told him at all. Wasn't like he had to know everything. Starting out, he'd just been a ride along. Supposed to be watching more than doing.

Though it hadn't taken much time for him to turn into more of a partner than a mentee.

That's how he was—embedding himself until all of a sudden, you'd turn around and wonder how he got right in the thick of it. It was in the way he saw things. Nothing was off the table for him. He felt he was owed an explanation for everything. He was lucky that way. I never felt like I was owed anything.

The day of the boy's funeral, of course, it had to go and rain. I laid out my old church loafers cause I knew they'd get messed up as all get out. Only one cemetery in town. It always had way more mud than grass, and the rain didn't cool it off but a few degrees. All the weather did was seem to remind us God was turning a blind eye to what was happening. Couldn't even spare some sun that day.

"Wish Daddy whatin hell bent on all of us goin'," Stacy told me as she slipped into her black dress. She only had the one. Wore it to funerals and out to eat on our anniversaries. Always meant to get her a second one so we didn't have to set there across from each other at Red Lobster once a year thinking about the last person we knew who'd died.

"If it helps you feel better, I don't think they let it be open casket when it's a kid," I offered.

She hated open caskets. Said people weren't meant to see each other like that, all plastic and fake looking. "Unnatural," she said, and unnatural was worse than dead.

"That ain't it," she said. "It's just Daddy gets real down after funerals. More than most. Harder an' harder to pull him out of it. Member last year when his cousin, Les, died? Took Daddy a couple weeks to get outta bed 'cept to go to the bathroom. I cain't take that again."

I pulled my navy blue tie out from the back of my closet. Only tie I had that came close to matching my suit. Brushed the dust off it. I couldn't quite place the last time I'd worn it. We'd missed Les's funeral on account of Stacy's last miscarriage. I've come to see if you can't remember the last time you watched someone be laid in the ground, you're a privileged man.

46

Stacy stood in front of me, reaching up, using her delicate fingers to knot my tie. Her perfume put me at ease. Vanilla cookie body spray. Still to this day, anytime I smell anything that comes close, I picture her in her pretty peach dress, holding a plate of her Snickerdoodles in our kitchen.

"Daddy says every time he sees a casket at the front a the church, he wishes we'd had somethin' for Kelly. Says it'd given him closure," she told me.

"Too tight," I said, pulling at the neck of my shirt.

"Sorry," she whispered, fixing it right away. "I tell him we oughta be glad we hadn't had to have no funeral for her."

At the time, I'd assumed she said it cause she held out hope for Kelly's return. People's need to believe what they believe never surprises me. Didn't never matter to Stacy how many *Law & Order* episodes we watched and the detective would tell the family the first forty-eight hours were crucial. How if you don't find a person by then, it's more than likely they're dead.

Never mattered how many times I'd nod slow when Stacy'd lean over and ask me, while we watched, if that was true. None of those times killed her hope. That was one of the things that held us together. Her with all her sweet, blind hope and me with none.

Her Daddy was already warming up a pew in the back for us by the time we got to the church. I could see Rae and Ms. Florrie setting up in the front row. You could hear Ms. Florrie wailing from all the way by the front doors. She was hunched over. Rae had an arm around her. You'd have thought Brandon was Florrie's.

If Hogue had been there, I thought to myself, he'd have noted that right off. It bothered me how I was thinking more and more like him and less and less like me. It was as troubling to me as the little boy laying in that casket, right at the end of the aisle. There front and center under the altar—the sacrifice of an innocent to a calloused God.

The service was a long one. Pastor Chris took full advantage of people's vulnerability, having more congregants than usual. He delivered a salvation plea instead of a memorial, making sure to get an altar call in at the end. Some preachers are always just itching to preach that hellfire sermon, get a few notches in their Bible belt.

At the end, we all formed a line, followed behind Rae, Ms. Florrie and a young guy. Didn't take a genius to figure out it was Brandon's Daddy. He wasn't from Sanford. Knew that by looking at him. Had too many artistic tattoos and earrings to make much of a comfortable life here. Hogue would've marched right up and talked to him. That's why captain's advice of leaving him at home was followed.

Hogue thought he was onto something when he'd say I was coasting. He could make those kinds of calls. Never could say that about him. The young always like to dole out their judgements on those ahead of them. They got no idea where we've been. All the places life'll drag you. If young pups like him make it past thirty, they see. They see just how time slips away from you before you even know to wish for more, and that's the thing. There's never any more. Besides, it wasn't that I was coasting. I had no interest in him digging. It was the last thing I needed.

There wasn't any lack for those who wanted to line up outside the fellowship hall. The family'd asked that everybody stay behind to get the lunch started while they went to the graveside. They wanted to be alone there. I was grateful. Didn't want to see that little box lowered in the ground no how.

"Horrible. Whatin but three, was he?" Stacy's Daddy said to me as he lit one of his Marlboros.

I nodded.

"Worse when they're young," he went on.

"Yes sir."

"Times like these, make God's plan's all blurry. You question if he's got any," he said blinking back tears. "Why'd he let that boy be born just to cut his life short? Don't make no sense."

I leaned against the cinderblock wall, biding time with him while he smoked. The Dumonts walked up two by two and into the fellowship hall. The oldest, Shane, stopped in front of Hicks.

"What you say there, Hicks?" he greeted, sticking his hand out.

48

Hicks switched his cigarette to his other hand and shook it with his free one.

"Not much to say, Shane," Hicks replied.

The two stood looking out at the church parking lot. The rest of the Dumonts walked on. The food line adapting so as not to lose momentum. People gave the two old timers a wide birth, proceeding around them to the entrance. Having that kind of respect of your community may be the last currency a man has after everything else is taken.

"Somethin' I thought I'd never live to see," Shane put it out there.

None of us outright wanted to talk about why we'd been brought together.

Hicks shook his head. "I've lived to see a whole lot I didn't sign up for," he admitted.

"I feel you, brother."

The two talked a minute longer. At no point was I acknowledged. This was how it was when I was off the clock and on this side of the tracks. Their silence, ignoring me, was their own protest. I got the message loud and clear. No matter who I'd married, my skin color and badge made me a lifelong stranger.

The last of the line shuffled by, each of them dressed in the best thing they could find in their closets. Some of them were like Stacy and must've had only one black piece of clothing to wear, cause I recalled their outfits from the last funeral.

"Felt that way about our Kelly too," Stacy's Daddy picked back up once Shane went inside. "Wondered why God let us have her just to let her go an' disappear."

Even though Stacy'd been talking about her sister before we left the house, there was something worse about him talking about Kelly. Something about Hicks saying her name made my chest tighten and head throb. It was an awful thing to lose a sister, but losing a daughter cut deep.

"She got fourteen years longer than this here boy," he commented like he was again having to make some kind of peace out of a thing that could never offer any.

"That's true, sir," I replied.

The side door flew open. Stacy poked her head out.

"Y'all comin'?" she hollered. "All a Layla's Macaroni Pie's 'bout gone."

"On our way," her Daddy answered holding up what was left of his cigarette where she could see he wasn't done. "Make us a plate."

The rain had cleared. Sunlight speckled her face through the leaves of the tree by the door. It was one of those times I couldn't believe she was mine, that anyone as beautiful as her had gone and married me. She winked. I smiled back. The pain in my chest instantly snatched up with that one look.

Her Daddy took a last puff, dropped his cigarette, and took to rubbing it out over and over with the toe of his wingtip til it blended into the pavement. I braced myself. It was clear we weren't just out there so he could smoke.

"I hadn't ever really asked much a you, Mitchum," he started in.

The way his voice was firm, I knew that was about to change.

"No, you hadn't," I agreed.

"Maybe it's this thing happenin' to this baby, or y'all losin another one a yours, maybe it's both. It's sure made it so Kelly's on my mind more than usual. Lately, all I can do is go over an' over that night she went missin'," he confessed.

I looked over at the side door where Stacy'd just been, praying she'd come out again to end the conversation. It stayed shut. Turned out God don't answer prayers that might play a hand in you not getting more of what you deserve. I guess I should've been grateful I'd gone that long without having to pay any dues with her Daddy.

"See, I been talkin' to Lawrence, Lawrence Keys over at the mill. Now, he works legal for us there. I was talkin' to him in the break room last week 'bout how long Kelly's case has gone on. Long as it's open, we cain't see any files or anything. Now he's a business lawyer, but he knows a little about all types a law. Helped Thelma at the front desk get out a her speedin' ticket, an' he says if I get Kelly declared dead, that ends the investigation, closes the case, then we'd get to see the files. They'd be public knowledge. Is he right? Could we see 'em if we do that?"

Our eyes met. My mind was clouded with wondering if mine were giving me away. Could he see how terrified I was? Part of me was oddly relieved though too. Relieved that no matter what files he ever got hold of, he'd never see what my eyes had seen. How beautiful and sleek Kelly'd been, making her way in those woods ahead of us. How strong she'd looked when she threw rocks. How she'd looked like one of those people who'd survive anything, who'd live to bury the rest of us. Looks don't just deceive—they lie with certainty.

"I hate to say, Hicks. Cold cases are tricky," I told him, his face instantly looking years younger. "May not be anything to speak of in those files."

"I get that. I do, but if we declare her dead, we can see 'em?"

"Yes, sir. If a family declares the missin' person deceased, they can gain access to the files an' whatever evidence was catalogued."

I did that sometimes, still do I reckon, hide behind police jargon. Try to sound real professional. The phrases and words making it more like something I'd read about in the paper than something that's actually happening.

"Well, that's good to know," he said. "Real good."

But I knew it wasn't what he was getting at. It was only part of it, and I felt myself getting as worn out as if I'd worked a full day.

"Now I just need you to talk to your wife for me," he admitted.

And that was it. When it was something about Stacy he didn't like or didn't want to have to handle, she went from being his daughter to being my wife. *Talk to your wife.*

"She won't do it," Hicks said. "She told me long as we keep that case open, there's a chance Kelly's gonna come home. Strangest thing to me, Mitchum. Stacy's smart as a whip, but she seems to have gone plain dumb on this. It's like she just cain't accept that there itn't any chance Kelly's still livin'. None. She holdin' out those little girl hopes she's kept. Beats all. Stacy said to me she's sure she's alive, but I cain't keep doin' this, Mitchum. I need to know. I got to see what's in those files. We got to have some forward motion."

My hands gripped the keys in my pants pocket. Bobby'd had my keys that night. *Why hadn't he driven Kelly home? Why?* That same question rolled around like a pool ball looking for a pocket in my head nearly every time I laid fingers on my keys.

"Alright," I agreed. "I'll see what I can do."

He took one big step, crossing the distance between us and hugged me to him.

"Thank you, son."

I can count on my hand the times that man ever even shook my hand or patted my shoulder. Just wasn't his way, and that was one of the few times he ever called me son, that one day out there after that boy died. One man, graveside, burying his son on down the hill, and there I stood, becoming a man's son.

We walked into the fellowship hall. Stacy was still over at the buffet table making us up a couple of plates. She chatted it up with everybody in line. Everybody knew her. They were drawn to her with that beautiful, wily smile and ageless face.

Both of those attributes always did make people forgive her for tying the knot with me. There wasn't forgiveness enough to trickle over my way. Cain't blame them. Every person in that room either had kin or a friend who I'd touched the head of as they got into the back of my squad car. They saw me, they saw dollar signs, money they'd had to pay for bail or lawyers. They saw Stacy, they saw another Black person who got snatched up by the law in one way or another. None of them would've ever have believed she'd come looking for me.

"Stacy's got high hopes," Hicks had told me a few weeks before I married his daughter. "She thinks you're the man to deliver on 'em."

I nodded.

"Not just hopes. She's got plans. Wants a life we never had," he went on. "When Stacy's got plans, well, I probly don't have to tell you, it's in your best interest to make 'em happen."

"I'm sure gonna try," I'd assured him.

"You're about the best bet she's got at seein' 'em through. Knew that the minute I laid eyes on you," he told me, putting a hand on my shoulder. "Don't mean I like that fact, but I know there ain't a brother in Lee County who can get that girl the life she's wantin', an' you sure as hell ain't the worst a the crackers."

I fought back laughing at that one. He'd been the first to call me a cracker to my face.

"Just the truth of it," Hicks went on. "Don't like it, but my not likin' it don't change it bein' true."

Watching Stacy dish out food for me and her Daddy, I thought about how he'd said that. It came to me that after all our lost babies, me working the beat and not yet captain, and all the protests for Black Lives Matter in 2020 after all that went on with the Floyd fella too, he might not've said the same that day at the funeral. Yeah, if I'd have been standing there that day requesting Stacy's hand after all that, he might've told me no. Can't say as I'd have blamed him one bit.

That's why I knew I had to come through somehow. I had to either try to steer him away from closing Kelly's case or figure out a way to help actually close it. I had no idea how I was going to do either. As I reached to pull a chair out for Hicks at a table, I caught sight of the bald spot forming on the top of his head when he sat down. It aged him to me, making time seem urgent. Seemed wrong to let a man get old and die without knowing something you had the power to let him know.

Stacy brought us over our plates. Not long later Rae and Ms. Florrie came through the doors, all red faced, makeup streaking down cheeks. Rae's looked a bit better than her mama's. Looked like she'd stopped off in the car mirror to fix her face on the way in. They made their way over to the card tables that'd been set up getting pats on their backs, hugs, condolences and promises of help.

Pastor Chris attached himself at their hips. He'd turned forty that year and his wife had left him for a car salesman the year before. I'd heard several of the ladies of the church gossiping about his attention toward the younger women and even teens. He'd been a youth pastor for years under his Daddy's leadership. Hadn't thought much of it, but seeing him there doting on Rae, I was leaning towards believing the old gossips.

Wouldn't be a couple months after that funeral until he went on and proved all the slander right when he ran off with one of the deacon's barely eighteen-year-old daughters. On that day though, he was still just browsing, feeling out how it felt having that youthful gaze on him. Never was too hard on him. Me and him were often only one of a few white people in the room at most church gatherings.

He wasn't my concern then and he didn't seem to be bothering Rae none. She smiled at him, ran her hand along his arm at one point in line while he dished up some food for her and her mama. He must've said something funny too, cause right there at the repast, when she was supposed to be the picture of grief, she laughed.

Had Stacy's Daddy not sprung on me what he had before we went in, I might've read more into that like I should've. I might've sided with Hogue about her right then and there. Even when Ms. Florrie made it around to us, while Rae made sure to steer clear, avoiding us like the plague, I still couldn't register it for the tell it was of the hand she was holding.

All I could think about, setting there eating the last of my macaroni pie, was how I'd outright lied to Stacy's Daddy, and I knew it. I couldn't help him. I knew good and well I wasn't ever gonna talk to Stacy about claiming Kelly'd died, closing the case. There was no way because if she were to agree and her Daddy was to get those files, he'd see my name right there along with Bobby Olsen's as the last two people here on this earth to have ever laid eyes on his other daughter.

91°F

It was so steamy out, he swore there was smoke billowing out from under the hood of his Corolla. But it was just another signal of the encroaching summer. His armpits provided another sign as they soaked his shirts the moment he stepped out the door. Indeed, the thick Carolina air rendered him more like one of the flies that hung wriggling in the fly paper over his Mamaw's picnic table than a teenage boy in damp clothes. Being the biggest lineman Lee High had ever seen, he accepted that he had no hopes of keeping his pits dry and just bought new t-shirts every so often.

Pulling up to the Olsen house in his already drenched shirt that day, he was glad he didn't have to get out and go in. He never felt at home in such a place—the biggest house for miles, he guessed. What did they even need all that space for?

"God damn, Mitch!" Bobby shouted as he got in the car. "Get that air crankin'! Won't be g'ttin' any bitches ridin' in this furnace. Jesus!"

As his friend fastened his seatbelt, Mitch caught sight of Mrs. Olsen standing on the porch, her face flush with embarrassment. A good church going woman like her would've stomped out and dragged her boy inside to wash his mouth out with soap had he not been a few months shy of being a man.

"Hey there, Mrs. Olsen," Mitch called with a big smile so as to make up for his passenger's crassness.

That was the nature of their friendship—one making the mess, the other cleaning it up. Bobby whipped his head around, stared at her, tongue tied.

"Hey there, Mitchum. How are you, hon'?" she called back as she made sure to stare right at him and not acknowledge her own or what he'd just said.

"Cain't complain. How 'bout you?"

She leaned on the railing, her dress moving slightly in the breeze revealing sheer panty hose clad legs. Mitch thought on occasion what it must be like for Mr. Olsen to try to get those off, but the vision of it ended up being more comical to him than anything. He didn't know another woman in town who wore hose in the summer.

"I guess I can't either," she said, her gaze turned acutely to Bobby. "Well, I could, but I won't."

"I know what you mean."

Bobby punched his leg down low enough, out of his mother's line of sight.

"Be back soon, Mama. Headin' to Sonic."

She looked back over at Mitch, and he knew what she was doing. She was looking at his face for reassurance this was true. Hopeful that it wasn't a meager alibi for something she'd hope to never have to hear about second hand from one of her friends at the Junior League. From the time the boys were in Pee Wee football together, she'd recognized who was the more honest of the two. Though it pained her it wasn't her Bobby, she chose to act as if it was.

Mitch smiled back, nodding and knowing as he did that the motion wasn't an out right lie, as much as it was a gamble. Everything with Bobby was. It was 50/50 they'd go to Sonic, shoot the shit with the girls, then head home. It was also 50/50 she'd be calling the cops, when come 2:00 am, there'd still have been no sign of them because they'd ridden all the way to somewhere like South of the Border on the border of South Carolina. If that happened, he'd drink tequila under a bridge while Bobby, and whoever he'd talked into it at a gas station on the way, fucked in the backseat. It wouldn't be up to Mitch where the night would lead. That he did know.

"Well then, y'all be good now, you hear?" she told them waving as she stood up, smoothed her dress and opened the screen door.

She stood half in and half out warily watching. Bobby rolled up the window on his side as fast as he could.

"Come on!" he hissed, punching the driver's leg again.

Backing out slowly, Mitch glanced up seeing her still staring. He gave Mrs. Olsen a small, conciliatory wave. She nodded, then went all the way inside, yet stood behind the narrow glass window in the door, her eyes not wavering from them. He thought this visual, her behind the glass, most accurately pictured how it was for the Olsen's—a layer between them and everyone else.

For this reason, it was always strange to him that Bobby hung out with him at all, what with how rich his family was and how, well, *not rich* he and his were. His own father worked at the mill way over in Aberdeen and both his uncles did as well. He knew his place would be secured there when his *glory days*, as his father referred to them, were done.

"Enjoy 'em while you can, boy. Let me tell you, it ain't never gonna get no better than runnin' plays out on that field an' plowin' pussy in the backseat a your car after. Not ever," his father'd admonish him when his mother wasn't around.

Mitch would laugh and agree, but he made sure his father never knew the latter of that scenario evaded him. No, he knew his dad needed the thrill of considering him a *poon hound* though he most decidedly wasn't. Oh, he had plenty of girls who were friends, just no girlfriends. This was a predominant reason he put up with Bobby Olsen.

He hoped, if he was patient, some of the girls Bobby quit having time for might naturally slip on down and consider him. He was damn good at consoling. One of these days, one of them would look up from crying and think "Hey, Mitch is really nice." When they did, he'd be ready.

That was the primary reason for their camaraderie, the secondary one being that they always started at every game. Bobby the running back, and him, the lineman clearing the way. Their positions were yet one more cliché thing that made the two of them the southern smalltown archetypes they were. Mitch was well aware they were living the photos that in a decade the kids of Lee County High would see in the display cases that lined the main hall outside the gym. Trophies would hide them partially, but there they'd be, he and Bobby, the Zeus and Apollo of the nineties.

"Laura still comin'?" Bobby wanted to know as they neared the Sonic.

"Far as I know."

His passenger lit a cigarette before rolling down his window. He'd talked to him about that before. No sense in revisiting it. Bobby lived by his own code.

"What do you mean, *far as you know*? Y'all didn't set it up?"

"Yeah, I mean, we talked about it. Last I knew she's comin'. Said she an' Kelly'd be there 'fore eight," Mitch explained.

"Kelly Diamond?" Bobby perked up.

"Mmm hmmm."

"Shit. That girl's a waste a time. Stone cold bitch."

"What? Come on now, she's been nothin' but nice anytime I been around her."

"*Nice*! Now that's exactly what you don't want," Bobby exclaimed. "I got dibs on Laura."

Dibs. It was always a mystery to Mitch when Bobby said things like this as if the girl involved wouldn't have a say.

"Sides, Kelly's from over there near the Food Lion. Hell, we don't even drive over that way if we don't absolutely have to for kegs. Damn sure don't wanna be datin' nobody from over there. She might *pass*, but her Daddy's Black as they come. You know that?"

Mitch shook his head. He hadn't known, and he guessed he

hadn't really given much thought to it. Now that it was told to him, it made sense. She was more tan than other girls and had whitish blond but kinky, curly hair she often kept pulled up in a ponytail. Bobby started back up joking around about *nice* girls as they pulled into a parking spot. There the two sat in front of the Sonic, just as Laura'd agreed.

Both were in short skirts and tight t-shirts. Laura seemed more at ease in hers than Kelly who pulled at her Green Day shirt trying to keep it from hugging so snugly. As they stood, Laura smiled; Kelly's mouth remained a flat line across her pretty face.

Mitch turned off the car and was first to open his door. Bobby stayed put taking a few last puffs, looking at the girls, then putting his cigarette out slower than usual in the car's ashtray. He always played it like he could care less. It had worked well for him so far.

"Y'all hadn't been here too long have you?" Mitch asked walking over to the girls.

"Naw, Kelly's aunt just now dropped us off," Laura told him.

She wobbled a bit, and he looked down to see she had borrowed her older sister's heels for the night. He'd never known her to wear them. She was a novice when it came to acting like a woman. She'd picked tonight to test her skills.

They'd been friends since grade school, him and Laura. Every time they'd ever hung out, she'd looked like she just came from feeding goats at her parents would-be-farm.

"Goats are good for makin' soap with their milk an' butter, an' you can eat 'em if you have to," she'd told him.

He'd learned not to question her about things like this. Why they'd have to resort to eating goats and all. Her family went to a prepper holy roller church in the backwoods. Her mother especially always struck him as a few bricks short of a load.

Bobby finally got out and came striding up like he was making an entrance on a men's cologne commercial.

"Hey y'all," was all he offered as he sat at a table.

When the rest of them joined him, Laura took her place beside Bobby. *So, he'd been right* was all Mitch could think. Not that he wanted Laura, but for just once, he'd have liked Bobby to call dibs and have it not mean a thing. It wouldn't be next week, and Laura'd be calling Mitch crying about how Bobby wouldn't call her back, and how she had a raw place on her back from the leather upholstery of his car seat. The way he saw it, some girls were hell bent on drama. He'd just never figured Laura for one of those.

Kelly lingered close to their table for a few seconds before sitting a little ways down from Mitch on his bench so she was facing Laura. On a Friday night in Sanford, they'd been lucky to secure a table at all.

"How're you, Kelly?" Bobby asked with an unmistakably caustic tone.

He hadn't directly addressed Laura yet, and Mitch knew this game. His pal liked ignoring them first, then they'd want him all the more. It worked for rich handsome boys like Bobby. The kind who looked like they stepped right out of all those old photos in their social studies books of the Kennedy brothers. It didn't work for schlubs.

Due to this, Mitch had grown up with the knowledge that he'd have to be nicer than most. He'd have to get A's and be as good an athlete as he could. His parents' muted features had found him early, and by third grade, he'd even gotten a bit of a gut. He would not be afforded the luxury of playing games with women. He understood his life was not to be one of social or any other ease.

It didn't bother him much. Most of the time, he could push this sad state of things from his mind. When he was with Bobby, however, his awareness was heightened. He was acutely cognizant that there were those who lived better. Those for who life would be full of open waters and smooth sailing. Bobby and his ilk would not encounter hardly any of the barriers that had been assigned to him at birth.

"Fine," is all Kelly replied.

Everything about the way she'd said it, even her body language gave off an irritation at having been spoken to by Bobby. Mitch liked her immediately. Yes, the girls had been divvied up well.

There'd be no going back on it. Jenny Lynn skated over to take their orders. She'd worked there for as long as they'd been alive. Mitch marveled at how someone as old as she was could still roller skate.

Once their orders were in, and Jenny Lynn was out of earshot, Bobby mimicked her accent. Laura laughed unwarrantedly loud. Bobby blew his straw paper at her. Mitch and Kelly looked on with mature disgust. They unknowingly shared the wish that they could be anywhere but there in Lee County. That they could have any other friends but the ones seated across from them. They also unknowingly shared the belief that Lee County didn't offer much else other than what they were experiencing.

The revving of an engine announced Lester Boyd's arrival behind the wheel of his muscle car. He could be found there every Friday night. This time, from what they could tell, he'd had a custom paint job done. All the kids collectively got up and walked over as he parked, entranced by the bold purple body of the automobile and fiery orange flames along the doors.

"What's Lester gone an' pawned now?" Bobby scoffed. "I swear, I bet his Grandma hadn't got a thing left in her place after all his pawn shop visits. Hope he lets her ride in it. God knows she's paid for that tacky thing."

Mitch took joy in Bobby's displeasure. He'd never known his friend to be the jealous type. Most of the time, Bobby was the one people were jealous of, but he was glad to see he could feel such a thing, even if it was Lester, and not he himself that had made him feel it.

Succumbing to his curiosity, Bobby hopped up and started across the parking lot with the rest of the patrons. Laura took off behind him.

"Y'all comin'?" she invited.

Mitch waved her on.

"Y'all go ahead. We'll wait for the food," he told her, hoping this would give him time with Kelly.

"A'ight. Make sure she brings us some ketchup. Cain't have fries with no ketchup."

"We will," Kelly shouted.

Mitch caught her stealing a look at him as she turned her head away from her friend. She was pretty. Not old school, readying-for-cotillion pretty like most of the southern girls he knew aspired to, but pretty all the same. Like many thoughts and feelings he had, he could not articulate them, he just knew what he knew. Kelly abruptly looked down at the table, fidgeting with a straw paper between her fingers.

There they sat—the two of them in a moment. The waitress serving those around them, kids shooting the shit next to Lester's car, loud music blaring from his open windows. It was all happening just for them and yet not at all happening for them alone.

A familiar feel crept in. Where had he seen all this before? Yes, he remembered, he'd seen this exact picture in his mother's yearbook. The kids all out at Sonic on a Friday night. As soon as he placed it, it soured things. The idea that not only was his life unoriginal but that their town, what kids got up to, hadn't changed in over twenty years. A new song started. Suddenly, Kelly smiled. She liked that one, and he focused in on her. He saw that if he wanted them to be, they were two stars in a galaxy of their own making.

Then she spoke.

"Why you hang out with him?" she demanded, looking out at Bobby and Laura.

Her smile crinkled the same way the waxy paper on the burgers they were getting ready to be served did, sending them plummeting from their place up high. They were not stars in a galaxy, but meteors hell bound for destruction.

"Bobby? Aww he's a'ight," Mitch protested, knowing the statement held little in the way of validity.

It was another one of his good old boy adages he repeated, a familiar song on his jukebox. At that precise second, as if to intentionally prove his buddy wrong, Laura screeched, and they looked over to see Bobby pulling at her tank top as he yelled "Let 'em breathe!" while she slapped at him. Bobby cackled. Laura laughed nervously but laughed all the same alerting Kelly. She was okay, so she kept her seat.

"Is he?" Kelly snapped.

"Awe, Bobby's just playful. You gotta think a him like one a those chimps at the zoo, the one racin' back an' forth along the bars makin' the most racket cause he's got the idea that if he keeps at it, the bars'll part just for him."

This made Kelly grin, and the sound of Lester's engine accompanied by him cranking up his rap took up any silence that might've lent itself to further conversation between them. It wasn't long til Jenny Lynn skated out again, their food balanced on her tray. She barely bumped the table as she sat it down, being sure to include a bottle of ketchup as she de-trayed their meals.

"Y'all set?" she shouted to them over the Friday night hubbub.

"I think so. Thanks, Jenny," Mitch shouted back, smiling up.

He could feel Kelly watching him as Jelly Lynn skated off. She was studying him rather, until he glanced over at her. His eyes meeting hers briefly. She looked away. Lester's revving quieted, and only Eminem's *The Way I Am* pouring from his speakers was left to contend with.

"Yeah, I heard you're all nice an' stuff," Kelly remarked before stuffing a fry in her mouth.

"Nice an' stuff?"

"You know, like a boy scout?" she teased, hand up over her mouth so as not to seem unladylike while she chewed.

"I'm not sure that's a compliment," he teased.

She finished chewing, swallowed and took a sip of her soda, then looked right at him.

"It is."

He did not look away. His apple red cheeks a contagion causing hers to redden also. She was the one to break the gaze by looking over her shoulder.

"Food's gonna get cold," she called to Laura who was rounding up Bobby, taking his hand, leading him over.

As they approached, they looked more like teacher and child

heading in from the playground than a potential couple. They flopped down across from their friends. Bobby narrowed his eyes at Mitch, then rolled them towards Laura. She caught this cue instead, and let go of Bobby's hand, elbowing him.

"What?" he screeched pretending it hurt more than it could have.

She cut her eyes at him. He shrugged, feigning an innocence he'd never possessed. This caused Laura to laugh and throw her arms around his shoulders giving way to being the awkward schoolgirl she was. She leaned over and whispered in his ear. Her game was sweetly amateur. Mitch felt pangs of guilt as there was no way for Laura to know she was no different than Little Red Riding Hood standing on the precipice of a dark, dark wood.

The longer they sat, eating, laughing, joking, the more his dread grew. Bobby was pulling out all his usual tricks. His hand on Laura's back, arm around her shoulders. His hand making its way to her thigh, tickling her a bit too close to her bra straps. Mitch had been present for enough of these dates, if you could call them that, to accurately chart the progression.

"What's he like?" Laura'd asked him on the phone many times, but also the night before.

They were in the habit of chatting at least once a week by phone even though they saw each other daily at school. It was as if they were siblings who no longer lived together but maintained a connection with modern conveniences.

"Think he'll like me?" she'd pestered.

He'd ignored this first question and given a less than exuberant *yeah* as his answer to the second. As she talked on about how she couldn't wait, how she'd had a crush on Bobby Olsen for forever, he wondered why it was girls always seemed so concerned about who would like them and unconcerned as to who they would like.

All he had to do was mention to Bobby that morning that Laura had been asking about him again. For whatever reason, even though he'd said it in passing to Bobby many times before, on this particular day, his friend wanted him to set up a double date. No doubt he'd be blamed however if Laura didn't follow right along with what was supposed to happen. What anyone who knew anything about Bobby would know was going to take place. Everyone knew Bobby Olsen didn't *date*. He fucked. He bypassed all the niceties the rest of them had to undergo. It was a luxury unearned, much like his whole existence.

Because of this common knowledge, Mitch wouldn't take responsibility for Laura. This was Bobby's M.O., and she'd persisted in pestering him about setting them up. She must've been itching for it. Who was he to judge?

But as Laura nervously blathered on, Mitch couldn't help wonder *why*. Why any girl who had any self preservation at all would subject themselves to Bobby Olsen. Surely, she'd stood in the bathroom after a dance or been at a cheer practice with at least one of his dejected leftovers. Hadn't she had to console at least one of them in the back of the auditorium after they'd been dumped by him? That was their mistake too. *You cain't get dumped if you're just gettin' fucked* Mitch thought.

"You don't talk much," Bobby accused Kelly, cutting Laura's blabbering off mid-sentence.

The brashness of it nearly caused Mitch to choke on a bite of his burger. Kelly was unphased. She took a long sip of her soda. Her eyes never left him as she delivered,

"Don't see the point."

"Of talkin'?" Bobby shot back.

At this point, Laura squirmed on her end of the bench, clearing her throat, looking at Kelly, then away. What was Laura fearing Kelly might say?

"No, just talkin' to you," she explained.

The thick night air sat in the middle of them, a presence all its own. It heightened any offense that might be taken, pressing on them, egging Bobby on. Mitch thought about how his Dad had mentioned that every time it got hot, they could count on a suicide, and definitely a homicide or two, at the mill. Each and every single summer.

Bobby shocked them all by laughing. He broke into his half-evil half-ornery cackle that every boy born below the Mason-Dixon was known for. As soon as he stopped long enough to notice only Laura had started laughing with him, and Kelly still held her evil eye on him, his laughter ceased.

"Now why wouldn't somebody want to talk to me?"

Kelly picked her drink up, sipping the last of it. Laura jumped up, hurrying over to Kelly's free side, tugging on her arm.

"Let's get refills. Come on," Laura begged.

Her friend obliged her. The two of them walked up to the window. Laura giving Kelly what for on the way over, nearly falling off of her heels as she did.

"Told you. Don't ever mix with anybody from over by the Food Lion. Crazy as fuck!" Bobby went off.

Mitch shrugged. He wasn't exactly sure which particular beef Kelly'd have with his pal. He'd never seen them even speak to each other at school. There was the chance Bobby'd messed around with one of her friends, but she was fairly new to Lee High. Always a chance of that, though. If you randomly selected five girls from Lee High, he bet 4/5 would have reason to hate Bobby. Might be she'd heard all the girl's locker room sob stories. That alone would be enough to turn her sour. Yes, it was good the two of them were seniors. Bobby was coming up on having outstayed his welcome, and it was beginning to be harder for Mitch to not come under scrutiny just by proxy.

The girls made their way back over, Kelly reluctantly having struck a deal with Laura on their way to be sweeter. Mitch eyed their return as though it was happening in slo mo, like in one of those 80's love story moments from classics like *Say Anything* that his mother loved. The ones where the underdog got the girl. Maybe tonight was his night?

Before they could make it all the way back to the table, a station wagon zoomed up so close, Laura almost had her hand nicked by the side mirror. By some strange stroke of chance, she'd put her hand up just in time to move her bangs. The driver's door flew open.

"So, this is where the devil's brought you!" her mother blasted her as she stood, shaking her fists next to the car.

She quickly crossed her arms tight, as if she was trying to hold the violence inside her. She had the look of a woman who'd spent so much of her life trying not to give way to any desire, that she had no love of anything. Everything a threat of temptation.

"Mama!" Laura cried.

The two boys stayed put. Mitch had met Laura's a mother a time or two over the years. She reminded him of the mother from Stephen King's *Carrie*, otherworldly in ways with her dark hair and pale skin. It was odd to him that some people got so vehement about their love of the Lord, that they started to look more like they were in Satan's camp.

"I knew you weren't studyin'! I knew it! Told your daddy you're not to be trusted. Told him outright I been a teenage girl an' they cain't be trusted further than you can throw 'em." She waved her backhand towards Kelly. "An' here you are out with this…"

She stopped herself from saying the word out loud. Likely her rigid Evangelical side winning out in its wrangling of her hateful sinner side. Kelly's mouth was agape, bracing for it. Though less and less acceptable in parts of the country, so they saw on the news, it was not a term Lee County folks had at all let fall out of their vocabulary.

"G't in this car!" Laura's mother demanded.

Laura's father slumped down in the passenger side, looking out his window like an escape con who'd gotten himself rounded up and told the warden where to find his partner so as to not be alone in his misery.

"Daddy!" Laura wailed.

Her mother took hold of her arm. Kelly moved aside knowing wars between family have no room for enlisters.

"He cain't help you. Come on!"

She continued manhandling her daughter til she wrangled her all the way into the backseat. Laura's sobbing could be heard over the music. The mother wriggled out of the backseat, and slammed the door, doing little to lessen the sound of Laura's fit. She then turned to face the rest of them.

"Your Daddy know you're out?" she put it to Kelly.

"Ye-yes ma'am, my uh, my aunt—" Kelly sputtered. "She—she dropped us off."

"How you gonna get home?"

"I'll call her," Kelly told her.

"A'ight then. Well, go on. Call her an' get yourself home. Ain't got nothin' bad to say about your kin. What you're doin' here's between you an' them, but Laura ain't no fast girl," the mother informed her.

"Neither am I," Kelly said.

Her response surprised the mother. Few in her life had ventured to push back when she shoved. She grunted something to herself, got in and drove off. Mitch thought Kelly talking back to the woman had shown real guts. More balls than most of his whole football team had and right in that second, he knew he could love her. Indeed, theirs might've been a clandestine love story for the ages, that is, if he'd ever seen her again after that night.

80°F

Hogue

I can see from here that their columns need a paint job. They needed one last time I saw this place. I remember thinking that way back then that night as we drove up, Evette whimpering in the backseat next to me. Mama and Daddy setting quiet as stones in the front. I wasn't sure you could trust a place to fix your head if they couldn't keep up with painting. Seemed off to me then. Seems even more off to me now.

Told Cobb he should have come instead of me, but he said he was already knee deep in paperwork this afternoon. Lord knows I'd rather walk across hot coals than do that pencil pushing shit. Sides, Rae's asked for me. So here I am, a place I said I'd never go again. Older I get, the more I'm finding, you wanna have to revisit something, just say you won't. It'll be happening again for certain then.

I gotta admit when Cobb told me she wanted me to visit her here and not wait til she got sent home, it gave me the creeps. Why couldn't she wait? Far as I know, from what her doctor told us, she's only got another week in here. I was willing to hold onto what I got to ask her about. What cain't wait til next Monday on her part?

"How long?" the parking lot guy leans out of the booth and barks at me.

I stare at him in his baby blue uniform with a name tag spelling out Dorothea Dix before his name.

"How long you plan on bein' here?" he says louder, standing up straight, squinting at me.

His posture makes it evident he ain't fond of the law.

"Hope not more than an hour," I say.

I clear my throat.

"Maybe just a half hour."

He chuckles to himself, leans inside his booth, brings a ticket out with numbers across the top.

"I'll give you least an hour. Wouldn't believe how many people say a half hour, an' I don't see hide nor hair of 'em for a week solid."

I open my mouth to argue, but I can see in my rearview a car's pulled up behind me, so I take my ticket and stick it on my dash. The bar across the entrance goes up. The attendant's already turned away from me. I pull on through.

Grass is greener than I recall. Then again, we came at night. The whole yard looked like one big ocean then, and I imagined if Evette could have worked her magic and snapped out of it, she'd have run barefoot across that yard.

"They got a pool. See it honey?" Mama'd called to her as we drove closer to the entrance.

Evette didn't look. She stayed in her fetal position hugging her door.

I'd been a little jealous. I'd rarely gotten to swim in a pool. Only person we knew who even had a blow-up one that held water more than waist high was Preacher Loomis. He'd only get it out for vacation Bible School a couple weeks a year and for baptism Sunday every six months or so. The more I looked out at that chlorine blue water, seemed to me like having a breakdown mighta been the way to go. Felt like maybe my sister had known something I hadn't. Like she'd found a way to get time off, have herself some leisure.

I pull into a parking spot, take my vape out of my pocket, take a few puffs on it. Cobb hates the peach pit tobacco smell of this one, and I've told him I'll quit. I just never say when. Figure while you're nursing a divorce, ain't a time to take away your vices. Already quit smoking to appease Jolie, but we were already passed appeasing by then. Wish she'd have told me she wanted to sever things before I gave up cigarettes. I don't miss much but, damn, I miss a good Pall Mall to round out my shift.

An orderly is walking with a big old fella twice their size over to a picnic table where they sit down. Wonder what he's here getting his head shrunk for? Cain't have too much going on upstairs. If he did, he'd know right off, he could outrun his keeper and make it over that brush a few yards away, be home free. But what then? Guess that keeps most of us doing what we gotta do. That question of *what then.*

The big fella looks back and spots me in my cruiser. He immediately frowns, says something to the orderly who stands, looking my way to see for themselves. Soon as she spots me, she frowns too. Probably thinks I got somebody in the back, ready to up their enrollment numbers here.

I nod to them. They just stare. Taking my last puff, I put my vape in the cup holder and open my door. I can do this. It's just a place. That's all—a place. All that with Evette was a long time ago. Won't be a soul here who was here then. I can do this.

The sidewalk up to the big front doors is a long one. Did I walk up this that night or did Daddy just take Evette up by himself?

"Afternoon," a voice calls.

A woman dressed in baby blue dress suit, all smiles, is holding the door for me. She has the whitest teeth made only whiter by her navy hair that's curled up in this leftover 50's hairstyle. I take that back. She might be a soul who was here when my sister was. She looks like she came with the place. The Donna Reed of Dorothea Dix hospital.

"Afternoon," I parrot.

Once I'm closer, I see the telltale signs of age on her heavily made-up face—the creases in her cheeks from years of that unnatural smile, crow's feet coming out from the sides of her eyes. Her beauty regimen don't seem to take the summer into account. Her thick war paint is showing signs of dripping off what with the top of her lip accumulating sweat across it.

Her skin has a strange yellowish tint. Maybe she's been sneaking patient's pills. Definitely same coloration pillheads get over time. They get close as they can to the shade of those pharmacy pill bottles they like so much.

"How can we help you this afternoon, officer?"

And even though she's asking how she can assist me, I cain't help but see how I had it wrong. She isn't holding the door as much as she's standing in front of it.

"Just here for a visit."

This doesn't pass her test. She looks past me like she's searching for back up she's gonna need if she tries to make me leave.

"I'd say you're a couple hours too late. Visitin' hours are mornins from 9:00 am to noon."

We both stand here. Her knowing that's not the kind of visit I'm talking about, and me knowing I don't need an invite to go in. She fiddles with her skirt then clasps her hands behind her back, looking me in the eyes then looking back down at her shoes.

"A patient a yours requested that I come, ma'am. Rae Doomis. Won't take long," I tell her.

The woman keeps her hands behind her back. She looks over her shoulder at the inside then out at the parking lot, takes a second to smile and nod at somebody she knows. Finally, she moves aside. Not a word from her, just holds the door, and that's my cue to enter.

An orderly at the front desk is talking on the phone.

"Mr. Phillips, Mr. Phillips, yes we understand, but...well, alright, sir. Yes...yes that's fine," she finishes as we walk up.

"He's sayin' we're stealin' her candy again," she says to Dorothea Dix Donna Reed.

"Who'd want that cheap candy?" is all Donna Reed shoots back. "Lee Ann, this is officer..."

She looks over at me raising her penciled-on brows.

"Hogue. Officer Hogue."

"Yes, well, please check him in, an' I'll be right back."

As Lee Ann catalogs my phone and types in my info, she talks a mile a minute about how Mr. Phillips is always thinking his wife's candy's disappearing, but if he'd pay more attention to her, he'd see she's the one eating all the candy, cause she's sure enough popping out of her pants.

I half listen, but my mind's caught on the chest high countertop my arms are propped on. I wasn't quite tall enough back then to rest my arms up on it, but Daddy was. I see him here that night and me looking up at him. Mama didn't come in. No, I remember now. Daddy'd made me go with him.

"Does she have a history of self-harm?" the nurse had asked Daddy.

"What?"

"Has she—has she—hurt herself or threatened to before?" she clarified.

Daddy shook his head, and that was his truth, but it was a lie. He and Mama always did seem to have their own truth only the two of them shared. It wasn't mine.

I opened my mouth to say so, but Evette tugged on my shirt. I looked up at her. I couldn't believe she wouldn't want me to tell something that might stand in the way of her getting back home quicker. Those sad almost turquoise eyes she had pleaded with me. I knew what she wanted, what she was demanding.

She wanted another chance to finish it. She wanted what had happed that summer to stay our secret. I knew it shouldn't, but I was only twelve. I wasn't old enough to go against her. There was also the fact that I was tired, so tired of all the drama with her and Mama and Daddy. The early morning hours waking up to the sounds of her crying on the other side of the wall there in her bedroom, Mama begging her to get up and go to school. Yeah, by the time we came to stand at this counter, I was as ready for her to have a *vacation* here as everybody else was.

So, I let it go, didn't say nothing. Didn't tell Daddy then just like I hadn't told him when it happened. I never told anybody about finding her that week of July 4th when we were up at the lake. She didn't show up with the other girls at the bonfire, so Mama'd sent me to look for her. Walked all over those campgrounds, thought I'd have to go back without her, then there she was.

Every now and then, when it's a full moon and I happen to get caught out in it, even if I'm nowhere near any lake, I see her. Moonlight shining down on her, out there in the water floating face down. And I cain't tell you how I did what it was I did in that second. I got no idea. I wasn't a real good swimmer, but I trucked it out there, grabbed onto her, and dragged her up on the shore. Laid her on her back, did quick pumps on her chest with my hands, in between holding her nose, and breathing into her mouth like our coach had showed us in P.E. I hadn't even thought I'd been paying him any mind in that class. When the time came though, I repeated what he'd done perfectly.

Before long, her eyes popped open. Evette started coughing up water. She sat up quick as lightning, wild eyed, looking all around trying to figure out if she'd gone on to the afterlife or she was still stuck in this one. I yelled at her, slapped one of her arms, mad as hell. She turned to me, tears streaking down her cheeks. They made thin lines through the dirty film from the lake that covered her skin.

I hugged her tight. She felt as cold and stiff as when winter'd sneak up on us and Mama's washed sheets would freeze on the clothesline before she could bring them in. She put a hand on my back, turning her head away so she could hack out what was left in her lungs. There was a second there, feeling her hand on my skin, I was mad she thought she got to leave. That she'd thought she could leave me alone with Mama and Daddy and the whole damn world.

Never said thank you. Never, and we never did talk about it, not even there by the lake. About what she was trying to do or what she'd have wished I'd done. I knew. Anybody who really knew Evette at all knew she wasn't long for this world. She always struck me as having one foot already out of it, and everybody's job was to pull her back in.

"You all set?"

Donna Reed is back.

I nod.

"It'll all be here when you come back down," Lee Ann assures me with a smile that makes me glad I only have a flip phone. Foils any of her usual snooping.

I follow Donna Reed up a long flight of stairs. Maybe the elevator's broken. Maybe it doesn't go all the way to the top. I look to my right where Cobb's usually at and smile like I actually said that out loud and he's there to appreciate it, then I remember I'm solo on this one. Donna Reed's already at the top of the last set of stairs, scowling down.

I make it all the way up and follow her down the hall to a big rec room. I spot Rae right off. She's over in a corner with a group of women, her face all done up like one of those old 80's music video girl. A perky woman in the middle's wearing regular clothes standing next to a patient who's holding a light pink Mary Kay makeup case.

"With this pink on your cheeks, now I know I'm right. You're more of a summer than a winter," she's telling the patient sitting in front of her, putting more pink powder on her cheeks than David Bowie ever wore.

Donna Reed gets sidetracked by a worker leaning out behind the glass window of what has to be the pharmacy and motioning to her to come over. I hang back and let the Mary Kay lady finish up. I don't like being here a minute longer than I have to but I'm doing my best not to let Rae get wind of it. Doing my best to play it cool. If I get amped, she might too then I won't find out a fucking thing.

The other patients who aren't getting made over are mostly gathered around a TV watching cartoons like I used to on Saturday mornings when I was little. Kids these days got cartoon channels all the time. I remember I used to be the first one up when I'd stay the night at Jimmy Crowder's down the street. We all loved staying at his place cause once his daddy got a check from getting hurt at his work, he had the biggest TV on the block. Smurfs were huge on that thing.

"My daddy lost his hand for this," Jimmy leaned over and whispered one morning when we were watching *Tom and Jerry*.

I looked back at his daddy in his recliner, pill bottles on the table next to him, feet up, sleeping open mouthed, a long line of drool dripping from it all the way down to his shirt. I remember wishing my Daddy worked out at the chicken plant where his Daddy did instead of at a grocery warehouse so my Daddy'd have had more chance of losing something. We'd get ourselves a big old TV then too. Didn't want him to lose a whole hand no ways. I figured a finger might've been fine. Surely a finger's worth a 50-inch.

Rae stares past the Mary Kay volunteer, right at me. She bats her thick mascaraed eyes at me under eyelids heavily caked with glittery eyeshadow. Natural is a dirty word to Miss Mary Kay here.

"Now don't y'all all just look lovely!" she exclaims packing up her supplies.

From the look of her, she ain't over forty-five. Second generation Mary Kay peddler; a family legacy of barn painting. My how Mary Kay's disciples have fallen. There was a time they could get themselves a fancy pink Caddy. Here this saleslady's in the nut house. She's worse than her mama cause these women ain't got nowhere to go except out back to the fenced in picnic area to mill around like a bunch of defunct sheep. Puts a whole new meaning to the phrase *captive audience*.

Patients go their own ways. One real tall gal who looks like she got done up in browns more than pinks, leans down and says something in Rae's ear. With the way her hand is on Rae's arm, how she's got her eyes closed, I bet anything she's telling her she's praying for her. Hugs her neck before she walks off.

"You comin'?" a short little gal in a white bathrobe calls to Rae from the back door where she's realized their herd's one short.

"I'll catch up," Rae answers her with a smile.

With her makeup like that, her standard looney bin issued scrubs with a neckline hanging low showing a small line where her chest ends and breasts begin, I'm betting about ten years ago, I could've seen the same scene at her high school. Only difference then would've been that they'd all have been wearing regular clothes and a door wouldn't lock behind them when they came in to go to bed at night. Yeah, Rae's that girl who runs things. All the girls want to know what she's thinking and doing so they can do it. Evette was the same. Everybody looked to her. She looked to nobody

"You're just born with it, little brother," she told me not long before life landed her here. "Just plain born with it."

Rae stays seated. She knows I'll come to her. That's how her world goes.

"Officer Hogue," she greets, nodding as I sit in the plastic chair across from her. "Sure 'preciate you comin' all this way."

She crosses her legs real elegant like we're on a date at a fancy restaurant. I get situated and notice my chair's all one piece of plastic. No screws holding it together. People come here with screws loose, guess they don't want them finding any stray ones to replace them with. I'm on a roll. I'll store that gem away for Cobb later.

"I think sometimes you joke so you don't cry," he's told me.

He don't take to my humor as much as I think he does. Catching myself before I crack up, I sit back and rest my arms on the arms of the chair. I figure laughing to yourself in here won't help you get back out without a hitch. I bite my lip.

"Well, we need to wrap up a few things. This is as good a place as any," I say. "How come you didn't ask for Cobb? Thought y'all go to the same church an' all?"

"Goin' to the same church don't mean nothin'. He's married to a Diamond. I got no use for 'em," she says, adding a little catty snarl at the end.

"Why's that?"

"Stacy Diamond always thought her shit don't stink. Likes to pass whenever she gets the idea it'll give her an advantage. Soon as it don't, she's back wantin' to be one a the *sistas*. Not all of us get the luxury a bein' Black when we need to then white when we want.

She always had a mind to marry up. Only surprise to everybody was she actually invited any a her daddy's side a the family to the weddin'. Not a one a them could pass if they wanted. They all Black as midnight," she tells me.

Slipping a note pad from my front pocket, I'm glad I went with Cobb's advice on bringing one since he was right about them confiscating phones.

"You got guts," Rae says. "I'll give you that. Cain't anybody else I know seem to set foot in here. Creeps 'em out."

She scoots forward, puts a hand on my knee, pats it, leaving it a little too long before she slides it back over on her lap.

"Not you though. I asked for you, an' here you are," she gushes.

"Yeah, well, a case is a case. I don't get to pick where it takes me."

This don't set well, me calling her situation a *case*. She uncrosses her legs, putting both feet firm on the ground. She reaches up, making a fist, kissing her hand then showing me the bright lipstick print.

"Lord knows! Woman put more lipstick on these lips today than they've had on 'em in my whole life."

She can go on and laugh. She's the one locked in here, not me. The room's nearly cleared out now except for a few orderlies.

"Cookie time," Rae says noticing me looking around.

There's a line outside the doors down the hall to a window where orderlies are handing out little cups, pints of milk and two cookies with them.

"Only time they give out Oreos. Helps their meds go down," she fills me in.

"Hate for you to miss that," I say.

She leans towards me again. I lean in too. I'll be damned. She already smells like cookies.

"Not me. I don't take meds. Not a thang wrong with me. Now, I up an' start takin' that shit, I'll be back here next month for more."

Her eyes go to something behind me.

"See that lady?"

I turn slow. An old lady plays solitaire at a table. Chocolate cookie crumbs on the side of her chin. Every time she lays a card down, she clicks her tongue. She reaches up, itchin her scalp with a long scaly finger.

"That lady's been in an' outta here ten times in the last two years. Her son told me. Visits every chance he gets. They cain't keep her off the oxy, an' he says it was the doc in here that first ever give 'em to her. A factory. That's what this place is. They make people crazier so they can keep their jobs. Not me. Nuh uh. Not g'ttin' those pills in me. I'm gonna pass that e-val the judge ordered, an' I'm gone. They got a shrink, some lady from Raleigh, who's got to do it comin' Monday. All I got to do is hold out til then. Gotta keep my eyes on the prize. Ain't gonna be in here a minute longer than I have to. You know you cain't even get water worth drinkin' in this place? Ain't hot. Ain't cold, just tepid. Like drinkin ol' bathwater."

Something about her confidence, her certainty about getting out, really sticks in my craw. The big fella who was setting outside with his own personal orderly's being led up to the cookie window. He don't have a leash on him but might as well. The orderly walks him over to the nurse handing out the drugs. He takes a small cup of pills, two Oreos and a pint carton of milk. The kind you'd see in a school cafeteria.

Rae keeps going on across from me, but all I can see is this fella, milk carton in hand as a little boy in the cafeteria line of his elementary school holding his milk the same way. I tell you, I don't know if it's God's doing or the devil's, that we cain't see the future. That boy he once was would've run screaming out of that line right out into traffic if he'd have even gotten a glimpse of this big old guy with only cookies on his mind in here today.

"Did I mention I'm, how shall we say? Familiar with this place?" I ask not giving two fucks if Rae's mid-sentence, and from the look on her face she was. "My parents brought my sister here. Whatin but seventeen. Went an' had herself a breakdown, an' this is the only place they could think to take her."

"Oh yeah?" Rae says.

I lean up, elbows on my knees, like we're gonna have us a heart to heart, and we are, just not the type she's thinking. She leans up, crosses her legs again, gets a real Oprah readying to interview somebody face on. I scribble in my pad where she can't see. Her glare could burn a hole through my pad with how hard she's eyeing it. She's just dying to see.

"Yeah, an' I tell you, if it's anything now like it was then, that there eval might not be the breeze you think it will. They got a lot a hoops you gotta jump through to get on the other side a those front doors again," I say.

This itn't what she's wanting to hear. She gets jumpy, tapping one of her feet against the bottom of her chair.

"I been jumpin' through hoops my whole god damned life. Don't reckon they got harder ones here. Bring 'em on," she boasts, sitting up taller, real pleased with herself.

I scribble just a little more, then sit back in my chair, bringing one of my legs up, crossing my ankle over a knee, clasping my hands across my stomach, settling in like we just had Sunday dinner and a nap's coming on.

"Theirs won't be the only hoops. Might just be I've got some for you myself."

Her cheeks heat the rosy powder on them up to a hot pink. Her small brown hands make fists she does her best to hide in her lap. She stares me down. Tries her hand at intimidation.

"What hoops?"

"Well, there's the matter a the palm print," I deliver, real calm like. Just like she's a waitress taking my order over at the Applebees.

"Palm print?"

"A prominent greasy one right on that back passenger door a your car."

She reaches a hand up to moving her hair out of her eyes, her hand all shaky making it so she barely gets it done.

"So?"

Her arms and neck are taut. Every vein answering roll call, popping out for all their worth. She's more muscular than I'd noticed before. Itn't that she's manly, just fit. Toned enough to signal she takes care of herself, probably always has. Maybe enough to indicate she's a borderline gym rat. I'd bet my coin jar stash, she's in her room here nights doing sit ups and burpies til lights out. Maybe toned enough to hint that having a kid didn't fit into her regimen. Don't really fit into anybody's. Once that hits them, some are just prepared to do more about it than others.

I stand up slow, flip a few of the pages of my pad, I squint like I'm studying it before I stick it back in my pocket. I walk around behind my chair, grip the back of it, massage it a bit with my hands.

"Ask Mitchum. He's got about ten years on me, but like you said, we went to the same church all growin' up," she offers, and I know where she's going with it cause Cobb tried to take me down this same nice church going girl trail of hers and I wouldn't bite. Shit, who're they kidding?

Gotta hand it to her though, bringing it back around to church probably seems a smart way to go. I'll let her think she's leading the way for a little while. Most fun I've had lately.

"Oh, we talked," I goad her.

"We go to Roberson Baptist. Mama's gone there since she whatin but just a little thang. She an' Daddy met there an' took me an' my brother. I guess you'd say I'm a third-generation pew setter," she jokes real nervous like.

The big fella's finished his cookies now. He's positioned himself right in behind Rae looking out the window. Cain't look at her without seeing him. The chocolate crumbs smeared on his face make him look like a wild thing that's roamed all night and rolled in dirt. Seeing them both, her in front a him, I cain't shake the notion that there ain't much difference between the two other than she's wearing makeup and he's got chocolate smudges.

"Way Preacher Tullis over there tells it, he ain't seen you settin' on any a his pews in months," I throw at her.

Even back in Lee County, I was known for this—verbal grenades. And it does exactly what I want it to. She crosses her arms, screws up her Mary Kayed lips.

"What's he know? Tullis ain't there every time the doors are open. Got the youth pastor fillin' in for him when he's out with his Ulcers. A real nice guy. Pastor—"

"Chris," I say before she can. "Pastor Chris?"

"Yeah, now if you ask me, he's the one should be the head pastor. Got more sense than any of 'em. Rest of 'em's judgemental pricks most a the time," she huffs, showing more of her true colors.

Big fella's orderly finds him, and I feel of tinge a relief in my chest that he's back under a watchful eye.

"I ain't here to pass judgement. Ain't darkened the door of a church in a dog's age myself. Don't have much use for make believe," I confess, leaning against the column behind me.

She uncrosses her arms. I see I hadn't lost my touch. Cobb says that's what I'm good at. I throw the bombs then slink around, staying for the clean-up. Says I'm a damn near pro at messing with heads, making people think surely they're wrong. Surely it wasn't a grenade at all.

He comes at it different. I can understand why the captain thought we'd get on though. Cobb likes to put people at ease. Says when people're at ease, you slip them the rope, they'll hang themselves. I think that sounds better to him than admitting he's a pushover. Guess I'm playing it a little of my way and a little of his today, seeing just what Rae'll do.

"I mainly go for Mama," Rae adds, without knowing by doing so, she's getting a tight grip on the rope I'm slipping her. "Brandon hated goin' in the church nursery. Couldn't get him to set still with me either. Told mama he was too little to set still for those long ass sermons."

"Hard for the little ones," I chuckle. "I use to get my grandma's pocket mirror outta her purse. I'd get it just right under the big lights a the sanctuary so I could reflect it in the preacher's glasses. Man probably thought it was the second comin' a Christ every time I visited."

We both share a laugh. She's setting back easier in her chair now. Takes me back to when I'd hang out on the bleachers after practice making jokes for the for the cheerleaders, all the while, thinking of nothing but what was under their little skirts. I bet Rae was a cheerleader. Had to be. Yeah, I'm guessing she's used to everybody making jokes for her to laugh at and drooling all over her.

The big fella by the window gets a wild hair with us laughing and joins in, clapping his hands. His laugh fills the room, drowning ours out. Rae and me get quiet, hoping he'll simmer down. His orderly pats his shoulder, whispers something to him. He snaps too, stops laughing then follows her. More cookies I'm guessing. Once he's gone, I see my way clear.

"Yeah, little ones can be ornery, a whole lotta work." I let the rope out just a little more.

"You're right about that. Cost about a thousand a month just for daycare. I'm on the wait list for a voucher, but I told Mama I bet Brandon'll be in kindergarten for it comes through—"

She stops real sudden, staring right at me. It's registering all over again that Brandon won't need a voucher. Behind her eyes, her mind is catching back up to the reality that he won't be going to kindergarten. I do my best to steady my poker face, but I feel my lips curl just the slightest little bit. I know we're done. That's all I'll get out of her, willingly anyway. She shoots up out of her chair. Her arms cross tight again. My rope hits the floor.

"I'd better get out to group. They got a therapist that comes an' does meditation an' shit. She don't like it if we're late," she tells me taking a few steps backwards towards the double doors her friends went out.

"Anything to that?"

"What?"

"Meditation?"

She nods.

"It's helpful. Gets your mind right. Helps you think clearer," she does her best to sell me.

"Sounds good," I say. "An' don't worry, we can wrap all this up once you're out. We'll have you come down to the station, sign off on your statement, tie things up neat."

Her mouth drops open and her arms fall to her sides.

"You didn't get what all you need?" She wants to know, using that syrupy voice I'm sure she used hanging out on the bleachers.

"Not quite," I answer with a little wiliness to my tone.

If she won't pick up the rope, I'll loop it around her neck one way or another.

"Well, what else you wanna to know?"

I walk backwards a few steps, putting more distance between us.

"Never did get around to firmin' up about that palm print. The one on Brandon's side?"

"I don't know what you want me to say. I don't have any idea. I—"

I raise my hand, waving her off.

"Nothin' to get all riled about. I'm sure it'll come to you. Might be somethin' for you to meditate on. Yeah, I'm bettin' if you set outside, Indian style in the grass, chantin' whatever it is that shrink has you chantin', it'll all come rushin' back."

Her eyes tear up. Oh, she's feeling that burn of the rope against her neck now. She bites her lower lip, reaches a hand up slow, itches at a place behind her right ear.

"See you on the outside," I say all smiles.

I make sure to step high enough my shoes come down hard as I go, the sound carrying all the way back to her. I want her to remember that sound, the sound of me walking away, and know I might be the first person she's ever met who don't believe one word of her bullshit.

51°F

Cobb

They say you don't know anything about somebody til you meet their better half, that is, if they've got one. Sure was true about me and Stacy. I'm not exactly sure what it is people knew about me when they met her though. Maybe that I was nicer than they thought I'd be? Maybe that I wasn't that bad after all? That's what I knew when I met her—that she could make it all better. That she was the kind of girl who righted all a man's wrongs. Certainly this man's.

That first day I saw her up close, I could hardly talk just looking at her. Saw her first thing in the rows of kids in the gym. Had those tight whitish blond curls like her sister, though I didn't put two and two together right off. Just felt like I knew her from somewhere. With her stark pale skin, she looked like a baby doll in her hoodie. She wasn't but a freshman.

Combs had taken me with him that day to run the D.A.R.E. class at the high school. We hung back as the students watched the video about what types of drugs there are and how to spot if someone you love is addicted. Sometimes I thought those videos were more "how to's" than cautionary. The government was hell bent on educating all the rural kids especially about the trials you invited if you decided to take narcotics. We were just the messengers. Combs said in the long run, it'd trickle down and help us too, cause we wouldn't lock up so damn many crackheads. Never really panned out. The illegal drugs changed to prescriptions. Intake numbers went up not down, but back then, we thought we had the magic bullet.

"What if the doctor gives 'em the pills?" was Stacy's question when we allowed time for students to ask some.

Combs looked at me. I looked at the floor. It was only my second time tagging along. I wasn't about to take that one. I looked up at her. She was standing just that way Kelly had that night out at the Sonic when Laura's mama was yelling, like she meant business. Even Stacy's posture demanded you treat her like she did too.

Clearing his throat, Combs replied, "Well, hon, don't matter where they get 'em. It's still wrong."

"Even if it's the doctor?"

"Even then," Combs told her.

She sat down, but I could tell by the look on her face, this didn't help her none. All the doctor talk made Combs real uncomfortable. He immediately went to handing out the buttons we'd brought. I walked over, handing Stacy her button, gave her a smile. She took the button from me, our hands grazing each other's, looking up at me with Kelly's eyes. It was like meeting her all over again. Like all those years were erased in that second.

"Thanks," Stacy said real soft.

I nodded. That was it. Didn't matter that I was ten years older. I knew I'd wait. Turns out, I didn't have to wait long. Next afternoon, there she was outside the station.

I was headed over to my car, minding my business.

"Hey," a voice called.

Didn't stop at first. Wasn't expecting no one then there she was standing by my trunk.

"You the one at the school yesterday, right?" she asked.

My mouth wouldn't make words. I couldn't believe she'd be there. I looked past her at a couple of the guys getting off shift at the same time. Even if I was excited to see her, there wasn't any good to come from her visit. Didn't feel wrong to me, but I knew it'd look wrong to everybody else. Wasn't as much about her age as her being from where she was from.

"Weren't you?" Stacy persisted.

I nodded.

"What can I do for you?" I asked.

"I'm hopin' you'll help me."

"Okay."

Hendricks was two cars over. He pulled out, and rode by with his window down hollering at me, egging me on. I shook my head.

"Don't mind him," I told her, my cheeks all hot.

"I won't."

She situated her backpack up higher on her shoulders. Strands of her hair fell down over one eye. Beautiful! Everything made her look so damn beautiful. I wondered if it was lonely, her being in this town, with only eager girls either hoping to be along for the ride and be her friend or other jealous ones gunning for her, trying to take her down a notch. Thin and fragile as she looked, I knew she still probably had to be tough. Her sister had been.

The boldness she'd had to come all the way across town to find me had up and left her stranded. She bit her bottom lip, balanced on the heels of her shoes, waiting for me to decide what it was that came next.

"How 'bout I drop you at home?" I offered. "On the way you can tell me how it is I can help you."

She nodded. I unlocked my car doors, and we got in. Her jeans were tight making her legs look more like a kids, but her shirt was snug enough to remind me she was only three years or so away from being a woman. Three years wouldn't be long. I'd waited my whole life for her. Three years was nothing.

Pulling out onto the road, I knew which way to head. It was common knowledge where anybody with any Black blood lived in Sanford.

"I'm over off St. Charles, by Wilheim Place," she told me.

The lights were in my favor. Each one turning red just as I got to them so I could steal looks at her. Caught her glancing over a couple times too. Closer we got to her house, the more I started thinking she didn't need help. She'd just wanted us to be in that scenario.

Pretty as she was, I still knew nobody who ever claimed me would be for us. She might pass to strangers, but long as both our families had lived in Sanford, they likely knew of each other. My kin would know her for the Black girl she pretended not to be. All my Mama and Daddy'd be thinking about was the brown babies that would turn out. No pretending could whitewash those.

"Member yesterday I was askin' about doctors?" Stacy started.

"Mm hmm."

"Well, I want you to go see my Daddy's doctor."

Her fingers traced the pink skull patch sewn to her backpack sitting on her lap. Pink socks. Kelly'd had on pink socks that night. I hadn't recalled that til just that second. It scared me how the brain can just go and ruin a moment.

"Why's that?" I asked.

She looked out the window at her reflection in the side mirror, blinking over and over to ward off tears.

"Cause I've been to see him a couple a times, an' he don't listen. He don't care that we want Daddy off pills. He keeps writin' prescriptions. Daddy cain't hardly sit up to even watch the damn TV. He hurt himself at work last year, but he shouldn't still be takin' 'em. He shouldn't!"

By then, she was gripping the sides of the backpack so tight her knuckles were whiter than the rest of her.

"I got a feelin', if a cop goes over an' tells him, he'll pay attention then," she said.

Wilheim Place was a frequent stop for us boys in blue. So much so, it was strange to me that we'd never seen each other before that day in the gym. It wasn't anywhere anybody'd be proud to live at. I felt sorry for her.

"Just let me out here," she said, pointing to the curb before the turn to the entrance.

I pulled the car along the sidewalk, close as I could get. I wanted so bad to reach out, put my hand on her arm, tell her to stay. Tell her to never get out, let's just keep riding down to S.C. That we could get hitched and get a place. That her daddy wouldn't care if he was as bad off as she said. I only sat there watching as she got out.

She leaned down, leaving a slip of paper on the seat in her place.

"That's the address a his doctor's office," she said with her full, pink glossed lips. "If you go Thursday, he's closed half a day an' won't be nobody but him there doin' paperwork after lunch."

"You got it all figured out," I teased.

I chuckled at that. She'd really staked it out.

This made her mad as could be. She slammed my door and stomped off. I rolled the window down, driving slow alongside her.

"Hey, now. I didn't mean nothin' by it," I called. "Really. I'm impressed. I mean it."

Stopping in front of the Wilheim sign, a hand on her left hip that was jutted forward, she looked like a gorgeous alien that'd been dropped down into our ugly world.

"Either you're going or you're not!" she demanded. "Ain't like I'm askin' you to kill him, not yet anyways. I just need you to make him understand."

Her fire pierced my already tender heart. I was no match for her.

"I'll go. You just gotta do me one favor."

She cocked her head to the side, pooched out her lips, narrowed her eyes. Her whole body saying *what?*

"Meet me over at the D.Q. day after tomorrow. We'll talk it through, make sure I get it right," I bartered.

Lowering her hands, putting them in her pockets, her cheeks turned pink as she looked down at her feet.

"You shouldn't be seen with me," she said.

"Any guy'd be damned lucky to be seen anywhere near you," I assured her.

She blushed brighter.

"Fine. 3:30 cause I got band."

"I'll be there," I told her and got back out on the road, leaving her in my right-side mirror.

Day after next, when I drove up to the D.Q., there she stood by the takeout window. The goon working the register was leaned halfway outside on the little metal counter, swatting playful at her, flirting away. Soon as I walked up, he ducked back inside.

Stacy stared at me. I was back standing under the lights of the Sonic with Kelly studying me. I knew that's what had brought me there that afternoon. Being with Stacy was time traveling. When we were together, I was a teenager again. I'd just helped win a game and the only other boy in town all the other boys dreamed of being, besides me, was Bobby Olsen.

The two of us standing there, I knew all my years since that night with Kelly, I'd been on autopilot. I'd just been trying to retrieve something it was impossible to get back. Do overs that would never be offered.

Seems like the south breeds a kind of nostalgia, a sweet melancholy yearning for what was. My Grandaddy used to talk about how southerners are inflicted with this want, this desire to return to the past cause their way of life was taken from them, not given up but taken. He said our hands are stuck reaching out, hoping it will all be handed back over.

Stacy was first to break the silence.

"Whatcha gonna get?" she wanted to know.

"I'm partial to strawberry sundaes. What about you?"

"I'm all about those Oreo blizzards," she said. "Biggest one they got."

I ordered for the two of us. The goon took our orders and rung them up, hardly looking at me as he did. He knew the deal. He didn't have a chance with Stacy.

She thanked him when he handed her the blizzard. He grunted. I took my sundae from him without a word. We walked out through the field behind there. It had a small pond and an old picnic table. Stacy didn't question why we were going to set out back. Went without saying. The fewer people who saw us together the better.

"He thinks I'm white," Stacy said out of nowhere. "Just about everybody at school does."

"Does it matter?" I asked her.

Her head went back. She laughed loudly.

"Spoken like a real white boy," she sassed.

The picnic table was covered with moss. I thought about taking my shirt off and laying it down for her to set on but couldn't think of her seeing my belly. She didn't pay the moss any mind, hopped right up on the table. Didn't seem sturdy enough to hold me, so I half sat on it, propping a foot on the bench while keeping one on the ground. I watched as she dipped her long spoon in the cup, taking a big bite with a chunk of cookie in it.

"Mmm! I could eat these every day!" she said.

I smiled, watching her lips moist with vanilla ice cream as I took a bite of my own. Always loved digging down, making sure I got strawberry syrup in with the first bite. That was the best part. That thick red gooeyness.

"Where's your daddy think you are?" I wanted to know.

"He ain't worried," she answered too quick to put me at any kind of ease.

I looked on as she shoveled a couple more heaping spoonfuls of her treat into her mouth. The rabid way she went at that blizzard showed her age. I felt shame creeping in. She set her cup down. Her right hand found my knee.

That first touch excited me and scared me senseless at the same time. I feared it meant she knew more about men than she ever did about boys. That she'd rest it there, no questions asked, it was like she assumed I'd want her. It made me sad for her. Mine wasn't the first man's knee she'd touched, that was for sure.

"You thinkin' you're gonna see that doctor tomorrow?"

I moved my knee slightly. Her hand slipped off. I saw it for what it was—coercion. I wanted the next time she touched me to be about more than that. Besides, there was plenty of time for touching more than knees. We had the rest of our lives.

"Won't your Daddy go on an' get his drugs somewhere else?"

"He don't have a car. Closest place he could get 'em is over in North Raleigh, an' he in't gonna walk 20 miles."

I used my spoon to swirl the syrup around, turning my ice cream bubble gum pink.

"No tellin' what a man'll do to get what he wants," I kept on, not totally against the idea of visiting the doctor but not really relishing it either.

"No tellin' what I'll do if I don't get what I want," she snapped.

"Alright now," I laughed, playing off the razorblade sharpness she delivered it with.

She didn't laugh. It wasn't a joke to her. I got the idea not much was. The sound of her scraping the bottom of her blizzard was all she had to say back to that. A bird flew overhead landing on a branch over the pond, dangling more than perching.

"You always lived here?" she piped up again.

I nodded finishing the last of my sundae.

"Only two kinds of people live in Sanford."

"Yeah? How's that?"

"There's the people who want to get out but cain't, an' there's the people who could leave but don't. They choose to stay cause they want to be the bosses a the first kind. They own the place."

The second it came out of her mouth, I registered it as truth. Thought it was pretty insightful for a high schooler. I also immediately knew which of the two I was. She'd known it too the minute she laid eyes on me.

"Daddy had his mind made up to go to his cousin's in California an' work on cars out there."

"How come he never made it?"

"My sister went missin'. She whatin but a couple years older than I am now. Hey, maybe you remember her? Kelly Diamond?"

However I played it would determine our future of that I was certain. There was no good I could do for Kelly by saying anything about her having hung out with me and Bobby, but there was her sister. She was sitting right in front of me needing my help, needing what my life could do for her life. Her lips so full and pink. I needed them to greet me every morning, to kiss me goodnight every night. Nothing else would do.

"Kelly Diamond? Yeah, seems like I heard that name. I don't recall too much from back then, though. I mostly played football an' drank more than anybody ever should."

It was the truth, but not the whole truth. That was always my comfort zone—that ravine between the truth and a lie.

"I don't remember her much. I was five when it happened. Daddy had plans though. Grew up hearin' all about how he'd been set to go to California that next week. Had his bus ticket. He was gonna work out there, save up, then send for us. Every time we gotta clean him up, my aunts go on an' on about it. How we wouldn't be seein' him that a way if he'd a just made it out there."

Her Blizzard cup was empty. She let if drop to the ground at her feet.

"Which one are you?" I asked her.

"What?"

"Which a the two kinds? You wantin' to go or wantin' to stay an' rule?"

Hopping off the picnic bench, she strutted out into the field and did a perfect cartwheel. On her landing, she posed arms up like she was a gymnast. I clapped, smiling away. She bounded back over, put both hands on me, one on each knee.

"I'm stayin'," she announced. "Stayin' right here. I'm gonna show everybody. I'm gonna have a house, an' a nice car, cute dresses, an' a baby. Might have two. I'm gonna be the queen of motherfuckin' Sanford."

I looked into her eyes. She was steadily making me part of her plans, and I let her.

"I bet you will," I agreed, laughing, patting her hands.

"An' you know what else?"

I shook my head as she leaned in.

"You're gonna be my king," she decreed softly.

Her lips felt warm on my cheek as she gave me a peck. Stepping back, releasing my knees, she winked.

"Soon as you go see that doctor."

And I did. I went to see him that very next day. Wasn't hard.

Roughing up a doctor's nothing like roughing up a meth head or a seasoned criminal. He bent easily to my will. Stacy and me started being an *us*. That's all it'd taken—a large Oreo Blizzard and knocking around a doctor.

There are still days that image of her in my rearview as I dropped her off, just watching me go, gets me through. She was never so bright as she was that day in that mirror, the sun reflecting in the background. It was right that minute, I knew. I didn't care one way or the other what color our babies would be. She was my second chance. She and I would follow through on what Kelly and I never got the chance to start. I would be her king.

I thought about that afternoon with my Stacy as I drove over to the Waffle House. While I sat in my car outside waiting, I wondered if Jolie had ever shone as bright for Hogue. They'd met in high school. That's about all he'd told me. I found myself ate up with curiosity as to what kind of life a girl would've had for Hogue to be the knight in battered armor who she let sweep her away from it.

Everything in me told me to go back home. Told me Hogue hadn't really messed up over in my neck of the woods. That I had no business heading over there, but I kept on. I couldn't get away from the gnawing feeling that it wasn't but a matter of time. He'd unravel it all. I'd known for a while who Rae was seeing, but til the boy died, there hadn't been anything I could really take issue with about it.

I quieted the part of myself that wanted to avoid conflict at all cost, that wanted things to stay like they were, even though that was its own kind of misery. I admitted that it was highly likely that the more measured side of me was an idiot. I bet nobody'd ever gotten Hogue on a different path once he took off on one. Nobody.

You never really know a man til you meet the person who's signed on to be with them day in and day out. She wasn't hard to find. Only one Waffle House in Clayton. Called the one in Benson first. They said Jolie'd transferred. I'm sure it gave her a change of pace, and it was still within driving distance of her house. Didn't have everybody coming in asking her about that night or if her new man was out of the hospital yet.

Didn't have to wait in the parking lot long til her little Toyota Camry came zooming into the spot a few down from mine. She was prettier than I thought she'd be. Her hair was long and shiny blonde. Couldn't have framed her face any more perfect if she tried. Hogue hadn't done her justice with his description. He was probably downplaying what he no longer had access to.

As she got out and walked to the door, she stuffed her keys down inside her purse causing the strap to break. All contents spilled to the ground. I got out of my car, hurried over to help. She glanced up, eyes wild. I remembered I knew about her, but we didn't know each other. I stepped back to lessen the creepiness of invading her space. She scrambled around on the ground picking up everything fast as she could. I took it she had practice at making quick work of a mess.

"Here I was thinkin' you might need help, but looks like you got it covered," I broke the ice.

Closer up, I could see she had real smooth skin with only the start of wrinkles around her eyes. The kind women get from worrying too much, squinting too hard to fight back all the words they can't say. Being married'll do that to you. Her collarbones jutted through her Waffle House uniform. Not much in way of happy mediums for those living hand to mouth. Long as I can recall, blue collar women either eat all the time, or rarely at all.

She stared at me then down in her purse, reaching in, retrieving a cigarette and a lighter. I looked past her at the windows that showed full tables behind them.

"Y'all sure stay busy," I said.

"Yeah, everyday's fuckin' Easter Sunday 'round here."

Cigarette in her hand, she could've passed for ten years her senior. Couldn't have been smoking long with her complexion. Soon enough her smooth skin would give way to the nicotine's dull yellowing.

"Got to be a tough gig."

With her free hand, she smoothed the skirt of her uniform. With those white athletic socks and nursing shoes waitresses wore, showing off those long stem legs, I bet her tips were hardly ever the standard ten percent. Those legs of hers probably garnered at least fifteen most of the time.

"Jo-lie." I read her name tag out loud. "Hadn't ever heard it before, but sure is perty."

She laughed.

"Had it all to myself 'fore Angelina came along an' made it famous 'fore I could," she told me.

An old woman exited the diner, her cane steadying her as she stepped down into the parking lot.

"You sleep in, hon?" she called to Jolie.

"Had the mornin' off, Ms. Jessup," She answered, winking at her and waving her cigarette.

"Hope I won't miss you tomorrow," Ms. Jessup said.

"Naw, I'll be here. I tell you what, if I ever get two mornins in a row off, you better start prayin' cause it's got to be the end a the world," Jolie joked.

"God forbid," Ms. Jessup said to herself as she got in her Buick.

Jolie and I watched as she backed out so slowly, I had to blink to make sure the car was actually moving. When she finally got all the way out, she smiled big, and waved to us, nearly hitting the car parked closest. Her brakes squealed. She nodded to us then headed out of the parking lot onto the road. We turned away. Some things you can't bear to watch.

"Her son cain't bring himself to take her keys. Just a matter a time," Jolie muttered, then took one last drag before dropping her cigarette.

As she stamped it out, she caught sight of my Lee County badge. I'd clipped to my pocket. Should've left it in the car. If she hadn't seen that, she'd have seen my patch on my sleeve though. If I'd have been thinking at all, I'd have worn plain clothes, but I was headed to work afterwards.

"Sanford's got one a the best Waffle Houses in the state," she told me.

I knew what she was fishing for.

"Yeah, but I heard from a reliable source that y'all got the best hash known to man, an' we cain't say that for ours."

She smiled wide. There it was. Had to have sealed the deal for Hogue too. A man'd be willing to live better or die violent for one smile from her.

"We do," she confirmed. "Stay late most nights choppin' potatoes myself."

"Well then, it's a no brainer. That's what I'm havin'," I said as we walked to the side door.

I weaved my way through the retirees, and a sprinkling of community college kids who clustered together there mid-mornings. Jolie shot straight for the back. I heard two or three people in the kitchen start in on her with their demands soon as they saw her.

A man next to me scraped his fork on his plate trying to clean off every last bit of whatever he'd ordered. A young waitress came to stand in front of me. Couldn't have been more than twenty, but with so much make up on, It was a certainty she grew up watching Dolly and Loretta Lynn on the Grand Ole Opry with her grandma instead of the Kardashians.

"What're you havin', hon?" she asked.

"I got him," Jolie shouted.

"A'ight." The waitress conceded stepping over to another patron.

"Be right there," Jolie told me.

I nodded. I felt for her. From what I could piece together of what Hogue rambled about, she'd grown up hard. They both had. Though he was more tight lipped about what all that meant for him. He'd told me she'd quit high school senior year to nurse her stepmama who got into a car accident. Woman only lived another year. Jolie'd gotten her G.E.D. After that, the two of them got hitched, then all her earnings went to putting Hogue through the academy.

You could still see that girl in her. As she bustled around the kitchen, prepped my hash on the grill. I picture'd her doing the same for him. My mind went to what kept her tied to the area. She had what many of us pray for—a clean break. No siblings to speak of. Only Hogue left once her stepmama went. Maybe that had sealed them together more than anything? There's no telling if sorrow'll drive you away or bind you to each other til you face it.

The flames flashed, she turned the gas down, raised her eyebrows at me. I smiled. I decided Hogue wasn't the type you face things with. No, I reckoned, with what little I knew of him, that he had things on her, that they were tied to one another with a heavy tether. Same way Bobby Olson and me, no matter what I did, were tied. Tied in such a way Hogue would never understand. I didn't understand it fully myself. The smell of the hash reminded me, good as it might be, it wasn't what had brought me there.

A few minutes later, the hash was presented in a mound on a plate in front of me.

"Hope it's worth the drive," Jolie said as she handed me a ketchup bottle from under the counter. "I'll come back an' check on you."

"Thank you," I told her, but she was already over by the register helping get the drawer unstuck.

The hash was better than good. Haven't had any as good since. Moist as a greasy pound cake and whatever butter they were using made the whole experience unforgettable. Hogue had to have kicked himself over and over to lose a hash-making woman like her.

The lunch crowd started up around me. I texted Pat back at the station that I'd be in later, that I was handling family business. With all Stacy's miscarriages, nobody accounted for my time much. I got the pity pass. Only perk to be had from losses as awful as I'd endured.

I thumbed through an *Our State* magazine, waiting for things to slow, hoping they would as I didn't see her coming back outside with me. I didn't want to really talk in front of so many people about what I'd come to say.

"You hang out long enough, I'll put you back there on dishes with Jake," Jolie teased, coming over and sliding my plate into a tub of dirty dishes balanced on her hip.

"My wife'd be first to tell you I'm better on the broom."

"A man with a broom. Now that's a sight we don't seem much of around here," she said evil eyeing the busboy not far down the bar leaning against the counter chatting up another of the waitresses.

We had a bit of back and forth about how much I enjoyed the hash, and I sipped the cup of coffee I'd been nursing as she tended to a few other customers. The timing of it all was up to me since Waffle Houses prided themselves on staying open 24 hours. It was evident by her restless flitting around that the longer I stayed, the more suspicious she became. Soon as she got close enough again, I put my cup out.

"How 'bout a cup for the road?" I asked her.

She poured.

"You know," I started in on why it was I came to be setting there. "You an' me, we have what you might call a *mutual acquaintance*."

85°F

Jenny Lynn had already come by twice to ask if they were alright. Mitch could tell she was wanting to close up. Til that night, he hadn't been sure the Sonic actually ever closed at all. What with them serving breakfast and seeming to be open every time they passed. Bobby ignored the cues of lights being dimmed, background music being turned off, a janitor picking up trash from the parking lot. He rambled on about what he'd do if he had parents like Laura's and then football and who was coming up from the junior varsity team that next year. How he'd pay good money to see them try and play half as good and he and Mitch had.

Mitch watched out of the corner of his eye as Kelly looked over at Bobby and then back at Jenny Lynn just cleaning away, then at Bobby again. Her eyes fully disclosing that she was seething with something that had other origins prior to the night at hand. Though who'd have blamed her if the last hour alone had been what annoyed her? Not like anyone could get a word in edgewise once Bobby got on a roll. As soon as Bobby took to laughing too long about his de-pantsing of Holford Levitz in the cafeteria, that was Mitch's in.

"I bet Jenny Lynn'd let you call your aunt," he suggested to Kelly. "G'ttin' late."

She nodded but made no move towards the takeout window where Jenny Lynn stood counting out the drawer. Kelly bit her lip, glancing over that way as Jenny Lynn then hurried out the booth door with a rag and began swiping across tables with a quick lick and a prayer as if she worked at a car wash rather than a restaurant. Looking away, back out at the parking lot where Laura had been just minutes before, she wore a mournful expression as if she wished she too had a horror movie mother to come searching for her too instead of the one she had. *Did she have one?* Mitch wondered. He didn't know.

He realized he knew next to nothing about her or her people except that she had a little sister. He had seen them at the Exxon together. There was a rumor that Kelly went with a boy over in Candor. She certainly didn't go with anyone at their school. From time to time, Mitch had caught himself watching her in class or as she walked by while he practiced on the field and thought she might go with him, that it would be nice if she would, but nothing had come of it. They only had the commonality of attending the same school. People didn't go together with so little in common—not for long, especially for a Black girl from her side of town, no matter how light skinned, and a white boy from his side. This he knew.

"This itn't late!" Bobby boomed, jumping up, patting the residual fry grease off of his fingers and onto his jeans. "Night's barely gotten started. Don't go g'ttin' all limp dick on me now, Cobb."

This was what he did. Mitch recognized they were now at that point of their time with a girl, who on this night happened to be Kelly, when Bobby was seeing just how much she'd tolerate before getting offended and stalking off. He also knew his feral friend couldn't forego this. It was not in Bobby to go long around anyone without pushing. Kelly stared down at the table, unphased by his crassness.

"I'm gonna go take a piss. Y'all don't go nowhere now, you hear?" Bobby instructed, then bounded off to the side of the building.

It struck Mitch as silly. As if there'd been a time the whole world didn't wait for Bobby Olsen. As soon as he was out of earshot, Kelly turned, facing him.

"I cain't call my aunt. She's workin' third shift over at the mill. Dropped us off on her way," she told him.

"We'll run you home," Mitch assured her.

Her shoulders remained tensed. He felt somehow this offer hadn't put her any more at ease. Jenny Lynn's squeal, as piercing as a schoolgirl's out on a playground, erupted from behind them. They looked over to see Bobby had exited the bathroom and had taken to spinning her around on her skates. Mitch smiled. He had to hand it to Bobby. That boy could charm anybody when he put his mind to it, even old Jenny Lynn. Kelly did not smile.

"He's ridin' with you too, right?" Kelly asked, her lips falling into a disdainful grimace.

"Yeah, but you can set up front. Got plenty a room for him in the back," Mitch said.

Bobby let Jenny Lynn get back to closing and made his way in their direction. Kelly's face unchanged. She cracked her knuckles.

"Yeah, we'll get Jenny to give him a shake, stick him in the back. Won't hear a peep out of him." Mitch went on. "Once baby drinks his sugar, he'll go night night."

At last, Kelly's lips crept into a smirk. The two snickered about this as Bobby approached.

"What's got you two tickled?" Bobby wanted to know.

Mitch shook his head.

"Nothin'. Hey, you know what? I heard they throw out what's left back there an' seein' as you an' her are so close an' all, maybe Jenny Lynn'll give you some free shakes?" Mitch suggested.

It took no convincing. Bobby whipped around, making a beeline for the takeout window. Mitch and Kelly took the opportunity to get in the car. Mitch turned the air up high in hopes of making her comfortably cool. As Kelly situated herself in his front passenger seat, the parking lot lights illuminated her face, giving the eye makeup on her eyelids a dramatic sparkle.

He imagined the two of them in that same spot on a different night, all on their own. Dinners in their laps on the crinkly Sonic paper. They'd share a large order of onion rings. For some reason, with the girls he'd been around, he relished the thought of one who'd eat onion rings with him. They were usually too messy to hear girls tell it and any dates he'd had avoided them.

They'd talk about school, or they wouldn't talk about that at all and talk about family instead. He'd tell her what little there was to tell. How his father worked at the mill and his mother used to work there too. How after his father *stepped out* on his mother last summer, just that one weekend with another mill working woman, his mother had quit.

Most days since, his mother could be found in her bedroom. It was as if his father had done the crime and yet she was doing the time. With only one income, however, he figured his mother had sentenced his father in her own way. Trouble was, Mitch too was serving this sentence of scraping by. He didn't complain. It wasn't his place.

Kelly's seatbelt clicked into place, and he thought if this date he was envisioning ever happened, his parents' marital troubles shouldn't be a first date story. He did know that. Maybe a second or third date?

"That fool only got himself one." Kelly scoffed, watching through the windshield as Bobby approached.

She closed her eyes, leaned her head back as she sighed. Mitch looked up to see Bobby striding over, one hand holding a shake with its straw up to his mouth, the other hand free and swinging. Nothing less could be expected. Seventeen was far too young to expect someone to start thinking of others.

Arriving at the car, Bobby stood next to Kelly's door. He stared blankly at her in what was usually his seat. Kelly looked at the dash. Slowly, he came to grips with the spot they'd designated for him. Mitch hoped he wouldn't make a fuss but fully expected he would. To his shock, the back door flew open. Bobby flopped down in the seat gripping his shake so it wouldn't spill. Kelly sat up, glaring at him in her side view mirror.

"Shit. You called it Mitch. She said what they don't sell gets poured down the drain. Told her I'd be sure an' stop by this time a night an' get more. Shame all that goin' to waste," Bobby said.

"Yeah, *a shame*," Kelly noted.

She tugged on the hemline of her skirt. It had ridden up a bit as she'd gotten in. It seemed shorter in the car than it had at the table. Sudden pangs of lust caused Mitch to pull discreetly on the crotch of his own jeans, resituating so she couldn't see the effect she had on him. He hadn't felt this way in some time and knew a more gentlemanly southern boy would be ashamed. His hands firmly on the wheel, he could not help but think of what might happen if Bobby was not taking up room in the backseat, how he and Kelly might fog up the windows.

That image took him back to another night. That night with Anita. Yes...it finally came to him! He did know something else about Kelly. He'd heard that she and Anita were cousins. There was part of him that hoped Bobby didn't remember this fact. He had hoped neither of them would ever have to remember Anita. At least she'd left school before Kelly arrived. Gone up north to another cousin's. They hadn't heard exactly why. They hadn't cared.

Had Anita told Kelly all about him and Bobby? Surely not! No... he didn't think so. If she had, Kelly would not have dared get in his car. If Anita'd said anything about what had gone on that night, Kelly would not have ever spoken one word to either of them.

The better part of his mind dismissed this, instead playing slides of bringing Kelly home to Sunday dinner, if they still did such traditions like that. There they were in their church clothes, his mother coming out of her room, and talking as she made her Shepherd's Pie. Kelly again shifted in her seat. Her legs were so long and thin. He again let his mind wonder to how it would be to crawl over to her side, where she'd be waiting for him to lift her skirt.

"Let's go over to Ducet," Bobbly interjected.

He slurped down the last of his shake, rolled down his window, and dropped the cup outside it.

"Hey!" Kelly shouted as she turned, eyeballing him from over the seat.

"What?" he sniped.

She shook her head. In what little time she'd been in his proximity, she knew explaining to him about littering was a waste of breath. She faced forward.

"Man! I drank that too fast," Bobby said loudly. "Got a brain freeze."

Watching his tag along in the rearview, Mitch thought about how a brain freeze required a brain, but he'd never say that. It was one of the many things he'd never say to Bobby.

He hoped Bobby would let Ducet go. He knew what going there meant. Kelly was not the type. If he could just drop Bobby off, he could take Kelly home and have more time with her. The light ahead of them turned red. To the right was Ducet. To the left was Bobby's. Mitch put on his left signal. He felt a hard thwack to the back of his head.

"Come on, man. I bet she's never been over there," Bobby said.

"Where?" Kelly asked.

"Ducet. You ever been over to Ducet?" he asked back.

"The ol' crazy hospital?"

"The ol' looney bin!" Bobby laughed. "Tha's the one."

"Why'd anybody want to go there?"

"Somethin' to do in this shit town. Kinna spooky. Gets your heart pumpin'. Sometimes there's junkies hangin' out. Member that bum, man?" he says to Mitch. "That one who kept holdin' on to that dead rat callin' it Spot, sayin' it could do tricks?"

Mitch did remember. One did not forget such a thing. He also remembered how Bobby had poked at the rat til it bled all over the man's hands and how the man cried while Bobby cackled. And then there was that night there with Anita. Surely Bobby recalled the relation? Eyeing him in the rear view, his crazed and sinister grin, he felt he must.

He looked nervously over at Kelly. These were not tales for her. Most of Mitch's life, in fact, was not a book she'd ever want to read. Her nose crinkled up. She was horrified at what had been described. He cleared his throat.

"Naw, let's call it a night, Bobby. My mama'll be waitin' an' you know how your mama gets," Mitch pitched.

Bobby kicked the back of his seat like a toddler strapped into a car seat wanting his way.

"Come on, man! You know your mama's done gone to bed if she ever even got out of it. Shit, my mama'll get over it. Come on, let's go! Just for a little while," he whined.

"Maybe I don't want to?" Kelly remarked throwing a wrench in his plans.

Leaning up, Bobby's demeanor softened.

"You know you do," he whispered in her ear. "You know you're curious."

And for reasons Mitch could not in any way ascertain, Kelly's half smile reappeared. This did not go unnoticed by Bobby. He slapped the headrest of Mitch's seat.

"See! Told you, now come on!"

The needle of what moral compass Mitch had intact spun around and around inside his gut. He ignored it, turning towards their familiar stomping grounds. Kelly hugged her door, watching out her window as if she, like Mitch, had entered into an unsaid agreement she was not at all comfortable with.

Landmarks, she thought. Yes, landmarks were what you had to take note of. A pointer given by a policewoman who'd come to speak to their health class about the prevalence of assaults in rural areas.

"Don't ever not know where you are," the policewoman gruffly barked.

Neither Mitch nor Bobby had been in that class. She felt this may work in her favor. She, like all young girls, went about overestimating what can work for them and not against.

Even the fact that her situation reminded her of the class

should've, in and of itself, been a red flag to Kelly. That was one of the problems with being someone who'd grown up where nearly every flag that flapped in the air around them was red, they became no different than the grass underfoot, or the trees in yards. She'd quit seeing them for what they were. They'd long since changed from red to a muted burgundy, not to be worried so much about.

As they neared Ducet, Bobby's incessant talking grated more heavily than usual on Mitch's nerves. With the radio playing in the background, he could scarcely make out what Bobby was going on about and he didn't care. He found himself wishing he'd have had the wherewithal to pull the car over and leave his mouthy backseat irritant by the roadside.

This urge was immediately shot down however, as were many of his urges concerning Bobby simply because they'd have to see each other again. It was the threat of the aftermath that always caused the weaker side of his brain to whip out its pistol, taking aim then firing at any ideas he got about showcasing his bravado.

This was the way with them. People like Bobby, like his own father—the ones always poking, pushing and goading everyone else. Appeasement, placation—the only options left to those surrounding. They were the ones dishing out, and Mitch knew he was part of the ones taking. And for some reason, maybe what with having a witness next to him on this night, a witness to his pitiful existence, Mitch's annoyance with Bobby slow boiled into a hatred.

In that car, on their way to that abandoned hospital, the one that had housed the insane, Mitch had a feeling that they just might be headed the best place they could be going. A place where he and Bobby belonged. Where wolves were once caged right along with the same sheep who'd been too slow to ever have a hope of getting away.

86°F

Hogue

For the first time since I got the idea to come over here, I wonder what exactly it is I'm going to do. Standing in his room, staring down at him now, all I see his him on top of her. They're in our bed, on our sheets. He's breathing heavy and Jolie's moaning. My chest tightens. The sound of my back molars grinding against each other drowns out all the beeping and whirring of the machines keeping this son of a bitch alive.

His head looks bigger and more bruised to me under these fluorescent hospital lights. Maybe it swolled up more after that night. Took time for everything to set in. When I got pulled off him, he only had a black eye and a busted lip.

The intercom goes off out in the hall. Somebody's needing more hands on deck a room or two over. I duck over behind the curtain quick so the nurses rushing by the door won't see me. Didn't come here the first week or so after I heard they took one of our boys off the door. Truth was, once things kicked up with all the Black Lives Matter protests downtown, they didn't have enough men to spare one here at the hospital. Only reason he got one of us as long as he did was cause he's Black and his family feared given how things had been going with all the media and all, some Proud Boy or somebody'd come over to finish him off. Man, wish I'd be so lucky.

I'd given testimony several times. Told them I ain't a Proud Boy. Not that I disagree with them. Only went to that one meeting with Dawson and Riggs. They eat, drink and sleep it. They asked me to go right when I got hired. Saw a Confederate flag sticker on my bumper. Didn't know it was my uncle's truck and his girlfriend gave it to me to drive when he kicked the bucket. I didn't mind it enough to peel it off.

Most of the guys at that meeting were pretty friendly. Don't know if it was just the Johnston County chapter or what. Several of them seemed like they still lived with their parents. They all seemed to enjoy commiserating about the government like they were some sinister masterminds in charge. Even talked about a representative of theirs who got elected. The government folk I know couldn't crack an egg without asking for help. I don't give a shit about politics. They weren't my type to hang with.

One guy got up and talked an awful lot about how women belonged at home, and they nearly had me there, but it didn't seem worth dedicating a whole Saturday night twice a month to talk about it, even though I liked nothing better than the thought of Jolie waiting with dinner when I got home.

I ain't never been much of a joiner. Even in school, never saw the point of team sports. Rather do things by myself without other people getting in the way. Didn't shoot the shit with anybody after night school classes at the academy when I was getting my badge. Ain't my thing.

One of those meetings was all it took though. When all my shit with this fucker laying here went down, I still got lumped in with them. Dawson and Riggs had gone and gotten in trouble for getting rough at one of those protests just a couple weeks before I put old Leigh here in the hospital. With that, and me having shown my face at their Proud Boys shindig, there hadn't been any convincing anybody what I did to him wasn't *racially motivated*. Hell, this guy here could've been green, and I'd have still tore his ass up. It's about him fucking Jolie, more than what color he is. Don't help that he's Black, but that alone ain't a reason to make me cross the street.

His knuckles seem like they're healing up. He busted them on the sidewalk cause I rolled out of the way when he was on top of me throwing punches. I can still see the blur of his bloody hands pushing my hands away from his face. That's how fights go—quick flashes of blood and the sound of hard breathing and shouts.

The machine beside him is steady noting his heartbeat. Still strong. Got tubes coming out of his arm, some with what looks like clear fluid, a ventilator mask on his face. With all the stuff attached to him, he looks like a cross between a scuba diver readying to go under water, and all the car parts under the hood of my car that keep it running. Reminds me, I need to change my oil soon.

I could finish what I started, but I'm not really sure what it was I set out to do that night. My main mission was to keep him out of my house, and out of Jolie's bed. How that got done, I hadn't thought out, and now, well here we are. He may not be in her bed, but she's sitting by his every time she gets off work. All in all, I'd say I failed.

Only reason I could even come up here and get a peek at what's going against me, is she's working a double. Saw her in the window of the Waffle House before I came over. She was ringing people up with that smile of hers. Same smile that drew me to her. Had me setting next to her on the bus every day. Kept me coming back all our years of high school.

She'd gone to the same elementary as me. We'd had second grade then fifth together. Even in fifth grade, the other kids thought we were a thing, but then her mama and daddy split up and her mama took her over to Benson. She went to junior high there til her mama OD'd.

That's when we met again, once she came back to live with her daddy and stepmama. Went to high school over in Clayton with me. She recognized me right off that first day. I scooted over in my seat, making room for her.

"I found her," she'd told me that first day on the bus. "My mama.

I was the one who found her. Had this white foam stuff all around her mouth like a rabid dog or somethin'. Man at the funeral home said nothin' coulda been done, but you cain't help but wonder, you know?"

I didn't know. All I knew was that I was glad to see her. Even at ten, I'd been dreaming about her being my first fuck, but before I knew what happened. She'd up and left then there she was again! I scooted over closer, slipped my hand into hers. She didn't jerk it away. Neither had Amy Sauls the month before, and I was so glad all I'd talked Amy into was putting her hand down my pants to give me a tug. Looking at Jolie there on that bus, I was so glad she'd still get to be my first.

"Real glad you're back," I told her.

She stared at me, tears on the brim of her lower eyelids drying up and she smiled. It was the kind of sweet smile that told me what I needed to know. She was a wounded bird and needed a place to rest. I'd be that place. I knew then that's how I liked them—in no shape to fly, in need of taking care of, little birds with busted wings. Wings that'd be easy to break again if she got any ideas about healing up and soaring away. It was set. We were gonna be a thing. We just were.

Leigh's finger on his hand closest to me twitches, jolting me out of my remembering. The machine's beeps don't falter. Probably his nerves. If luck's on my side, that's the only kind of moving he'll ever do again—finger twitches.

Our bus ride was so long ago now. Way before this fella came along flipping burgers and making patty melts back on the Waffle House grill. Way before Jolie'd started waitressing there, even though I told her she didn't have to work, that we could get by on my salary. Should've stuck to my guns. I see that now. This is all on me and my giving in.

"Cy?" her voice breaks into my thoughts.

I turn slow to see her standing in the doorway. Her fingers grip the bottom of a vase of fresh flowers so hard it's a wonder it doesn't crack sending water and glass all over this floor.

"What the fuck, Cy?" she whispers like this vegetable laying here's gonna wake up if she's loud.

"I ...I just wanted to—" I start.

"No!" She shakes her head, plunks the vase down on the table at the end of his bed, makes her way around the other side, takes his hand in hers. His hand looks so dark against her skin. I see myself reaching across, ripping her hand away as clear as day and that feels like the best option.

"Just leave, Cy. Go!" she orders.

Her face is so red. Her eyes are fixed on mine in such a way, I know us being here and him laid out because of me, she's got the upper hand. I back out slow til I reach the hall. I hadn't thought we'd run into each other. I really hadn't, even though I'm sure she thinks I planned it this way.

The hall seems longer than it did on the way in. A nurse exits a room with blood covered gloves. I hug the wall railing to keep way away from her. I'm almost to the elevator.

"Cy, wait!" Jolie calls.

I stop but stay facing the fingerprint-smudged metal door in front of me, waiting for it to open. Got to stay facing forward. If I turn back, it won't be good. It won't. Fast steps click-clack behind me, and now she's right beside me. She presses the button for the cafeteria floor.

The doors open. An older woman coming out of the room diagonal to the elevator follows us inside. The doors close. I stare at the three of us, our funhouse reflections in the steel door. I'm taller than both of them. My face is long and drawn out. Looks more like that mask from those *Scream* movies than my face.

"Valve repair," the old woman suddenly says to us on the way down. "My husband's havin' his heart valve repaired."

I feel her eyes on me. I don't speak, shift my weight a little to lean against the wall closest to me.

"My boyfriend's on a ventilator in the I.C.U.," Jolie offers. "We're hopin' he'll be breathin' on his own soon."

I'm sure she said this to twist the knife. *Boyfriend. My boyfriend's on a ventilator.* What is this? Old home week? Jesus! This shitty metal box can't move fast enough.

"Sorry to hear that, hon," the old woman says, reaching over and patting Jolie's arm. "I'll pray for him."

"Me too," Jolie tells her. "For your husband. I'll be prayin' he'll be just fine."

We come to a stop. There's a ding. The elevator door slides open. The old woman goes left as we go straight. I guess Jolie's decided we can be closer than a hundred feet long enough to eat some stewed beef over rice or slurp up some tapioca.

"Y'all want a hot plate?" the cafeteria lady asks.

Jolie nods.

"Coffee for me," I tell her.

She hands me a mug, points down at the end of the aisle to a coffee maker plugged in next to the soda fountain. I walk down to the end and help myself while Jolie tells the lady what she wants on her plate. I'm sure she gets tired of Waffle House freebies.

One of the differences between us. I sure never did get sick of any of it. I'd love to get my hands on some of that fried fatback for making sandwiches that she used to bring home and smell all those smells in her hair and on her clothes from the grill. I'd give anything to hear her coming in my door again, to know she'll be collapsing next to me on the couch.

I pay for my coffee and Jolie's plate. She don't argue about it. So much for being an independent woman. Guess she figures I owe her. I suppose if I owe anybody, it's her. We walk over to a table in the corner in front of a wall made of thick windowpanes. People can look out at the woods behind the hospital. I can barely make out the dark outline of the trees in the distance mixed in with our reflections. She takes her food off of her tray just like she used to back in school, real careful, like it's all as fragile as she is. I take a sip of my coffee.

"Actually, not as bad as I thought it'd be," I say knowing that's not at all what I want to say. Knowing I'd like to tell her all about my new house, about Cobb, and how I like it real well over in Lee

County. How I might just have a lead on putting a baby killer behind bars. She'd like that. She loves babies. She'd be real proud of me if I lock up a baby killer.

She forks around her mac and cheese in its tiny plastic bowl. I can't tell her any of that. My lawyer'd have an aneurism just knowing I'm setting here. I'm supposed to steer clear. She's supposed to get to stay around here. I'm supposed to be totally disappeared til the hearing. Cain't even be on my email or doing shit online, calling anybody I know or nothing. Who can live like that? Don't see why I should have to.

Her head hangs. She lays her fork down on the table and plants both her hands on either side of her plate. She takes a deep breath and glares up at me. All I can think is how fucked up my life is that lately the last two bitches I spent more than five minutes with have both been in hospitals. Damn! I got to start getting my ass back on a barstool again on Friday nights if I ever hope to see any less crazy pussy.

"I figure you an' me are overdue for a talk," she says.

I don't speak. I sip. Best way to get anything I want to get out of this night is to shut the fuck up.

"See, I think you got the idea that Leigh is why I'm not with you," she says.

I stare at her.

"Yeah, I thought so, but that's just not true, Cy. Not true at all. If Leigh whatin never born, you an' me'd be callin' it quits."

"I don't buy it."

"Don't matter what you're buyin'! It's true, Cy!"

A man walks by us toting a little boy on his hip. They're carrying a tray over to the table not far from us. We watch the man set down as slow as he can, maneuvering so he can keep the boy asleep on his shoulder. Jolie waves. He nods like they've met. She's getting that bleeding heart I'm-about-to-cry-face.

"His wife's real sick," Jolie informs me like I give a shit about some dude and his fucking kid. "Itn't it sad his little boy cain't be home in his bed, that he's got to be here in this place?"

I empty a couple sugars into my coffee and stir. Her gaze comes back to me. I don't have any idea what she's talking about.

"I'll tell you what else is sad. It's sad we aren't home in our bed, me an' Leigh. Sad that I'm down here eatin' this nursin' home food again while he's up there needin' help breathin' all cause a you, Cy!"

I lean forward, letting my coffee mug hit the table hard enough some splashes out.

"If we really wanna go there, Jo. Really, truly, trace it back, I'd say it's cause a you. I'd say you leavin' brought all this on."

She laughs, picks up her spoon, lifting a big bite of mashed potatoes and gravy up to her mouth. Her neck looks so thin and beautiful as she swallows it down. My hands tingle like they remember all on their own what it's like to slip up around that throat of hers while we're fucking. Never was much her kind of thing. She'd do it for me. Whole hell of a lot she did only for me.

"That's how you see everything, Cy. You see all the wrongs a our lives as somethin' somebody else caused. That's bullshit."

"*Right*. You're always *right*, Jolie."

The little boy stirs from his spot on the man's shoulder. He whimpers having woken up. The man puts his sandwich down, gets up and starts lightly bouncing him trying to get him back to sleep.

Jolie leans in so they won't hear. Her greasy Waffle House signature scent wafts up under my nose, clouding over the smell of all this hospital crap. I think about the last time I held her close, breathed in that smell and nothing else. I think about her uniform dress falling on the floor.

"I don't blame you, Cy. Naw, you hadn't changed a bit. You know my lawyer asked me when you turned, what it was that happened that made you so god damned mean an' you know what I told him?"

I roll my eyes, take another sip of coffee.

"I told him you ain't especially mean. Not more than any other guy I knew growin' up. I told him there what nothin' happened to you 'cept bein' born here. That all you southern boys are just plain marinated in hate like those chicken breasts Tom barbecues out back a work on Sundays. You just soak up all the hate an' anger that's been around for years. You come by it natural. Didn't really have a choice in it. You just are who you are," she explains. "Those are the same excuses I told myself about you for years."

The man sets down with his boy again as he's finally gotten him back to sleep. He eyes us as he tries to eat the last of his food, hoping we won't get louder.

"So, it whatin you that went an' changed, Cy. Naw, I changed. I started g'ttin' to be around other people. I started seein' that everybody whatin ate up with anger. Everybody don't go around talkin' about Blacks g'ttin' everything handed to 'em an' how bitches cain't seem to keep their legs shut to quit poppin' out welfare mouths they got to feed with our tax money, how God's a fuckin' fairy tale or any a that other shit you spout. Yeah, bein' at work, I saw that some people choose another way. They choose to see the good instead a lookin' at the bad an—"

"People like your golden boy upstairs?"

"Damn right, people like him! Cy, you know Leigh's from here, come up right over in Smithfield? Graduated, then went up to Michigan to work with his mama's cousin at his restaurant an' go to culinary classes. He was changin' his situation. Only came home cause his brother, Demete, got in some trouble, somethin' with drugs. Got himself sent up to Central couple a years back. Leigh had to help support his mama an' his younger sister. Soon as Demete got settled, after g'ttin' out, Leigh was headed back up to school. Now Demete's out an' here Leigh is."

*Demete? Demete from over in Smithfield...*figures. I shoulda known I hadn't seen the end of all that. Gotta be the same Demete. Ain't many fellas in these parts with that name. Him getting an 8 x 10 at Central ain't all on me though. He'd been funneling me info after I busted him for dope slinging out back of Haverty's club on game nights. I'd always told him if he fed it to me straight, we wouldn't have any problems. Soon as he gave me the wrong location for a bust, I let Reinhold pick him up and slap a possession charge on him.

Way I see it, I just delivered on what I warned him would

happen. Now here, what I set in motion, brought his brother down south to fuck my wife, and I've gone and beat the shit out of that brother. Demete's going to see it as part of some kind of revenge. Soon as he lays eyes on me again at my next hearing, he's bound to know it's me who got him sent up in the first place. Damn it! I cain't catch a break.

"Are you hearin' me, Cy?" She hadn't quit talking. I'd just quit listening. "Leigh showed me there's another way. That we all have choices in how we act, in who we get to be, if we love, if we hate, an' I don't choose this. I don't choose you, Cy. I don't choose *us*. I don't."

Her mouth is in a flat line I haven't seen before. Seen her smile and her frown but not this. She means it. She means every word of this shit. She's done. Her wing got mended. My little broken bird of a girl from the bus rides, I knew like the back of my hand's become some high-flying woman I don't know at all.

Setting right here, I'm glad I did it. Pleased as can be I put old Leigh in the I.C.U. My only regret now is I didn't go on and really seal the deal. Should've gone on and got him hauled off to a drawer down at the morgue.

Like she's reading my mind, Jolie narrows her eyes, lifts a hand and points a finger at me.

"I choose him, you hear? I do. An' if I catch you here again, I'm callin' it in. Won't say a word to you, I'll just call your ol' buddies over there at the station."

I stand up, look down at her. She'd like nothing better than to see me in jail. I get that now. I put a hand on her shoulder. She tenses, readying to scream. I squeeze, and she holds off. Her eyes dart over at the man with his kid searching his face for help, but he's looking down at his phone.

"Here I am just tryin' to be nice. Stoppin' by to tell you I hope you'll be happy, Jolie. Really. Tha's all. I hope you'll be *real* happy now that you landed you a *brother*."

I remove my hand from her shoulder, letting it wind around to her back, rubbing it over the clasp of her bra under her dress.

"I know it whatin no accident, Cy."

"Awe now, I don't know if I'd go as far as to say that."

I lean down so my lips nearly touch her left ear.

"Damn shame, cause when it's dark, they all look alike. No way to tell who it was walkin' up on your porch," I whisper. "Yeah, I hope you an' him'll be happy an' have lots a little jigaboo babies to get underfoot."

Her hair slaps against my face as she whips her head around and hops up. Her back is against the window like an alley cat backed against a dumpster. Out of the corner of my eye, I see the dad's gotten up out of his seat, his hand holding his brat still sleeping in place. I reach in my pocket, pull out my badge and clip it to my shirt pocket staring him down as I do. Bring it on motherfucker. I'm sure the I.C.U.'s got room. He stays put. I grin. That's what I thought.

Jolie bolts, pushes right past me. I chuckle as I watch her go.

"Enjoy that badge while you still got it, Cy," she yells over her shoulder.

The cafeteria lady's standing out in the aisle, phone in hand like she's ready to film if something YouTube worthy pops off.

"Bye bye, Jolie. You take care now," I call with my perfect gentlemanly voice I keep on hand for occasions just like this.

She stops, but don't look back, just holds up a hand, flips me off then stomps off and rounds the corner out of sight. The cafeteria worker claps. The dad sets back down to his food. Lucky him. His kid slept through this whole little drama.

I cain't wipe the smile off my face all the way to the car. She'll be burning up about tonight for a long time. Next best thing to Jolie loving me is her hating me. Either way, I'm on her mind. Yeah, if that fucker starts breathing on his own, by some chance makes a recovery, she'll be fucking him, but she'll be hating me and that there takes a whole lot more time and energy than loving me ever did.

43°F

Cobb

I sat in the car in front of my house a while that night after my Waffle House trip. Through the kitchen window, I could see Stacy as she stood at the stove. It'd been at least two months since she'd lost a baby. Took longer for her to get back to normal after each loss so I wasn't moved to exit the car. I just wanted to sit there a while and enjoy the view. When she was cooking again, it was always a good sign.

Minute I walked in the house, I hoped she'd be glad to see me. A few nights before, she'd been on a crying jag and letting it all out more than usual.

"Just seein' you reminds me of what I cain't do for you. What I cain't do for us," she'd cried.

By then, she'd started rationalizing that her womb was somehow toxic and it was her fault. Seems that's the way with people—blame themselves when no one else steps up to take responsibility.

"Maybe God knows I'd be a bad mother?" she'd say from time to time. "Got too much bad in me."

No matter how I tried to refute it, I saw it was the years I had on her that gave me a leg up. Those ten years had shown me that there's so much that happens in this life with no doorstep to lay it on. Blame floats through the air without a home wreaking its havoc wherever it can. Heard one of the old boys at the station say one time that he thought most crimes were just all those horrible things we couldn't account for, that we couldn't understand, finally finding a way to show their faces.

"Hey you," Stacy exclaimed all smiles as I sat up to the table. "Just in time to be my taste tester."

She made her way over to me, holding her hand under a spoon full of whatever it was she was making. Taking a bite, her doe eyes staring up at me, I thought about how little, if any, badness she had in her. I thought about how if her line of thinking held any truth, what I'd just come from trying to orchestrate over in Clayton was likely worth at least two more dead babies. I didn't let that thought take hold. I reminded myself I was just a God-forsaken man, doing my best to bring other God-forsaken men to justice.

"Real good, hon," I told her.

I scooted up to the table, watching her work her wonders in that little light pink apron she wore. Nothing like Jolie's Waffle House one. Stacy's was all for looks. She tried to keep it clean. It was one of those nights I could look up now and then nod, half-listening as I mulled over the events of my own day.

Jolie's face hadn't changed when I told her who I was, handed her Hogue's address on the paper. It was like she'd been expecting me but was also disappointed I'd come. That part surprised me. I'd have thought she'd have been glad to get the upper hand in her and Hogue's mess.

"An' what am I supposed to do with this?" Jolie'd demanded.

"Your man's still in a coma, right?"

She bit her lip, fighting tears. She nodded.

"Doctors say there's still a chance he'll come out of it," she said. "Might breathe on his own if they unhook him. His mama's prayin' day an' night. I cain't hardly get her to leave the hospital some days. Other days I cain't get her to show up."

The lunch crowd had dispersed. Few customers remained. I'd done my best to get it down to brass tax before the dinner stretch.

"Cy had me come with him to that last hearin'. Stood in the back, just for good measure. From the way some a our own had to hold off your man's family from comin' at Cy, I'd say they're hell bent on rightin' wrongs," I told her.

Arms crossed, she leaned back against the counter behind her, looked out the window at the people pulling in, a mournful scowl like she'd trade anything to be one of them.

"Ain't never been one for rules," she finally started in again. "Showed right up at the hospital the other night."

That came as a shock to me. Hogue knew he'd been told he had to steer clear of her to have a chance at getting his badge back. For a split second, I felt pangs of failure. I was already feeling responsible for him like he was my own wayward brother.

"You know Mr. Cobb, men like Cy are a dime a dozen 'round here. He really itn't a bit different 'cept for the fact he went out an' got himself a gun an' a badge that gives him a right to carry that gun any time any place. Boys an' their guns," she grumbled shaking her head. "Give em somethin' to do violence with an' then wonder why they're violent. Crazy!"

"Thought he just beat your fella? Didn't shoot him, did he?"

Looking down at the floor she chuckled a bit. That really unnerved me.

"That itn't my point, but I'll tell you, I'm sure this ain't the reaction I bet you thought I'd have when you give me this. Maybe you thought I'd hug your neck an' thank you. Fact is, your comin' all the way out here, well, Mr. Cobb, that pisses me off."

I got up from my stool, laid my cash on the counter for the hash and coffee.

"Certainly didn't mean to do that."

"Well, you did an' you know the worst thing about it? Worst thing is, you think it's the right thing to do. That you're better than Cy somehow for doin' it."

The busboy couldn't read the room and scooted in between us. Jolie sighed long and hard.

"That's where you've failed, Mr. Cobb—thinkin you're in the

right an' Cy's in the wrong. Ain't no right or wrong about it. There's just hate an' how you deal with it. Before you walked in here, I didn't know where Cy's stayin' at. Didn't have a place to put my hate an' was havin' to handle it. Now, see, you've gone an' delivered a place for my hate to go."

Standing there, I breathed in real slow. The heaviness of what she was saying pushing down on me like the time my Aunt Carol's horse rolled on my arm when I wasn't but nine years old. Jolie came around the counter, her hips navigating on autopilot, untouched by the booth corners. Her right hand reached out. Thought for certain she was coming in for a slap. She stood her ground, landing her hand on my shoulder.

"Here I'd been havin' such a nice break. Nearly all but quit hearin' Cy in my head. Now you show up. What you cain't see is you brought him to me. Brought him right to me on this paper," she said, waving that address in my face.

"I'll take it back."

She lowered it, stuffing it in her pocket.

"Won't matter. I've seen what's on it. Remember it letter for letter."

I reached up, pushed the side door too, then her hand tightened into a squeeze.

"Now, you know what else? If I don't do anything with this, well that's exactly what he'd love. It'd mean he still has me under his thumb. If I do what it is I think you're hopin' I'll do with it, he still wins," she said.

"I don't think he—"

"He does! He wins! You cain't see! You cain't see that if I do that, it makes me just like him. You cain't see that Mr. Cobb, cause you're one an' the same."

"How was it?" Stacy asked from where she sat at our table across from me, breaking through my memory.

"Good. Really good, hon," I told her. "Maybe one of my favorites you've made."

She cleared our plates. I walked down the hallway to dress for

Wednesday night prayer meeting. I wasn't in the mood for prayer. That's when they say you need it most. Found myself hoping we could set in the back so her Daddy wouldn't start in again about declaring anybody dead or seeing any files.

Under the fluorescent bulbs she'd had me install in our bathroom over the sink, Stacy's hair was almost blonde. I liked watching her comb it. She was a light tan more than she was Black, like a Barbie doll. I often had to remind myself she was what she was.

"What?" she giggled as she caught me eyeing her in the reflection of the mirror.

"You're beautiful's all." I slipped an arm around her.

Staring at our reflections, I thought about how the world's made so none of us really get to be who we're meant to be. All of us misplaced warriors, with no worthy battles to fight, least ones we hadn't created all on our own.

"What is it, Mitchum?" Stacy cooed again, turning, kissing my cheek.

"Nothin', hon. Just tired."

And that wasn't a total lie, I was tired. But I was also frozen there thinking how glad I was that she'd never know what Jolie'd said that day right at the last. What she'd leaned in close to tell me, making it so the smell of her perfume mingled with hash overtook my nostrils as she moved her hand lightly to my shoulder.

"I take that back, Mr. Cobb," Jolie'd whispered. "You're worse than Cy. Far worse off cause you think comin' here makes you different, an' you don't get that your settin' foot in here means he's already got you."

She turned loose of my shoulder, took a few steps back, looked my face over then smiled this odd little smile.

"Hmm. You know the more I look at you," she said, "the more I think you were already just like him, an' y'all only just now found each other."

85°F

There were no other cars or signs of anyone else as they pulled in. He and Bobby got out. On one hand, Mitch was relieved there were no meth heads who'd set up camp that night. On the other hand, he knew what the three of them being alone would likely mean. He'd told himself it was that one time, that it would never happen again. It was not who he was. Did he know who he was? Yes, like a meth junkie in his own right, he'd promised, just that one time—the time with Anita.

Kelly opened her door slightly. She ignored the instinctual hesitation kicking in and followed them out of the car. She looked much darker in the shadows the old hospital created. With her punk band shirt and high-top tennis shoes, she wasn't like the other Black girls at Lee High. Mitch wondered if she, too, felt like a stranger in their strange land. Stranger in a strange land... his dad's favorite Iron Maiden song.

Bobby looked over at Mitch, his eyes twinkling. Mitch could tell he was already thinking about it—the threshold. That's what Bobby thought about them all. What would be their threshold of what they'd participate in. What they could stand, be pushed to without telling on him. No one had, to Mitch's knowledge, ever told on him.

Long ago, Mitch had accepted that being in Bobby's orbit meant you no choice but to think about this. You had to know your own threshold, your rules. For the last while, he'd come into the understanding that over the years, he'd become desensitized. His threshold a distant memory. What he felt sure he'd never partake in, he had. The muddled inklings of pride and shame that came with that were a mystery to him. *He used to know who he was, didn't he?* Yes, at one time, there was a time... That's what Bobby did just by being himself, wore your morals, your pride, your very self down. Bobby was the water steady and slow, dripping onto rock, reshaping it.

There was the sound of the pea gravel under shoes. Kelly appeared next to Mitch.

"Have some," Bobby offered holding out a flask to her. He often kept it hidden somewhere on his person or in the car for just such occasions.

Kelly vehemently shook her head. Mitch put a hand up, ready to wave him off as he'd figured he'd be the designated driver. The smell of the strong malt scotch called him though. He took the flask. Maybe if he sipped it, just sipped, he'd be fine. He had to really. If not, Bobby would only circle back, revisiting the offer until he conceded. That was part of his genius. Repeated exposure, circling back until what he wanted was done and who was Mitch to change him? Drip...drip...drip.

Besides, come next year at that time, he'd be getting off work at the mill. Bobby would be off kicking some cheerleader out of his bed over at NCSU. They'd have little to do with each other. In a life where there wasn't much Mitch could take comfort in, aside from the privilege that came with being a large white guy, he took comfort in this. He took a bigger than intended swig of the scotch, then handed it back.

"Go on an' hang onto it, man," Bobby told him.

The sky went more black than navy overhead. It was not an hour that they should've been out. This added to the trepidation of it all. Mitch could scarcely recall a time his stomach had been in more knots than it was at that moment. The alcohol slowly began having its way with him.

A quote Mr. Lowell had told them in history class surfaced from the recesses of his mind.

"The best thing about humans is they adapt. The worst thing about humans is they adapt."

Some man named Chomsky had said it first. Mr. Lowell shared it one class period towards the end of last term. The only year the man ever taught there. Everyone had been shocked to find out, he'd come back to Sanford to live with his Grandma, so he could go to one of the local twelve step programs several times a week. Word got out it had been the alternative offered him by his wife rather than a divorce. It had worked remarkably well. Mr. Lowell was so well rehabilitated that he quit teaching and headed home to his family at the term's end. Mitch had helped him carry some of his boxes out to his car when he went.

"Do me a favor, son," Mr. Lowell had said.

"What's that, sir?"

"Don't stay here, alright?" his teacher implored him. "I don't know where to tell you to go, but just don't stay here, Mitchum."

No one had ever spoken to him in such a forthright way. Mitch stood still, holding a box, uncertain of how to respond. Mr. Lowell said nothing else before taking the box from him, loading it in the car and driving off. He'd not required a response. Deep down, he'd known Mitch well enough to know that a response was too much to ask.

He'd only wanted to plant the seed, the idea of possibilities. Mitch had been mad at him ever since. He supposed this made Mr. Lowell the best teacher he'd ever had. He supposed you always had a distaste for your best teachers because that's what they did. They came into your life, dropped bombs into your existence, blew up life as you knew it.

Don't stay here...don't stay here... tunneled its way through his consciousness as he watched Bobby sprint ahead of him and Kelly, running a stick along the mostly broken out windows, alerting anyone who might be hold up inside as to their presence.

The scotch burned a little as it went down Mitch's throat. The good stuff. Bobby could always be counted on to siphon off the good stuff from his father's liquor cabinet. Watering it down worked until his father next poured a glass. Bobby weathered most any repercussions. It was worth it. Before he realized it, Mitch had sipped more than intended. He put the cap back on it.

"Looks like we're all on our lonesome," Bobby crowed from his perch on the edge of a large cracked cement fountain. At the top of it was a moss-covered cherub. One of its wings broken off. The wing left was chipped. A fitting mascot for the game to ensue in the coming hours.

Kelly went a bit further ahead of him than he liked. To Mitch's disappointment, she was not apprehensive, not at all scared. There'd be no grabbing for his hand in the dark if the wind roared too loudly or an owl screeched. No, she was an independent sort, evidenced by the way she went at her own pace, way away from both of them, peering into the half-broken windows at the building's end.

"Cain't imagine people bein' put in here," he heard her say as he got closer.

A pebble bounced off of her shoe. She whirled around. Bobby put his hands up, a robber in an old black and white shoot-em-up flick. He hopped off the fountain, bounding over right up next to her.

"What do y'all do out here sides torture guys an' their pet rats?" Kelly wanted to know.

Neither answered right away.

"Not much," Mitch finally said, licking the scotch from his lips.

"Mainly break shit," Bobby lied.

"Looks like your job's done," she replied.

Bobby leaned down and picked up a few more pebbles.

"Long as there's any glass hangin' on, there's still good times to be had," he told her, throwing another pebble at a jagged shard remaining in a window.

"God!" Kelly chastised.

"Here, you try," Bobby said. "Give it a go. Breakin' shit feels nice."

Mitch hung back, confident the girl would not continue to disappoint. That indeed she was wanting less and less to do with Bobby by the second. *That half smile in the car was nervousness*, he told himself. Only nervousness.

He couldn't explain why he did this, this retreating, preemptively letting Bobby take the lead. Giving him free reign to win them over. Maybe he was tired? Or maybe, just maybe, he'd reconciled himself to the fact that young love was not in the hand dealt to him. At least with Bobby, Mitch had a seat at the table, even if he only held a pair of fours.

At first, Kelly only stared at the pebbles in Bobby's hand, keeping her hands in her pockets of her jean skirt. Bobby raised his hand higher.

"You know you want to," he coaxed.

Oh, how often Mitch had heard this kind of double speak, teasing to be taken one way or another. Tonight, with the scotch swirling, having its way, the veil had been lifted off of Bobby's actions. Mitch saw clearly, there'd never been any teasing or coaxing, only grooming, readying for whatever he wanted next.

"Might not be her thing," Mitch called.

They ignored him, and it happened just like that. He became a prop, no different from the warped fountain cherub or broken windows. Kelly reached out, taking a rock, raring her arm back and throwing. The shattering sound that followed likely woke a dog or two keeping watch from their porches down the road. Who knew she'd have such an arm? Mitch and Bobby were equally smitten. She was a natural.

"Whew doggie!" Bobby whooped.

He turned looking at Mitch, eyes wide with wiley amusement.

"See that, man?"

Mitch took another swig from the flask. Kelly clasped her hands together, bouncing up and down, a pleased as punch girl in line to get her prize after knocking down all the milk bottles at a carnival booth.

"Tha's good. Real good, Kelly," Mitch said.

He couldn't bring himself to seem too eager. That part of him had been deadened. That part of him that would want to rush over, sweep her up and plant one on her as if he'd come home from war, and she'd been waiting for him. Seemed to him that's all life was, a ramping up then a deadening down.

"Give me some more," Kelly demanded, holding her hand out.

Bobby reached down, sifting through the soil until he had a fist full. Mitch again pocketed the flask, meandering over to them. His steps already proving heavy and unsteady. Beer was their customary Friday night staple. He held that like a champ, but the scotch was both a welcome elixir and formidable foe. It took out his senses one by one, dulling everything. Why had Bobby drank so little of it?

The three of them used up the first fist of rocks, aiming for the higher windows. There was a whole floor of smaller thinner ones they'd neglected on their prior outings there. They made quick work of them. The hospital resembling more and more those pictures from history class Mitch remembered of buildings in Germany after bombings in World War II. Everyone had their own private wars, he supposed. It struck him he was to be a soldier in only one war that would ever amount to much—the war between the man he wanted to be and the boy he allowed Bobby to make him.

Boredom quickly found Kelly once all the glass their pitching arm rock throws could reach was in pieces.

"What's down there?" she asked, pointing to a small trail that wound behind the building.

"The river," Mitch answered.

That was all that needed to be said to send her off down the path. All they could see as they followed was the white soles of her black and white high-top Converses. The moon was bright enough to light their way, more or less. Mitch feared getting too close to the water in his current state, though he also didn't want to wait alone at the car for Kelly's sake. The image of the billboard across from his uncle's house in Georgia by the Savannah River that stated *Friends don't let friends walk drunk* flashed through his head.

"Didn't ever know all this was here," Kelly exclaimed in awe as the three of them came to stand at the river's edge. "Bet it meets up with the part we swim in over behind K-Mart, over off Horner. Me an' Stacy, Anita an' Daryl'd go over there in the summers when I'd visit. 'Fore I lived here."

Anita... the name immediately creating a wall of tension wedging a divide even further between them all. Mitch stared at Bobby. His heartbeat pounded in his ears so loudly, he was sure the other two could hear it.

"You an' Anita friends?" Bobby asked, taking a leftover rock he had held onto, tossing it into the river.

"Cousins," Kelly said. "Why? You know her?"

The river gurgled, dark and thick, flowing around the boulders and branches. She watched Bobby then Mitch. He could feel it. She'd just cast out her line, just a hair and was seeing who'd be first to take the bait.

"Look at that!" Bobby exclaimed pointing across the way.

They looked up to see a deer slumped over a tree limb, legs hanging down like a limp towel over a laundry line. How it had come to be all the way up there was a mystery. Mitch felt pangs of *kindredness* with it—a misplaced creature being viewed by another misplaced creature. Bobby took his shoes off, then stripped down to his underwear. Kelly looked on, tongue tied.

"What're you doin'?" Mitch blasted. "We don't wanna see all that, man. God knows!"

Before anything else could be said, Bobby lit out down the bank.

"Yippeekayeahhhh!" In no time, he was out in the river, making his way across. "Shit! It's cold!"

The flask again called to Mitch from his pocket. He took it out, turning it over in his hands. Kelly watched Bobby get right under the deer, so close its decaying head nearly touched the top of his own.

"He's crazy!" she hissed.

Finding a stick from a branch that was leaning out from the other side of the river, Bobby pulled it loose, wielding it in his hand like a wand. He poked at the deer's head. Its eyes bulged as if they might pop out. For reason's Mitch couldn't quite name, it was a sad sight to behold. A once-majestic beast turned bloated and ranking.

The branch became tangled in one of the antlers. Its body rocked forward as Bobby jerked to loosen it again.

"Sick!" he shouted.

Kelly shook her head, taking a few steps back.

"Stop it! Leave it alone!"

His wand then freed, Bobby used it to jab at the side of the deer next. Blood dripped down, but it was not red. Not in the moonlight. It was more of the same oil color the water possessed. It dripped steadily, finding its way to the river's current. As it surrounded Bobby, Mitch thought it made him resemble a dark overlord immursed in pure liquid evil. He again brought the flask to his lips, working away on the scotch.

"Come out of there! Just come out!" Kelly cried.

And Mitch saw as he glanced at her that she was rubbing away tears.

"Aww y'all don't know how to have any fun," Bobby said, yet he oddly obeyed.

He threw the stick into the woods, wading back over to their side, emerging from the water. His cut abs rendered him more unreal than not, like one of those Calvin Klein ads from the Belk catalogs Mitch had seen hanging in Amy Bishop's locker.

Ads, like many of the billboards around town or fed to them on TV, something to aspire to. Something to make them dissatisfied, and they worked. Oh, was Mitch ever dissatisfied, everything around him reminding him, *here's what you aren't and never will be.*

Leaning down, he picked up Bobby's pants and shirt, handing them back to him, as Bobby worked his way up the bank. Kelly leaned against a tree behind him. Her sniffling an unwanted interruption.

"Floodin' last month musta stranded it," Mitch theorized.

Bobby slipped on his jeans, wiped his face with his shirt. He eyed Kelly.

"What's got you all bent out a shape? Shit! It's already dead."

"Guys like you always gotta mess with everything. Cain't leave nothin' alone! You think you can do whatever you want whenever you want!"

He and Mitch shared a look between them. It would have been evident even to the most emotionally impaired bystander that her outburst was not about the deer. Mitch held his breath. From where he stood, he could see Kelly's chest rising and falling. She was steadying herself, measuring her next words, her next step. He knew this feeling well. It wasn't unlike the show he'd watch as a kid, *The Hulk*, where scientist Bill Bixby had undergone a mishap with an experiment and forever after had to guard against becoming too angry or he'd turn into his alter ego, The Hulk.

What was the alter ego Kelly was guarding against? Though he himself, had been introduced to his on several occasions, Mitch was yet to name it. He felt that was a promising sign it hadn't taken over. *To name something was a whole nother level.*

"I don't know why I thought this would be a good idea," she said.

"What?" Bobby slipped his shirt over his head, struggling to put his arms through the armholes as if he was a toddler who rarely dressed himself.

"Comin' out here with you two!"

Damn the scotch! Mitch's hands felt as swollen as his throat. His head two sizes larger than usual. Mitch didn't like being part of this *you two* she was referring to but didn't have the wherewithal to formulate a rebuttal.

"Nobody made you," Bobby shot back as he put his shoes back on, taking his time to tie the laces.

"Laura wouldn't quit talkin'. *Bobby Olsen. Oh, that Bobby Olsen. We just have to go*, she kept sayin'. I told her I know all about you an' that I didn't want to be anywhere near you, but she wouldn't let up."

She had Bobby's full attention. Nothing had Mitch's attention. Only the moaning of his gut and the dryness of his mouth that he kept trying to assuage with sip after sip from the flask.

"You don't know shit about me."

Bobby took a few steps towards her, signifying he took these as sparring words. He hadn't hit a girl, that Mitch knew of, but he was up for a good verbal reaming out any time he felt it was called for. Kelly stepped forward, her crossed arms nearly touching his chest.

"I know about you an' Anita," she said coolly, a seasoned gambler admitting she'd held the winning hand all along. "She told me all about it."

As soon as these words came out of her mouth, as if on cue, Mitch went down, slumped over, grabbing at his gut with one hand, steadying himself on a stump next to him with the other. Bobby walked over.

"Mitch, you alright, man?"

Everything began to swirl around like the tilt-a-whirl ride they rode every year at the fair. He thought if he could just gag himself and throw all that scotch up, he'd be fine. Bobby picked up the flask from where it had fallen in the leaves, shaking it, laughing.

"Shit, you drink all this? Lord knows. Never thought you were such an' alkie," he teased, leaning down, batting playfully at Mitch's bloated belly.

"Leave him alone!" Kelly shouted, rushing to the other side of Mitch, supporting him as he rested his back against the stump.

Crouching next to his buddy, Bobby pretended to wax sympathetic.

"Aww ol' Cobb here's got an iron gut. He just needs to sleep it off."

She reached out, smoothing Mitch's hair out of his eyes. He was glad he'd talked his mama into letting him keep his Beatles haircut as she called it. He told her nobody knew who the Beatles were anymore. She'd replied that people would always know who they were.

"Mitch, just rest. A'right, man?" Bobby lightly punched his shoulder.

Kelly reached across, shoving him, causing him to fall back, his rear end meeting the dirt.

"Damn girl!" Bobby shouted hopping up.

"Just let him be. Quit aggravatin' him. I don't know how he stands you!"

Looking up at Bobby, the moonlight illuminating his shiny forehead making him seem less like a person and more like one of the plastic action figures they played with as boys. Mitch knew no one talked to his *compadre* this way. No one.

"How's he stand me? *Me?*" Bobby scoffed. "Shit, everybody's always thinkin' Mitch is some kinna saint."

He leaned down. Kelly shot him a look that let him know she had another plan of attack ready if he got too close.

"Your cousin forget to mention *Golden Boy* here? Hmm?" Bobby asked.

She looked at Mitch, his eyelids blinking slowly as if made of lead. Surely, he was as harmless as he looked. Surely.

"She should have. He was out here then too. Yeah, he was ridin' shotgun. I'd say she *liked* us both just fine, but specially ol' boy scout here," Bobby went on.

Kelly shot straight up, pushing him.

"Bullshit! You don't talk about her! I know all about it. She told me everything you did an' I believe her over you any day."

A gun shot went off in the distance. They froze waiting to hear more, and from which direction it came. Nothing. It was just the one like a lone firework. Gunshots like it were commonplace in the country. That's why people moved out there—to shoot guns when they pleased and have their privacy, sometimes one causing the other.

"I'm goin' home," Kelly announced, the gunshot an auditory affirmation that she should never have been there in the first place

Bobby stayed put. Mitch having no choice in the matter, did as well.

"How you think you'll get there?" Bobby called.

"I'll walk it," was what she shot back making him only more resolved to stand his ground.

Soon she disappeared, up past the building. There they were as they'd been so many times before, the two boys left to their own company. There she went, down the road, into the night—a brazen woman. The idea that her plan was unsound in some way did not hit her until she was well out of sight. As it turned out, it wasn't anything that lay ahead that would be the end of her. Oh, if only she'd known that. If only anyone had ever told her that it's when we abandon the voice of reason, embrace a fear of what's unknown and turn back in the direction of the familiar, that we run right into the very arms of treachery.

83°F

Hogue

We keep our distance as Ms. Florrie pulls her car in the driveway. We were on our way out to Buncomb Road when Cheryl came over the radio.

"Your girl's headed home. Processed her paperwork this mornin'."

Cobb snatched the radio off its holder.

"Thank you, Cheryl," he said.

He hadn't liked it that she'd radioed. Would've preferred an email or note on his desk. Probably what he and the captain had been hashing over earlier in the office. How they're going to get me on another scent. How I won't let go of all my ideas about how Brandon met his maker. I'd bet neither of them's ever owned an honest to God hunting dog.

Soon as he hung up the radio, I turned the car around. He knew me well enough to know where we'd better be headed. Rode the whole way over here without a word. Guess he figured he'd rather be in on it than let me go on my own.

And here's Rae, setting in the back of her mama's car. Ms. Florrie makes her way around and opens the door for her like the girl's some cripple. Cobb's watching keen as I am, one of his elbows propped on the door so he can rub his big old forehead. Bout time to turn the air back on; he'll roast quick.

"Really ain't much we can do with their shrink clearin' her," he reminds.

"Bullshit. All she had to do was waltz in there, bat those eyes at him an' he was a goner. Whatin a thing she even had to say after that."

I pull out my vape, take a puff and blow out a cloud of pina colada smoke haze. He rolls his window down a piece ruining my hopes of ultimate relaxation.

"You're aware that's barely a notch above just goin' on an' havin' yourself a cigarette, right?" Cobb grumbles.

"So you've said."

The two women make their way up the sidewalk. Ms. Florrie looks in her purse for her keys. Rae takes the opportunity to look behind her out at the street. Isn't us she's looking for. Naw, she's watching for him.

"See," I blurt, elbowing Cobb.

"Mmm?"

"She's lookin' for him."

"Who?"

"That fella I told you about. The one the nurse over at the funny farm was sayin' called every day like clockwork."

Cobb hadn't got anything to say about that, settles down further in his seat, situating himself for one of his after-lunch naps.

"Yeah, that nurse, Lee Ann, said he was always tryin' to sweet talk whoever picked up to get extra phone time."

Rae finally goes inside after her mama. She stands looking out the screen door a while before she shuts it.

"How long you thinkin' we'll set here?" Cobb pesters.

"Just a little while longer. That Lee Ann said I was the only one sides her mama who came to visit, but that he kept that phone line tied up. I figure he'll be chompin' at the bit to get over here. Won't be able to stand it."

"Well, maybe you can at least turn the air on low? Bout to have a heat stroke."

I oblige him. We stay put. Itn't long and he's off to snoozeville, snoring away while I'm watching. I hate being wrong, but I know we can't just camp here. I turn the car back off, the air goes with it. He itn't offering to pay for the gas. He'll live.

Cobb shoots up in his seat and right off sets to rolling down his window, already getting bent out of shape the air's off.

"Never showed?" he asks.

"Not today."

"She itn't married anymore. Cain't hang a case on havin' a fella. Pretty girl like her's bound to have a one or two. If nobody's told you, it's a woman's world now."

"I know that don't make a case. Jesus! I ain't that green."

Cobb leans his head over towards the window, about to put it clean out like a dog riding shotgun. Shit, he's pitiful. I start the car again and get the air going for this big boy's sake, but we don't move. Not just yet.

"Thing of it is, night the boy died, your pastor went over there. Ms. Florrie'd called him to come over to pray. He told me Florrie was goin' all to pieces over her grandson, but our sweet lil' Rae whatin sheddin' not one tear."

"You talked to Pastor Chris?"

I nod.

"Said Rae kept puttin' her head in her hands kinna whimperin', tryin' her best to look like she was all tore up. He told me he's seen a lot a people whose grief takes different forms. Hers whatin any form he'd ever seen. Thought her actin' was worse than the time y'all tried to have some passion play an' charge for it but the actin' was so bad he refunded everybody an' sent 'em out the back door."

"Grief don't hit everybody the same."

"Sure. You're right, but there's that thing she said out back by the grill that day we brought her in. Mighta said it 'fore you got out there. She said, 'He said I can bear it… He said but'—"

I'm halted by what comes into view at the other end of the street

141

—a Dodge Charger. Nobody within an hour of here's got money for a car like that, not anybody young enough to want one. It comes creeping down the road pulling up in front of the house two houses down from Rae's. Windows are tinted making the driver a mystery.

"Whatchew wanna say that's our boy now?" I tell Cobb, slapping him on the leg.

As Cobb leans up, gets an eye full, he frowns, looks back over at Rae's then at the car again. He's nervous as a pole cat.

"You know that car?" I ask.

Long as it takes him to shake his head, I know he's lying. He knows the car. More than that, I'd go a step further and say by his hangdog look, he knows the driver. Nobody gets out. We sit, our engine on. They sit with theirs on.

Itn't long til Rae's door opens. She looks out from behind the screen, her face lighting up like the second of Christ's happening just for her. The Charger engine revs. She turns and disappears back inside the house for a second. When she comes back, she leans out, waves, then shuts the door again. Her mama must be getting in the way of her little rendezvous.

The Charger pulls back out on the street. I don't even say a word to Cobb. I count to five so we won't be right up on his bumper, and I get us going in his direction. We tail him far enough back so as not to be seen but close enough we don't lose sight of his brake lights.

"An' the end game here'd be?" Cobb fishes.

"Won't know til we see who's drivin'."

He sighs but that shuts him up for the time being. The Charger takes us all the way out to the interstate cut off out by old Highway 1. A couple miles we'll be leaving Lee and entering Wake. We pass the sign for the county line. Cobb fiddles with his pant legs, clears his throat. Our jurisdiction's in the rearview now and maybe that's the best place for it. I'm well aware, but I don't give a fuck.

I'll be dog gone if the Mr. Dodge Charger don't know he's out of our reach too cause he picks up speed and zips in behind another car.

"Let's call it," Cobb protests.

I ignore him and get up close enough to see the plates. Should've done that first off. I'm getting rusty, like a gun that's been stashed in a cabinet and gone unused.

"Got one a those specialty plates – C-r-o-s-P-h-i-t" I spell out for Cobb. "Take a picture with your phone!"

He just sets there.

"Come on!" I gripe.

"If you cain't remember that, you're in the wrong line a work," he says. "Now, let's head on back."

Mr. Dodge Charger zips out of sight. I pull off down the first side road and turn us around.

"Got to be him. Gotta be Mr. Once a Day Caller," I say.

We're back over the county line before Cobb weighs in again.

"Hate to tell you, even if it is him, callin' somebody's not a crime. Nothin' to write home about in the way a evidence either."

"Gil said there's a lot a unidentified prints on her car. Ones that don't match hers or her mamas. Might match his," I say, thinking out loud to myself more than for his benefit.

"May not be a *him*. Couldn't see the driver," he says.

I throw a glance his way. What's stuck in his craw? I usually go on about a whole lot of shit, and he don't pay it any mind.

"It's *him*. Mr. Once a Day Caller," I repeat with a voice that lets him know I'm done debating.

Driving us back to the station, I think about how just last year, before everything went how it went, I'd have followed that fella all the way home. What would've happened then's why I am where I am. I'm supposed to be learning how to do better.

Part of me knows Jolie's right when she talks about how I cain't accept things. I get my mind set on a way things should go, and if it don't go that way I'll burn up the whole world trying to melt it down, fit it in my mold. That's what she'd say I'm doing now, with this Rae thing.

And I know she'd be right. I know it itn't about bringing a

woman to justice. It's about setting my world right. I know it the same way I know Rae's boy burning up in that car wasn't any accident. Yeah, that Rae's a fire starter just like me. Mainly, what I know is people like Rae and me don't even need any matches to keep the flames burning.

40°F

Cobb

A full week went by from the day Hogue tailed him til my phone rang. Stacy answered. Soon as she walked into the living room and handed me the phone, I knew it was him. Those old ties between us not at all worn down by the years we'd lost. I breathed a little easier. Glad to go on and get it over with.

"Mitchum," was all he had to start with.

I didn't say anything back right off.

"So, you have a spring chicken drivin' you around now, huh?"

"Looks younger than he is," I replied.

"Lord knows I wish somebody'd say that about me. Feels like I've lived a hundred years an' it's startin' to show."

"Hard livin'll do that," I told him.

There was only the sound of him breathing for a minute.

"Yeah, you're probly right. What about you though, man? You hadn't been livin' hard, an' you still look like an' old coot. What's your excuse?"

And just like that we fell back into our back and forth, like when we used to run the field and pass the pigskin. Just like that.

"Aww, I'd say mine's from payin' dues, tryin' to set wrongs right. That takes its own toll I reckon," I said.

"What kind of livin' don't?"

Stacy stood in the doorway, looking out at the driveway. The Dodd's little boys were riding their bikes up and down it. Painful how she watched over neighbor's kids as if they were her own.

"The honest kind," I answered.

"Well, that's a shame, Mitch cause that's the most borin' kind there is."

Another quiet lull found us. The weight of it felt over the phone line. All those years we'd been off doing our own thing piling up, all trying to get in a front door too small for any of them to get through.

"We gonna do this all night?" I pressed.

"Naw, we'll do a little more, but let's have some grub while we do. I know a place up my way you'll like. They have that grass fed beef. Man, I tell you though, once you have it, you'll be ruined for any other meat. Won't want to even get a whiff a anything corn fed," he carried on.

That whole way up to Raleigh, I popped Tums like candy. I'd lied to Stacy about why I wouldn't be home on time and to Hogue about why I was taking the afternoon off. I knew if I went, and Bobby got to jabbering on like he always did, we'd go way past lunch time. And I needed him to get to talking. That's how you get anybody to tell you anything you need to know, let them keep on.

Looking back on it, I have the awareness to know he wasn't the exact Bobby I remembered. He was the Bobby of our middle age. I figure any villain you deal with keeps coming back around. They're in a different body, with more years on them, just like you. But you recognize them right away—they're your villain.

On that drive up though, I really had no idea what happens when the image you've stored up in your head of the villain of your youth collides with who they are at present. I should've known full well, while I'd been getting weaker, he'd been getting stronger. That's the way with villains. I'd been off licking wounds. Bobby'd been off lifting weights.

I walked into the restaurant he chose feeling like a farmer drawn up by ray beams from out in his field, up into an alien's ship. Sanford didn't have any of those farm to table joints and never would. We had rusted tables sitting out on actual farms, and that's about as close as we came.

The walls of the place were lined with tin panels. I smiled to myself at the idea of what yuppies thought a barn looked like. Ceilings were real high with stained wood beams across them. It was a relief to meet there, cause not a soul I knew would ever happen by.

A laugh came from the direction of my left. I looked over to see a waitress hardly looking old enough to drive standing next to a table just giggling away, obscuring her customer with her body. Didn't matter. I knew who she was talking to.

She moved just a hair and there he was. Had on a tight t-shirt, his ball cap turned backwards, a goatee without one hair out of place framing his chiseled chin. You'd have thought he'd done little else since the last time I'd seen him ten years earlier but set there eating grass fed beef, only taking breaks to go to the gym, down supplements and lift.

I instantly checked my shirt was tucked and ran my tongue over my teeth making sure there wasn't any leftover breakfast stuck in them. My armpits were sweaty. They rarely weren't. I usually didn't pay it any mind, but right then, I was embarrassed. He'd mistake it for nervousness. I knew he would. Really, I just stayed hot as hell about May til September. Must've been how women felt around him, like they weren't presentable. It wasn't so much I was wanting to please him, I just didn't want him to think I'd totally gone to pot. Who was I kidding?

Anybody that compared the two of us right off would see a new kind of manhood had evolved. A kind that had men caring about their waistlines, how many pullups they could do, or how big their biceps were more than their work ethic. Man, our fathers had it good. Back when we were coming up, getting older came with a pass. Bellies were supposed to get soft. Men were entitled to sit longer in front of TVs. I'd followed suit.

Staring at Bobby, I saw that those passes had expired. He was a poster boy for a new era of modern men who pulled trucks with ropes then uploaded it to Instagram or YouTube after. His breed cared more about eating organic than hunting. A whole new model of men who got facials and manicures and took their cars in to be fixed rather than fixing them. I wanted to run out that door. If it would've taken me back in time to better days, I sure would have.

It was too late. His eyes met mine. He put a hand up, motioning me over. Once I got closer, he hopped up, pulling out a chair for me. As I sat in it, I saw he hadn't done it as much for me as he'd done it to get a chance to slide his arm around the waitress' shoulders, moving her out of my way. He hadn't changed a bit. He always had all the moves. I had to hand it to him. In a world that had made him over, nearly turned him inside out, he was still the same old Bobby. Still an old *poon hound* as my Daddy'd called him.

"Cobb, this here's Lisa. She's my go-to girl. Main reason I keep eatin' this shit, just to catch sight a her. Lis, would you believe this here's my buddy from way back in grade school?"

Lisa wrinkled her brow, looking me over, noting I could easily pass for ten years older than him.

"Y'all came up together?"

"Yes, indeed. Played Pee Wee ball back in the day, gave our mamas an' teachers an equal portion a hell. Didn't we, Cobb?"

He had that smile on that was never a precursor to anything you'd be glad you were a part of and that same light in his eyes. The kind that crossed over the line between mischief and pure deviance.

"Well, *you* did," I answered, putting my hand out for the menu she was cradling closer than a baby. She handed it over slowly knowing my arrival meant she had to get on with her work.

Bobby plopped back in his seat.

"Aww, you're modest. They screamed your name a fair share from the stands an' other places."

And so he began his usual pushing me to the edge, hoping I'd slip just so he could watch me dangle. I didn't budge, just looked over the menu. A tense silence gut punched its way in between us. Lisa got the hint.

"I'll be back by when you're ready," she tried to bow out, inching towards the bar.

"I know what we want," Bobby proclaimed.

I stared at him. He'd never known what I wanted. Not now. Not ever.

"We'll have two a the garden grabbers with sweet potato fries for the side," he told her. "You hadn't had better fries," he added to me like we were on a second date, and he thought ordering for me would seal the deal. Just like that, pulling me back in.

"Comin' up," Lisa said, then took off for the kitchen.

"They got your number here, don't they?" I told him.

"Yeah, I'm here more than I'm not most weeks. My gym itn't but a few miles away. Easier than cookin'."

He went on a while about how he'd started taking CrossFit classes not long before everything that'd happened with his wife and girls. How it'd given him new purpose, so he'd gotten certified in it, and he'd leased a building so he could give other people purpose. He'd never known it would become what it had. He'd never known it would save his life. A church of barbells and tractor tires.

"If your body itn't right, your mind cain't be either." He wrapped up his run down of what he'd been doing since the last time we'd seen each other outside the courthouse.

Couldn't help but notice as he said it, his eyes drifted to my belly pushed against the table, pressing the cheap, plastic buttons of my dress shirt to their limits. If the kind of mind he had came with that body, I'd keep my slouchy dad-who-wasn't-a-dad-yet body any day.

By the time Lisa brought the food, I was still unclear about where exactly it was all headed. I'd thought about coming right out with it, asking him what he was doing sniffing around Rae's, if they were still a thing or what. Depending on what his reply was, then I'd get around to whether or not if Hogue kept on, we'd find his prints on Rae's car. If they were an item, it wouldn't be long til Hogue'd be on his doorstep. All those years later, and Bobby was still what he'd always been—one big old pile of questions. Most of them you really didn't want to know the answer to.

He chomped down on his burger, and I watched as he chewed. It threw me right back to high school in the cafeteria before practice. They'd serve us whatever we wanted and as much of it as we could eat. Our hunger and our metabolisms equally charged. Sitting there, I came to terms with the fact that it wasn't that I missed our old days. I missed who I thought I would go on to be as I sat in that cafeteria. Our futures unknown, waiting to be carved out. Difference was one of us popped out of the womb with a whole hell of a lot better set of tools to do the carving.

"Thought for sure you an' your boy were gonna follow me all the way home the other night," Bobby finally kicked things off.

"Itn't our jurisdiction."

I unfolded my napkin and lifted a hand to tuck it in the collar of my shirt. Stacy'd have a fit if I stained another dress shirt. He had his wadded next to his plate having already wiped his mouth with it. I decided on putting mine in my lap instead. It was better to risk Stacy's fussing than look like a pussywhipped wuss.

"Yeah, well, I should've given her more time to get settled when she got home, but I needed to see her," he told me. "Had to risk it. I was just glad her mama whatin outside. The two of us don't get on too well."

I took a bite of my own burger. Minute it hit my mouth I knew it wasn't any beef I was used to or wanted to get used to. Eating the standard corn-fed cattle might take years off your life, but I couldn't see wanting to live if you had to eat that way.

"Her mama's got it in her mind I was what ended Rae's marriage, but they were already done," he kept on. "They were separated by the time she started comin' to my gym."

"She was drivin' all the way up here to work out?"

"A friend a hers who lives up this way invited her."

I chewed slow and looked past him out the window at the field in the back, doing my best to get him squirming, it just eating away at him what was going to come of it all. I knew it'd take time. Bobby never did break easy, if he ever broke at all.

"You know, you an' my mama were the only two people who never asked me about all that with Laura an' the girls," he suddenly changed routes.

"What is it I would've asked you?"

"Y'all never once asked if I did it."

Taking another bite, I didn't look at him, just chewed, kept my eyes on my plate. More I ate of it, the more the beef that wasn't beef grew on me. Didn't dare tell him that. He got to be right about enough in life as it was.

"Mama's still never come right out an' asked me. She still goes out to their graves every May 10th, calls me once she gets home an' just cries an' cries. I keep waitin' for her to ask but hadn't happened yet. Cain't bring herself to talk about it at all."

It came to me that he was lumping me and his mama in together. This got my blood boiling.

"I won't speak for your mama, Bobby but I don't ask you cause I don't need to."

Took another bite, chewed extra slow, staring him down.

"That's what I appreciate about you, Mitch. After all this time, how much we've changed, all life's dished out. You still know me, you—"

"I don't need to ask if you did it, cause I know you did." I laid it out and it felt about as good as anything ever did just to say it.

He dropped what was left of his burger back on his plate, just staring back at me, then picked up his napkin and wiped his mouth.

"Y'all doin' okay?" Lisa wanted to know as she bopped by on her way to wait on someone else.

"Fine, girl. We're fine," Bobby assured her, giving her a wink.

A couple came in and sat a table behind us. They had a baby with them that was sounding off, unhappy as the world they'd dragged them there and squalling for all they were worth. Bobby leaned in where I could hear him.

"Your parents were at mine an' Laura's weddin'. Sent your mama an' daddy a Christmas card with us an' our girls, those beautiful girls, sittin' next to us on it every damn year til they died, an' that's what you think? You think I'd do that? You think I'd kill my girls?"

I met him halfway, leaning forward myself, sliding my plate aside.

"I think you know I do, Bobby. I think you know it, an' that's why you knew better than to call me as a character witness at your trial."

The mother behind us quieted the baby with a jingling bell rattle of some kind and the sweet jangly sound of it made everything we were saying seem all the more awful. Bobby leaned back, puts his hands behind his head, resting his head in them.

"Shit, man. I never called you cause a you comin' to the house that night. Comin' over, leavin' your card for mama an' tryin' to warn me. Didn't want to get you in trouble."

I stayed put, elbows on the table, hands clasped.

"I whatin warnin' you. I was there for her."

"For her?"

"Soon as I got word of it down at the station, I wanted to get over there an' make sure she was alright."

His hands dropped. His head fell forward a hair.

"You thought I'd hurt mama?"

I pushed my chair out, stood and laid a twenty on the table from my wallet.

"For all I knew, it was finally all hittin' the fan an' whatever it was you did to 'em, whatever the hell it was you did way on back out at Ducet that night, you'd go on an' do it to the last woman left in your life."

His eyes searched mine all wild and crazed. Shoulders slumped gradual like the muscles holding them up were deflating slowly as a Macy's Thanksgivng Day balloon snagged on the corner of a high rise.

"I'll lay it out for you, Bobby. I cain't do a thing about not speakin' up senior year. Way I see it, your family's still got enough money to make anything I'd dredge up go away anyhow. Probly put me in the poorhouse an' the jailhouse doin' it. Hell, the Captain still goes on about how much the Olsens donate to the department. I'll tell you this, though, whatever you've got goin' on with Rae, whatever it is y'all have gone an' done, that kid I couldn't keep from followin' you's got a scent, an' he's hell bent on trackin' it, makin' sure this case won't be g'ttin' closed til he does."

"But I—"

"He's onto you. Plain an' simple. Best thing for you now is to turn Rae loose, distance yourself. I'm sure you've got plenty a other fillies at your gym who're chompin' at the bit to be arm candy. Heck, I'm bettin' you'll even find one dumb enough to believe your depressed wife killed your kids an' then herself story. She may even go on an' marry you just to make it all better."

I delivered that truth with an I-don't-give-a-shit swagger that I've rarely had access to since, a sudden lack of any fear of consequences. Right then and there, I saw that fear hadn't ever done me any favors. I'd been doing plenty for it and I was done. I wasn't doing anymore. Wasn't hard really. Once the first bullet was shot, the rest flowed easy, rapid like machine gun fire.

He wiped his mouth a last time, stood up, took out his wallet and plunked a couple twenties. Snatching mine up, he reached out, stuffed it in my front dress shirt pocket.

"I invited you."

His chest was puffed up, his pecs bulging under his t-shirt, nearly brushing against my arm. I could see he was still using the same tactics—use of his muscle to coerce and intimidate. I nearly laughed out loud.

"Mitch, I don't mind tellin' you that while I appreciate the heads up, Rae an' me, well, we're g'ttin' married. Soon as all this dies down, an' it will die down, she'll move up this way."

I took one step back, only one, but leaned in, placing a hand on his shoulder. I squeezed it like our coach used to if he had a point he wanted to drive home or if he had a mind to take us up to the office after one of our pranks in the locker room. All the time that'd passed between Bobby and me had given me time to pick up a few of my own tricks at getting the upper hand.

"You're not hearin' me. My partner knows it was you who was callin' the hospital askin' after Rae. Knows it's your prints all over her car. He's got a hard on for both a you. An' nobody, not even me, can put a damper on it."

"You know how many kids die in hot cars every damn year?"

"Don't matter. You're not thinkin' this through. He's probably sittin' back at the station right now runnin' your plates. Once he does, an' he has your name in hand, there'll be at least one person stuck workin' the desk who don't like me all that much that'll talk a blue streak about how me an' you used to be joined at the hip."

Lisa came up behind him, slipped a hand up on his other shoulder. Girl couldn't read a room for anything.

"Y'all headin' out already?"

Bobby wormed out from under my grip, took her hand down from his shoulder and kissed the top of it. She blushed like a freshman getting invited to senior prom.

"We're gone. Thanks Lis. See you in a few."

Dodging around me, he walked to the door, putting up one hand as he went, signaling for me to follow. I took the twenty from my pocket and laid it back on the table.

"We don't need any change, hon."

"Hey, thanks!" Lisa squealed like the giddy schoolgirl she was then set to cleaning the table off.

Standing at the door, ready to hold it open for me, Bobby shook his head, and scowled. He wasn't used to playing second fiddle. Before I joined him, I leaned in closer to Lisa.

"Can I ask you to do me a favor?" I said gentle as I could.

She looked up from wiping the table, her arm still circling with the rag as she did.

"Hmmm?"

"I want you to stay away from that fella there," I said, nodding back Bobby's way.

She laughed, assuming I had to be pulling her leg. I put a hand down on her hand and it froze.

"I'm not kiddin'. You want to keep makin' it home to the ones you love, you steer clear. I know he don't look it, but he's the worst kinna trouble."

She slid her hand out from under mine, patted my arm.

"Aww, not Bobby," she giggled. "He don't look like any kinna trouble my mama ever warned me about."

I walked a few steps backwards in his direction.

"Trust me, that's just cause your mama hadn't ever happened to meet bad as bad as that one," I said, then turned to go.

"You be good now, Lis," Bobby called, steady smiling, holding the door for me.

Lisa waved to him, but her lips kept a frightened flat line. Brushing right past Bobby, I made for my car.

"Mitch, come on. Don't go rushin' off. We hadn't gotten close to squarin' this mess away."

I turned loose of my driver's side handle, whipped around and stomped back over, put my face an inch from his.

"Which *mess* would that be? This one or the one out back a Ducet?"

He shook his head and laughed so loud I'm sure Lisa heard him inside. Throwing his arms up, he brought his hands down on my shoulders, one on either side. He gripped them like he would a softball. I hoped he wasn't thinking about how soft and flabby they were. I flexed, holding my gut in while I was at it.

"Come on. Don't be like this, man. Let's keep it on Rae. Let's figure out how to derail your huntin' dog, an' make sure Rae's in his rearview."

"He's not mine. You should know better than anybody, there comes a point that a dog's just too far gone. Itn't a soul who can call him off."

"Hey! Bobby!" a man called out from where he'd popped up in between my car and the one next to it.

Bobby dropped his hands from my shoulders, stuck a fist out to the man as he came closer so they could bump them. I walked back over by my door, propped myself against it, waiting while they had their old home week moment. A couple times the man looked over at me, probably trying to place me. There were no introductions. The man wasn't from Lee County. Bobby saw no reason his past needed to meet his present.

The longer they talked, I figured Bobby might not've been as riled up about Hogue digging around as I thought. His taking time to chat it up with that fella made it clear, he felt he had the situation under control like everything else in his life. I finally took the hint, got in my car and started it up. Whatever was coming he deserved it every bit as much as I did, probably more.

Soon as he heard my engine start, he fist bumped the man one more time then hustled over to my passenger side, and got in. I cursed myself for not being a quicker draw on locking the door and backing out before he even got a leg inside.

His back slumped into my seat like he'd never left it. We both looked straight ahead through the windshield and restaurant windows at the man he'd talked to as Lisa led he and a woman to a table.

"Would you believe I got no idea where I know him from? Shit, he just kept talkin' an' I hoped he wouldn't notice," he told me like I was someone who was interested.

Part of me wanted to shoot back that that was the least of what he didn't have any idea about, but at that point, I was too tired.

"Hey, you 'member that game we played over in Vass? The one against the Cougars. They had that big ol' boy, that Clay—Clay—"

"Dumas. Clay Dumas," I filled in his blank.

"Yeah! Lord, that boy was a damn hoss!" he kept on. "You were the only one of us who whatin scared a bit. Rest a us nearly shittin' our pants, but not you. You ran those plays without battin' an eye. Plowed right through that boy!"

The man and his wife got comfortable at their table. We didn't exist to them. It was only the two of them getting ready to eat dinner. Their world going on in there. Our world stalled in that car out there.

"Man, I always envied you that. No fuckin' fear," Bobby confessed.

Out of the corner of my eye, I watched him. *Surely he knows* was all I could think. I felt he must know I'd had fear—I'd been scared of him. Hell, I had been for most of our lives. More than just scared. I was terrified of the person I was when we were together. Not a minute could I recall that he didn't feel like quicksand I was sinking in.

"That your wife who answered the phone?" he fished.

I didn't answer.

"Pretty voice. Damn, sounds just like her sister," he kept on. "She look like her too?"

Still, I bit my tongue. My heart pounded like a train stuck in one spot on the track, engine chugging, going nowhere.

"Yeah, when I heard you married a Diamond, I couldn't believe it. Guess I didn't know you were that taken with Kelly. We never did usually bring any a those girls out in the daylight back then. Too worried about what people'd say. I get it, though. Once Rae came along, finally said fuck it myself. Somethin' about what's between their legs'll makes you go colorblind, won't it?"

My right arm shot out. My hand finding his throat—an arrow to a bullseye. He sat still, us just glaring at each other. I squeezed a bit then I let my arm drop. It wasn't in me. Not like that.

He put a hand up, rubbed his neck, cleared his throat.

"You're gonna do what you got to do, Mitch. I know you, an' I know however it's got to get done, well, it'll get done," he said. "We both know a dog that won't train, won't get rerouted, well, that dog's not doin' anybody a lick a good."

His hand came down heavy on my leg, a gavel delivering a judge's paid off verdict as he patted my knee, then just like that, he opened the door and got out. I saw nothing but red as I rolled my window down.

"Maybe I'm ready? Maybe I'm ready to go on an' see what he'll dig up. Maybe it's time to get it all out in the open!" I blasted.

His jaw was set. He was grinding his back molars as he stalked back over, dropping down on one knee so he could look up and into my window. Many a time our coach had taken the same posture while we'd been benched, downing Gatorade, trying to rally for the second half.

"Now, I think you know that wouldn't be good for either of us," he said stern but gentle enough to play on my sympathys. "I think your sweet soundin' wife would tell you the same."

I just glared back.

"Cain't really say as it'll affect me near as much as it will you. Might lose my badge for not comin' forward 'fore now, but I'll go work security, be a P.I. or somethin'. My wife might hate me. I'll deserve it. Might even have to pay for a divorce, but I'll make due," I told him, my heart pulsating in my chest so hard by then I was sure it could be seen through my shirt.

His eyes narrowed. A genuine confusion overtook him.

"An' what is it exactly you think you should've come forward about, Cobb?"

"That night at Ducet. That night out there with Kelly."

He put a hand on my car door, stood slow and then backed up, folded his arms across his flexed pecs.

"See, now, I'm g'ttin' the feelin' what you think happened out there don't at all match what really went down."

I kept my mouth shut. He was partially right. I didn't remember a thing about how the night ended. I had hours missing that I'd filled in, and he'd never had the chance to set me straight. Hours I'd made stories for. That's the problem with stories—tell them enough, and they become your history.

"Your wife bein' Kelly's sister, agreein' to marry you," he said, head cocked back. "About damn certain she has no idea you an' me were the last to see Kelly, does she?"

He already knew the answer.

"Fuckin' bastard."

"That's a no," he laughed. "Oh, I can see it now. The nice plea deal I'll get once I tell whoever I need to tell that I'll give them the information they've been wantin' about an unsolved case from over on the west side. What with all the riots an' protests, after that Floyd dude got it, well, I think Lee County would love nothin' better than to have a cold case about a missin' Black girl, all wrapped up an' handed to the press. Might make national news. Yeah, I'm thinkin' it might just be the perfect time. You know, I think you're right. Let your boy hunt. Let's go on an' let this play out."

I rolled my window up. He gave me a wink, nodded. I put the car in reverse, didn't even look in my mirrors, then sped off down the road.

The whole way back to Sanford, my head was a pinball machine flitting that metal ball around. The stories I'd repeated in my mind for years about Kelly, about what went on out there, all blurry. The middle and the ending all fading on that drive home. I knew Bobby was right. I knew I would have to do what had to be done. I found myself wishing how it would have to happen was as foggy as the past, but it wasn't. What had to be done next was somehow always so crystal clear to me.

85°F

His hands were cracked and dry. She was glad she'd remembered the lotion. Things were finally falling into place enough at work so that she could take a couple days off.

"That feels nice, don't it?" Jolie murmured as she rubbed the cocoa butter into his chapped skin.

The doctor hadn't been able to say for sure if Leigh could hear them, but he'd told her and his family there was no evidence he couldn't. That had been good enough for her to keep talking to him every time she visited. Not that what the doctor had or had not confirmed would have had much bearing. Jolie had always been one to talk to herself if she was alone. Her dad once told her he'd heard it said that talking to yourself was a mark of intelligence. She wondered what it was if you started answering yourself.

She'd expected to walk in and see Leigh's mother sitting bedside. That had been the plan until she was able to get there. His mother had promised. The room was empty save the orderly who darted out just as she walked in. Promises meant nothing in their world. That was a certainty. The empty room was a reminder of that.

Leigh had told her this was the way it was with his family. Before they were even a thing, way before he landed in the Moore

Regional, he'd tell her all about them as he flipped meat on the Waffle House grill.

"I can count on me. That's all I need," he'd tried convincing her.

In that second, she knew she wanted him to count on her too. A few light green and sealed blue envelopes lay on his nightstand. Someone had brought cards yet failed to open them. Maybe he was wrong? Maybe he could count on someone other than himself and her? Maybe his mama'd just left a few minutes before?

The room was lit mainly by the parking lot light not far from their window. It shone so brightly through the blinds they rarely turned on the overheads. She liked it that way as it made no sense having more light in such a dark place.

"You like that?" She rubbed in the last of the lotion she'd brought. "Yeah, that's real nice. You'll feel so much better."

A soft knock on the door sliced into their intimate moment. She looked up to see Leigh's brother, Demete, duck inside. He had that look of dodging someone and indeed he was. The head nurse wasn't taken at all with him after he'd decided to blare Leigh's playlist of rap and metal on his last visit. Metallica and B.O.B. were not appreciated in the I.C.U. He was usually good with the ladies but not that nurse. When he tried to turn things around by roping her into dancing with him, she reared back, informing him she'd seen his type before.

"Hey," Demete said.

"Hey."

Demete turned his hat backwards, so the brim wasn't shielding his eyes. Hangdog eyes. That's what Leigh called them. Eyes that told you he'd done something you were going to have to forgive him for, and if he hadn't yet, he would soon.

"Smells like a damn beach in here, girl."

She held up the bottle of cocoa butter. He smiled.

"Now if that smell don't get him stirrin', I don't know what will. Moms used to lather us up with that every day 'fore we went to school. Woman might forget our lunch money, but she didn't want no ashy boys leavin' her house."

Jolie patted Leigh's hand. She watched him keenly, wondering if his brother's voice might cause a reaction. His brother's presence wasn't necessarily a calming one. The way Leigh had described their relationship, it was one of keeping Demete close to keep an eye on him more than because they enjoyed each other. By the time Demete got out, Leigh'd been hospitalized so he hadn't seen Leigh since the last time he'd visited him at Central months ago.

"Least if he's in there, I know he's safe," Leigh said to her once about his brother's stint in prison.

"Yeah, boy, me an' Leigh were the slickest, shiniest dudes at West End Elementary. Probly coulda slid right under our back fence without a scratch on us."

A woman's voice interrupted them from out in the hallway. Demete jerkily turned to see who it was, on the lookout for his *hater*.

"Chill. She itn't workin' tonight," Jolie teased.

His shoulders instantly relaxed. He slouched in the chair like a teen on his buddy's basement couch.

"That's one stone cold bitch. I'm tellin' you."

"Awe, I think she's just not a Metallica at work kind a girl."

He vehemently shook his head.

"Naw. You cain't be that shit. Everybody loves 'em."

Leigh's index finger twitched against her palm. The first time this happened she'd jumped up, yelled to the nearest nurse to come, and immediately called Leigh's mom. She wished she could go back to that time weeks ago. That time when there was hope. Before the doctor informed them that this was only nerves. It happened to everyone in Leigh's condition. That was the last time she'd felt the least bit excited about anything until she had her visitor at work, until she'd run that slip of paper he'd given her between her fingers.

She was unsure what exactly her excitement over now knowing Cy's whereabouts said about her. If you go without feeling anything long enough, you won't care what causes it the next time it happens. You'll just be so glad you're able to feel again. That, she decided, was what she was—excited to still be able to feel something. Anything but sadness.

The noises from the breathing machines created a background mix to Demete's rambling. He was a talker. She looked over at him now and then. Mostly kept her eyes on Leigh. Once she'd rested his hand next to him again, it struck her that he looked like her Uncle James had in his casket. This panicked her. She immediately picked his hand back up taking it in hers, placing it across Leigh's stomach as if he'd just eaten and was relaxing, not readying to die, laid out at the mortuary.

Demete regaled her about how he and Leigh used to breakdance on cardboard in their backyard. She got up and moved to the other side of Leigh's body to rub lotion into his right arm and hand. This was her favorite part of the visits, the caring for him. She'd done the same for him when they'd laid in bed together on those long Sunday mornings they'd take off together. There'd been exactly twelve of those Sundays.

Twelve before that night that Cy wrecked the life she'd dared to make without him. Her mother had always called her a smart cookie. Apparently, not been smart enough. Somehow brains had never translated to better decisions, and this she'd come to think, was the real mark of a child who came from poverty like theirs— this inability to make decisions with the head versus the codependent heart.

Demete resituated himself in his chair causing his sneaker to squeak against the linoleum floor. He cleared his throat.

"You usually workin' aren't you?"

"Been missin' him so I took a couple days."

"We all miss him," Demete seconded.

As he'd said it, she couldn't help but notice, he was looking past her, out the window. She tried to think if she'd seen him look at Leigh even once. It was strange to her, what with where he'd come from. Surely there'd been worse to see in jail? Maybe it was worse seeing it done to someone you cared about.

Demete's skin was so dark, much darker than Leigh. They didn't have the same Daddy, he'd told her. The same mom was all that mattered to bind you, he felt. She had no siblings to speak of so she took his word for it, though the longer she knew Leigh, she felt he may have just been the only person she'd ever come close to truly being bound to.

"Your mama said you got a job parkin' cars over at the hotel," she tried her hand at salvaging any conversation.

"Been a while since I clocked in anywhere, but my P.O. knows a guy over there," he said. "I told moms I'd be sure an' get by here, 'fore she has to—"

He stopped abruptly, looked at the machines churning, whirring, keeping his half brother alive.

"Told her I'd come 'fore I start work tomorrow," he pivoted. "Won't be able to get by as much after that."

Studying Demete's reflection in the window as she rubbed Leigh's hand, her eyes were drawn to her own next to it. Bags had settled under her eyes. Dark roots had broken through at the base of her scalp corrupting her blond die job. She hadn't had the time or money to go to the salon. Her eyebrows were in bad need of tweezers. She'd never looked worse and yet it was fitting. Her life had never been worse. Her beauty burning away like chaff from a life where it served no purpose.

"When's she gonna have to do it?" Jolie questioned with no emotion, as if calling out orders to the fill in fry cook back at work.

He didn't answer right away. They stared at each other's reflections, car lights from cars whizzing by outside blurred them. Life in the room arrested in a cocoa buttered stasis of impending gloom. Life outside the window not missing a beat.

"Doc told her by next week he's got to know one way or the other. Got to see if baby bro can breathe on his own," he finally replied, leaning forward, his elbows resting on his knees, hands clasped in front of him like he was readying to pray. Jolie scowled. She didn't want to know a God that listened to men like him. He certainly hadn't listened to her yet.

"Why wait?" she snapped. "Hmm? Why not go on an' get it over with? Let's just do it tonight. Call her up!"

Demete unclasped his hands, reaching one up and touching her shoulder. She shrugged it away, grabbing one of the many chords hooked up to Leigh.

"I mean why not? If she's gonna kill him, ain't no use in waitin'."

The able bodied of the two brothers stood, methodically and softly taking the chord from her hand, placing it back where it came from. He patted Leigh's arm. It was the first time she'd seem him touch his brother. She went to pieces, gripping the side bed railing, leaning over, sobs erupting from a deep, sorrowful place she thought her own family had nailed the doors shut on years ago.

"Jo," Demete whispered. "Come on, now."

His hand found her shoulder again. She let it stay. In a week, they'd never have to see each other. There was some comfort in that. Their only connection in the world laying between them. This had always struck her strange, these rickety bridges haphazardly erected when strangers have a mutual aquaintance.

"Moms says we'll pick a time. We'll all come in an' be here together, okay?" he assured her. "Day's comin' in all the way from Oakland, an' Aunt Pat'll drive from up from Atlanta. Everybody who can's tryin' to get here."

She released the railing, running her hand along the chord again instead, ensuring as best she could that it was back to its job. The shame she felt for having grabbed it as palpable as if it had taken the empty seat in the corner and was shaking its head at her.

"He could still wake up, Demete. He could. I was readin' about this guy in Oklahoma who fell fixin' powerlines. He was in a coma for five years an' then one day—"

Demete shook his head.

"Doc says that's a one in a million shot, Jo. One in a fuckin million, an' I'm sure Leigh's done told you, our family ain't never had much in the way a luck."

The siren from an ambulance pulling up to the main doors, blared. More lives being interrupted. There were times, on her visits

166

when she heard this sound that she wanted to run down to the emergency room and yell at them to turn around, go home. She wanted to tell them that getting in there didn't promise anything. It just hid the sick away from the well having to see them. That's all it did.

Walking over to the window, Demete looked down at the paramedics in their urgency, sliding a person out on a stretcher. It took him back to the prison cafeteria where he'd been shown how to slide the trays of bread out of the confection ovens. The person lay on the stretcher as lifeless as the warm rolls he's turned over with a hot pad to protect his hands. It struck him how people turn into things when they're down for the count. Rolls... just like those rolls.

He wished like anything Leigh could have seen him when he'd gotten out. Not that he could have seen Leigh. He was not that unselfish. He wished they could have cut up down at the Juke and done shots off Rooney Sil's flat stomach. *Was Rooney Sil's still around?* His mind wandered. He knew he'd have to Google her.

Jolie's heavy sigh filling the room. He was reminded they weren't done.

"Look at it this way. If he don't breathe on his own, your ol' man's g'ttin' sent up for manslaughter. That ain't nothin'. Some kind of motherfuckin' vindication, an' that's hard to come by."

Her *ol' man.* Yes—*her man.* He'd never been so much a man to her as a warden. It was odd to her given that Demete was Black and the state of things being as they were that he had such faith a white cop would suffer any punitive action. She, herself, did not have anything resembling trust in a system that had employed a man like Cy in the first place.

She made her way around the bed to her purse in the corner. It felt heavier than usual. Sifting through it, she felt in the side pockets for it, hoping she hadn't lost it. Silently cursing at herself for not having taken a picture of it with her phone. Finally, there was the feel of the paper against her fingers. She took it out, holding it up to Demete.

"What's this?" He wanted to know, his eyes appealing to her with a warm sincerity so similar to Leigh's.

Crumpling it back into her own palm, tears overtook her again. She folded into Demete's chest, a baby bird in need of sheltering. He leaned his head down, his chin on her hair on top of her head. Her voice so faint he nearly couldn't make out her response. When she was quiet again, they hugged. She then squeezed his hand and swiftly walked out and down the hall.

All the way to her car, she was tormented by the realization that she hadn't even told Leigh good-bye. She would go back the next day. She wouldn't go the week after, however. The idea of standing by while his air was taken from him, and watching whatever the results would be, was not something she could bear. Someone would call to let her know.

Her car seemed to drive itself, her mind preoccupied as it was. She was back in bed. On that last Sunday with Leigh. The two of them so full of hope and making plans. Oh, how many plans they'd had.

Pulling into her driveway, the headlights lit up the spot where Leigh had last breathed independently. She'd cradled his head in her lap til they came. He'd looked up into her eyes until he couldn't keep his own open any longer. Each night she saw that sidewalk, she felt like a cannonball shot out onto the battlefield of their love, landing hard followed by an explosion of emotions, the aftershock felt for hours.

A small bit of comfort found her as her mind turned to Demete, the paper she'd thought of handing him. How just this one time in her life, she wished she was a man like him. Oh, she wished she was a big armed man to do what she knew needed to come next. What had to come if her Leigh had in fact already breathed the last breaths he'd ever breathe unassisted.

86°F

Hogue

That cigarette she's smoking's got to be mighty enjoyable. My guess is the first time you have a smoke outside the nuthouse, it's as good as the very first one you have when you get out of the joint. Not that I'd know. I've managed to stay out of both except for taking people there in handcuffs or visiting them to get statements.

Jolie says that's just luck. Not long after she left, back when we'd still talk on the phone every now and again, she told me the only difference between me and the perps I lock up is that I haven't been caught yet. Said I'm a damn genius becoming a cop. That I'm like a dog wearing a dogcatcher's uniform.

"Don't matter what you put on though, Cy," she said. "You're still a dog."

That was one of the last times we saw each other without lawyers, til my little hospital stop in the other night. Should've left well enough alone, steered clear. Somehow, I never do.

Cain't help but think Jolie wouldn't be a bit surprised at where I find myself tonight, standing outside Rae's. Watching through the trees like a hungry dog would. Don't know what I hope to see. Maybe I'll catch sight of Mr. Dodge Charger since it's a night her mama's gone on to church and left her all on her lonesome. Yeah, he'll be chompin at the bit to see her. What with all those calls the nurse talked about. He's been missing her something fierce.

Maybe I don't care as much about him as I'm just mad as hell she's out and about like nothing happened. Keeping an eye on her feels like I'm doing something about it. They couldn't have brought my shrink in for her eval. No way she'd be writing any baby killer a pass if she hadn't written one for me. Yeah, I bet they got some real winners over there giving out those evals. So full up they need the beds. Unless Rae just roamed the streets with that baby bleeding out in her arms, with a knife stuck in his gut, they don't got room to keep her, and we don't have enough to charge her.

"You're gonna have to let this one go, Cy," Cobb kept saying just yesterday. "There's nothin' concrete. Not a thing to prove it whatin a simple case a absent mindedness."

"Evidence? Shit, we got that. What about that palm print that matches hers? Hmmm? Did you look at the pictures Dooly sent from forensics over there at county? He's got that good equipment. Now, why would somebody leave a palm print like that on the door a the car, pressed so hard you can nearly see every line? They were holdin' it shut hard as they could. That's why. An' the scuff marks. Did you see those? Scuff marks against the back a the front seat. That kid was kickin' for all he was worth."

Cobb wasn't having it. Went on and on about how any kid locked in a hot car, would be kicking. Don't mean anybody held that door, and how that palm print could've been from another day. That's Cobb for you. He could explain away anything. Most religious nuts can. Have to in order to believe some man upstairs is playing puppet master with us all.

Through Rae's back window, that she's got open wide, I see she's nearly down to the last bit of her smoke. With that flowered dress she's wearing, seems like she might've thought about heading to church with her mama then changed her mind. She's dropping ashes in the sink every second or two after taking a puff. Nervous as she is, no way she itn't guilty of something. I'm certain of that. Nothing but intentional. Maybe it takes one dog to know another.

She walks out of sight. The back door opens. I stand still.

"Makin' mac an' cheese," she calls.

I step out from behind the tree that's been a poor excuse for my cover.

"Long as you don't make it with too much milk. Cain't stand it all soggy."

She shakes her head, laughs a little to herself as she drops her cigarette on the deck and stomps it out.

"I make it thick. The thicker the better."

A fire truck sounds a few streets over. I look behind me. No flames visible.

"Come on then," she prods motioning to me to come up the steps.

She holds the screen door open, plants herself half-inside, half-outside. The light from the kitchen's cutting her face in two. Cobb damn well wouldn't be doing this. Not in a million years. As I scoot inside, her breasts graze my chest. Way she's standing her ground, I'm thinking she planned it that way. She's barking up the wrong tree.

To say she itn't my type don't touch it. Her scalp's showing in places. She's in need of her hair extensions being resewn. Lipstick's the only thing she has on her face that lets me know she didn't just roll out of bed. Her body's tight, I'll give her that, but this ol' boy never has been one to mix no matter how tight a body is. I ain't Jolie. Yeah, this game Rae's got going might work real good on backwoods Sanford hicks who like to watch all that *sista* porn in the privacy of their trailer bathrooms, but not on me.

Leaning against the pine paneled wall inside, I notice one of those old rotary phones hanging next to me. No telling how many people've gotten killed by whoever it was who'd broken in cause it took them for fucking ever just to dial 911. Rae dips around me, over to the counter. Her perfume mixes with the leftover smoke smell making my nose itch.

There's a pot in the sink. She turns on the faucet, fills it with water then totes it over to the stove and turns on the burner. Her biceps are taut. Clearly, she works out. Bet she was doing push ups in her padded room all week, probably trying not to lose what's left of her her tight ass or her marbles.

A highchair's still setting up to the kitchen table right up to the end of it like Brandon was the head of the house.

"Nice of you to come over an' make sure I'm gettin' settled back home," Rae purrs with just enough sass thrown in to let me know there's no mystery about what I'm up to.

"Guess I'm just ate up with curiosity's all."

"Curiosity?"

"Yeah, I'm curious as all get out how it is your crazy ass itn't still in there laid out in a padded room g'ttin' ready for your nightly Oreos an' meds."

The burner under the pot turns bright red.

"Guess they cain't be keepin' everybody. They'll run outta room."

She wipes her hands on a towel from the counter then turns around, faces me head on.

"Believe it or not, they've got bigger fish to dope up than me," she delivers with this sick little smile. First thing she's done that might spark any kind of fire for me.

Walking over, she stands smack dab in front of me, reaches a hand up, straightening my collar like we're playing house, and I'm readying to leave for work. I don't move a muscle. Don't even fucking blink. She leans in assuming I'm hard up, and she's just the action I've been jonesing for.

"You don't give yourself any credit. A baby killer, well, that's the biggest fish of all," I say real soft, then wink. "Hardest to keep on the line an' damn sure hardest to wrestle into the boat."

She cut her eyes at me. If she had a knife within spitting distance, my throat would be cut. The water's boiling, rocking the pot on the burner. She whips around, rushes over, turns down the heat, opens a box of noodles and pours them in.

I walk over, pull a chair up to the table. I balance the chair back on two of its legs. The creaks that start make me hopeful its stronger than it looks. From here, I watch her stir the noodles nice and slow.

"I like extra cheese in mine. Wanna hand me the cheddar from the fridge?" she asks.

I don't budge. She lays her spoon down, takes two steps to her right, opens the fridge and gets it out for her damn self. It's one of those huge Costco bags of cheese. You'd think her boy was still around to help eat it.

That big bag gives it away more than the tarnished linoleum floor does that they haven't ever had much to speak of. Jolie loves hoarding up big bags of cheese, cans of chili and bags of rice, face washes and body sprays. Part of growing up without two dimes to rub together that never stayed with me—the accumulatin of shit for fear you'll go without. Not me. I like my freedom. I just go on down to the Food King whenever I want. Don't keep more than a week's worth of anything around.

"I like knowin' it's there if I want it," Jolie'd say. "I work my ass off. No reason to be left wantin'."

But sometimes we still were. Specially when I was finishing up the academy. Went without a house of our own, nice cars, clothes from anywhere but Walmart, and a whole hell of a lot of other things. Finally, I guess we went without love. We were just going through motions. There wasn't anything she'd stocked up on could help with that.

"Mama'll eat hers cold when she gets home," Rae tells me as she knocks noodles off the spoon back into the water. "Spaghetti, pizza, her tuna casserole—she likes it all better cold. Got Brandon eatin' it that a way too. I'd have to wake up early, make it then put it in the fridge, so they'd eat it once it's chilled."

She laughs remembering this as she reaches up, uses her free hand to move her hair out of her eyes. The water boils, a few drops popping out and burning her other hand. She puts it up to her mouth, kissing the heat away. Looking over at that highchair, I can just picture her leaning over, those same lips kissing her boy goodnight on his cheek not three weeks ago.

It strikes me it's been I don't know how long since I've even been in a kitchen while a woman was cooking. Least six months. Had to have been that night when I'd just gotten shipped over this way. I went over to a hole in the wall brewery in Vass. Woke up in a house I didn't recognize without a stitch on. Looked down at the pile of my clothes on the floor, slipped them on, shoes too and crept down the hall to the kitchen. It was an old house with the floor lopsided in parts like the foundation was ate up with termites.

A girl stood by a stove. Barely remembered us talking the night before out back by the fire pit where a band was playing. There she was that morning, making me eggs with nothing but a wife beater on and some pink panties. Didn't take a genius to know the score.

Already had plates laid out on the table, glasses with orange juice in them too. Kind of made me sick her making that food, scuzzy as the place seemed and her with no more on than that. I didn't say anything about it. Just sat down and figured I'd get it over with.

That one was a talker, boy! Whole time we ate she went on and on about some other girl who'd been at the bar who'd pissed her off. The more I looked at her in the light of day, I knew I had to get the hell on. Couldn't have been more than sixteen if she was a day. Kept wondering if her daddy or her old man was gonna drive up any second. The smudges of dirt on her wife beater along with the dirt under her nails were enough to make me cough up what eggs I'd swallowed.

On my way home that morning was the first time the thought set in that Jolie might've cursed me. I got to thinking I might never have anything normal again. Like it all went out the door with her. That from here on out, I'm doomed to a life of filthy bitches who part their legs for anybody willing and eating their eggs in even filthier shacks.

Rae dumps the noodles into a strainer. I cain't help but wish I was back in that pink pantied girl's kitchen. Might've been scum but least she hadn't let a baby suffocate. Rae pulls a big mixing bowl out from a cabinet that looks more like a punch bowl than a bowl for hot food. The noodles fill it easy. She pours the milk, adds butter, cheese powder and some of that bag cheese, stirring it through. Enough there for an army. I sure hope she and her mama like it, cause I have no intentions of eating. I hate that cheap shit.

Her head tilts back. She closes her eyes and inhales.

"Smells good," she says as she spoons some up for the both of us.

Her hips swish back and forth like she's strutting on a dance floor as she brings the food over and sets it down. It don't smell good at all. Smells chemical and fake, not like anything anybody should fuel their bodies with.

She sits the bowl in front of me. I scoot back from it. The steam from hers rising up to her face giving it this sheen. If she was white, she'd look real pretty right now. If she was, this might be where I'd make a move. I clear my throat. Might have to anyway. That's how it always is with me—my bodily urges betraying me.

A couple bites in, she puts her spoon down and scoots her chair closer. Her elbows are on the table, hands clasped over her bowl. She rests her chin on them, batting her eyes at me. The sound of the window unit doing its best to keep up is our background music. Thing's so old and loud. If she screams, nobody'll hear.

"Can I be expectin' you regular? If I can, I've got to warn you, mama's not much on people showin' up unannounced."

She throws a wink in there, unclasping her hands and wagging a brown finger at me. She thinks she's funny. Yeah, her whole god damn life men've been nothing but one big joke to her. She's got the wrong one now.

"I wouldn't go so far as to say *regular*. Soon as I get what I need, won't be any reason for me to keep comin' around," I reply real smooth.

She cocks her head to the side, pushes her chair away from the table, opening her legs a bit, running a hand along the outside of one of her thighs.

Cain't even help myself. I laugh right out loud.

175

"Shit! That's got nothin' to do with what I need, gal."

Those legs snap shut like a bear trap set off by a fallen branch. She scoots back up to her bowl, her face turning a redder shade of brown.

"Well, then I'd say there's nothin' for you here."

I reach around behind my back, taking out the photo stashed in my jean's pocket. I unfold it, lay it out flat right next to her bowl of mac and cheese.

She looks down at it.

"What am I lookin' at?"

I grab her by both wrists. She jumps, tugging at her hands, trying to jerk away, and then clenches her fists up tight. It don't take long before she gives up and sits still. *That's a good girl.* I force her fists open, release one hand, lay the other palm up on the table beside the picture.

"This right here, is a picture a your palm print, see? Your palm print that was pressed hard on your back passenger door. The door you nearly like to put your hand clear through cause you were hell bent on keepin' it shut. Did he scream? Yeah, I'm sure he did. Probly screamed his head off for you, an' there you were, just pressin' an' pressin'."

Soon as I loosen my grip, she yanks her hand away. She stands feet apart, arms out to her sides like she's thinking about knocking me off this chair, trying her hand at choking me or whatever else she can pull off. I lean forward, give her a grin. Bring it, bitch.

She grabs her bowl and mine, stalks over to the trash and pours what's left of our mac and cheese in it, before taking it over to the sink. She turns on the water and starts rinsing out dishes like it's any other day. I guess it is for a baby murdering cunt like her.

"Hit a nerve?" I sneer as she puts Saran Wrap on the punch bowl of leftovers, beginning her clean up.

"You ain't hit nothin'."

Her shoulders are all relaxed. She's already back to being cool, calm and collected.

"Way I see it, you got a lot a time on your hands, what with you bein' so far from home, not knowin' anybody or anything. Got a lot a extra time to sit an' look at pictures an' start comin' up with things," she tells me. "Must be a real nice way to keep your mind off your own shit."

"What shit would that be?"

She turns resting her hips against the counter. Those hips that've opened for too many men to count to enter and for only one little man to exit. Just looking at those hips kicks up a rage I can't put words to. They also spark a heat I hope to never put action to and this, just being around her, reminds me no matter what, I am what I am—a dog in a dog catcher's suit. An animal ruled by primal instincts.

Hands on her hips, standing up tall, with her chest out, she's trying her best at getting the upper hand.

"That whole shitstorm over in Johnston. All that business that got your ass sent over here," she says. "Ain't sure what gave 'em the idea that Lee County ain't got enough of its own problems without you addin' to 'em. Hell, seems like everybody wants to put their horses out to pasture over our way minute they come up lame."

Her lips curve into a half smile that goes straight to my gut. Before I know what's happening, I'm out of my chair and right up in her face. So close I feel the air coming out of her nostrils. Her eyes get wild, but not scared. She's either too stupid to be scared, or she's so used to being the one causing fear she hasn't been on the receiving end enough to know how to act.

In the inches between us, a regret sets in that Cobb came after her that day in her back yard. Would've been better if she'd gone on and bled out after slicing open both of her wrists with that meat fork. Hell, is that thing still out there? I'd gladly hand it to her right now. *If at first you don't succeed, try the fuck again.*

"You don't know a god damn thing," I growl.

She gets gutsy and moves her hands up to my chest, trying to put a little more breathing room between us. I let it happen, but I don't move an inch.

"I know as things go right now, you're lookin' at an assault

177

charge. I know if that man don't come out a his coma, cain't breathe on his own when he gets unplugged, you're lookin' at manslaughter."

I stare at her and wonder how long til her mama walks through that door. Is it long enough to shut this bitch up, I mean really shut her up? Pieces of her hair slip down covering one of her eyes again. She reaches up, pushing it back, blowing at it with her big lips.

"Manslaughter…" she repeats. "Puts us on the same playin' field don't it?"

A moth flaps against the outside of the window behind her head. Beating its wings something fierce, dying to get in at the light. Doesn't even register that the glass is in its way. It keeps on and keeps on. I step back, lean over and pick up the palm print photo, returning it to its rightful home in my pocket.

"Well, look at you. Went an' got your shovel out an' dug up some dirt on me. *Bra-fuckin'-vo*," I say, clapping a couple times, a smile setting in on my lips. "That's all it is though—dirt. Itn't a soul in the state with a third-grade education who cain't read the same if they have a computer or a phone to Google it."

She's the one laughing now.

"Oh yeah? Dirt huh? Well, I tend to think you dig long enough, you're liable to find a body."

I chuckle.

"Keep diggin'," I goad her. "Go on ahead, but if I were you, I'd put your shovel down an' get real concerned about what it is I been busy unearthin'. Maybe I'm better at excavatin' an' this picture itn't the only thing I've got? Maybe I have what we call an evidence recovery tech who'll testify about all the scuff marks on that upholstery on the back a your passenger's seat an' the back passenger door. So many scuff marks, like Brandon was tryin' for all he was worth to kick that door open, an' there's the loose handle. So loose, like he pulled an' pulled at it."

Her arms drop limp by her sides. Her knees go soft. Her hips resting against the counter and it's all that's holding her up.

"Your Brandon was pretty big for his age whatin he? Yeah, his legs reached the back a that seat. His arms reached the handle. Most kids his age couldn't have, but he was a big strappin' boy." I press. "Poor little thing, just couldn't quite get it done. Sure tried his best."

I hold a hand out, palm facing up, then raise it to eye level like I'm gonna wave to her, but I don't. I just leave it in the air.

"Naw, he wasn't never gonna be able to pull that off, not with you pressin' so hard, workin' against him." I wrap up, motioning with my hand like I'm pressing my own palm on an invisible door.

Her hips give way. She goes all dramatic, sliding down, landing slumped back against the cabinet doors. Her flowered dress covering her legs all buckled under her on the floor. She slides her knees up to her chest, hugging them to her.

"Motherfucker," she hisses. "You think I don't lay in the bed every night thinkin' a him in that car, kickin' an' screamin'. Just kickin' an' screamin'—"

She trails off. Whispers something only she can hear.

I crouch down in front of her, put a hand on one of her knees. She doesn't even flinch. Feeling the heat coming off her body, I know I'm in dangerous territory. I'm standing at that line again, one I've crossed more times than I haven't.

"I'm sure you do. I'm sure some nights you cain't think of nothin' else. There's other nights though, ones when you're with your Mr. Dodge Charger—"

Her eyes meet mine. *Yeah, I know all about him.*

"On those nights, I'm pretty sure y'all are thinkin' of anything but little boys bein' burnt up in cars."

She wipes her eyes with a hand and scoots over so my hand drops off her knee. I let her, but I stay at her eye level.

"Mr. Dodge Charger...got a past all his own don't he? Shit. How do people like you find each other? God knows," I laugh. "Cain't be too smart a fella to get off for doin' in his own wife an' kids an' be slinkin' back around here pokin' around for pussy. Too many dead kids an', hell, even a rich white boy's luck'll run out."

She pulls herself up by the cabinet knobs, storms past me over to the back door, and throws it open. I take my time getting up, tuck my shirt in tighter, adjust my belt buckle before I follow her unsaid orders. I'm halfway out the door, when I stop and look dead in her eyes.

"That day out back a here, you said somethin I cain't shake," I say.

She glares a hole through me.

"You said, 'He said I can bear it, but I cain't. *He* said ...' An' with us bein' down here, smack dab in the middle of the Bible belt an' all, I thought you were talkin' about God. That whole verse about him not givin' us more than we can bear? But once I caught wind of what you an' Mr. Dodge Charger got goin', I'm thinkin' he's your god. He's the one who said you could bear it."

Taking a step back, she tries to slam the door shut. My boot stops it. I put a hand on the doorknob, showing her it'll close on my terms.

"Thing is, I know how hard it is when you find out there itn't any God. That there's only each other an' that the one you've looked at to replace him is full of shit," I say real soft, tucking her in for the night with my own little bedtime story.

She reaches out for the rotary phone next to her on the wall taking it off the cradle. I move my boot, nod to her and leave her with one of my smirks. I hear the porch banister rattle as she slams the door hard. There's the sound of the deadbolt clicking, like that could even stop me. I head down the porch steps and through the woods back to my car.

Well, there he is—Mr. Dodge Charger, parked so close to my front bumper, his car's nearly touching mine. His paint job's darker in the moonlight. Looks like the Batmobile. I'm a little jealous. A clean-cut meat head wannabe of a fella gets out and shuts his door. He doesn't look my way yet. Just walks over like he owns the fucking world and sits on my hood. Nah, he's no Batman. He's got to be the dumbest Joker to ever live.

As I approach, he dangles his legs off the hood like a wily kid who knows damn well he's not supposed to touch dad's car, but don't give a flying fuck. He grins wide at me like we know each other, and I reckon we do. So, this is how we're gonna meet—on his terms. Me and the god who tries to talk Rae into bearing whatever he doles out.

43°F

Cobb

Before Hogue and me caught Rae's case that summer, I did my best to let Hogue hang back when we went out on calls. Even though he wasn't but from two counties over, it was no different than if he was from somewhere out in the sticks, a village way out in the Amazon. That's just how different the south is, county by county, town by town. Rules of one place don't translate over the miles. If you're a badge and you assume they do, you're good as dead.

A few things carry over wherever you go below the Mason-Dixon. Don't knock a man's religion. Itn't any separation between the Almighty and this U.S. of A. You love God then you love this country. Don't go shooting a man's dog, even if it's coming full force at you. Everybody has rights to shoot his own dog. No matter what. And don't get in between a man and his woman if they're already in the thick of it. Try to stop it before it starts, or you just have to let it end then help clean up, but once it's on, well, it's on.

It was a few days after my Waffle House visit with Jolie that we got a refresher about that last one. Lisa and Harold's neighbor called in. I'll go down as saying I tried to let Leland take it, but he was tied up with an errand the captain had set him on. At least, that's what he claimed.

Hogue had been antsy all morning. Something eating at him. By lunch, he was chomping at the bit. Soon as that call came in, he was telling Leland we'd take care of it before I got a say.

"Come on. You scared? They gonna come out with AKs or somethin'?" Hogue jeered. "Any domestic I been on's usually just a lot a bark an' no bite." I wondered if that was what the officer who'd showed up at the last one between him, Jolie and her boyfriend would've said. Seemed all bite and no bark applied in Hogue's case. That was one of the worst and best things about him. He had no forewarning and no middle ground.

A few minutes of his carrying on was all it took to wear me out, so I let him have what he wanted. I got my keys, and he followed me out to our car. Thing is, you can't really stop a man hell bent on action. No point in pretending you can.

Every town has a Lisa and Harold. At least we didn't have more than one. Well, most of the time. Once in blue moon there'd be some couple out at the Star Motel on Highway 1 who'd get all riled and one of us would have to head over. Most of the time, Lisa and Harold cornered the market on our resident wannabe Bonnie and Clyde.

I'd been out to their place more than my fair share. They didn't have an AK or any gun that I'd seen. Still, they were what we called *wild cards*. There'd been one or two of us who'd had to dodge a bottle, or Lisa getting in a methed-up craze and running towards us with a knife. Faulk put in to transfer the year before due to one of their nutty late nighters. A brick had landed right through his windshield before he even got his car turned off.

"What can be so bad?" Hogue wanted to know, the closer we got to their place.

I rested my elbow on the door frame, putting a hand up over my mouth to cover a big old smile.

"I guess you're about to see for yourself."

From the end of the driveway, I spotted Lisa pacing on the

porch, yakking away on her cell. They had all their windows open. I'm sure the heat hadn't done anything by way of cooling off whatever argument had ignited. Open windows made their yelling trickle more easily into their neighbor's houses.

"Pull up real slow," I instructed.

Hogue listened, which he rarely did. I tried not to take that in and of itself as a foreboding sign. He took the driveway inch by inch. Lisa looked up, screamed into the phone, then stuffed it in the back pocket of her jeans nearly causing them to fall off her bony hips. Hogue stopped, put the car in park. I opened my door.

"Hey, Lisa," I called, barely poking my head up outside of the car.

She clenched her fists, jutted out her jaw like a gnarled bulldog guarding a scrap yard. We'd gone to the same elementary school. She had that exact stance back then when she wanted the jungle gym all to herself. Once she positioned herself like that, you knew the slide was off limits to everybody else.

"Now you know good an' well, you ain't gonna do nothin' but poke a hornet's nest, comin' up in here, Mitchum."

"Lisa, now, fact of the matter is, we've had calls," I said, easing out a little further, standing slowly, keeping my door open, propping my left arm up on my side of the roof of the car, trying to look casual. Didn't work.

That little bit of a thing rushed over so fast, I'd have sworn she was a Tasmanian Devil not a 5'2 woman who I'm sure could still wear her high school cheerleading outfit when she got a mind to.

"Oh, you've had calls?" She wagged a bony finger in my face. "Whoever's got time enough on their hands to be callin' you, g'ttin' in our business can go straight to hell, Mitchum Cobb! I got plenty to make noise about! As you know, Harold's a tweaker motherfuckin' son of a bitch, an' he deserves whatever he g'ts!"

With her getting in my face, I turned my head slightly, noticing Hogue's door open. I dropped a hand back down in the car waving him off. The door stayed open, but he stayed put.

"I won't argue with you on that. I won't, Lisa. Just don't want to see you be the one g'ttin' dragged in for dishin' out whatever it is he's got comin'. Hardly seems fair." I took a step away from the car, shutting my door in a show of good faith.

Her jaw relaxed a little. I saw I might just be getting through to her better nature. On that day, I was foolishly still under the delusion everyone had one. It was hanging on by a thread, mind you, but the belief was still there. I put a hand gently on her shoulder.

"Why don't you wait out here, let me go in an' talk to him?"

I might have gotten somewhere had the good Lord been on our side. He must have been in another part of town right then cause Harold came busting out of the screen door nearly taking it off its hinges. It was like he'd been sitting inside and some meth head sixth sense he came by told him things were calming. Calm is the last thing a revved up tweaker wants.

"Don't listen to her!" Harold hollered right off the bat. "She'll get your mind all twisted!"

Lisa shrugged me off, whipping around setting her sights on the man she'd loved and hated equally ever since we all could remember. Only a brief second passed between the two as they faced off. From the way she was all out growling and the way Harold was narrowing his eyes at her, I knew we weren't there to head anything off. Much too late for that. We were there for the clean up.

Lisa stamped her foot and took off, hurdling most of the porch steps as she went. She knocked Harold back through the door he'd just come out of. She leapt in on top of him like a squalling cat falling out of a tree. Watching the two of them reminded me of clicking through my View-Master slide of my cousins when I was a kid. It was of King Kong and Godzilla in an all-out brawl, the tiny city stamped to death underneath them.

Hogue rushed around to the front of the car.

"We're just gonna let 'em go at it?"

I stepped forward, putting my arm out. The sound of them rearranging their furniture with their bodies came flowing out like rancid metal music that's really not music at all.

"We'll see who comes out first, take that one in for the night, give the other one a break. That's how we'll play it."

Pushing my arm down, Hogue decided that wasn't how he wanted his playbook to read. He rushed up the steps stopping in the doorway, yelling in at them before busting in. I took my time. I was already thinking about how in another hour, I'd be home with Stacy having dinner. I hung back, teetering on the top stoop that separated the porch from the living room. I stayed ready to bolt depending on what or who came flying out that door.

Watching Hogue wedge his way between the two of them was the funniest thing I'd seen lately. He was a weight class above the couple. They still nearly took him down.

"Stop this shit!" he ordered. "Stop it! Now, come on!"

He squared off putting one of his hands in the middle of Lisa's chest holding her off, and the other hand on Harold's chest. Harold still trying like anything to slap at Lisa. For the first time since we'd met, Hogue looked stressed. *Welcome to Lee County*, I thought. My next thought surprised me. *I hadn't needed to go to the Waffle House an' talk to his ex. I could've just come out here. Lisa an' Harold might wrap it all up for me.*

"You better be glad that old cronie next door called us in! Better thank her. She saved your fuckin' life!" Lisa shrieked at her man.

Harold flapped his skinny arms a few more times then dropped them having tuckered himself out.

"Now y'all go on an' take a seat over there," Hogue instructed.

Lisa scowled, stepping back from him causing his hand to drop from her chest.

"Mitchum, who the hell is he?" she wanted to know.

I leaned in a bit further from the doorway, leaving the door wide open for any of us who'd need it. I prayed all the while there wouldn't be any running that day. I'd barely recovered from giving chase over at Rae's and carrying her to the car when she'd sliced up her wrist with that fork.

"Officer Hogue. We've been partnered up for a bit."

"Oh, yeah? You so old they're sendin' out the young bucks with you to do the heavy liftin'?" Lisa sneered.

"Come on an' sit down," Hogue tried again, motioning to her to sit in the only armchair they hadn't turned over next to the couch.

She looked at the chair, her scowl went into a peaceful trance kind of stare, then her lips formed a little smirk. When I go back over it now, I fully recognize I should've seen it. I should've given the room a good once over and seen what Lisa saw there not far from that chair. At the time, I didn't. I missed it. In my defense, so did Hogue. The woman's compliance alone should've been a red flag. She hadn't given him any lip, just strutted over and plopped down.

"What now, *young buck?*" she put it to Hogue.

The three of them, Hogue, Harold and Lisa exchanged looks. Harold no doubt shocked as hell along with me that Lisa'd listened to anyone tell her what to do. He should've seen the red flag too, but I don't know if meth heads see color anymore. Best I can figure, tweakers lose all ability to see the colors of any flags. Their singular focus is on that next fix.

"Let's talk about *what now*, alright? Let's just talk. How about that? Some good ol' fashion *co-mmun-i-ca-tion*," Hogue offered in this Mr. Rogers tone I hadn't heard him pull out before.

My radio went off interrupting his little intervention before it even got off the ground.

"Whatcha say, Cobb? We reservin' a room for one or two?" Leland boomed from where they had him minding the desk, proof his errand had been a farce.

Harold had been around long enough to know what *reservation* was code for. He had no intention of being booked.

"Take her! Leave me here! Hell, a man cain't defend himself?"

Hogue put his hands up to keep what was left of any personal space he had between him and Harold, trying his best to talk gently. With his back then turned just slightly away from Lisa. God bless her, she took her chance. She reached to her left beside the fireplace and grabbed a fire poker. She barely raised it above Hogue's head before I tazed her.

That was only the second time I'd used it on the job up to that point. I'd like to say it was my last, but that'd be a falsehood. The fire poker fell from her hand down onto Hogue's shoulder. He whipped around.

"God damn, Cobb!" he gasped.

The electricity only took a second to take Lisa to the floor. I let up quick. She was such a little bit of thing. No way she'd be getting up til we were ready for her to. She lay at Harold's feet, arms and legs gyrating like a fly thwarted by a bug zapper.

A genuine look of shock came over Hogue's face. Don't know if he was surprised I could act that quickly or that I'd cared enough to do it. I stared down at Lisa, my own true motivations not clear even to me. In that second, I'd made a choice. I'd decided right there that Hogue might get what was coming to him, just not on my watch. The paperwork alone I'd have to fill out if my partner bit the dust with me watching his six, was enough to sway me. Besides, I'd set other things in motion. Didn't see a need to let Lisa go down. Not for hurting the likes of Cyrus Hogue.

Overall though, I've come to attribute that moment to the fact that it takes a lot to go against instincts. If your training for the badge takes at all, that's what it becomes—instinct. Second nature to protect your brothers in blue. Even if they're making your life a new kind of hell. You protect them. No questions asked.

Now you would've thought Harold would've rather I gone on and put a bullet in Lisa what with her hell bent on getting him either locked up or buried. I honestly looked for him to have something to say about my choice of a lesser weapon, instead of what he did next. Soon as she quit twitching, he dropped to the floor sobbing and carrying on, sad as anything that I'd acted at all.

"Why'd you have to do that?" he wailed. "She's all talk. Hell, you sat two fuckin' desks away from us in the god damn first grade, Cobb! Cain't believe you! God damn!"

Before Hogue knew what was happening, Harold raised up,

hurdling Lisa's still twitching body and sucker punched me right in the nose! Hurt like a son of a bitch, I won't lie, but I stood my ground. No way was I going to let him see me fall.

Snapping out of his stupor, Hogue rushed Harold getting him in a hold. Both of them cursing a blue streak as they knocked around like two wild bulls in the same rodeo shoot. At first my whole face felt numb, then came the pain. I put my hand up to my nose. Blood dripped down my hand into the sleeve of my shirt, pooling at my elbow.

There wasn't a thing in that house I'd have wanted to come in contact with my open wound. God knows, Harold's filthy fist meeting my nose was bad enough. I rushed out to the car, grabbed a clean shirt from a change of clothes I kept in the trunk.

"I don't know how he got that punch in, but I got him now! He won't get in another one!" Hogue called from where he'd wrested Harold out onto the front porch and forced him to sit.

We waited with Harold til the ambulance came. Him sniveling like a baby the whole time. Hogue sat right next to him, elbowed him every now and again. I held my head back, leaned against the stair railing trying not to pass out. Didn't take long for the red lights. Larry was usually on call that time of day. He was always ready for something other than biding time in the Walmart parking lot waiting for an old lady to have cardiac arrest on the way out to her car. Weekdays were slow.

"God knows, Mitch!" Larry couldn't help but holler as he got out of his ambulance. "Dispatch didn't say it was you I was comin' for."

I waved him off.

"Naw. I'm fine. Hogue'll drive me on over to the urgent care. Lisa's inside. Had to taze her. Couldn't be helped. She'll need a once over. They'll probly keep her over night over at Central Carolina if they got a bed," I told him, motioning to the open living room door.

Lisa's eyes were wide open by the time Larry loaded her on the stretcher. Her jaw was clenched shut. As they wheeled her past me, I swear if she could've moved her hands, they'd have been around my throat. Harold was still crying soft as Larry got her situated in the back.

"Jesus," Hogue griped shaking his head. "Can you shut the fuck up? Be a man."

The way he delivered this, I gathered it was a line Hogue had heard many a time himself. A well-rehearsed bit and he felt he was carrying on a manly tradition of some kind by barking it. Harold only got louder, a line of snot dripping from his nose threatening to slip down into his mouth. I turned away.

"He goin' with y'all or what?" Larry wanted to know nodding Harold's way.

It hurt to even blink. I dabbed at my eyes with my shirt sleeve and looked down at Harold. I knew he'd wake up tomorrow and be lucky to remember a thing. Something about the way he was sitting there in cuffs, hands behind his back, took me back to our days out on coach's bench. He was always last to get picked, every single time. A wave of pity overtook me.

"Uncuff him," I directed Hogue.

This fired him up. "You're talkin' crazy! I cain't—"

"Come on, now," I boomed louder. "He's Larry's problem."

"Well, I don't know how I like the sound a that, Mitch," Larry piped up.

"Aww, he'll probly pass out on the way over. No need takin' up room down at the station," I muttered, motioning to Hogue again.

Grumbling as he did, Hogue uncuffed Harold and led him up into the ambulance.

"Will she burn me if I hold her hand?" Harold asked Larry.

"Only one way to know," Larry smarted off.

The doors shut before I got to see if Harold gambled it or not. Since then, any times we get calls to go out there, I make sure somebody else goes. Figured Lisa's done with me til the day she dies after sparking her up that like that.

As Hogue drove us back down their gravel drive, a hog wandered out in front of us from the pasture to the right. He blared the horn at it. It looked up from rooting and sauntered on in its own sweet time.

"This country ass place with country ass idiots," Hogue mumbled, rubbing the shoulder Lisa's poker had landed on.

I don't think Hogue'd ever had a broken nose, or he'd have known even a bird chirping'll make you feel like your head's coming apart, needless to say a horn blaring. He'd probly been more on the giving end of nose breaking than he had on the receiving end.

I sat back, rested my head against the headrest, rolled my window down, gave him a few minutes til I said another word.

"How's it going with wrappin' up things over back over in Johnston?"

His arms tensed. His hands tightened on the wheel. Evidently, he was bringing out the balances in his head, weighing what I could be trusted with. Who was I to tell him *nothing*. Not to trust me with a single thing. I didn't owe him that. It was his job to figure it out.

"They'll take that fella off life support Wednesday. Guess we'll know after that."

"Which way'd you say it's leanin'?"

A car pulled out in front of us from a side street. Hogue was quick on his horn again. I looked down to see the blood on the shirt I was wearing and my pant legs and thought about how Stacy'd think what I'd been through was a whole lot worse that it was. That wasn't always bad, garnered a syrupy sympathy.

"Motherfuckers," he griped at the driver ahead before answering. "Hard to know. Hell, he might *shock the world* an' start breathin' just fine or he might croak the second they do it."

I looked at him driving, unphased by those words. We both knew if Jolie's fella croaked, it'd change everything. He'd be looking at manslaughter instead of assault.

"Well, I'll be prayin' he'll hold his own."

"Can't say as I've decided which way I hope it goes."

"Come on now. He up an' dies, you'll be g'ttin' issued a jumpsuit."

Hogue loosended his grip on the wheel with his left hand,

propped his arm on the door, leaned back into the seat like we were high school boys readying to cruise the local strip.

"When'd you know you wanted to wear the badge?"

Seemed a strange time to be getting more personal. What with him just narrowly escaping having his skull cracked in by a tweaker with a fire poker, I humored him though. I figured something about me being infirmed, made him want to open up.

"Senior year. This officer came to our school for the D.A.R.E. program. We got to talkin'. Knew me from church. Told me he'd help me get a scholarship if I'd consider the badge instead a linin' up for the mill like my ol' man. Said they needed guys like me. The mill didn't need me so much as I needed it, so I took him up on it." I summarized as best I could with a bloody shirt up under my nose.

"I was ten," Hogue started right in like he hadn't heard me at all but had been waiting to press play on his own tale. "Cops came to our house on the regular, just like with those two fuckheads back there. They knew our address. My Mama an' Daddy couldn't go a day without one threatenin' the other. Nobody ever went to the hospital. Mama came close a couple a times, but would you believe that woman learned to sew her own lip up? She was a real go getter when she needed to be. Most a the cops just stopped by, did a quick check, made sure everybody was breathin'. Bout half of 'em stayed on the porch or in the yard, didn't even come inside. If Daddy was passed out an' the cop got pushy, Mama'd let 'em in, but she mostly tried to keep 'em outside in case Daddy woke up an' raised more hell."

"Your daddy was on the bottle?"

"Weekend roller mostly. Hard workin'. Worked all week a 9:00 to 5:00 at a produce warehouse drivin' a truck for 'em. Come Friday nights, he'd stop by the corner store, get enough liquor an' beer to last him til Monday. Swear that man spent half his paycheck on it. Anyways, this one cop whatin but a few years younger than I am now. Mama must've thought he was nice to look at. Opened the door wide right off. He came in an' sat down on the couch like Sunday company. The two of 'em talked a while. I pretended to play with my Legos, but I was listenin'. Listenin' an' lookin' at that gun in his holster. When Mama got up to get 'em some sodas, I stepped right over Daddy who was still laid out on the floor, an' eased up next to that cop on the couch. Asked him if he'd fired it. He laughed, told me, 'No, not yet.' An' then you know what my next question was?"

"No tellin'."

"I asked him if I could. Can you believe that? Asked him if I could fire his god damn weapon. There I was just ten an' already jonesin' for it," Hogue said.

"I take it he said *no*."

"Yeah, he did, but this'll blow your hair back. He said I couldn't fire it, but I could hold it if I wanted." Hogue went on. "Course I wanted to. Hell, what boy wouldn't? He had me lay my hands out flat, unholstered it, put it right in my palms. Just for a few seconds. 'That's lives, other people's lives in your hands, son,' he told me."

I stared at him, envisioning little Hogue's eyes bright, loving a thing for the very first time there on that couch.

"That's all it took. I knew what I was gonna be right then an' there. I knew I wanted that. That there whatin nothin' that would ever give me more power. Holdin' a gun; holdin' lives."

We were back in town by then. The sounds of people blaring their rap at the Quick Mart parking lot flowed through my open window. When we stopped at the light, Hogue looked over at them, a smirk formed on his lips.

"Way I see it is when you have power like that, you've got to decide what's worth losin' it over. Just a given. You ain't gonna be able to keep it your whole life. I don't mind tellin' you, Cobb, cause I get the feelin' you'll know what I mean. That night outside Jolie's, I made my choice. An' now, I just may have to give my power up over it. I know," he informed me as we pulled into the Urgent Care parking lot. "But I wouldn't change a thing. Wouldn't do it any different."

I had nothing to say to that. Nothing. I was relieved my nose needed reset so I could get out of that car. The waiting room was filled with mostly young mothers with their kids and old people looking worse for wear.

"Mama!" a boy shrieked taking one look up at my face, scrambling up into his mama's lap.

Brennan Phillips eyed me from her spot up at the front desk. I smiled as best I could. Brennan'd been nursing people about as long as I'd been arresting them. I was glad to be in her capable hands.

"Mitchum Cobb, good Lord!" she exclaimed shaking her head. "Come on. A room just now opened up."

"I'll wait out here," Hogue called.

I wished he wouldn't. I wanted to tell him, go on home, that I'd call Stacy, but I didn't want to have any back and forth about it there. In no time at all, Brennan reset my nose. No pain like it. Hope to leave this world without ever knowing its equal. All they had was purple tape to bandage me up like the kind they used for kids. I told her I was in no position to split hairs, to go on and do what she had to do.

She only got through one story about her mama's gout and next thing I knew, we were done. You wouldn't ever get out of being treated by her without hearing about some of the off duty nursing she was involved in. Poor thing. Never got a day off what with invalid parents and working at emergency. She never complained. Guess some people's sweet spot consists of putting other people's lives back together.

"He's all yours," Brennan announced to Hogue as she led me out.

He took one look at that purple tape and didn't even try to hide his snickering. I just walked right by him on out the front to the car. He caught up to me.

"I ever tell you about this nurse I'd fuck over in Johnston? We'd get right to it in a janitor's closet. Next time, introduce me," Hogue said. "Don't have nothin' regular over this way yet."

"Hopin' there won't be a next time," I shot back as he unlocked the doors and I got in.

"Hate to tell you, man, but that right there's some damn wishful thinkin.'"

He got in, started the car and drove towards the exit. My chest tightened.

"Stacy's gonna have herself a real fit. Don't take me home just yet." I sighed.

"I gotcha."

As if he was a mind reader, he drove us over to the Dairy Queen. He knew me better than most. Pulled us through the drive through. We ordered and sat in a parking spot over to the side to wait til they brought out my strawberry sundae and his Coke. The way he started fidgeting, I knew I was going to hate whatever it was that was coming. Whatever'd been on his mind that made him want to get tangled up with Lisa and Harold was still there waiting to bare its teeth.

I started eating on my sundae. Whatever he had cooking in that head, sugar'd make it better.

"Now I ain't one to kick a man when he's down—" he started.

"You ain't?" I said, starting to laugh, but squelched that quick due to the pain.

"Okay now. I mean with your nose being broke an' all, I'd usually give you another day or so."

I looked over at him. He reached up to his face, like he was my mama, dabbing at his own chin showing me I had something on mine. Didn't even feel the ice cream dribbling down with the Novocaine Brennan'd shot me up with. I reached my napkin up, wiping it off.

"No use waitin'," I told him.

He looked out at the D.Q. and a man making his way inside decked out in full camouflage.

"Had a run in with our Charger driver the other night."

I felt all the color leave my face like cold bathwater taking me under.

"A Bobby Olsen, I believe he said his name was. Says y'all know each other. Says y'all go way back."

Using my plastic spoon, I dug at the syrup that'd sunk to the bottom of the cup wishing I'd have just let him take me home. Facing Stacy would've been the better choice.

"Do you?" he asked.

"Do I what?"

"Go way back?"

I took a couple more bites.

"Where'd you run into him?" I asked, deciding to be the one doing the interrogating rather than the one getting interrogated.

"I-I-a-I was over there at Rae's."

My head throbbed. I overrode the pain, turned his way so quick, thought it would fall clean off into his lap.

"Now why the hell'd you be over there?"

He set his Coke down, rubbed his hands on the tops of this thighs, still not looking at me.

"I just didn't want her to think she was in the clear. I wanted to make sure she knows it ain't over."

I slammed my ice cream cup on the middle console.

"An I'm guessin' you wanted to tell her all about your little theories you been cookin' up, hmmm?"

"I told her about the palm print on the door an' the scuff marks on the seat. They aren't *theories*. Those things were on that car, Cobb an—"

"Fuck it, Hogue! Fuck it all to hell!"

I leaned forward propping my elbows on my knees, holding my head in my hands, then raised up quick.

"Bet her Mama whatin home for this little meet up, was she?"

He didn't answer.

"Yeah, you went over there when she was all alone to put some fear in her. An' all the while you've got nothin' but cockeyed ideas. Not one damn shred a proof, of actual, take-into-court-evidence that would hold water with any jury!"

I didn't even wait for his reaction. I threw open my door, and got out, slamming it behind me. He hopped out, scurrying around his side to the front of the car.

"Cobb! Come on now. Let me run you home."

Turning around, I kept walking backwards making for the side door of the D.Q.

"No! Go on," I barked. "An' tomorrow, we're gonna talk all about how you're gonna close this one, you hear? You're gonna close the file on that kid an' we're movin' on."

"But I—"

I stomped back over, put my face right in front of his, purple tape and all. He looked down at the pavement. I wasn't quite old enough to be his Daddy, but I could sure enough play the heavy-handed older brother.

"You ain't g'ttin' it, Hogue. This job itn't about power, about people's lives in our hands. It's about what we can god damn prove! That's it!"

And with that, I did an about face and headed for the D.Q. door.

"You know Bobby Olsen or not?" he kept on.

I froze.

"Are y'all *old buds* like he says, man?"

"Go home, Hogue."

Didn't turn around. Waltzed in that D.Q. and texted Stacy to come for me. I'd determined to weather whatever she'd say about my clothes and my nose. That's the thing about going home. You have to do it sometime.

Hogue sped out of the parking lot. As I watched him drive off, I hated my instincts. I regretted using my tazer. He wasn't anybody's brother in blue. Didn't care a lick about proof or anybody's lives. It was all about the chase for him. A cop like that, gets that craving for the chase, they're never satisfied. Never. And there's always gonna be another rabbit.

85°F

The day before had been the only day of his entire school career that he'd remembered being out of school due to rain. The flood watch had turned out to be a fluke. The sky had been so black, he'd felt sure it was what his grandpa meant when he'd get to talking about the ushering in of Armageddon. This seemed an ever-present concern when Mitch visited him at the old folks home. His parents rarely accompanied him. He made it there every once in a while and then gradually at least every couple of weeks.

"Smells like piss," his Daddy'd complain when he asked if he'd want to come along.

"You could put some vapor rub under your nose," Mitch suggested.

"It ain't him anymore. That ol' man settin' in front a that TV. It ain't him, an' won't a bit a vapor rub make it him," his daddy delivered with finality.

Mitch thought that if you quit seeing everyone when they became unrecognizable, you'd eventually damn yourself to a life of solitude. He didn't want that, and so he continued to visit his grandpa. The failed son turned ever faithful grandson.

The old man's ramblings weren't all about the onslot of

Armageddon, and how to be ready. Every now and again, there was talk about how the *filly*, as his grandpa had deemed her, down the hall in room 112 who liked to fuck like a rabbit in springtime. This made Mitch stifle a smile. It gave him a hope for the future that his own father's day-to-day grind at the mill did not provide.

That morning, after the forecasted flood turned out only to be clouds and rain, he'd gone by his grandpa's before school rather than after. He knew the increasing frequency of these visits weren't about their closeness as they hadn't had much. That morning, as he walked the hallway, following the scent of powdered eggs and freezer burned sausage patties, he was aware that he was there to take his mind off it all. He'd resorted to doing anything he could not to think about Bobby, or Kelly and that night last month out at Ducet.

Kelly's family had plastered up posters on every telephone pole in town. They'd also taken out a couple adds in the local paper. Only a couple, as that was an expensive way to find someone. On his way home from school the week prior, he'd seen one of the posters blown down, hanging over a chain link fence. Something about seeing Kelly's face splayed over the top metal bar had nearly brought him to his knees.

It called to mind that deer out over the river behind Ducet, draped lifeless, staring down at them. That river where she'd swam with Bobby. At least he thought she had. Had they swam? For the life of him, he could not recall it clearly.

The police had visited both he and Bobby the day after, once it had been twenty-four hours and Kelly's father had called her in as missing. It was determined by the canvassing the officers did of those who'd been at the Sonic that she had stayed late there with the two of them and then been given a ride at the end of the night. Mitch had gone to Bobby's house right after the police and he knocked and knocked on the door. No one answered. He pictured Mrs. Olsen in her dress and panty hose, watching him from her bedroom window. *What had Bobby told her? What was there to tell?*

These two questions ate at him daily like lions feeding on the lame gazelle of his psyche. It seemed no one wanted to help him answer them. Laura had refused to take his calls. She gave him nothing but cutting looks as they passed in the school hallways until just yesterday when he'd waited for her after second period.

"Stay away from me," she hissed, tossing her books inside the bottom of her locker, quickly taking out the others she needed, stuffing them in her backpack.

"Why?" he blurted. "What's wrong?"

Looking up from her packing, a fury he'd never witnessed took over her face.

"What's wrong? *What's wrong?* You fuckin' lost Kelly!" she blasted. "That's what's wrong. Don't you get that? Why'd you let you her go off on her own out there anyway?"

He only stared at her. He did not get it. According to what Bobby told the officers, Kelly had insisted on walking home. Why did that make him responsible? It crossed his mind to retort that Kelly had lost herself. He knew this would not assuage things.

"An' stay away from Bobby too! You hear? His mama said he cain't talk to you, cain't be seen with you, or nothin'. So just quit callin' me an' quit callin' him!" She slammed her locker door then stomped off to her last class.

The slamming of the metal echoed in Mitch's head. He marveled at Mrs. Olsen warning her son against him, as if he was automatically the guilty of the two. What tale had Bobby woven? It couldn't have been good. The abhorrent truth was that any counter he'd offer, what with his foggy recollection, would not be an adequate rebuttal. He simply could not remember. This truth rested, immovable, residing in his gut.

Decades later, Mitch would come to know that it was not Bobby that Mrs. Olsen was protecting. She'd call him from that same home his grandpa had been in and confess to him that she knew she really had no way to know what her Bobby was capable of. That even in his playground dealings as a boy, she'd seen when hemmed in, he lost all logic, erupting into a creature she did not recognize. *A mother knows these things.* she'd told him. *A mother knows when she's birthed a monster.*

Unfortunately, that morning, Mitch was left to his own assumptions—that Mrs. Olsen, thought he was a golem to be plucked from their lives. And so, he put one foot in front of the other on the tile floor of his grandpa's residence and he tried, for a few minutes, to forget. To just be a grandson talking to his granddad.

"You here to see your grandad again?" Eden, the main floor nurse on the hall asked Mitch as he neared his grandpa's door.

"Yes, ma'am."

"Ain't you the golden boy," she christened him. "He's just g'ttin' up. Let me tell him you're here."

She called in to his grandpa.

"Well get on in here, Mitchum," was his grandpa's response. "You can help me get the other leg."

"Yes, sir," Mitchum complied, making his way inside and over by the bed to help the old man slip on the other leg of his pants.

"Everybody thinks Armageddon's gonna be this big bomb sent crossed the ocean or a meteor rainin' down. Some shit like that." His grandpa was off to the races before Eden could even bring in his coffee. "That ain't it at all."

"Yeah?" Mitch went along. "What's it gonna be then grandpa?"

The old man leaned forward, his eyes boring an invisible hole in Mitch's head, a sniper site honed in. Their eyes locked. Mitch swore his grandpa could see. That age and experience had endowed him with powers to look past his pupils and see right into his brain. That he could see what eluded even him—what it was that had become of Kelly. Reaching out, the old man broke his gaze. He patted Mitch's shoulder.

"That's just it, Mitchum. It's already happenin'," he whispered.

"It is?"

"Yes, boy. It's happenin' inside every man, woman an' child. That epic battle between good an' evil. The very fight for one's soul. Good versus evil! Right in here." He delivered with emphasis like an old-time televangelist, beating his own chest one good time. "Right in here!"

And with that, he unclenched his fist, moving his hand over to Mitchum's chest.

"In here," he repeated.

In here...in here... was the updated soundtrack to Mitch's day as he opened his locker an hour later. The small square mirror hanging from the locker vents accosted him with his reflection. As he smoothed his hair away from his eyes, he stared back at himself wondering what the old man was privy too. If God had indeed given him a window to souls and he had called Mitch out.

His day went on in an uneventful haze until third period. As they all sat listening to Ms. Schnell go over importance of the Declaration of Independence yet again, there was a knock at the door. Ms. Schnell walked over and opened the door to a policeman. Mitch's heart pounded out a guilty refrain. They'd come for him!

"Class, this is Officer Holmes," Ms. Schnell introduced.

The officer needed no introduction however, as once Mitch found his breath, he recognized the man from his family's church. They'd never spoken, and the officer wasn't a regular. He was certain he'd seen him there on holidays though. The pastor would have him direct traffic for the bigger celebrations like the Christmas pageant and the Easter sunrise service.

"How is everybody?" the officer greeted.

A low chorus of *fines* went up from the students. Holmes had one of those kindly smiles. He was younger than most policemen Mitch had seen. Certainly younger than the one who'd come that morning after to question him about Kelly.

The officer stood in front of the class detailing that he'd been selected to be their school representative for the Lee County D.A.R.E program.

"I *dare* you to show us your gun!" Doug Ellison yelled out.

Ms. Schnell hurried over next to him pressing on his shoulder with her bony fingers.

"Ow! Jesus!" Doug yelped.

"Not exactly that kind a dare." Holmes played the disruption off well. "This dare stands for Drug Abuse Resistance Education."

Mitch studied the man's mannerisms, determining what it was that had his superiors send him to fend off the unwanted snarky comments of teenagers instead of being out arresting criminals. *Had it been a punishment?* Half the class remained unimpressed, working on homework when Ms. Schnell wasn't watching them, or passing notes to each other. A few were catching up on sleep.

The more Holmes talked, the more Mitch was all ears. The more the officer talked about abstaining from the temptations that others may present, the more Mitch felt this was exactly what his grandpa had told him about that very morning—the epic battle for one's very soul. He became certain that if he let Holmes leave without talking to him, he'd have let the evil in him win. This was so strange to him as before that morning, he wouldn't have said out loud to anyone that he believed in good or evil really.

When it came time for questions, there were a couple about drinking and how much was too much. Carl Mammot mustered up courage and asked if Holmes himself had ever tried any drugs. Holmes, unphased, answered noting that he too had been where they were once. That being a teenager had never been more difficult in his opinion due to the access to so many things that could wreck lives. A cherry tomato cheeked Ms. Schnell shut down the questions early, making the excuse of readying for the next class to cover up her mortification that children she instructed weren't of better moral fiber. She led Holmes to the door. He raised one hand ready to wave goodbye and placed his other hand on the doorknob.

"Officer!" Mitchum called out.

Time played its usual trickery, seeming to freeze them all right where they were. All eyes on him. Mitch cleared his throat. Officer Holmes looked at him, a kind smile intact, waiting, simply waiting. Ms. Schnell glared.

"You go to Roberson Baptist?" Mitch finally asked.

"I sure do. My mama's got her own pew there. Try my best to

make it when I can," Holmes told him. "I've seen you there, right? You're Larry's boy, Mitchum, right? Mitchum Cobb?"

Amazed that he knew his name, Mitch nodded.

"Thought so," Holmes stated. "Anything I can do for you, Mitchum?"

Leah Reynolds was seated next to Mitch. He'd never thought one way or the other about her, but as he felt her eyes on him, she moved to the forefront of his world. All the many eyes on him wondering, like Holmes, what exactly it was Mitchum wanted. He felt his own eyes get hot with tears. He didn't know. He had no idea what the officer could do. He only knew something needed to be done. *A girl was missing, surely someone had to do something!*

"Uh, yeah. I was… a… I was—" Mitch sputtered.

"Come on, Cobb. I'd like to go home in the next hour," Leah Reynolds sneered.

Ms. Schnell snapped her fingers, pointing at Leah then lifting her index finger to her lips demanding silence. Leah slumped in her seat, sighing loudly, like a bull bedding down in its pasture for the night.

"I'm wonderin' how it is you become a cop," Mitch blurted. "How long it took an' all."

Ms. Schnell looked at Mitch, her eyes taking on a pride. She'd never heard him talk about anything further than the mill line after he graduated, and this had only been because she'd outright asked him when he'd been contented with C's.

"Won't matter, Ms. Schnell. My Daddy made D's an' F's in school, an' he's got ten guys takin' orders from him over at the mill," Mitch had informed her.

She'd been unable to mount a sound argument against that, yet there he sat, showing interest in serving his fellow man by enforcing the law. She fought the urge to rush over and hug Mitch right then and there.

"Well, you have to get your criminal justice degree. Most fellas take four years, but a buddy a mine knocked it out in three by going to summer school," Holmes explained.

Mitch's lower lip quivered. He realized his mouth had remained open, the real words he'd wanted to say unsuccessfully trying to push their way out.

"Not Cobb. It'd take him least eight years to be Po Po," Colt Slopes snickered from his seat in the corner.

Laughter from several classmates reaffirmed Colt's identity as the class clown.

Ms. Schnell repeated her snapping and silencing gesture to him. Colt playfully put his head on his desk, pulling his shirt up over his head to hide his face, a toddler who'd been caught with their hand in the cookie jar.

"Why don't you stop by the station, Mitchum?" Holmes commented. "I'd be glad to show you around, tell you more about it."

"Sounds like a good plan," Ms. Schnell told Holmes while smiling and nodding to Mitch.

And with that the officer waved himself out. Mitch closed his mouth up tight, feeling the opportunity missed, the truth again quieted, the threatening clouds of Armageddon encroaching on his soul there in his desk.

91°F

Hogue

I'm writing up the report from the whole tweaker fire poker fiasco when in she comes. She's gripping her purse like she thinks we have criminals running loose in here and slinks along the wall to the far right. Looking out over our desks, don't take long til her eyes meet mine, and she makes her way over. Rae had to go spouting off at the mouth about our little mac and cheese dinner date. Fuck!

"Officer Hogue," Miss Florrie greets me. "Lord, some days if I didn't know better, I'd say the devil might've gone down to Georgia but he left a few a his demons here to keep things hot."

"Sure is a scorcher," I agree.

There's a chair across from my desk. Hadn't had a use for it, but we all have one. She sits in it, loosening up her hands, popping her knuckles then cradling her purse on her lap like a grandbaby. I clear my throat.

"Cobb ain't here yet, an—"

"I'm here to see you."

Through the glass wall that separates the captain from the rest of us, I see him in his office chair having his coffee. He's jabbering away at somebody on his phone. If I play this right, I'll get her out of here before he even sees her. Don't need him knowing about any of my *extracurricular* activities.

"Well, Miss Florrie, I'm not sure exactly what Rae told you but I—"

"Rae don't know I'm here Officer Hogue, an' she don't need to," she informs me, scooting her chair up.

I do likewise and lean up, resting both elbows on my desk. I drop my head a bit so I can hear. Turns out Rae can keep her trap shut after all.

"Alright," I say.

Her knuckles are large showing her arthritis as she clutches her purse tighter, leaning up close as she can. Her face is scrunched up, tension building in her shoulders. Whatever's got her all revved up, she's hell bent on letting me know about it.

"Officer, I came to talk with you specifically. I don't want to get him in any trouble, but Mitchum isn't returnin' my calls. I even tried catchin' him after church last Sunday. He passed right by me, ducked in to talk to the pastor. The one an' only time we did speak a week or so after Brandon died, he did his best to convince me it's an' open an' shut case a Rae bein' forgetful. Told me all about how it's common, more common than I'd imagine, babies suffocatin' in cars. Said nearly thirty kids a year die that a way in this state alone, an' how there's even things you can put on your phone now, if you have one of those kinna phones, to remind you to take your child out a the car. Never thought I'd live to see that day. Women havin' to be reminded they have a child! My whole life, I've never known one other person this happened to, Officer Hogue. Not one. Have you?"

I look past her at the door watching for Cobb. He's bound to show up any minute. Would've thought the man would call in sick with his broken nose and me calling him out in the D.Q. parking lot last night, but he hadn't. I know exactly what he'd want me to say if he was sitting here. He'd want me to have his back and repeat those stats he told her. Name some case from elsewhere I read about, even make it up if I have to.

"Had one last summer over in Johnston and the summer before that."

"Well, I've been alive near 68 years, an' I hadn't seen the beat of it. Not in this county or any county around here. I've got people in Clayton an' over in Vass. Not one of 'em mentionin' anything like this where they stay at either."

She sits back against her chair, then moves forward again. It's clear she hadn't exactly made up her mind what it is she's willing to say. Sometimes people are trying to give you clues so you'll say it for them, take the pressure off. She inches up, arms nearly touching my desk, eyes darting to the side and behind me, clocking who's going to hear whatever it is she's chomping at the bit to spit out. This pony's liable to bolt if I don't rope her soon.

"Where's Cobb at?" McAfferey shouts over from the coffee counter. "He been in?"

"Hadn't seen him," I answer. "When he g'ts in, I'll tell him you're lookin' for him."

This seems to appease McAfferey. He stalks off down the hall to the Highway Patrol's designated part of this shithole.

"My Rae was a preemie. Did you know that?" Ms. Florrie blurts.

Where the hell's this coming from? Shit.

"Well, that's silly. Course you don't know that, but she was. Felt like we spent our whole first two years a her life with our own designated chair right in Dr. Mason's office. Lungs weren't developed. It was like they had to learn what to do."

She keeps on but my mind wanders to O'Donnell who's eyeing us from where he's gone over to get the last of the coffee. He's up every chance he gets checking the pastry box for another pastry that Lois brought in from Dunkin today. Aww hell, by the time I can get up from here, won't be a damn thing left. He lifts the coffee pot, raising his eyes at me. I shake my head. Don't care about the coffee. Sure would've liked to had me a bear claw though.

"Her second-grade teacher said she—oh, now how'd she put it? Empathy. Said Rae lacked *empathy*." Miss Florrie's still just talking away. "Said Rae didn't seem to be able to care about how others felt."

I nod. Maybe there'll at least be a glazed one left.

"At the time, I kind a took offense to it, her sayin' somethin' like that about my Rae, felt like she was pickin' on my little girl, but it stuck with me. Seemed like every time somethin' came up from then on, with Rae an' other kids, or with her an' me or her an' her daddy, I'd think about what that teacher said. Even when I had breast cancer, you know Rae only came to see me a handful of times?"

This breaks through. A handful...I try to focus, push my hunger to the side. She sure is telling me something. Might just be telling me everything I need to know.

"All my friends thought that was so strange, her bein' my only child an' all. Said they thought with all I'd done for that girl, made over her, always makin' sure she looked picture perfect, that she should a been right by my side any chance she got. She whatin though. I'd have to call from the hospital an' track her down at friend's houses, her knowin' I was havin' the chemo."

"How long she lived back with you?"

"Ever since Brandon was about a year. She an' Brandon's Daddy married, but they couldn't get along. Meth got a hold of him. He'd be on again, off again. I told her bring that boy home. I'd be glad to have 'em. Been just the three of us since. Rae's Daddy, you know he's been passed goin' on fifteen years. Just dropped over of a heart attack leavin' the mill one day. His Daddy same thing bout the same age as him. Maybe that's why I tend to spoil Rae? Afraid she'll go young like her Daddy. Rae always was a Daddy's girl. Cut from the same cloth those two. Least that's how it looked to everybody."

"Sorry to hear about your ol' man."

Something takes hold of her making her face fall, exposing all the sorry she's been carrying. Her hands clutch her purse so hard I think she's liable to rip it in two. She looks right at me, tears plaguing her eyes.

"Day her Daddy died, she got off the bus, came inside the house, an' I was settin' at the table waitin' to tell her, eyes all swolled up from all my cryin'. She didn't even ask what was wrong. She bebopped around that kitchen in her little cheerleadin' skirt makin' herself a snack. No matter how many times I asked her to set down, that I had somethin' to tell her, she wouldn't, so I finally just hollered out *Rae, your daddy died today!* An' you know what she said?"

I shake my head, having no earthly idea.

"She said she knew. Said the guidance counselor had called her in an' told her. I was madder than a wet hen once that set in what they did over at the school, but then watchin' her just standin' there makin' a PB & J, I was so shocked I couldn't be mad at 'em. There she was, actin' like life hadn't skipped a beat."

Miss Florrie scoots all the way up in her chair.

"See that's the thing, Officer. Rae's life don't skip beats. Her Daddy can die, I can have cancer, her boy can burn up in her car, an' she keeps on," she whispers. "She just keeps on keepin' on."

I lean back, picking up a pen, putting it down again.

"Miss Florrie, I'm not sure what you're g'ttin' at, ma'am?"

She looks to her left and her right again like she's wanting to cross a street but she's making sure nothing's coming. And more than likely that's what's happening here. She's getting ready to step down from the curb of denial and cross over the street to the side of the truth.

"She's got this boyfriend," she starts back up. "Bobby Olsen."

"We've already been in touch," I tell her. "Are you sayin' you think Olsen's got somethin' to do with your grandbaby?"

"I don't know what I'm sayin'. I—I—well, did you know he was on trial? It was a while back, 'bout ten years or more. He got off, but plenty a folks think he did it. They say they knew his wife, an' whatin no way she'd have killed their babies, maybe herself, but not her babies. No way," Miss Florrie tells me. "Now don't you think tha's strange? A man whose babies were killed g'ttin' together with my Rae, then her baby up an' dies?"

"Miss Florrie, I understand your concern, a man like that takin' up with your girl. I can. If I had a daughter, I sure wouldn't want 'em takin' up with a fella like that. Thing is ma'am, we have no way to link him to what's happened, him or Rae at the moment. Unfortunately, 'round here, we can't go by just what we think's strange. Hell, if we could, those cells back there'd be standin' room only."

I stand up. She takes my lead rising out of her chair. I come around the desk and put a hand on her shoulder, gently guiding her over towards the exit. Was sure hoping she'd have something more concrete. She stops walking, looks up at me.

"Officer Hogue, I'm afraid I've beaten around the bush. It gets hard not to do that at my age. You'll see, but I've been callin' Mitchum about that Bobby. I think he may know somethin' about him, about his past. A friend a mine over at the church was just talkin' a couple Sundays ago about how back in the day, Mitchum's wife Stacy, had a sister went missin'. Soon as she talked about that, it came right back to me too. My Don, Rae's daddy, he went out with some a the other men in town to help look for that girl. Came home that night, tol' me he'd heard some a the officers talkin' 'bout how there whatin much to go on an' how the Cobb's boy an' the Olsen's son had already been talked to. That those two were the last to see the Diamond girl. I recalled that real clear soon as she brought it up. It was a big deal in this county back in the day. That's what Don said to me, *they'd been talked to*. Somethin' itn't it?" she ends with a question.

"What's that?"

"How poor kids get called *boys* an' rich ones get called *sons*," she says.

I see through the glass door that leads out front, Lois is hanging up the phone and spots us coming. She gets up and opens the door to us.

"Miss Florrie, I didn't see you come in," Lois tells her. "How are you, hon?"

"Not as bad as I could be. Not as good as I wanna be," Miss Florrie answers.

"I hear you. I'm so sorry about Brandon," Lois cain't help but say.

Miss Florrie's eyes well all up. She takes Lois' hand.

"He was too good for this world. Too good."

Lois walks with us to the front door, holds it for us too. I help Miss Florrie down the stairs. She digs in her purse for her keys handing them to me. I walk ahead and open the car door for her like her personal valet.

"I don't know exactly what it all means, Officer Hogue. I wish to the good Lord I did, but I don't. I just have this horrible feelin'. Horrible! I cain't help but feel like this Bobby Olsen comin' 'round's brought all this down on us." She goes on as she gets in and gets situated in her seat. "Now I'm not sayin' my Rae is blameless a any wrongdoin'. No sir, I'm not, but I think he's got some kind a hooks in her, filled her head with all kinds a ideas a what her life could be if she whatin tied down. She spends all her time since she got out a that hospital up at his gym up in Raleigh. Has it in her mind, he's gonna be makin' her a business partner or some craziness."

I put one hand on my waist and look back at the station. Lois is still standing in the doorway looking out the glass doors at us.

"I'm sorry, Miss Florrie. I'm not sure what else I can tell you other than that we hadn't closed Brandon's case just yet. I can dig a little more, but I sure cain't arrest anybody for not havin' *empathy* or for datin'a free man people think might've killed his family. I just cain't do it."

She leans forward, closes her door but rolls down her window.

"Cain't shake my feelin', Officer. I cain't. I fear if my Rae stays with him, she'll end up like his wife or like that Diamond girl. They never did find her. Turns out she had a boyfriend over in another county. Everybody decided she ran off with him, but I don't think so. I just don't." Miss Florrie frets, shaking her head. "A shame how people'd rather cling to a lie than live with unanswered questions."

Leaning down, I put both hands on her driver's side window frame.

"Now, Miss Florrie, I won't make you any promises, ma'am. What I will say is that I'll do my best to get to the bottom of it."

"What can I do? You tell me Officer, Hogue. What is it I can do?"

I stand up, move back from her car, drop my arms, put my hands in my pockets, try to look relaxed so Lois won't get worked up.

"Keep prayin'," I reply. "Just keep prayin'. The truth'll surface. Always does."

Remembered that one all of a sudden. My old C.O. used to say it all the time. Cain't believe it was waiting in there with everything else I've got clogging up this head of mine.

"Yes, Lord. Yes, it will," she agrees, nodding.

She rolls up her window. I watch her put the car in reverse and ease slowly out of our parking lot. The fact that she's still got a license and hadn't killed anybody, might mean there's a man upstairs after all. *The truth'll surface...* always did wonder how anybody believed that shit. It's a nice thought for most, I guess. Better than reality. Hell, works in my favor that's all it is—a nice thought.

51°F

Cobb

In one of our classes back at the academy, a brain researcher came all the way from Duke University over in Durham. There was a big push at that time to have better community and police relations. Guess they thought starting with the head doctors would help.

That they'd have better ways to say it than our instructors. The only thing they'd say that resembled any kind of caution about how we were out in public was *watch yourself out there*. Always struck me strange. You watch yourself, well, you'll repeat what you're watching.

The brain researcher talked to us about how our brains fit our lives into stories. How it's built for it. The way it connects people into roles, fits them into the categories of villains or heroes. How we'll often interpret what people do in a way that reinforces these roles we've assigned. How in our line of work we have to be mindful of doing that because maybe people aren't always just one or the other. How this whole life's all about what tales we tell ourselves. Really stuck with me.

There's always been two stories about that night out at Ducet that I rehearse depending on the day. Stories about why Kelly didn't ever make it home. In the first one, she did exactly what Bobby'd said she'd done. She set off, alone in the night, to the closest gas station, and whatever mystery boy she was rumored to be seeing came and picked her up when she'd called him.

This first story puts her off somewhere, living a different life than the one her family had planned. Maybe the two of them got married? Maybe they made their own way in the world, had some kids? Maybe she's happier having left the rest of us behind?

The second tale is one where Bobby made sure no one would ever find out what it was that went on with Anita and me and him. In this account, while I was passed out, he went to whatever lengths he had to in order to save his hide, *our* hides. In this version, Kelly didn't make it home cause she's buried somewhere out there behind that old head shrinker's hospital. I don't like this one, but it's easier, wrapped up cleaner than the possibility Kelly'd ever show back up.

When Bobby said that to me outside the burger joint about what I was thinking might've happened having not been what went down, I tried not to let that in. I didn't have any room for a third story. Didn't know the characters and ending in that one. If she didn't walk off, if he didn't do something, what the hell happened? My brain locked it out.

What would we do without our stories? These things we tell ourselves when someone we know disappears or leaves us. Narratives helping shield us from the truth, lessen its impacts. They make it so we get through the days. Way I see it now, most of my days may just have been kept afloat by lies.

Thing is, we really don't want to know the truth. Part of us is plum terrified about which character we are. The villain ...the hero. If the first Kelly story is true, and it well may be, that she somehow slipped away in the dark, I'm off the hook. I'm neither.

Still doesn't take away that guilty sting I have inflicting me when she comes to mind. The stabbing thought that what if I'd have never offered for Bobby and me to ride her home from Sonic. If I hadn't done that, there'd have been no need for either account. Our stories would've diverged right there and then.

That's just it though. That's why our brains start weaving the stories. It makes the God-awful reality of what we've done into something we can stomach. Something we can look at behind our eyes in the mirror. These two tales—mine and mine alone.

Not long after we got married, I realized my Stacy had her very own tales her mind crafted about it all. Should've known she would. Her brain no different from everyone else's—needing and feeding on stories.

"You know she's never called us? Not once. Hadn't sent Daddy a birthday or Christmas card. Not word one lettin' us know she's still breathin'," she'd say every now and again, mostly on holidays or Kelly's birthday.

I never quite knew what to say when she'd start in on this. After the most recent miscarriage when I picked her up from the hospital, she'd latched on to what it was that had become of Kelly even more than usual. Especially after naming our latest after her sister, she had a new reason to need to know. Maybe she wanted to think of our lost baby up in heaven being cradled by Kelly. We all yearn to know somebody's waiting on the other side.

"If she's still alive, she'd a contacted Daddy. They were tight. She was always his girl," she went on as we rode home from visiting Hicks one afternoon. "I was young. She didn't hardly know me, but Daddy. She just loved Daddy."

"You never know," I tried to console, patting her hand, hoping the spell would pass like it had other times.

"Someone might," she muttered. "Someone has to."

I kept my eyes on the road offering up small prayers the light ahead would turn green, so I wouldn't have to stop.

"Sometimes, Mitchum, you know sometimes, I think these babies we keep losin' keep on dyin' cause of somethin' we—cause of somethin' I've done. That it's cause my insides are all ate up. They're a mess from all the years a not knowin'. All my wonderin', hopin' an' prayin'. All this time, wantin' any kind a sign one way or the other about her."

"Awe, honey, don't think that."

"Miss Lynn says I should come to church more an' get prayer. She invites me every time she rings me out at the Piggly Wiggly," Stacy added, tears trickling down her light skinned cheeks.

"If it'd help you feel better, might not be the worst idea."

"I cain't do that, Mitchum! I cain't!" she wailed.

I pulled the car over to the shoulder, turned it off, and gave her my full attention.

"Why not, honey?" I whispered, slipping a hand up to her wet cheek.

"What if that pastor was to lay hands on me, an' God tells him right off about all the evil in here," she said pounding her chest with a fist.

I scooted over closer, took that fist gently in my hand, putting it back in her lap.

"Now, hon," I murmured softly in her ear. "Not a bit a evil in you. Not one bit."

She pushed me away back towards my side of the car.

"There is! There is, Mitchum! I got all kinds of evilness an' selfishness in me. I've been wishin' she was dead! Do you hear me? I've been wishin' Kelly was dead! I just want somebody to find her body so we'll know. We'll finally know. I need to know, Mitchum. I need it so bad!"

Her small body contorted in a seizure of rage and sorrow too much for it to contain.

"That's not evil, Stac."

"It is, Mitchum! It's evil to wish your own kin dead! My own sister! An' if I'm bein' honest, I just want Daddy to shut up about her. I want him to think about me for once. I want people to think about me. That's why God won't give us any babies. He won't let any pure good thing stay alive in here, in my evil, selfish body!" She cried, leaning forward, rocking herself.

Inching close again, I slid my arms in around her doing my best to press her to me. Cars passed us. A couple blew their horns likely recognizing our car.

I reached one arm up waving them on and just held my girl.

When she couldn't cry anymore, I started up the car again. She fixed her face in the side mirror, wiping her eyes with a tissue, and putting on her pink lip gloss. We continued our drive home.

"You think about me don't you, baby?" she asked slipping her hand over onto my thigh. "All you ever think about is me."

I lifted her hand up and kissed it before putting it back on my thigh.

She only ever told me that story about her evil insides on that drive. Only the one time. I was so glad she never said it again. Didn't want to think about it. I couldn't imagine if someone as sweet and innocent as my Stacy was ate up with evil. If that was true about her, well then, I didn't know what in the world my insides looked like.

80°F

It took him two more visits to see his grandpa, a weekend of heavy drinking with his buddies and five miserable days of school before he found the nerve to stand at the front desk of the police station. The cop manning the desk used the phone to call back to Officer Holmes, then showed Mitchum where to wait.

The lobby had gone unchanged since the fifties, like much of the town of Sanford itself, with its brown paneled walls, old wooden magazine rack screwed into the wall and clunky wooden chairs with pleather seats each bearing a rip down the middle showing they were past due for being replaced, it was clear no taxpayer money was being allocated to keep up appearances. The longer he sat, the sicker Mitchum felt. He rubbed his sweaty palms on the thighs of his jeans.

Everyone who walked by took notice of him. Indeed, not many boys his age sat in that lobby. They were usually escorted to the back and locked away til their parents could come claim them after cow tipping or other intoxicated ventures country boys got up to at night. He caught the front desk cop watching him warily while answering calls. Did he think he'd done something? He had, hadn't he? When the cops who'd visited his house had questioned him and he'd attested to Bobby's version of events about Kelly walking off to meet a more preferable boy, that in and of itself was a crime was it not? A crime of omission.

"An' when you woke up, she was just gone?" the cop had asked, sitting across from him at his kitchen table.

Mitchum's mother stood behind the officer, biting her lower lip, her fingers pressing so gruffly into the skin of her neck that she left splotches.

"Is that right, boy?" the cop pressed.

Mitchum nodded.

His mother's hands slipped back down to rest in the pockets of her robe. He swore he could hear her exhale.

From what the officer clumsily disclosed, Bobby had told them that he and Mitchum had drank too much for either of them to drive. Kelly'd gotten frustrated after Mitchum passed out. She'd informed Bobby she was hoofing it. That she had a fella over in Vass who'd be happy to come get her once she got to the gas station a mile or so away and she'd give him a call. Bobby said he'd been too far gone to tell her it was a bad idea. The last he remembered was Kelly, rounding the bend of the long Ducet driveway, and then she was out sight.

And there'd been no evidence to the contrary. The only hitch was that she'd never made it home. Once her Daddy called it in, all the officers they could spare had already been out at Ducet and given the property a once over. As to whether she'd made it to the gas station, the attendant there really couldn't say. Their security cameras were props at best. Few businesses had them at that time and even fewer actually kept them in working order.

So Mitchum had not gone against Bobby. What could he have said? That he had a horrible feeling? And to say this, to talk about this, would have been to admit his own complicitness in all he'd witnessed and simultaneously be confessing to that one time he participated. Anita. Oh, what they'd done to poor Anita! It had so sickened him, he'd vowed to never do so again, yet found no matter how much you obstained, the one time you caved in could never be erased.

It didn't matter. Once was all it took and then Bobby had that over him. Bobby and possibly Kelly were the only ones who knew about his slip up aside from Anita herself. From what Kelly told them, Anita was in no state to tell anyone but her. Anyone but Kelly, and she'd not told her cousin about both of them, only about Bobby. This had perplexed him.

"We'll let you know if we need anything else," the cop had said as he'd gotten up and readied to exit their kitchen.

"Would you like somethin' to drink 'fore you go?" Mitchum's mother meekly offered.

The cop surveyed the surroundings, unkempt and borderline unsanitary. Mitchum couldn't recall the last time his mother had cleaned.

"No thank you, ma'am," the cop replied.

And they'd never contacted him about anything else. He'd seen the signs that Kelly's family put up in the community, heard tell of the men who'd organized a search for her, but the cops had never again come back to his house. What Bobby Olsen said had been all that was needed. What Mitchum had always thought proved to be true—when a rich person speaks, it's taken as gospel.

"Mitchum?" Holmes' voice infiltrated his stupor of remembering he'd fallen into there in the station lobby.

Mitch stood up so quickly he nearly toppled over into the man. He felt all the strength and balance in him leave. He feared he'd collapse into a puddle at the officer's feet. The room spun for a second and he thought it might all be a figment of his imagination. That he'd not made it there after all, but then reached up feeling for his forehead reminding himself that was nonsense. He'd never had any imagination to speak of.

"You alright, son?" Holmes asked, putting a hand on Mitchum's shoulder.

"Yes, sir. I'm fine."

"Well, I'm glad you came by. Didn't know if you'd take me up on it."

"Been busy. My grandpa's over at Trinity. I been tryin' to get by there every chance I can 'fore graduation an' all."

"Sure. I remember what it's like at your age. A lot on your mind," Holmes assured him. "A lot ahead a you."

They walked around the station. Holmes talking to anyone who crossed their path. He was well liked, that was clear. It wasn't at all how Mitchum had pictured a police station. It seemed more like an office, each of them with their own desks and computers. Their uniforms muting their separateness. The guns holstered to their belts reminded him it was not at all an office but a place where the law and those who broke it were accounted for.

A few of them noted they'd seen Mitchum play ball.

"Man, you took 'em down that night against Moore."

"Plowed right through."

"What're you benchin' now, boy?"

Their accolades and praise meant more to him than that of other adults at church or at school. He indulged them, embellishing his bench press numbers just a bit, smiled and took their heavy-handed back pats good naturedly. Holmes gave him the full tour, even walking him by a holding cell where a tweaker, an old elementary school classmate of Mitchum's who could usually be found begging outside the Galaxy Mart, was detoxing for the afternoon. The boy interrupted his pacing to growl at them like a rabid zoo animal as they walked past.

"Settle down now, Harold," Holmes warned. "It'll be supper time 'fore you know it."

"I don't want no fuckin' supper!" the boy lashed back.

Three desks to his right, was all Mitchum recalled about him. He'd sat three desks to his right in Mrs. Milner's first grade classroom. Harold had dropped out by ninth.

"You will. Trust me. You will," Holmes said with a smirk shaking his head.

The more minutes that passed, the more Mitchum felt the

reason for his visit slipping away. He knew he had to rally his courage. He'd summoned all he'd had to get himself there, but now he had to muster it again to say what needed to be said. Looking over Holmes' shoulder as they left the hallway still in view of the cell, Mitchum gulped back the paralyzing fear that he would soon be joining Harold if he got up the nerve to open his mouth.

"Got time for a cup?" Holmes asked.

Mitchum nodded and followed him into the break room. An ancient coffee pot with its power light faintly glowing sat half empty in its holder. The smell of the coffee was reminiscent to him of the mechanic shop where his daddy took their car for oil changes. Holmes held up the pot, sloshing the coffee around. It was too thick to do much in the way of drinking.

"Aww, I think I've got somethin' more your speed," he noted, setting down the pot, reaching over and opening a mini fridge on the counter. He pulled out a couple of cans of Coke.

They sat across from each other at a rickety table held somewhat steady by the folded-up paper towels under a couple of the legs.

"What're your plans for next year, Cobb?" Holmes asked, addressing him by his last name as if already prepping him for a badge. "Thinkin' a playin' ball over at State?"

Mitchum took a sip of his soda then shook his head.

"Daddy says there's no money in it. Not long term. Ain't a livin'."

"Might be some pro ballers who'd argue with him on that one."

"Yeah, I guess, but my playin' days are done. Been a good run. The old man's got a place for me over at the mill. His boss has me on the schedule startin' the beginnin' a next month."

"Is that what you want?"

This took Mitchum aback. He shrugged. This wasn't a question he'd been asked. Certainly one he had not asked himself. His entire life, he'd been told what to do, what he should want, like hand me down clothes he'd just put on. They'd barely fit, and were often worn, but he hadn't complained. He'd known nothing else.

Holmes gulped down a big sip of his drink putting his can on the table, then leaned forward, resting his arms on the table, hands clasped. Whatever it was he was about to pitch, he was going all in.

"I'll tell you, Mitchum, that itn't really a shruggin' matter. Now if I was askin' you if you want pizza or a burger, that's somethin' to shrug about, not your future."

"Yes, sir. I guess not."

Mitchum downed another drink from his can. *Now!* he told himself. *Tell him now! Tell him everything you remember about that night. Tell him about Kelly!* Holmes reached down into his back pants pocket, bringing out a glossy pamphlet and laid it in front of Mitchum.

"See, the reason I'm g'ttin' all nosy, is the precinct gives out one scholarship a year. We offer it to a high school senior who we think might just have a future in law enforcement."

The shiny paper reflected the neon light from overhead right into Mitchum's eyes. If it was indeed his future, it was brighter than he'd ever expected.

"Full ride over at the academy at Central Carolina. You'd still be a stone's throw away, an' you might still be able to go on part time at the mill, if that's what your Daddy's set on. It would all come down to how much hustle you have in you, enough to pull off school an' work," he continued.

A scholarship? Be a cop? Mitchum felt a laugh bubbling up from inside, and yet also oddly felt like he could cry. No one had ever seen anything in him. Not anything substantial. His coach had seen a powerhouse. That'd had nothing to do with who he was, rather what he could physically pull off. Here this man was offering him something, seeing something in him. Holmes slid the brochure closer.

"They have a real good program. It's where I went. Big state schools got nothing on 'em. Kids come from all over," Holmes bragged.

Mitchum picked up the pamphlet. There were pictures of young men and a few women not much older than himself all decked out in their cop duds. All with vibrant eyes and hopeful smiles. He'd never seen any of these pristine youths around town. He didn't recognize a one. He wondered if they'd brought in people from somewhere else to pose.

A smile began on his lips as he looked at the poser cops. Could he be one of them? It came to him, he'd been posing his whole life. Posing as a compliant son, a good boy who did what he was told, as a friend, a football player. He'd shut up, beefed up, and done what it took.

"You learn football, boys! We studied the plays now get out on that field an execute. Hell, you can do that, you can do just about any damn thing in this life," their coach was fond of shouting at practice. "Some a the greatest men in our country started out just like this—learnin' plays an runnin' them. Look it up!"

He'd never say who exactly. It never mattered. It sounded good to them. They were eager believers of his vague sermons. The proof was in their wins, and oh, did they ever win!

"So, what do you think, Cobb?" Holmes pressed. "Think this could be for you?"

Looking down one last time at the glossy future police force, he knew the answer. He'd learn it. Being a cop would be no different than running plays. Sure! Why not?

Mitchum opened his mouth, but looking at the man across from him, an upstanding man like Holmes, he felt he should get up and run. He should take off for home and pray they'd never cross paths again. He felt sure that's what boys like him were made to do—run and hide. Men like Holmes did the chasing and the finding.

He didn't run, however. He stayed put. There was no way, now that he'd gotten on his radar, that he'd ever avoid Holmes. They'd see each other at church, or around town. His running at that moment, once they'd sat, had sodas and he'd taken him on the tour, would only incriminate him.

And before he could ascertain what the best alternative to fleeing the scene would be, he heard himself say,

"What if you've done things?"

Holmes turned his can in his hands, holding it up, taking a shot at the trash can behind Mitchum. The can went in making a clanking sound at the bottom.

"Done things?" he regurgitated Mitchum's words.

"Yeah. Things that wouldn't—well, that wouldn't make you a good cop. Things it wouldn't be good if other people found out about."

By the way Holmes squinted his eyes, it was clear this was not what he'd expected from his pitch. He leaned back in his chair, crossed his arms, then uncrossed them again. He took his time wanting to be sure not to scare off his young recruit.

"I'd say if you're out in the free world, son, how bad a thing could you really have done?"

The answer to this didn't come readily to Mitchum. He stared again at the brochure. The truth was... well the truth was, he didn't know the truth. For all he knew Kelly had made it to that station. She'd called that mystery boy. She had. That had been the rumor that had grown legs and walked around town.

Yes, there were nights he lay awake imagining just that- her out there somewhere starting her new life. It could be what happened... it could. He'd assured himself of this many times over the last few weeks. His mind had taken to it, but his whole body had shunned it like ipecac, expelled from his stomach. His whole being could not make peace with it. He wondered if he could. Over time, would his body bend more to his mind's persuasions?

"Look, Mitchum, everybody's done somethin'," Holmes continued. "It's like pastor says, 'Each of us born into sin, not a one of us blameless.'"

He proceeded to rehearse a few more of their pastor's greatest hits. Mitch was surprised he could tease out bits and pieces of so many. Holmes finished his closing arguments with sliding the brochure even closer to Mitchum so that it brushed against his shirt.

"Way I see it, this is your opportunity. A way to balance the scales, do some good to make up for any a those things you're talkin' about."

One of the light bulbs overhead buzzed then flickered on the verge of going out. Looking up into that wavering bulb, Mitchum thought about the other scholarship kids who'd come before him, went on to become real cops. Maybe they'd even sat in that very same seat, hearing this exact same speech. He wished he could talk to one of them. Had it helped balance their scales? Had the good they'd done outweighed their bad? Maybe they had less bad to outweigh?

"How about you take this with you?" Holmes finally proposed as he stood, scooting his chair back in under the table. "We got a couple weeks til we have to turn in our candidate for the county. Last year we didn't even have one. Caswell County always does, an' the captain don't want us bein' shown up again, but I got a good feelin' about you, Mitchum. I do. I think come next week, you'll have some good news for me."

He patted Mitchum's shoulder as the boy rose, tossing his own can over towards the trash bin, missing it altogether. Mitchum hurriedly picked it up, dropped it in the trash, then followed after Holmes. They walked together out to the lobby, the brochure still clasped in Mitchum's hand like a field trip permission slip he was eager to show his mother. Back when she'd have been eager to see anything he had to show her, before his Daddy had destroyed any eagerness she'd managed to hang on to.

"Take that on home, show it to your folks, see what they think of it. Then give me a call or catch me at church Sunday. Alright?" Holmes suggested.

"Yes sir."

And as Mitchum made his way to his car, he knew he could never show it to them, especially not his Daddy. That man who had his heart set on his joining him at the mill like an inmate hoping for a cell block buddy to do time with. No, Mitchum would only tell them once he'd made up his mind. Even then, he might just wait til he walked out of the house in his uniform for the first day of class.

It would be nice to show it to at least one person though...his grandpa. He'd show it to him. The old man couldn't remember much from one hour to the next. This was the small spark that ignited hope in Mitchum as he laid the brochure on the passenger seat of his car. He hoped his grandpa might just tell him it would be a good idea. He hoped he'd tell him it could be the only way to stave off the Armageddon of his very soul.

88°F

Hogue

I lay on the asphalt looking up at the sky. I wonder if those are the same birds flying over that flew over the day Brandon was kicking the shit out of the backseat of Rae's car. Cobb's right. Itn't nothing out here. Itn't any proof. Not a shred of evidence. I stay put, letting the sun push my limits, bake me a bit.

Old dogs like him like to see it that way. Works well for them. They can fill out the paperwork, withstand the wailing and cussing from families of the next of kin and get home in time for dinner. I don't have a home to get to, not really and I'm more of a breakfast guy.

The fact that there itn't proof right off don't mean anything's clear cut to me either. Sometimes I just know things. I know if somebody's off. If this'll be just the first thing they do. Whether or not I'll be reading about them on down the line wishing I'd have had the balls to put them where they belong to begin with whether that would've been in a cell or in the ground. Takes one to catch one and I'm alright with that.

Cobb on the other hand spends his life placating people, soothing his nerves with food, playing the good old boy, church going husband and all. He cain't accept what he is. Learned a long time ago, a wolf trying to be a sheep'll starve himself to death. Knew by the time I was in tenth grade what I was. I'm a wolf. Could be why Cobb's so thrown about this Olsen fella lurking around again. Might just be they were once wolves together, back before Cobb tried to put on his white wool getup.

Even my mama knows what I am. Used it to her advantage more than once. That's all you can really do with a wolf. Cain't love it, hold it to you and pretend it's a pet. You keep it chained, wait til you need a wolf, then you let it loose.

"Get his legs!" she hissed at me that afternoon when I got home from Jolie's.

It was nearly three years after Evette did herself in. I'd turned fifteen just that week before. Daddy'd whooped it up, drank himself silly at a family party. He was a fun drunk that night. Standing in the doorway watching mama drag him across the kitchen floor, knife in his chest, I figured the mean drunk in him had reared its head while I'd been out.

He was heavier than I thought he'd be. Even now, I wonder if in death we're fully who we've always been—our true mass setting in. All that weight everyone around us was carrying, the slack they picked up for us finally coming home to roost. Nobody'll ever find him. Made sure of that. Daddy didn't have much kin to speak of. Only a cousin ever came asking about him. Whatever mama told him sufficed. He never came back. One cousin...says something about a man don't it? When wolves drop off from the pack, they aren't missed. The pack keeps hunting.

The hot parking lot pavement feels like it's about to burn a hole clean through the back of my shirt. I sit up quick. A camera from the corner of the building's pointed right at me. Don't matter. Woman who runs the beauty shop, Judy, said she hadn't had it working since her husband died. He was the only one who knew how to run it.

When I asked her about it right after it all went down with Rae and little Brandon, Judy said after her man was gone, wasn't anybody else left to do her any real harm. She figured why bother with a camera. Guess it never dawned on her that that security itn't so much as for yourself as it is for everybody in the vicinity of your place. Bet she thought Sanford's a town that don't have much happening in the way of crime. She'd be wrong, but that's why cops have jobs—so people can keep being wrong.

I stand real still in that exact parking spot where Rae's car was parked that day. In front of me is the beauty shop. Judy's closed on Mondays. Whole slew of trees and brush to my left, an old vacant warehouse is across the street and an empty mechanic's shop is to my right. Well, it was empty last time I was here but hell, if I don't see a light on. I dust off the back of my pants and walk on over.

The windows are caked with dirt and grime. I rub a patch off the corner of one. Definitely a light coming from inside, not a bulb light neither. More like a flashlight or a fire of some kind. A shadow moves across the wall. Music kicks up.

I hear a door open. I walk over to the left side of the building, crane my head around the corner. A tall, lanky guy props the door open with a rock. His back is to me as he walks out a few feet away from the building then stops. A thin line of piss goes out in front of him between his legs. I ain't totally heartless. I let him finish, zip up before I say anything.

"Got to come all the way out there to drain your hose?" I call. "Plumbin' ain't workin'?"

The guy jumps so high, I cain't help but chuckle.

"Shit! You fuckin' scared me, bro."

Bro. He's one of *them.* Just great. One of those Wonderbread white boy wannabe motherfuckers who came up listening to Tupac, 2 Live Crew or some shit. Goes around calling everybody *bro* now like just by doing it he'll eventually change the pigment of his god damn skin. I look over towards the side door making sure we're alone. Nobody. Appears he's a lone squatter.

"My uh... my brother in law... he uh... he owns this place an—"

"He know you're callin' it home?"

Cain't be too careful with these tweaker types. His teeth. Dead give away. Look tiny and rotten like he's spent a lifetime eating

Halloween candy and never seen a dentist's chair. When somebody's got so little regard for their own body, they shoot it full of who knows what, they sure as shit cain't be expected to have an ounce of regard for anybody else. Just as soon kill you as look at you.

"He uh… well, he likes me to keep an eye on it. Had some break-ins."

He rambles on. I stroll over to the door, peer inside. The smell alone about knocks me backwards. Could take out an army! Ain't no way I'm stepping in. He itn't just squatting. There's a meth kitchen somewhere in there.

"Don't matter to me, son. I don't really give two fucks if you even know the fella who owns this shithole. You could a never laid eyes on him for all I care. I'm not here about you."

Son. One of my go-tos even though he's probably a couple years older than me. Hard to tell. Meth makes everybody look ready for the old age home. You call a grown man *son*, puts them ill at ease. Automatically creates a hierarchy. In this line of work, you don't meet too many men who were ever real happy with the first person who used that term with them. Whole lot of paternal grudges ride in the back of every cruiser.

We stand here, him trying to act like the bowels of hell odor itn't slapping me in the face. I itch my nose not letting him forget some of us haven't lost our sense of smell.

"What is it I can do for you then, officer?"

"See that parkin' lot over there?" I ask pointing to where I'd just come from.

He nods.

"You member 'bout a month ago, a bunch more cops bein' out here, an ambulance, a hearse, a whole lotta carryin' on?" I paint the scene for him.

His boots scrape against the cement as he shifts what little bit of weight he's still got on him. He slides his hands into his greasy pockets.

"Let's both keep our hands front an' center, alright?"

He pulls them right back out.

"Sure. Sure thing, bro," he babbles hands at his sides now like he's already lining up to walk single file to the prison cafeteria. He clasps his hands, then returns them to his sides. Jittery as they come this one.

"I uh, I whatin here for any a that, but I did get home, I mean here, in time to see a tow truck towin' the car. Driver an' me got to shootin' the shit. He said a kid died or somethin'. He was towin' the car over to y'alls station."

Shootin' the shit. Bet that wasn't all they were shooting.

"But you weren't around when it happened?"

He shakes his head.

I put a hand up to my chin, rub it a bit, and look at the spot where Brandon breathed his last.

"You got a suit?" I ask, still staring out at that pavement.

"A suit?" he says.

Ain't too quick on the take this tweak freak.

"Yeah, you know like somethin' you wear on holidays or when your girlfriend drags you to church with her family, or at least the girlfriend you had. Cain't see a man pullin' much in the way of tail with this bein' home base."

For some reason that's totally lost on me, he smiles. Guess he's happy he's got an answer to this one.

"I got one I keep at my brother's storage. He holds on to a few things for me there, but I ain't sure he's paid the fees," he answers, face falling. "Might be hard to get it out."

"Aww, I'll bring you one," I say, turning back, staring him down. "You'll get cleaned up, look like you come from the land a the livin'."

"For what?"

"Court."

"Hell, you hadn't even arrested me yet," he shouts puffing out his chest like a rooster readying for a fight.

I get the feeling it's not the fights he's seen coming that've put him where he is.

"I'm not arrestin' you," I explain. "You're gonna testify."

"Testify?"

"Lord, son. I'm beginnin' to feel like there's an echo out here," I jab. "Yes! Tes-ti-fy."

"An' what is it I'm testifyin' about?"

I open the door a little wider, peering in a bit further, only peering. God damn that smell! There it is to the right. A long plywood counter with beakers and containers—a mad scientist meth head's wet dream.

"Well, I'd say you're testifyin' about anything I want, wouldn't you?"

40°F

Cobb

When the call came, it was one of those summer nights we didn't even pull the sheets up over us. Our air conditioner barely kept it much cooler than 80 degrees. Stacy always liked it hotter since she was just a little bit of a thing. The phone stirred her even though I'd picked it up on the third ring.

I tried to do more listening than talking as the captain detailed chaos that had gone on. To hear him tell it, Hogue's house was burnt to the ground. Three vehicles were out front: Hogue's, and running plates had revealed the Charger belonged to Bobby Olsen and the Honda Civic was Hogue's ex-wife Jolie's. The fire was still cooling after the fire department put it out. They were pretty sure they had at least two bodies in the ashes. More action that Lee County had seen in months.

"I shouldn't have ever taken him on," the captain berated himself. "If I hadn't owed Dewitt for takin' on Harris, I wouldn't have. That's for damn sure."

His breathing was labored. I wasn't sure what he wanted me to say, or what I could say that would ensure I still had a desk in the morning.

Harris. It'd been a while since I'd thought about him. He'd gone off at one of the protests over the Robert E. Lee memorial out back of the courthouse. A losing battle that one. Our county was named for Lee after all, but we tried to keep the protests civil. *Let em have their say*, our captain was always reminded. *Most people just want a say.* Harris wasn't having it. Pepper sprayed one of the Black choir members from over at the First Presbyterian.

We didn't see Harris again after that. Til that night's call, I wasn't sure what'd happened. Apparently, DeWitt, the captain over in Johnston had taken him on to keep things quiet. Should've known we got Hogue on a favor. Our captain was a moral enough fella, but he wasn't what I'd call benevolent.

"What the hell'd Bobby Olsen be doin' all the way out here? They know each other?" The captain finally broke up the quiet.

I knew exactly what Bobby was doing. He was putting the pressure on for Rae's sake. He was taking care of his own. Our talk hadn't had his intended outcome, so he'd turned up the heat on a different burner.

"Strange," I replied. "Last I knew Bobby stays up in Raleigh."

"Well, from the looks of it, he was in Sanford last night. Cain't be sure who the bodies are exactly yet. One's got to be the ex-wife, but the verdict's still out on the other. Don't know if we're lookin' for Hogue or Olsen. Too burnt up. Right now, I just went on an' put out an A.P.B. on 'em both."

As Stacy rolled over, I held the phone closer to my ear. It crossed my mind whoever the second body was, whether it was Bobby or Cy, it'd mean a whole lot of trouble for me.

"You sure his ex is one of 'em? Just cause it's her car doesn't mean it's her. I'll tell you, I went to one a his hearin's, sat in the back an' the victim's family was chompin' at the bit to see him get his. One a them could a borrowed Jolie's car. Boyfriend's brother hadn't been paroled but a few weeks."

It was just enough chum to toss in the water for the sharks on duty. Leigh's family. It was obvious. I could tell the captain felt foolish he hadn't thought of it.

"True enough," the captain said.

"You need me to come out there?"

"Naw, now you stay put. I got Hendricks settin' tight over at Rae an' Miss Florrie's in case Olsen's the one on the run. If it's Hogue, no tellin' where he's headed. He's in the wind for now."

We hung up. I sat there on the edge of the bed watching Stacy sleep. Her face never seemed to age. No matter how old she ever got, her face had an angelic innocence. It was a reason men loved her and women hated her. Just looking at her made my heart swell up with ample portions of pride, and fear. Pride she was mine. Fear she wouldn't always be.

That night though, I was more fearful of all the things Stacy didn't know. About how well I'd known Kelly, why I could never help talk her into closing the case like her Daddy wanted, all I'd done on the job and off it.

I sat on the edge of our bed paralyzed, waiting up for one or the other to show. I knew either way, no matter which body the second one was, it was a certainty I was getting a visitation. Sometimes, you get yourself in such a spot that's all you can do. You wait for the devil and pray you can handle him when he comes.

The longer I waited, the more I knew I should've taken care of things myself. That's exactly what Bobby had gone to do. I'd been here at home. It had been the coward's way to hope it all would get washed clean on its own.

It wasn't an hour til the next-door neighbor Gene's dog, Sally, sounded off. I listened for a car to pull up or a car door to shut, then recalled the captain had said the cars were all there so they had to be on foot. The dog quieted for a few seconds then started up again. From where her barking was coming from, I knew I needed to check out back.

I stood up, smoothed the bed spread on my side, holstered up, securing my glock in its place, pulling my shirt over it the best I could. I stepped careful over the creaky boards in our bedroom. Stopping in the doorway, I took what I thought could very well be my last look at my Stac.

Making my way down the hall, the streetlight next to the house caught my eyes as it beamed through the window of what was still a guest room, lighting the way. I peered to my right into the room at the empty crib all pearly white, and unused.

"It's somethin' called law of attraction, Mitchum," Stacy'd informed me the day I came home to her putting it together. "By bringin' in a tangible thing, you call to you what you want. Your actions an' words, all of it, call it to you, so I'm not going to keep saying *if* we're parents. I'm going to say *when* we're parents. We're gonna be like magnets to metal."

I didn't comment much at the time. Sounded nice enough. I assumed it was probably her cousin Lila's doing. She was always filling Stacy's head with all that newfangled New Age nonsense like channeling your thoughts and such. Things I never gave much credence to.

Law of attraction, calling things to you... If there was something to it, I didn't have the heart to tell Stacy we were already as good as doomed. I'd called enough darkness out of the woodwork to leak over onto the both of us. That's the thing about all those bad deeds, even the ones we can't quite recall, they spread over anything and anyone you touch. Staring in at that crib, I knew I'd even called that to us—a lonesome baby's crib.

A commotion out back by the window broke me out of my stupor. Soda can bin. It was the sound of the cans scattering over the sidewalk. They'd tripped over it. I'd done that more times than I could count. Time and again, I'd told Stacy I'd bring home a better one, but I hadn't yet. She'd asked me repeatedly, but it went undone.

Our back door latch was always getting stuck. I tried to press against the door as I turned it so me opening it wouldn't wake Stacy if the cans and Sally barking hadn't already. I took a deep breath. I didn't know which one of them I was praying harder to see—Bobby or Cy.

When I finally got it open, there he was, sitting on the bottom step up of our porch, cans scattered at his feet. He was making no effort to clean up his mess. From the look of him, it seemed it was all he could do to be sitting upright.

In the moonlight, I could see the blood all over his shirt. And I don't know why, but the manila folder with his name on the tab, the one the captain handed me a day or so before he actually showed up flashed in my head.

Cyrus D. Hogue...

I'd held that folder and even then, felt I was holding trouble. There trouble sat, bloodying up my porch steps. Sally kept on and on causing Gene to come out onto his back porch to see what had her spooked.

With the height of our gate and from where he stood, all Gene could see was me from the shoulders up.

"Y'all alright over there, Mitchum?" he asked soon as he saw me. "Hush, now Sally girl. Hush," he scolded the dog.

"Sorry, Gene. Just takin' out the trash. Knocked over these soda cans. Stacy's been on me to get a heavier recyclin' bin. I'll get around to it one a these days."

"That's a'right, Mitchum. Sally's a nervous wreck. Only gets it right about fifty percent a the time." He called over opening the back door for Sally, standing looking out at his yard for a minute. "Damn humidity won't let up, will it?"

"It's been a scorcher."

"Used to be you could at least count on the nights to get a little cooler. Not anymore," he went on. "Come on, Sally. G't inside. Night, Mitchum."

Sally yelped and the sound of her claws scurrying off the deck, let me know she wouldn't be back out. I waited for him to shut the door before I walked closer to the steps. I could see then not just his shirt was covered but also his hands and his face were spattered with red, like he was one of those paintings Mr. Pierce showed us slides of in art appreciation junior year. Abstract ones that're supposed to make you think of something but aren't really anything recognizable.

He looked up at me. The whites of his eyes a starker white with being surrounded by all that red. His sweat and the blood melded into lines all meeting at his chin then dripping down to his shirt.

"I'm bettin' they called you," he whimpered.

His eyes told me. He knew they had. He also knew I couldn't be on his side and there were always sides. Anybody lives long enough, they've got that down.

"Come on," I told him. "You cain't stay out here."

He stood slowly, looking out into the yard then back at the open door behind me, neither option a more comforting one. I felt sorry for him. I knew it was only just hitting him right then that that's all life is—choosing the least bad choice.

As I closed the door behind us, I thought about his manila folder, how the contents of any folder can't tell you anything. Records, typed words, all of it, just a way people use to try to make sense of each other. You can never truly make sense of any human being.

I was reminded that night in my house, what with him standing there, blood soaked on Stacy's good rug, that on that day with that folder, I'd had a strange and horrible premonition. I had it and dismissed it like I'd done most honest feelings in my life. I'd stood there outside the captain's office, folder in hand and I'd understood in that moment that I wasn't holding a folder at all. No, in my hands, on those papers lay the sledgehammer I'd attracted, and it would bust up everything I held dear.

83°F

A pale, yellow stain trailing across the worn comforter caught her eye as she sat biding time on the end of the bed. She didn't want to think about what it was on the bedspread, or who had been there before her that caused it. Her last summer of high school, she'd spent her days cleaning motel rooms at the Motel 6 off Highway 1. If the motel she was sitting in was anything like that one, the bedspreads were rarely cleaned. The expense of washing bedspreads was not in the budget.

"They'll lose color the more you wash 'em," the manager had told her when she'd questioned why they didn't clean them after every guest checked out.

It was then that she purposed when she grew up, she'd visit fine places with duvet covers and high thread count sheets that were washed regularly. The fact that she kept having to meet him at places like this was a signal to her that either she had not grown up yet, or she had lied to herself, maybe both.

She finished one cigarette and lit another. He was late, but late was on time for him. Other people's standards did not apply where he was concerned. No, he hadn't had to have any standards whatsoever in regards to when to be somewhere or how to act once you got there. This was a quality she admired. She herself had been so constrained, bound by schedules and opinions of others.

Her whole life, she'd been surrounded by drones, weak men who punched clocks. Ones who ruled over kingdoms of worn-out recliners, cheap beer and bad television when they weren't punching those clocks. This wasn't his M.O. Yes, she liked this about him, til it bit her.

"That bitch gets nosier an' nosier," he blasted announcing his arrival, letting the flimsy door slam behind him.

"Kim? Oh, she don't mean nothin' by it," Rae defended the front desk girl. "She's just bored."

"*Doesn't*. She *doesn't* mean *anything* by it," he corrected.

She took a puff from her cigarette, letting his condescension slide. She chalked it up to the price a southern girl pays just for being born, especially a Black southern girl in Lee County.

He collapsed beside her on the bed.

"What's so urgent you couldn't wait til Friday?" he demanded. "You need a *fix?*"

Taking her hand, he put it on the crotch of his jeans, scooting over closer to her. Leaning in, she felt his lips start his customary neck nibbling. He liked to joke that she was his tasty little riblet. That's indeed how his kisses felt, as if he was savoring a barbecued rib. She craned her neck further from him.

"I ain't here for that, Bobby," she told him.

He paid no her no mind. She scrambled out of his reach accidentally dropping her cigarette on the shabby carpeting. He saw it hit, and immediately stomped it out.

"God damn, Rae! I don't wanna be havin' to buy any two-bit motel."

"We gotta talk!" she scolded, pulling out another cigarette from her purse then lighting it.

Collapsing back on the bed, he sighed loudly. The popcorn ceiling was peppered with stains of its own from a leaky roof. He didn't mind it. Over the years these filthy places had become respites for him from his mother's high society country club crowd and elitist church going friends.

He'd never felt comfortable on his side of town. Even in high school, he and his pal Mitchum had driven to the beach to cruise seedy bars. No one carded them. He came to love those places. Where age and laws didn't matter. All that mattered was if you could pay and he always could.

Propping up on his elbows, he watched Rae pace. Her brown skin looked even darker juxtaposed against the backdrop of her smoke, and he wasn't sure how that struck him. He just knew that it did.

She hated this place. She'd told him many times. It had never stopped her from meeting him, however. He knew she wanted to please him. What she didn't understand was that while she was hoping he'd be her ticket out, he was using her as his ticket in. Into a kind of life, a part of town that he'd never fully embrace. She was a recreational indulgence more than future wife material. This information would always elude her and this contented him.

He patted the covers next to him as if she was his lap dog.

"Damn it, don't you hear me, Bobby. I need to talk to you!" Rae said.

"Awe, what's so important we can't wait til after?"

She quit pacing, tapping the ashes from the end of her cigarette into an ash tray on the table.

"They ain't closin' the case."

"What?"

"Just what I said. Turned it over to the D.A. yesterday. Mama got us an appointment with a lawyer this mornin'. Some fella goes to our church. He already had all the evidence they got on me sent over to his office."

He sat up fully, edging up to the end of the bed.

"What's he got?"

She stood leaning against the counter of the small kitchenette across from him. Crossing one ankle over the other, she took a drag, blowing the smoke in the opposite direction. He hated smoke, what with being a health fanatic. He rebuked her regularly for the habit. Uncrossing her ankles, standing up away from the counter, she faced him in a more stern stance.

"He says they got a witness."

"A witness? Who would they've gotten that could've seen a damn thing? Thought you said the shop owner was inside, that it was just you out in the parkin' lot."

A hickish accent took over when he became angry. His redneck alter ego, she called it. Never to his face. Just to her friends.

"We cain't know who. We only get to know that they got one."

Leaning up, he rests his elbows on his knees, rubbing his temples with his hands.

"What else? What else they got, cause I've been around long enough to know one lousy witness itn't gonna cut it with the D.A."

Smoke trailed behind her as she crossed the room, looking out the window. She slid the curtain slightly to the right to see the parking lot better. Was he watching? Her cop hell bent on justice? If she stayed out of prison, was the rest of her life to be lived with glances over her shoulder? Could she live that way?

"What would anybody've seen? Huh? You g'ttin' out a your car goin' into the beauty shop?"

She wished she hadn't come, that she'd never called him, that they'd never even met. This wish caught in her throat causing her to cough. Hacking, leaning down, bracing herself on the back of the chair, she knew the fact that she hadn't wished this til this moment exposed her for the debauched soul she was.

His eyes were on her. He did not ask if she was alright or move from his spot to check on her. There was just the feeling of his glare, him staring a hole through her in the same way her son had done many times. A look of sheer all-consuming irritation.

"I mean if they heard him screamin', it'd say more about them that they didn't try to help, wouldn't it?"

Her throat clear, her cough subsiding, she stood up, back still to him.

"I held the door," she whispered.

"What?"

"I didn't know he could reach the handle. I-I had to hold it shut."

An invasive clicking alerted them a patron was opening the door to the room next to theirs. The walls so thin, they heard the steps that followed as the person entered. It was a welcome interruption. She didn't dare turn to face him to see what he thought of her ignorance. The holding of Brandon's door had been a most moronic deviation.

His arms slid in around her waist as he moved up behind her. Though she knew it was his preferred way of holding her, an observer may have deduced that she was trapped.

"They might've seen me holdin' it an' heard him in there. He was kickin'. Kicked so hard, an' screamed. Screamin' in there for all he was worth."

Ashes from her cigarette dropped onto her arm. She let them. She did not even flinch. It was the least she could do in the way of penance. Her recognition of such things was evidence that though she'd left the religion of her youth, it had never fully left her. There was always a part of her who felt God was watching and that when the time came, he'd also dole out the rewards or punishments.

That's how it was coming up in the fixed faith of the south—a knowing without any bearing. No bearing at all on how life was lived. Sins still committed. His blood then needed to wash them away. Debts owed. Praying mother's knees worn and calloused.

"You saw it happen?" Bobby asked.

"No! God No! Only til he let go of the door," she quickly answered, then went quiet, stifling sobs.

His arms slid in further, tightening their hold on her. He laid his head on her back at the base of her neck. He could hear the faint thump of her heart, feel the hard top of her backbone against his warm cheek.

"Don't worry. It's gonna get ruled an accident. Witness or not, you'll have 'em eatin' out of your hand," he soothed. "Just like you did me."

Her shoulders dropped. She leaned back, body nearly limp

against him. A sickly rabbit giving way in a wolf's mouth, resigning, and releasing. She let his arms keep her upright.

"Sometimes, when I wake up, he's still screamin'..."

"Shhhhh. Shhhh, now," he whispered. "Don't let that in."

Her chest heaved in and out as she sobbed. He didn't understand. As he held her tighter, a fear coiled inside her; a copperhead in its dark den. A fear that there was no letting it in. It was already there, inside and she was left only with the dread that she'd never get it out.

95°F

Hogue

I stand still. All froze up right here in the aisle of the Quik Mart, using the cooler door glass to stare at the couple behind me. They cain't be out of high school yet. So perfect looking they don't seem real. It's like they stepped out of one of those commercials for first day of school clothes you see around the end of August. She's got her arms up around his neck, kissing him while he's trying to pay. He's laughing and hugging her to him with one arm, paying with his free hand, then they head out to their car.

Jolie never loved me like that. Cain't say as I can blame her. I never loved her like that. Nothing personal. I've never loved anybody. I look out the window to see the couple make out a little in their front seat before they pull off. I've never wanted to be somebody as bad as I want to be that school clothes commercial boy right now.

That Black ass fry cook got all Jolie's love. Yeah, I saw them the night before I took him down. They were out back of the Waffle House between the back door and the dumpsters. Jolie's arms around his waist, his around her waist. They were slow dancing. Both of them in their greasy work clothes, not a care in the world. From where I stood behind the trees across the street, I could hear that Aerosmith song *Angel* playing. Didn't think that'd be the kind of music he'd play for her.

Her smile was all big and bright. She was laughing at something he was saying, burying her head in his chest. I knew right then I'd lost her. More than that, I knew I'd never really had her. That's all I ever wanted—for her to stay mine. Whatever had joined the two of us was nothing like what I was seeing that night and I hated his guts. Guess that was the last thing Jolie gave me—a direction to drive my hate.

Minute I leave the Quik Mart, six pack in hand, I'm well aware I shouldn't be anywhere but in my house today. I know it, but this heat and having no air conditioning yet is pushing me to have bad judgement. Today's the day—the day that fry cook either breathes when they unhook him or he don't. I'm testing fate to even step off my property.

All things considered, I've been good. Hadn't been on any of my phone apps, no matter how bad I've wanted to. Tracked Jolie a long time that way. You can still stay up on your ex as good as talking to them if you got a smart phone. Worked for me that there really itn't any stalking anymore. These days it's called *staying connected*. You're only called a stalker if you go and do some loopy shit that gets you on the news. It don't work for me that beating up your ex's boyfriend qualifies as loopy. Now I've got no way to keep tabs on her. Flip phones are of no use for that.

Thought ahead and got my Mama's cousin to put my new house in her name. I've done everything so I cain't be found til I have to show my face for the final hearing to get the judge's word on if we'll go to trial. Well, everything, I guess, but kept clear of Jolie. I'd thought she'd be at work the night of my little hospital drop by so technically that's on her.

Tried reading up a little about fry cook's chances. There aren't a lot of stats on who survives and who doesn't after they get unplugged. Seems like the man people think they're talking to upstairs is in charge of that. Never can get my mind around how the deeds are down here, but when it comes to the outcome, they push it all off on him. Setting God up to get a bad rap.

Soon as I round the curve in my driveway, I see it—his Charger. Parked out here plain as day. My front door's wide open. Gotta admire the balls on this fella. He cain't know today's not the day, but maybe, just maybe, today is the day. Maybe today he starts getting back some of the shit he's been dishing out. I'm more than happy to serve it to him.

I pull up behind him. With deep ditches on either side of my driveway, he'll have to leave when I get good and ready for him to. I get out, toting my six pack up the front steps like I'm headed to a college frat party. Only ever went to a couple of those with a girl I was seeing up at N.C. State. They were partial to pony kegs but any alcohol would do. Strikes me funny, I have a frat boy inside minus the party. Not the kind he came for anyway. Door's already open. I step in, being sure to leave it that way.

"I was hopin somebody'd bring booze," Bobby booms. "Hot as all get out in here."

He's setting up to my cardboard dining table like this is his house. He's leaned back on two legs of one of the old wooden chairs that were left here when I moved in, holding a can of my soda in his hand. Yeah, he's doing all he can do to show me he's been here long enough to get real comfortable. In his fucked-up head, he's king of the whole god damn world. I understand this line of thinking. By the time he leaves, he'll see he's trying to fill a position that's already been spoken for. I got no plans to give up the throne.

He'll have to make peace with it, or we'll have us a problem on our hands. Might have to tell him, as of today, the I.C.U.'s got an open bed over at the hospital. Wouldn't be any trouble making sure he gets it.

I pull up the chair across from him, tear a beer off its six-pack ring then slide it to him.

"Coors?" he sneers.

"Didn't know I'd be havin' company."

"It'll work."

We both pop ours open, keeping our eyes on each other over the tops of the cans as we gulp. Cain't make out if he's carrying. I assume a fella like him always is.

"You like it all the way out here?" is his first ask once he sets his Coors down.

"Wouldn't a bought it if I didn't."

"Bought it? Oh, see, now here I thought you might just be hidin' out," he says with a grin starting across his lips. I want to punch it clean off.

I take another swig. He leans up, his chair landing so all four legs meet the linoleum.

"You probly thought this is a place where all those people from over there in Johnston who're itchin' to find you wouldn't think to look."

I stare at him, sloshing my beer around in its can.

"Aww, don't mind me," he chuckles, shaking his head. "I'm not here about all that. We all got our skeletons. Some of us've just been able to keep 'em in the closet longer than others. I gotta say though, man, you picked a hell of a time to beat a Black guy senseless. I mean in the history a bein' a cop, this is about the worst time you could've gone all Rodney King on a dude."

Leaning my chair back, I don't divert my eyes. I keep my lips in a flat line. Don't let on that he's shaking me one fucking bit, cause he's not.

"So you went an' got Dell Whitford to come out of his meth haze an' go on down to the station, huh? Gotta hand it to you, man. Didn't know Dell could even formulate a full sentence these days nevertheless be a witness," he says.

I take a long last swig, then crunch my can down on the table as loud as I can.

"Oh, Dell cleans up real good. You'll see."

This really tickles him. He full on laughs.

"His rap sheet's as long as a football field. No way anybody'll give two shits what he's got to say, if he even stays clean long enough to make it to the stand."

I lean forward, all four of my chair legs hitting the floor.

"You're bankin' Dell's the only one who came forward."

His grin flattens out. Whatever intel he's gotten, it didn't include anything about more than one witness. All I have to do is look convincing enough to rattle him with it. The bluff'll do its job all on its own.

He looks past me out the open door at his Charger. He's deciding his next move. Maybe he's more of a meathead than I'm giving him credit for being and he's just thinking how much he loves that shiny thing. Could be the humidity's going to his head. Sure working its wiles on mine. His gaze falls back to me.

"Way I see it, you buyin' this house, pushin' on the case, doesn't seem like you're a man eager to go back where he came from. Maybe you think makin' some case on Rae'll help wipe your slate, secure you a permanent position on Lee County's force, an' you can be a brand new man over here. Could be you're just wantin' a new place to stay the same old one you've always been."

I lean back my chair again, stretch out my arms, lift my hands up behind my head, cradling it. I'm relaxed as they come.

"Not that it's really your business but since you're interested in my real estate dealin's, this house was just too good a steal to pass up, an' everybody's been so nice an' welcomin' here. Who wouldn't want to stay?"

"I hear ya."

He reaches for the beers and tears another one off the six-pack ring. He doesn't open it yet, just sets it in front or him, moves the can around in his hands a bit. Bet he won't even drink it. Just doing it to show he takes what he wants.

"What if you could solve a case a whole lot bigger than Rae's?"

We look each other in the face—him wondering what my answer will be, me wondering where the hell this is going. I put all the feet of my chair on the floor again, scoot up and rest my elbows on the table. I clasp my hands together like I'm a little boy ready for a Sunday School lesson and he's the deacon ready to give it.

"I got to thinkin' it might help your plight even more to find the body of a missin' Black girl, close a cold case, than it will to go pinnin' the *accidental* death of a little Black boy on his mama right about now."

I rub my hands together. God damn. I hate it that he's right.

"Did Mitchum ever tell you about his wife's sister?"

"We mainly stick to the job."

"Oh, I'm sure you do," he laughs. "I'm sure between the two a you, if you ever got to talkin' much in the way a personal history, you'd be about neck an' neck as far as past sins go."

"Past sins? Sounds like you've been thumped by more than a few Bibles. Fuck it, I don't go in for all that religious bullshit."

He scoots his chair back, stands up. I slip one hand down in my lap and the other on my holstered glock. I never leave home without it, even on my days off. He puts his hands up to show he's not doing anything shady. Not yet.

"Easy. Just gettin' some water," he says, walking over to my sink.

Turning on the faucet, he sticks his head under, drinking from it like he's at a water fountain. I could offer him a glass, but it ain't that kind of visit. When he's done, he turns, leans on the counter, crossing his arms, being sure to flex his biceps.

"Mitchum's wife, Stacy, had a sister bout ten years older than her named Kelly. Their cousin Anita went to school with us through most a high school. Now, we didn't know Kelly too well. She only went to our school a few months at the end a senior year, but we knew Anita. Yeah, we *knew* her," he reminisces, a strange smirk creeping up on his face.

His cheeks are beet red. Could be the temperature, could be shame. I get the idea though that this fella and shame ain't never been introduced. Hadn't ever met it myself to know what it would look like. He reaches a hand up, massaging his jaw, snickering a little. God knows! He's one crazy fucker.

I scoot my chair back readying to stand.

"Ever occur to you I might not want to spend my day off listenin' to you goin' on about you an' Cobb's glory days?"

"Aww, come on now. I think you'll want to stick this one out.

See, Kelly went missin' right before graduation. Every Black person in town was out lookin' for that girl. Never was found."

Moving away from the counter, he walks over closer to the table again, leans down closer, puts both hands on it.

"Not many people know, but me an' Mitchum were the last ones to see Kelly. Cops came to our house couple days after it happened, talked to us. Me an' Cobb stuck to the same story—that she got mad when were out there messin' around at the old hospital, out at Ducet. Said she told us she was walkin' to the gas station to call some boy she knew to come pick her up an' then she stomped off. Told 'em both of us were too drunk to go after her, that we'd slept if off out there an' by mornin' there was no sign of her. Both of us've stood by that account."

"I'm guessin', what with your proposition, that whatin exactly the truth."

He stands up straight, puffs out his chest. This must be the stance he gets in at the gym when he's readying to pick up a big ass barbell. Something tells me, the truth's heavier than any of that weight he's been lifting there.

"I'll show you where her remains are, an' you'll lay off Rae. That's the deal I'm offerin'."

I'm the one shaking my head now, chuckling to myself.

"An' who am I gonna say told me where to find her?"

"Cobb. You're gonna say Cobb felt guilty, confessed to you one night about killin' Kelly then told you where he hid her. You'll say you just didn't feel right keepin' that secret. You agree to say that an' I'll take you out there to the body."

"And did he?"

"Did he what?"

"Did he kill her?"

A car door slams. Both of us whip our heads in the direction of the door. My hand instantly falls again to the grip of my glock. I hop up and head to see who it is.

"Cy!" A voice squalls. "Cy, you motherfuckerin' bastard!"

Jolie's car's parked behind mine. I spot it before I do her where she's bent down, digging in her backseat. She raises up holding her grandaddy's shotgun. As she storms through my yard up the walk to the steps, I cain't help but think about how I've never wanted to fuck her more than I do right now. Her skinny arms holding that gun, the fury she's wearing. So god damn beautiful!

The closer she gets to the edge of my porch, it's clear from her tear-streaked cheeks that she's been crying. The unplugging of her fry cook must a went south. Here I thought, if that was the outcome, she'd send Demete or another of his family. Got to hand it to her, nothing like a woman who does her own dirty work.

She stops at the bottom of the porch, raises the shotgun, aiming it right at me. A breeze comes out of nowhere, tousling her hair like she's starring in some low budget action movie. Damn if she don't have the upperhand. I close my eyes without saying a word, taking my right hand off my glock. I let both hands drop to my sides. Sometimes you just gotta take what's been coming whether you think you deserve it or not.

A shot fires. Don't seem loud enough for it to have come from her shotgun. My hands clutch my chest out of instinct. I feel all over my pecs, my gut, my sides. Nothing! Jolie's shrieking. I look up to see her writhing on the ground, holding her shoulder, gun lying next to her.

"God damn, you got enemies comin' an' goin', man," Olsen says.

He's standing to my left, arm still half raised, gripping a 9mm Luger in his right hand. I go for my glock but stop short of shooting him. For once, I gotta think this through. It's about more than just me. Jolie stands to catch some heat. I take the butt of my gun to his head knocking him down in one fell swoop. He slides down a few steps til his head's touching the bottom one and his shoes are still touching the top step.

I run over to Jolie, crouching next to her. From what I can tell, it's a clean shoulder wound. Bullet went right through. She'll live, maybe a surgery to sew up anything severed inside. Other than that, she's real fucking lucky. She's steady slapping at me with her arm that itn't shot up.

"I'm tryin' to help you, Jo!"

"You ain't never helped nobody!"

"Be still. Damn it! I'm g'ttin' you up."

"Call the ambulance an' leave me here!"

I let go of her, take my flip phone out ready to call, but catch sight of Olsen there on the steps. If the ambulance comes, I'm not sure what kind of tale I'll weave to explain him being here, and I cain't have him leaving. I need him to tell me all about Cobb. I pocket my phone again.

"Let's get you inside," I say as soothing as I can. "You don't want 'em pullin' up seein' you out here with this shotgun an' him lyin' there, do you?"

The pain is too much for her to keep fighting me. I ease an arm under her back, then the other arm under her legs. She slumps against my chest, settling in, whimpering away as I walk us up the stairs.

Never carried her across any other threshold. We got married at Myrtle Beach on a weekend cause we both had to work the Monday after. Only threshold there would've been was to our room at the Emerald Shores Motel. Just wasn't a call for it, but here we are now. She feels so light and tiny in my arms. We step over the threshold of my house into the kitchen. It feels right. This could be our house. It could.

Pulling the chair Olsen had been in out further, I set her down in it then grab a couple kitchen towels and some zip ties from the kitchen drawer. You can hold anything together with zip ties, even a shot up ex-wife. I stuff a towel into her wound. She wails something awful. I wrap another around her arm, string two ties together then zip them tight to stop the bleeding. Half out of it, she looks down at me tending to her wound, just shaking her head.

"God knows, Cy. You always got those handy." She laughs through her tears. "World'll be fallin' to pieces an' you'll whip out zip ties to fix it."

Her laughing makes her cough. She grips her shoulder moaning.

"Ssshhhh." I do my best to keep her calm.

Hadn't really hit her yet what all's happening. She came here to end me and here I am saving her ass. That restraining order'll be null and void come tomorrow, I'm guessing. All these last few months, everything that's led up to this, it'll be what binds us now.

Cain't be sure yet. Got to figure out which way the wind's blowing. The soles of Bobby's feet out on that top step catch my eye. From the look of the soles on them, looks like he's wearing brand new Nikes. Wonder if he's my size?

"Did you call 'em?" Jolie reminds. "You call the ambulance?"

I pull the other chair closer to her and sit across from her.

"I will. I just... see...I gotta take him to show me somethin'. Won't take long. I gotta take him. Soon as I get back I'll—"

"No fuckin' way Cy! Call 'em now!" she screeches.

She takes a breath, confusion washing over her. The pain's taking her over. I take full advantage and quick as lightening zip tie her hands behind her right to the slats of the back of the chair. Can't take any chances. Her eyes get big.

"Hey! What the fuck, Cy?"

My hands fit over her kneecaps just like they used to. I gently rub.

"Now, Jo, I promise you, once I take care of what it is he an' I had goin' 'fore you showed up, I'll make the call. Bullet went clean through. Those towels'll hold for a good while. I just need you to hang tight."

"Unzip me! Give me your fuckin' phone! I'll call 'em!" she orders, kicking at me.

I barely touch her bad shoulder and she slumps down in the chair, but still keeps her legs going for me. It's clear it itn't gonna be peaceable. In a flash, I get her in a hold, zipping her ankles to the chair legs. She's squalling all the while. I just tune her out.

"I cain't Jolie. I cain't. Now you don't see, but I'm tryin' to help us. That fella out there, he knows somethin' that can clear me, help me stay outta jail an' keep my badge. I have to see it through," I lay it out plain. "Have to."

Olsen's groaning now. Any minute he'll be sitting up. I hurry over to the door. His head's barely moving.

"You got that wrong, Cy!"

I turn back to Jolie. With her sitting all bloody hogtied to that old wooden chair in this big old house, she looks like something out of one of those Saw movies. Did a decent job on the tying. Hogtying a person's no different than doing it to an animal, except the animal can't mouth off while it's happening.

"What?"

"Help *us*. There never was an *us*. There's always *you*. You, Cy, an' only who's of any damn use to you. Don't you get that? Why do you think I finally used the address your partner gave me to come out here, an' kill your ass. There's fuckin' no such thing as *us*!"

I'll be damned. Cobb went and gave her my address? Didn't really think he had it in him. My mind won't take this in. It's pain talking. She's wrong. There's never not been an *us*. We've been destined since we popped out of the womb. No matter what's gone on, we've always ended up together. She knows it.

I look down at Olsen. His foot's twitching.

"Be right back," I tell her.

"Cy! Don't you fuckin' leave me here, Cy! Call the ambulance! You call 'em!"

Standing at the top of the steps, surveying the scene, I see the shotgun not far from Olsen's head, laying in the grass, it all just comes together. It usually does. I know what has to happen. Cain't take him out there looking for a body. Naw, we don't live in a world where that'll work. He'd run off in a minute, or he'd be trying to add my carcass to the pile.

"Call 'em!" Jolie's still carrying on in the background.

Her restraining order'll hold. From what's gone on here today, I can see she's got no interest in keeping me out of jail, letting me have my badge or even seeing me live. This won't ever be our house. Hell, no reason it should be anybody's house.

I turn Olsen on his side then step over him and walk down in the yard. Should've thought of it before. From what I know of Cobb, I can tell him Olsen snitched, then he'll roll over and take me to the body himself. This motherfucker just became unnecessary.

"What the fuck, man?" Olsen murmurs trying his best to sit up. Picking up the shotgun, I position myself right in the same spot Jolie'd been in. I cock it. The sound of it reaches her inside She goes quiet. A downright spooky silence surrounds me. Olsen sits up enough to face me, scrambles and pushes his back up against the stair railing.

He don't say a word. He knows the deal. I pull the trigger. The kickback sends pain through my shoulder. Been a long time since I used one of these. Wouldn't surprise me if I missed and blew off a piece of the porch instead.

Lowering the gun, I see I'm just as good a shot with it as I am my glock. His head's cracked clean through like a rotten Halloween pumpkin. His body's draped over the stairs. I step forward. Hadn't ever seen the inside of a man's head. My stomach don't lurch. Not even once. I hook my arms under his arm pits and hoist him up.

Jolie's whimpering starts up the minute she gets a look of what's left of Olsen. Her face all confused, white as paper just like it was the night her Black ass fry cook got what he deserved. I can still see her out there under that streetlight scared shitless as the E.M.S. fellas loaded her man in the ambulance. Saw it all from the back of the cruiser. Nobody handcuffed me, but they made me get in the on-duty officer's car, just to be sure to look like the law was doing due diligence.

I drop Olsen at her feet, pull the shotgun out from where I'd tucked it in the waist of my pants so I didn't have to make an extra trip. I lay it on the counter. Blood's covering my arms. I'm relieved it's not mine. Hadn't ever seen much of my own.

"Oh God! Cy, what... what did you do?"

She leans forward what little she can what with being tied, pressing on what's left of Olsen's neck with the toe of her shoe like it'll stop some of the bleeding. I'm reminded she's not the sharpest tool in any shed. Always needed to go to tutoring back in high school. Sitting straight up, she looks at me like she's begging. I don't

bat an eye. She gets the message and slumps in the chair, starts
bawling, and whispering to herself. This is what she does when she's
overwhelmed. Don't take much to get her that way. Many a nights
at our place, she'd cry herself to sleep doing nearly this very same
thing.

I walk over, reach down and rub her back, same way I would if I
was trying to burp a fussy baby.

"Awww, now nobody's gonna miss this one," I assure her. "Hell,
him bein' gone probly saves at least five bitches in the long run."

I nudge Olsen with my right foot. His body slides over further
onto Jolie's feet. I cain't help but laugh at how quick she jolts,
pushing her own chair back so fast she lands, flailing like a turned
over turtle just to get away from it. She rolls around on the floor.
Blood leaks steady from her shoulder. Olsen's body is right up
against her now making her lose what's left of her mind. Her mouth
opens but she can't breathe well enough for any noise to come out.

"Come on now," I say standing over them.

"Get away from me!" she finally shouts for all she's worth.

I lean over and take Olsen's Nikes off his feet. I look at the
tongue tag inside. Well, what do you know? They're my size. Didn't
even get much in the way of blood on them. I take off my boots off
and lace them up on his feet. I slip my feet into his shoes.

"I said get away, you fucker!" Jolie shrieks out, glaring up at me,
wiggling around, trying to put distance between her and Olsen.

I step around her and pull out a few more zip ties from the
drawer. Leaning down, I get a hold of her, reinforcing the ties on
her wrists and shoring up her ankles while I'm at it.

Her screaming nearly busts my eardrums. I'm grateful she's
making it easy. Any desire I ever had for her is gone.

"Go on an' let it out," I coo, smoothing her hair out of her eyes.

Her wailing turns into hacking and couging. I leave her there,
walk down the hall and take a minute to look at each room. Man, I
could've turned this place into something. Had a lot of ideas. Shame.
A damn shame.

My eyes fall on the lighter on my dresser. I'd still been lighting those pound cake candles from the mall over in Durham. If you cain't have a home, having your place smell like home's the next best thing. Covered the mildew smell of this place and reminded me of how our house always smelled. Jolie loves candles. Anything that smells like things you shouldn't eat is what she likes.

Taking the lighter in my hand, I remember I hadn't gotten around to getting gas for the mower. That would've come in real handy right now. Old as this place is though, the plan'll work without it. Jolie's somehow situated herself on the floor so she can look down that hall at me. I act like I don't see her and make for the back door.

"Cy! Cy!" Jolie's calling. "Don't leave me here, Cy! Please! Don't you—"

I slam the back door then take the porch steps two at a time. Turning, looking up at the old place, I click the switch on the lighter. I put it up to the edge of the stairs. It takes to it like it was waiting for it. In a few seconds flames climb up, covering the whole porch and engulfing the door.

If it wasn't already so damn hot out, it might feel good to stand this close to it. I've never seen anything burn but a fire in a fireplace or one of those controlled burns over at the nature park a time or two. Watching fire overtake the house one board at a time, my thoughts go back to what Jolie'd said about Cobb giving her my address. He'd gone out of his way to get it to her. I was wrong about him; he hasn't given up. I feel a little proud. Guess my being here's given him new lease on life. Not the kind I'd like, but we don't get to pick what spark we ignite in anybody.

What kind of partner does that make him, though? Only reason I can think of he'd do a thing like that is cause he knew Bobby'd turn on him. He knew Bobby'd give him up, and I'd be listening when he did.

The flames rise. The heat pouring off the house, the crackling of wood, Jolie's screams, all point me to what's next. I back up, crouch down, tighten up the laces on what were Olsen's Nikes. These have to be the most comfortable shoes I've had. It's true. The rich really do live better, right down to their footwear.

I whip around and set off running through the field. Going on foot'll send them in circles for a while what with all three cars out front and my boots on his feet. I know right where I'm going.

Yeah, it's time Cobb answers for everything, whatever it was that happened in his past, and for what he's caused to go down today. If he gets what's coming, I still might end up the hero. Ain't a much bigger fish in this town than Cobb. I take him down, hell, they'll probably give me his desk.

Picking up speed, I get into that track breathing coach taught us in junior varsity track and field. Only lasted one semester, but I still remember how to do it. Funny what's available to you when you need it. Things you think you've lost like how to run, how to help drag a body, how to destroy evidence or hogtie someone. I pump my arms. I'll be there before Cobb knows it.

43°F

Cobb

First year at the academy, a social worker came and talked to us about officer/civilian relations. That was when I learned the term *confabulation*.

"You mean lyin'," one of the other cadets smarted off to our guest.

"Not exactly," the social worker corrected. "Confabulation is when someone makes up stories to fill in gaps in their memory or replace something too painful. They rehearse these so much, they come to believe them. So, if you're questioning them, the way they see it, they're telling you their truth."

"Lyin'." The cadet leaned back and whispered in the direction of those of us sitting behind him.

Confabulation...that word fixed itself in my mind. My thoughts never wander far from it. I've looked back on that night out at Ducet a million times searching for whether or not that's what I've done—created a story to fill in or cover up. What do I remember? When did I last lay eyes on Kelly? Was it up by the stump where I woke up or back by the fountain where we threw rocks?

What was it Bobby said to me about what she'd told him? Why would any girl in their right mind walk in the dark alone on that road? There'd been the dirt on his clothes, on his arms and hands. His daddy's liquor had cast a haze over all of it that can't be denied. Not an excuse, just a fact. Maybe they're one and the same?

As a bloodied Hogue stood in front of me that night, I was again accosted with the reality that my version of the events back then differed from Bobby's. That whatever he might've told Hogue, I couldn't honestly refute it. I had no way to know if his truth was a lie or if mine was. Confabulation could've taken over both our minds causing us to believe our own versions. Each of us equally right to ourselves.

Since Hogue was standing there, it was a certainty Bobby's was the second body the captain had found in the ashes. I should've been happier about it. Picturing him laid out, burnt to a crisp. I somehow couldn't conjure up any emotion one way or the other. I'd known him my whole life. Bobby Olsen...*the* Bobby Olsen...gone.

Come the week after, there wasn't a soul within an hour of us who hadn't gotten wind of it. The devil'd broke the mold when he made Bobby. In Lee County, someone like him passed, they left a hole in the fabric of what it was that kept our world together. Wasn't anyone or anything sufficient to stitch it back up.

"Olsen was wantin' to make a trade," Hogue told me there in my dining room.

"A trade?" I echoed.

"So Rae's case'd get dropped. Said he knew where there's a body. Your wife's sister's body, out there at Ducket."

My eyes darted over to the hall for any signs of Stacy stirring.

"*Ducet*," I corrected.

"Yeah, that's it. He said he'd show me where if I close Rae's case."

I leaned against the doorway between our dining room and living room.

"He tell you how he knew where the body is?"

He shook his head again.

"We didn't get to that," he answered.

Of course they hadn't. I didn't know if I was more downtrodden that my torture was to continue or that I finally knew without a shadow of a doubt that Kelly was dead. Hogue set to pacing, tracking up Stacy's rug just spilling his guts. I couldn't keep focused for the life of me.

Watching him ruin that pretty carpet, I stood there, on the verge of a full-on heart attack. Bobby had said what I thought happened out there might not be what happened. While I was passed out by that stump, had he tried his antics with her, she wouldn't have it, and he got too rough? Had he?

"An' Jolie—Jo, she just showed up in the middle of it." Hogue went on. "Raced up in the yard. Jumped out totin' her grandaddy's shotgun."

It dawned on me they'd unplugged Leigh that day. Jolie's man must not've made it. A damn shame. I couldn't believe she hadn't sent her man's brother to serve Hogue up the justice due him. Couldn't blame her. I'd have wanted to see it through myself if I were in her shoes. I'd have wanted to see the look on Hogue's face as I blew a hole clean through him.

"Got no idea how she even found me," Hogue said.

He paused, staring at me blank faced, seeing what I'd say. I could tell he knew how she did.

"House sale, records?" I told him.

"No chance. Itn't in my name."

"Mitchum?" Stacy interrupted. "What's goin' on?"

I stared at her, raising my hands slowly to wave her off. She was propped against the door frame between the kitchen and dining room in an unnatural kind of stance. Her slightly opened mouth and furrowed brow showing outright bewilderment. Her right arm tucked in behind her. She was reaching into the kitchen. Knives. We had a butcher block of knives on the counter by the light switch. Her Daddy didn't raise no fool.

"I—I'm sorry to wake you, Mrs. Cobb," Hogue apologized.

He smoothed his shirt out of habit, not recognizing the ignorance of it what with all the blood. There was no making himself more presentable. There'd be nothing presentable about him anymore, if there ever had been.

"You must be Cy," Stacy said, all the while looking cautiously over at me, trying to get a feel of the situation.

"Yes ma'am."

She slipped her arm down. From where I stood, I saw her slide the knife into her robe pocket quick as lightning. I hoped that's where it would stay and even though I'd holstered up before I'd come down the hall to open the back door, I was glad she had her own means of protection. She stepped forward extending a hand.

Her hand looked so small hanging there mid air. Hogue reached out but stopped short registering the red stains on his hands. Stacy slowly let hers fall. She clasped both of her hands in front of her stomach, very mannerly like she was waiting in the line to talk to the pastor on the way out of church.

"Looks like you've had a night," she remarked. "Come on in the livin' room an' sit down."

Eyeing our beige couch, she immediately opted for the least stainable thing we had, pointing to the wooden dining chair closest to him.

"Naw. Tha's alright. I've ruined enough a your house."

The three of us stood, shifting slowly from one foot to the other. Her glancing nervously at me then at Hogue whose eyes were glued to his muddied Nikes. I swear Bobby'd worn the exact same ones when we'd met up in Raliegh for lunch.

Headlights shone in the front room window as a car turned onto our street outside spooking Hogue.

"Why don't I go an' get you one a Mitchum's shirts?" Stacy proposed.

"You don't have to," Hogue said.

"It's okay. Won't take but a minute. It'll be a little big, but it'll be better than what you got on."

As soon as she was out of sight down the hall, Hogue stepped closer, leaning in towards me so Stac wouldn't hear.

"Let's take a ride out there to Ducet," he whispered. "If Olsen was gonna show me, surely you an' me can find it together. We solve this thing, it'll look good on us both."

The faint smell of smoke came off of his clothes like bad cologne, and all I could see was his pretty Jolie who'd made me hash, screaming, beating on that old farmhouse door. I knew there was no helping her. Stacy was my concern. If he'd burnt up his own wife, he'd have no problem hurting mine.

"Itn't any need for her to be involved," I ordered, motioning in the direction Stacy'd gone.

We both looked down the hall, watching for her to reemerge from the bedroom.

"Sure, I gotcha," Hogue assured me.

Stacy didn't hurry. Eventually, stepping nearly without sound, she all but floated back to us like it was any other day. She always could play it cool. I loved that about her. Then again, sometimes it scared me to death.

She handed Hogue one of my t-shirts. He took it from her putting it on over the one he had.

Stacy and I looked at him.

"I uh, I hate to ask, Mrs. Cobb, you bein' so hospitable an' all, but I need to borrow Mitchum for an hour or two," Hogue told her.

"Oh?" Stacy questioned. "Where y'all off to?"

"Well, we—" Hogue stammered.

"Bobby told Cy about a lead we should follow up on," I explained. "Won't be long."

"I'll get my shoes," Stacy said, giving Hogue a polite smile, nodding to me.

"Stac, I don't think—"

"You're not wakin' me up this time a night an' leavin' me here, boys. I'll sit in the car," she told us. "I wouldn't get a lick a sleep no how. Why I'd just lay here all night, with my wheels turnin'. You know how I hate that, Mitchum."

Both of us stood, arms at our sides, dumbstruck, neither prepared to protest.

"I'll just be a minute," she said. "You won't know I'm there, promise."

She went back to the bedroom, slipped on a pair of boots. As we all three headed for the side door, I don't know how I had my wits about me to think of it, but I did.

"You already woke my neighbor up with those cans," I reminded Hogue. "You better sneak out the back, meet us on the Corner of Front an' 6th. We'll pull around an' pick you up."

"Good thinkin'," he agreed.

We walked to the back door. I opened it for him. He whipped around.

"Won't be the captain who pulls up will it?" He asked with wild little boy eyes.

I put a hand on his shoulder looked right at him.

"You know me to do anything underhanded like that?"

Stacy stood in the living room behind me, side doorknob in hand. He looked past me at her. It was a foolish question. Between his ex showing up at his place and whatever Bobby'd told him, he couldn't say he knew me atall, but now Stacy, with her baby doll looks, he was thinking surely, she wouldn't dare steer him wrong. I turned towards her and caught her up to speed.

"You know how nosy Gene is. I was tellin' him it's best for him to go on ahead of us out the back an' you an' me'll pick him up at the corner of Front an' 6th."

"Sounds smart. We'll see you over there, Cy," she confirmed, smiling at him.

This was Stacy's way, using first names, treating people like they were hers and always had been. An ease fell over Hogue. He nodded, giving her a half smile and nod in return.

From the way he bit his lip, I thought he might cry. I wondered how long it'd been since a woman had been the least bit kind to him. His feet no sooner hit that bottom back step when Stacy grabbed my arm.

"What in the world is all this about?" she demanded.

"He's in a bad way, Stac. Captain called earlier. They're lookin' for him. I gotta keep him calm an' soon as I can, I'll take him in."

"I'll tell you right now Mitchum, from everything you've told me, I know we've come too far to lose anything over this racist son of a bitch! He's not part of any future of ours."

"Let's just let him think he's got the upper hand til I can figure it all out, alright?" I asked.

Looking back on it, I should've wondered why Stacy just nodded and didn't make sure I called the captain before we left the house. We walked out to the car together. She in her pajamas and robe with boots on and me looking like I was ready to take my place in the unemployment line in a t-shirt and jeans. No one who knew us would've ever thought we'd leave our house looking that a way, but it wasn't a time for worrying about appearances.

We got in, me in the driver's seat, her in the back passenger side. We did our best to pull the doors closed gently instead of slamming them which would've brought Gene right to his front window. Not a soul was out and about. The night belonged to us.

Had we been out at that hour for any other reason, it would've taken me right back to those summer nights when we dated. When Stacy'd and I'd have to sneak around to meet up. Just the two of us cruising in my car, planning our lives, looking for the best gravel road to pull down so we could make out uninterrupted. Those nights were the last ones where I felt truly alive. So much ahead of us, crowding out what had come before.

"Remember when you used to pull around behind Daddy's over on Holt?" she asked. "We'd get to talkin' 'bout how life was gonna be an' we'd kiss some more."

I nodded, winking at her in the rear view even though I wished she was anywhere but setting there. I wished she wasn't going to be party to whatever it was Hogue had in store and what I'd have to do about it. In the midst of all that, her memory reminded me we shared one mind. Always had.

Rounding the corner, I saw him come out of the bushes and take his place on the curb. Under that streetlight, Hogue seemed like he was an extra in a rap video. My big shirt hung nearly to his thighs, his Nikes cementing the look.

"What's he think you're gonna help him find?" Stacy asked.

"God only knows. He's desperate, just reachin', Stac," I told her.

Slowing the car, I barely came to a stop before he reached for the handle, opened the door and jumped in.

His gaze immediately went to Stacy situated directly behind him.

"You could a had the front, Mrs. Cobb," he offered.

"I'm alright," she replied. "An' call me Stacy. Mrs. Cobb was Mitchum's mama. She wouldn't like me to use it. That woman never could stand me."

"Aww, don't feel bad, Stac. My mother-in-law hated my guts too," Hogue said. "Told me I was trouble from the word go."

"Were you?" Stacy prodded with a chuckle.

He put his arm up on the seat, nearly touching my shoulder, getting comfortable.

"Don't really like that word. I prefer to call myself *spirited*."

"My, that does sound better," Stacy shot back.

She leaned up, patting his arm.

"Sounds like somethin' trouble would say," she teased softly.

They shared a laugh. I smiled trying not to let my nerves get the best of me.

My hands were sweaty as they slid around the wheel, steering us down the vacant roads to Ducet. As we turned onto the street leading to it, I watched in the rearview while Stacy scooted up closer to the driver's side of the backseat. She looked out the back window like we were at some drive through zoo.

"This is where my sister disappeared," she said.

"What's that?" Hogue asked.

"My sister, Kelly. Went walkin' home on this road middle of the night one night. Never made it home," she said.

I could feel Hogue's eyes on me. I just drove. There was a disturbing feeling that whatever was transpiring, there'd be no heading it off. Oddly, I didn't want to. I had the notion that whatever justice was underway, it had been a long time coming.

Hogue cleared his throat.

"Well, Stacy, I may as well tell you that's why we're comin' out this way. See, Bobby Olsen, an old friend a Mitchum's, came to see me. He—uh, he said he could show me where Kelly's body's at."

My heart went silent. I fought cursing Hogue right then and there. I had no idea what Stacy'd do with this news or how Hogue'd spin it, if he was going to, so I wouldn't come out every bit as guilty as Bobby. The yellow lines of the road ahead kept coming. The engine never sounded quieter. I watched for Stacy's reaction in the mirror, sending up silent prayers to the Almighty. Those ones we all save for when our world is ending.

"I wish you'd have told me that at the house, Cy," Stacy said coolly, shocking the both of us. "Might've saved us all this whole little trip."

Her eyes met mine in the rearview. I knew that look. It wasn't one of surprise or anger. It was one of resolve.

"Bobby—well Bobby seemed pretty certain," Hogue sputtered. "He said—"

"Whatever he might've said, we have no way to know if it's true. Half this town, includin' my Daddy an' his friends, came out this way lookin' for Kelly. They all roamed these woods for days, Cy, an' nothin'," Stacy informed him. "Not a sign a her."

He faced forward watching the headlights reflect off the white lines ahead.

"Can't hurt to check one more time," he muttered.

The faint sound of the only R & B station to speak of in Lee County played over the radio. I hadn't registered it was even on when we got in. There was some rap playing that I didn't recognize. It was better than the silence.

Stacy edged up from the backseat, brushing her breasts against Hogue's arm to reach up and turn off the radio. He quickly put his arm down, his hands in his lap. She resumed her seat, though not as far back as before. I'm sure he could feel her breath on his neck.

"Cy, I know you say your mother-in-law hated you, but I bet it was nothin' like the way Mitchum's mama felt about me. Whew! That woman wouldn't a spit on me if I were on fire," Stacy circled around to mama again.

"Now that's not true, hon," I said out of habit.

She playfully popped my shoulder.

"Mitchum, you know it is! Hate itn't a strong enough word for it. If she saw me out an' about, she'd look the other way. You'd a thought I was trash the way she carried on. Couldn't stand the thought a her boy takin' up with a Black girl."

Hogue stared ahead, nervous as I'd seen him. From time to time, he'd rub his hands on his jeans, but it did little to take off the blood. I bemoaned the car cleaning I was going to have to spend my weekend on.

"She didn't help plan our weddin', didn't even act like it was happenin'. Wouldn't hear tell a his Daddy attendin' without her either," Stacy said.

"That's a shame," Hogue interjected like a full-blooded southerner does when someone admits something sad.

"Never said two words to me til about a month 'fore we were due at the altar. She was ate up with cancer by then. Mitchum's Daddy'd stayed with her as much as he could, but his boss told him if he didn't come back to work, his job was g'ttin' given away. They didn't have a soul to stay with her. I'd just graduated high school, had the summer off so she agreed to let me sit with her. That's how it goes. People'll stuff their hate down when they got no one else."

"True enough," Hogue agreed.

We were a mile and a half from Ducet's entrance at that point. The only stoplight on the road for miles turned green, clearing the way.

"Treated that woman sweet as pie. Watched her stories on TV with her, gave her a sponge bath, got her some clean clothes on, changed her bedpan, still, that whole mornin', she hardly said two words to me."

"Whatin as personal as you're makin it," I added. "She hardly said three words to me the whole last year a her life, Stac."

Stacy scowled. I couldn't blame her her. I was as taken aback as she was to find the good ol' Lee County boy in me still ready to defend his mama long after she'd passed.

"Oh, I wish she would've kept that up, kept her mouth shut. Wished I'd a made it out a there without her sayin' a word. I whatin that lucky. By the afternoon, she turned into a chatty Cathy."

Keeping my eyes on her in that rearview in between glances at the road, I had no idea where she was going with it all. I'd never heard about mama chatting her up and I sure as the world had no idea what bearing it had on the matters at hand.

"She wanted to tell me all about how shocked she'd been that Mitchum became a law dog. Said he'd had a place with his daddy at the mill an' he'd never mentioned the law to 'em before he up an' went to the academy. No, she said the only time Mitchum had even had any contact with the police was when they came out to their house couple mornin's after that girl went missin' his last month a high school. Said the cops talked to him an' his buddy Bobby cause as it turned out, they'd been last to see Kelly. *That girl* she called her. *That girl*."

As we neared the Ducet turn off, she slid up to the edge of her seat again, leaned in and put her left hand on Cy's shoulder.

"Now, Cy, that woman knew damn well *that girl* was Kelly an' that Kelly was my sister. She knew an' I knew damn well she only told me that to make me leave her son alone. She'd saved it up til the month 'fore we were due to get hitched to put it right in my face," Stacy explained to Cy softly, pain in her voice that I'd only ever heard when she talked dead babies.

I didn't look over at her. I couldn't. She tightened her squeeze on his shoulder. His eyes widened.

"But she didn't come between us, Cy. No, she didn't. See, no one comes between me an' Mitchum an' our plans," she hissed loudly in his ear. "No one's gonna mess up anything for us."

The sensation of liquid spattering across my face was what I felt next right before I felt Hogue's arm thwack me across the chest. Squinting my eyes clear, I rubbed a hand over my face. Looked down at my fingers and saw they were bloody! You don't ever forget the way another man's blood feels on your skin. It's different than how your own feels, thicker somehow and warmer.

I looked over to see Hogue's neck slit clear across, blood gushing from it. Stacy had him in a head lock against the seat for all she was worth, but she wasn't unable to keep him still. I took my foot off the gas and coasted to the shoulder, shifted into park. I threw myself over and held his arms before he could get a hold of her. I held his arms. His wild little boy expression gone from his face. A scared to death one taking over. He eyed me as he gurgled then breathed his last.

It was a labored kind of gurgling. Stacy's head was right up next to his as she hung on for dear life. In the weeks that followed, when we made love, I'd see his head next to hers right on the pillow beside her, even when I'd shut my eyes. Pretty soon, I saw that image no matter what I was doing—Hogue gushing blood.

Once he was limp, we turned loose of him. Stacy flopped against the back of her seat, the kitchen knife still in her small right hand. I moved over behind the wheel. We didn't talk. I started the car up and eased back onto the road, Hogue's body slumped over. His head landed on my shoulder like a bowling ball hitting hardwood. I left it there; the weight of it surprised me. Turned out it held more than I'd have guessed.

I turned into Ducet and parked by the fountain. The angel that had been on top of it from what I recalled, was gone. Only a partial broken off leg remained. Wherever it had gotten to, it was in a better place. Ducet was never a place for angels of any kind. There are times I wonder if the south itself is a place for any human being to call home what with all the demons who've staked their claim and made a home here.

Looking at Stacy in her bloody robe, I couldn't help but wonder what was left of the angel I'd married. Had she ever been that girl or was she just better enough than the rest of us that we assumed she was saintly? All the while, had she been this frightening child underneath? A bruised apple whose skin looks all shiny red, seeming ripe for eating til you get it home, cut it open and find rotted mush.

Stacy opened her door, gripping onto that knife. I pushed Hogue aside and opened my own door. The moon shone bright behind my bride as she walked over to the empty building and surveyed the broken windows. She didn't know her sister had helped break them. She did know her sister had broken us all.

"What was she like?" Stacy asked.

As soon as a reply started forming in my mouth, I knew that even though it was strange to flesh out after all that time, it would feel good to talk about her. I couldn't even remember the last time I'd said her name out loud...*Kelly*.

"Kelly? Well I—I didn't know her real well. I—" I hem hawed around, anxiousness taking over.

"What you did know of her, Mitchum. Just tell me about that."

"Well, she was tough."

Stac turned, moving her hair out of her face, and narrowing her eyes at me.

"Tough, but real funny an' sweet. Yeah, she was sweet, an' pretty. Kelly was very very pretty."

By the way she wasn't frowning, this seemed to suffice. We stood there in that moonlight taking each other in. Two strangers meeting for the first time. In retrospect, I think she was only a stranger to me. She'd known me all along.

"You know why I had to do it?" She asked, "Do you, Mitchum?"

I shook my head.

"Course you don't," she scoffed, looking at the ground, kicking at pieces of glass and gravel.

She took a few steps towards me. We walked slowly back to our car together.

"You never sat in the dark cause your Mama an' Daddy couldn't pay the light bill or wondered when your Mama might be back, if she was comin' back, an' if your Daddy'd come home too high to make it up the steps on his own. You never had your sister lie to you an' tell you that you were eatin' beef stew when you'd already seen the dog food cans in the trash an' not say not a word cause you knew she didn't have nothin' else to feed you, that she was doin' her best. Yeah, you were poor but not our kinna poor, Mitchum. Y'all hovered right on that poverty line. Me an' mine? We suffered way down under it. There's no way you could understand," she detailed.

"I'd say that's as fair an assessment as any."

We stood by the car, Hogue's body just next to us through the passenger side window. Stacy put a hand on the door handle, rubbing it with her bloody fingers.

"He wanted you to come out here so he could be the one to find her an' you know full well he'd a come out the hero one way or the other. For all he knew, you'd get locked up. It would've saved him, though. Sure would've saved his hide."

"I hear you, Stac, I do."

"I won't go back, Mitchum. Not to all that worryin', not knowin' where the next dime's comin' from. You hear me? I don't care what you know or don't know about Kelly, what you did or didn't do. I really don't. That may make me bad in some people's eyes, but I think it makes me a survivor. I'm a damn survivor, Mitchum."

She looked down at our reflections in the window, Hogue's body the backdrop behind them.

"You are too," she decreed. "You're a survivor."

There wasn't any going against her. She'd made up her mind.

"Let's get on with it," she said.

We pulled Hogue out, propping him up against one of the front wheels like a spare tire. I bent on one knee, leaned over, got his waist up next to my neck and hoisted him up onto my shoulders. An old move the coach showed us in workouts when we'd use sandbags at practice. Hogue felt just like one of those. I've always been stupefied by how a man can become no more than just a mass of weight in a matter of seconds. No more than a sandbag.

I could hear Stacy's boots snapping twigs as she walked behind me, feel the pressure she was applying by putting her hand up on Hogue's back to steady him. She needed to feel like she was helping. Didn't need the help, but I let her.

Up ahead of us, I saw the stump. It was still there! I saw myself setting up against it, could nearly smell the liquor. Kelly standing by it, her long beautiful legs so close I remembered wondering what she'd do if I reached out and touched one. Why had she come along? What would've possessed a girl to go off with two boys like me and Bobby?

We reached the riverbank. I knelt again, sloughing Hogue off onto the dirt by our feet. Looking to my right, I half expected to see Bobby and Kelly, running off down to the water. Had they swam? Had we all swam?

"I want you to know, the minute your mama told me that about you, Mitchum, about how the cops came, an' about you bein' one a the last to see Kelly, that it didn't matter. You hear me? It didn't matter," Stacy said. "It was forever ago, an' you're my sure thing. You're my ticket to food in my belly, a roof over my head, an' a life, some kinna real life. I knew then you were damn sure gonna be of more use to me on the outside than in some cell. Still are. You hear? You still are. An' you love me. Hadn't nobody else ever loved like we have."

We stood side by side, the stagnant summer humidity pooling on our foreheads. I knew I must look like Hogue had there on our back steps, blood streaking down my cheeks.

"Think anybody'll come lookin'?" Stacy asked wiping her own brow, smearing the red spatters into blurred lines with her sleeve.

"All Captain said on the phone was that he's in the wind," I said, still in shock of what all had transpired in the last hour.

"I hate it when you do that! I hate it when you answer a question with somethin' that itn't any kinna answer!"

Her hands were on her hips. She grew up in that second. I never saw her as a girl again. I wished I'd have had a warning so I could've truly gotten all the joy there was to be gotten out of my girl I'd loved.

"They might send out an A.P.B. Probly already have, but they don't have any reason to think he'd have come over our way."

"Good," she murmured, calming a bit. "That's good."

She stepped around behind me, slid her arms in around my gut, pulling me to her, nestling her head against my back. I stiffened up at first, not knowing the throat slicing woman latched onto me. The longer she held me, the more I softened. I'd always felt like I hadn't deserved her. That night, I came into the understanding that we deserved each other. More than that, we were meant to be.

"This is just one night. Just like that night out here with Kelly was one night. Just one. We're gonna keep livin' our lives. We'll keep livin' 'em an' try to help Daddy through it when he gets his mind set on ghost chasin'. He'll forget all about closin' the case when we have a baby. You'll see, Mitchum. He will. Babies make you forget everything bad."

I put my hands up on top of her arms, hugging her deeper into me, getting acquainted with my new Stacy, the new us. We'd been born again and though it had been a birth rent from violence, and we had no way of knowing it at that moment, it was the only birth we'd ever know.

"I want you to understand that I truly don't know," I said out into the night, more to the river than to Stacy.

"Don't know what?"

"What happened to her. I have no earthly idea. I'd had a lot to drink that night. I—"

"Sshhhh. Ssshhh. It's alright." Stacy assured me, "It's alright."

And it was. We used rocks and tied them into my big shirt, weighing Hogue's pants down as well, then we sent him out into that river. He sunk quickly. Watching him go, the branches out past him conjured visions of the dead deer. That night, in the trees, Kelly'd been disgusted by it. She had. I remembered that plain as day. A dead deer. That was something.

For whatever reason that was the only image from all those years ago that came back. How the mind picks what to keep hidden and what it throws back at you, I'll never have a clue.

Hogue wasn't found. The current had to have taken him way out. Not that anybody looked too hard for him. When people aren't worth looking for, well, they'll stay hid.

It was highly convenient for both of the police departments of Johnston and Lee County that he became just another of their mysteries. One of those rarely talked about southern quandaries that people mention in hushed tones every now and again, whisper about on sidelines of parades, or at church barbecues but that they never talk on long enough to pursue solving or bringing any closure to.

Stacy and me drove over to the all-night car wash in Vass. There was only one attendant on duty and luckily, they were busy on their phone. Didn't pay any mind to the two of us as we cleaned the car and sprayed ourselves down. We scrubbed and scrubbed on the blood in my front seat. It wasn't as hard to get out being so fresh, but I knew I'd have to take Stacy's car to work til I could do several more rounds of scouring the next few nights. It was a small price to pay for both of them being gone. I didn't quite know what to do without anybody left out there with potential to menace me the way Bobby and Hogue had.

In that moment, it felt freeing, yet there was a sneaking suspicion, that there'd come a day I wouldn't know what exactly to do with that freedom. Stacy hummed as she wiped down the hood, a reminder I'd never be totally free. She'd always know what all had gone on, at least with Hogue anyway, and that was okay. Too much freedom makes a man a god, and no man's prepared for that.

A wild hair came over me as Stacy finished wiping off her door. I sprayed her with the hose. She laughed, squealing a little. We laughed together. It felt good. Both of us playing around out there, fully knowing each other, as much as two people ever can. We owned the world—our little piece of it anyway. Nothing could touch us. I'd never felt like that with anyone. Don't think I ever will again.

I drove us home, our wet clothes saturating my front seats. We pulled in as far as we could in the driveway, snuck around back and stripped down on the porch, hid the clothes in a trash bag til we could dry them then burn them. The sun was peaking up over the trees. The two of us stood there in our underwear, taking in that sunrise.

I wondered by that time next year if confabulation would have again worked its dark magic. What story would we concoct to fill in our gaps, cover our pain? Would there be gaps, or just things we didn't talk about? If we didn't choose to remember, did any of it happen?

"It's beautiful itn't it, Mitchum?" Stacy asked, closing her eyes, the bright yellow rays of sunrise warming her face.

I reached down, taking her hand in mine, leaned in and kissed her cheek.

"Yes, it is."

The months that followed seemed a brutal punishment for what we'd done. Her Daddy died somewhat sudden. We thought he'd made peace with Stacy still not wanting to close Kelly's case, but turns out it wasn't peace at all. He went and fell off the wagon. OD'd in a hotel over in Smithfield.

I thought it'd nearly kill Stacy, but there was a part of her that was relieved. She said one of her Daddy's N.A. sponsors mentioned to her at Hicks' funeral that an addict's family never rests easy. There's no way to turn off the wondering, the questions of when or if they'll go back to it, he'd told her. I reckon it's the same for the family of someone who goes missing, always wondering if they'll come back the same way an addict's mind's always on that next dime bag. Addicts make addicts out of the people they love Hicks had told me this one time when he came back from N.A. He'd said your loved ones get addicted to worrying over you.

Though we didn't talk about all the business at Ducet with Hogue again, it made itself at home with us. There wasn't any need to relive it out loud. Not long after that last miscarriage, the doctor had told us it might be best if Stacy went on and had a hysterectomy so as not to do any further damage to her body. Once we got home, she'd wanted to soak in the tub.

"Soon as that doctor said that, Mitchum, I knew it was truth, but god damn it! I hate the truth! Just once I want to believe a lie. Just one time!" she cried, as she smacked the bathwater.

I didn't know how she'd overcome the verdict that her womb would be bare. I feared living with it would kill her in its own slow cruel way. As we drove home from the hospital after her hysterectomy, I thought she might dredge up Kelly, Ducet and Hogue. Wrap it all up as part of the darkness in her speech she'd usually give on those rides away from the hospital. Her speeches all about what kept her from being a mama. She didn't though. Didn't say not one word about it. I think by then it went without saying.

She died three days later of what the doctor deemed *unforeseen complications*. I didn't even get to say goodbye. I'd rushed her to the emergency room and pulled the car around after. By the time I ran into the hospital, the nurse up front had some confusion about where they'd taken Stacy. Once they got me to her in the E.R., she was gone. One of them had already pulled the sheet up over her. Only a foot stuck out from under it.

I gingerly lifted the sheet, moving it over, rubbing it. I thought of our Kelly…baby Kelly. About how I'd asked the doctor if I could see her and there her little foot had been, the only part that resembled anything looking like a baby. I couldn't help but notice Stacy's foot looked just like baby Kelly's had. I knelt down, leaned over, held my head in my hands. I cried for all I was worth.

Not long after Stacy's funeral, one of her aunts came by the house. I'd let the family have her ashes. Felt it was only right. She'd brought some of them back to me with a letter Stacy'd mailed to her right before her hysterectomy.

"If things go south with my surgery," the letter stated. *"I want my ashes scattered. Mitchum'll know the spot."*

"Thought it was real morbid, her talkin' bout dyin' at her age. I mean a hysterectomy itn't a operation most die from," her aunt remarked. "When I called her up an' asked her was she alright, she said she was just makin' plans was all, that anytime anybody goes under the knife it's best to leave some directions just in case. Said everybody should get a say about where they're laid to rest. Like she just knew. Beats all don't it?"

So I took my Stacy to that river. For the third time in my life, I stood at its edge out back of Ducet. Cradling her remains in an urn under my arm, I knew her punishment had been the loss of being a mother, the loss of all those little lives, and finally the loss of her own. I knew in that moment, mine was to be the loss of her, of everything that'd ever meant anything. I crouched, poured her into that tar colored water, watching as she swirled through it.

Staring at its murky depths, it became clear no matter what I'd done or hadn't done, remembered or hadn't remembered, this life had made damn sure I paid up one way or the other. Sure as anything, nobody, not even an old law dog like me, ever gets off easy in a world like ours.

91°F

I
t was pitch black outside. The deep charcoal kind of blackness
that swallowed up girls making sure they were never heard
from again. Kelly was too young and optimistic to know this. She'd
left the boys and set out down the driveway with every intention of
making it to the road then the gas station. Daniel would be up. Yes,
she'd call him.

They hadn't talked on the phone in a couple of weeks, but he'd
answer. They all answered when she called. He'd drive over to pick
her up. He was what her dad called a good ol' boy. He wasn't at all
like the jokers she'd been with all evening. It was too bad he lived a
town over. All the ones worth their salt, lived at least a town or two
away.

As she walked, she tried to exude the same don't mess with me
type of strength she did in the daytime. Each step strong and steady,
though her mind was anything but. The reasons she was out there
on that back country road became more and more hazy. She'd
wanted to tell Bobby about Anita's news. She'd wanted to see his
face when she told him. That plan hadn't really gone the way she
wanted. Her fear had gotten the better of her.

From the woods to her right there came the distinct sound of twigs snapping. She froze. It happened again, only louder. She turned and took off back down the road in a full-on sprint. She'd heard the way back to anywhere seems longer than the way there. On that night, she experienced it first-hand. The entrance to Ducet seemed to elude her. She wondered if she had missed it, and then it appeared just ahead of her. A dim streetlight shining on what was left of its sign:

Ducet
A place to grow and change

An age-old dilemma took hold. The one of the known being less terrifying than the unknown. Pumping her arms, she flew right past it. Mitch's car was still where he'd parked it near the building. She slowed a bit, taking deep breaths, looking all around for the boys. A bright red *Exit* sign shone over one of the front doors to the hospital. She was surprised she hadn't noticed it before. Had she not been so arrested in her fears, the sign might've served as the warning it should've been.

As she neared Mitch's car, she saw the passenger side door was open. A leg was dangling out with a Nike on the foot. She crept close enough to peer inside. Bobby. Sure enough, there he was, slumped against the seat, snoozing away. The slovenly position suited him.

The leaves and brush bent under her high-tops but didn't snap. Her Converse were not made for any real treading, not made for walking miles. They were for school halls and shopping centers. The stark white laces were so bright, they glowed, lighting her way back to Mitch. She washed her laces on a regular basis. Cleanliness was something a poor girl, a girl like herself from the apartments over behind the Food Lion, could maintain if she had access to a washer and some soap. Her cleanliness was one of the few things Kelly could hope to ever control in her world.

Mitch hadn't moved an inch. She assessed that Bobby and he

must've finished off the liquor and Bobby'd left him there to make off for better sleeping arrangements of his own.

"Mitch!" she hissed, shaking his shoulders. "Mitchum! Wake up!"

She wasn't certain why she was doing her best to be quiet, except maybe to ensure Bobby didn't wake. She hoped they'd make it all the way home without him stirring, until she was ready to talk to him again, approach him about her offer, hers and Anita's. Shaking Mitch's shoulder once more time, she did not succeed in waking him, only caused him to slide over, head meeting soil, his lower back still against the stump.

"Jesus," he groaned.

She sat down atop the stump, reaching over, helping to right him again.

"Sorry," she whispered.

A leaf stuck to the side of his neck. He reached up with his stubby hands and swatted it off.

"What time is it?" he asked, once words found him.

His head felt as if it was not attached to his body, as if he could remove it and hold it out in front of himself like a jackolantern.

"Don't know," she answered.

And she instantly wished she'd have agreed to wear the watch her aunt had given her last Christmas. With it being from the Dollar General, it hadn't made the cut of what she'd actually want to be caught dead in. She'd left it on the dresser. There were lines she'd drawn in her life. Not many, but a few. Looking less fortunate with a junkie watch was not one she was willing to cross, not yet.

His right hand slowly found his forehead, a headache from the liquor setting in, already working its torture.

"Guess you don't hold yours too good," Kelly mused.

Mitch shook his head much like a dog who'd hopped from a tub would shake off its body after a bath. This made her laugh.

"After games, we usually stick to lightweight stuff. Coors, Buds, even some a those Mexican beers from La Hacienda over on Highway 1."

"Better stick to that from now on."

An owl hooted from across the river several times in succession. A glint of silver shone through the leaves. He reached over, recovering the flask so it didn't get lost. Bobby'd be wanting to sneak it back into his dad's cabinet. He shook it hearing nothing. It was empty.

"You finish it?" he asked her, holding it up.

She shook her head.

"Nuh uh. Better ask your boy about that," she shot back.

"Where'd he get to?" Mitch grumbled looking behind them.

"Up there. He's sleepin' it off in the car."

Mitch grunted, opening the flask, turning it upside down over his mouth as if he was a man who'd been stranded in a barren desert. Nothing came out. He huffed, setting the flask on the stump. His head pounded. Only another stiff drink could set him right. The poison and the cure...

She walked out ahead of him all the way to the embankment, surveying the river. The water made Kelly think of Ms. Essex, her science teacher and how she'd taken up money last month for the oil spill cleanup off the Gulf of Mexico. When the bowl had been passed Kelly's way, she'd not put in a dime. She'd fought the urge to take a bit for herself to feed her and her sister that night. The teacher'd raised an eyebrow, passing it to the next student. Kelly recalled thinking that it was real nice of Ms. Essex to care about the animals dying there and all, but she and her little sister, Stacy, still had to eat. What about them?

What Kelly felt Ms. Essex didn't know was that caring was a luxury. Being able to think about other things besides where your next meal will come from, or if your Dad's friend might stay after your dad goes to bed one night and force his way into your room, or if your Dad's car will break down again causing him to lose another job, was not her reality. She'd felt a happiness creep in that day in class, that there were those like Ms. Essex who could take up such causes, yet wondered when someone might take up her and her family's cause. It seemed a certainty to her that she and she alone had to take it up.

"A little help?" Mitch called.

She walked back, extending her hands. He braced himself against the stump letting Kelly pull on his arms as if they were a tug of war rope. Her palms felt so soft and smooth. It hung over him that this was likely the only touch he could expect from a girl as pretty as she was. Gradually, he found his way to a standing position. A dizziness mixed with a nausea threatened to take him down to the ground. Sheer will ferried him over by her, however. He stood next to her looking out at the river.

Stealing glances of her, there in the moonlight, he was awestruck by her. So light skinned. The kind of light skinned that made her own hate her but not light enough to open any doors far enough with his kind. Her features were small and petite. To him, if he hadn't know better, she looked white. He wondered if she'd *pass* if he up and decided to take her to see his mama. First, Kelly'd have to give him the time of day.

"I'm guessing Bobby's got the keys," she said.

He felt his pant pockets hurriedly sticking his hands down in then whipping them out again. Nothing but his wallet. Every movement heavy and difficult, feeling as if it was the last movement he'd make.

"That's alright. We'll let him sleep," she sighed.

"Won't anybody be wonderin' after you?" Mitch asked.

"My daddy won't be home from his shift til nearly eight in the mornin'. My sister Stacy's stayin' over at our Aunt Sheila's. She itn't old enough to be left alone. They don't trust me with her by myself yet," she explained. "I'm glad. Shouldn't have to take care of her. I whatin the one who had her."

"Go on with your bad self," Mitch teased elbowing her.

"Don't you worry. Nobody's *wonderin'* after me. You're stuck with the pleasure a my company."

Out of the corner of her eye, she saw his boyish smile. She liked him. Yes, she'd like him ever since they'd moved to Sanford, watched how he was in their classes. Always respectful to the teachers. When others lunged, he hung back. When someone yelled and carried on, he kept his tongue.

No, her beef was not with him. No, she was intent on holding Bobby's feet to flame not Mitch's. After all, Anita hadn't mentioned him. How Mitch had ended up with a friend like Bobby, she was sure she couldn't understand. It was Bobby, she could simply not abide.

A breeze blew the smell of the dangling dead deer in their direction. The odor much like the night's unfolding events—at first barely discernable then strong and putrid all at once. They looked out at it, both dismissing what a fitting metaphor it was. Both fearing, what with its limp legs and rotting flesh, that it said everything there was to say about life in their county.

"I do wonder how that ended up there?" Mitch said aloud, covering his nose with his hand.

"How's anything end up anywhere?" Kelly replied.

The river gurgled over rocks calling her, beckoning her. She and her sister rarely swam. Her family could not afford to be part of any club and in Lee County, the country clubs had a monopoly on pools. *One day...* she often thought, one day she'd wear a bright red swimsuit and walk into one of those places wearing big glamorous, red framed sunglasses...*one day.*

In a moment of unfettered spontaneity, the kind most teenage girls are prone too, Kelly put her bag down on the bank. She took off her Converses, slipped off her skirt, next her top. Mitch did his best to look away.

Before he knew it, she stood next to him in her underwear. He felt she must want him to look. She was muscular, more like one of the Amazonian warrior women in his Wonder Woman comic books. The ones he kept hidden under his mattress as a boy, that he still ogled on occasion.

"Come on!" she beckoned as she took off down the bank and into the river.

His headache was unrelenting. He knew he wasn't sober enough to swim. He also recognized this was not an experience a young man like himself should pass up, hungover or not. Some things were worth the risk of drowning. He would not deny himself this fodder for locker room banter, even though his days in the locker room were numbered. It was also a tale that when retold would stick in Bobby's craw. He'd never let it go that he'd slept through it in the car while it took place.

In short order, Mitch's clothes lay next to Kelly's. In only his boxers, he made his way down the water. The river bottom felt slimy between his toes. He tried not to grimace as he made his way out to her. For a summer night, the water's cool temperature was perfect, offering slight relief from the heat.

Kelly was out ahead, not far from the deer. Mitch reached her vicinity, keeping a few feet between them. He joined her in gazing up at it.

"Makes me sad," she told him. "Thinkin' about it drownin' in the flood water, seein' it up there like that, where it don't belong."

"Yeah," Mitch added, not having the faintest idea what she was going on about as he was preoccupied with stealing eyefuls of her breasts, barely hidden by her wet bra.

"That's sposed to be one of the worst ways to die," she said. "Water g'ttin' all up in your lungs. Awful! Don't it make you sad?"

He nodded, though didn't have a real reply. It made him sad for different reasons he knew would sound stupid to her. That deer could've fed him and his for a week or two. When he looked at it, hooves dangling above them, he saw waste.

"You know what else'll make you sad?" Kelly asked, moving her arms through the water.

"What?"

"Goin' up to Dorothea Dix, seein' all those crazies," she replied. "That's where Anita is. Up at Dorothea Dix."

Nausea joined in with his headache. Even his stomach seemed intent on causing him embarrassment. He rubbed it with one hand underwater to calm it. Anita...in the nut house? And he knew without asking anything further what had put her there. The instant feeling of her legs around his hips in the backseat of Bobby's car came over him. He was glad Kelly could only see him from the shoulders up. It was one of those times he hated his body, with its sick mind of its own and its sleezy reactions.

"That's why Bobby won't talk about her. He knows she's settin' up there with his baby in her," she said wading a bit further from him.

"What'd you say?" Mitch asked.

"You didn't know? He don't know that I know, but she wrote him a letter. Told him all about it, asked for his family to help. He didn't give two shits," Kelly informed him.

Mitch ran a hand through his hair, slicking it down with the filthy water.

"Well, maybe he didn't get it, maybe—"

"He got it. He called her house pretendin' he was just some friend from school an' when she picked up, tol' her she was crazy. Said his family couldn't be havin' a half breed baby in it an' not to ever write him again. Tol' her to forget she knew his name. He said she was nothin' to him an' that's how it'd stay. Had the nerve to tell her it might not even be his for all he knew." Kelly fumed.

He pushed the water with his hands, creating swirls next to him, wishing they'd take him under, carry him down the river, spit him out anywhere else but there.

"How does she know it's his?" he questioned.

She whipped around.

"A girl god damn knows these things, Mitchum. You hear? A girl knows!"

Raising his hands up, he nodded. He couldn't argue with her. No, he'd never tell her about that night. A night when Bobby had again brought his Daddy's flask. What was there to tell really? He knew they'd both done things with Anita in the car, that she'd whimpered at first. They all whimpered at first. They all liked to seem like they weren't up for it. His father passed that tidbit along to him, that girls can't act like they want it. Not the nice ones anyway. As she'd grabbed for the door handle, Bobby'd held Anita's hands together and laughed. Those were things Mitch knew readily, those and how her legs had felt around him. She had not whimpered then. She had not made another sound. She'd stared of out the window til he finished.

"Anita hung up from that call an' lost her mind, Mitchum. She just lost it. Her mama had to call the cops to come get her. She was tearin' the shit out a their place, talkin' like she was gonna kill herself. Didn't even tell nobody 'bout the baby til we visited her up there. They gave her some kinna drugs cause she looked calm as could be settin' there. Tol' me all about it. I think I'm the only one who knows how it happened," Kelly continued.

"You saw her?" Mitchum asked.

She nodded.

"A couple times. When we was by ourselves, she talked all about what he did. Said she kept yellin' no, an' he wouldn't let her out of the car. Won't tell her mama or daddy who her baby's daddy is, just me. Soon as she said it to me, I knew I cain't let him get away with it. It's all on me. I'm gonna make damn sure he gets what's comin'." she decreed.

As she babbled on about the hospital, what it looked like there, how white everything was, Mitchum was transported. That night with Anita had been different. She had waited out back of the gym, there with the gaggle of girls who lingered like cattle at an auction, every game night, hoping to be chosen. Anita too was hoping to be picked.

Before then, she'd only flirted a little with them in class. He and Bobby hadn't even remembered her name. She was cute enough, though not particularly memorable. That night she had been. She had been because she was the only Black girl who'd ever dared mingle in amongst their usual waiting fans. Her bravery had impressed them.

"I wondered if y'all might give me a ride?" Anita'd asked after they'd done all the back of the gym flirting that could be done before evolving into more.

Mitch had been reticent. He had not wanted to be seen with her, but Bobby had grinned at him. It was that grin he had that promised more. Mitch knew it was already set in motion. Even as they helped her into the backseat, Mitch knew. He knew Anita was not aware of what asking for a ride home from them meant. She'd been feeling grown and had wanted to try her hand at being a woman. Not many of them ever bargained for the side of being a woman that Bobby showed them.

Before Anita, he'd never been in on that part. Most of the time, he'd had Bobby drop him off at home, or he'd gone for a walk and left them back at the car together. That night with Anita would have been no different, but Bobby'd brought along the liquor and Mitch had been unusually tired. He was tired of holding himself to a different standard than his cohort. He wanted to know what it felt like to live as if everyone was there to serve you—to live like Bobby. The liquor had helped him to do so.

A splash of water doused his face. Kelly swam by, splashing him as she put her feet down, standing upright.

"Don't you fall out in this water. I'm not that good a swimmer," she warned.

He splashed her back. She giggled.

"She keepin' it?" Mitch called to her.

It wasn't at all what he wanted to say. He wanted to apologize, for his friend, for himself, for all of it. Why had Anita left him out of the confession? Had she drank with them and hadn't remembered about him as well? Had she?

He knew the part of him that wanted to apologize, make amends, was not the bigger part. His go to modes of protectiveness, and self-preservation took the reins. His loyalty had an eerie automaticity. In that moment, there was not even a decision process between his ears, if there ever really had been. That's how it was being friends with Bobby. There was no apologizing, only loyalty, and damage control.

Her face hardened.

"That's what y'all always wanna know, itn't it? *Keepin' it*. Like it's a thing, an' not no baby. Like it's just up to us an' y'all ain't had nothin' to do with it." Kelly snarled. "All y'all are ever worried about is evidence."

"That's not—"

"Oh, I know. I know, you just want what's *best for everybody*," she mocked in a cruel, demeaning tone that took him aback.

Her hair didn't stay slicked to her head long. It sprung up in little tendrils around her face. He wished he could touch it, touch her. He longed for their night not to be going the way that it was.

"She just wants to forget the whole thing. Wants to give that baby up to the state. I told her that ain't right. That baby needs her, an' I'll help her. Hell, why you think I came all the way out here?" Kelly sassed.

And there it was, he thought. The reason she'd hung around with them when she'd never paid them any attention before. She was there for the baby. She was there to strike a deal.

"Once your boy wakes up, I'm gonna tell him how it's gonna be. He's gonna pay for that baby, send a check every month right to Anita's house. If he don't, I'm gonna tell his whole family an' everybody in this trashy town all about what he did to her. We're gonna get one a those tests, prove it's his. You got that an' a judge'll make him pay up. I told her if you're gonna go an' get yourself raped, least she went and got raped by a rich motherfucker. That's somethin'."

A paternity test? Was she talking about a paternity test? Raped? Who was saying rape? She became blurry as she flitted about again in the water, on her back and then doggie paddling. She was enjoying telling him how it would be. It was clear it all made her feel powerful. Something about that made him hate her.

"She was a fuckin' wildcat!" Bobby'd exclaimed about Anita that night when they'd finally dropped her off.

She'd stood in front of her house on the sidewalk, tear-streaked face, sniffling, staring back at them, a hollow shell of who she'd been outside the gym only hours prior. Bobby'd waved to her and smiled as they pulled away like they'd all been out on a big date. Though Mitch had been drunk off his ass, he did recall feeling how strange it was to have done what they did and then wave, acting as if it was nothing, as if it was natural. Acting as if it was what she'd wanted.

Anita's house had been pitch dark that night. That was vivid in his memory as well. No one was waiting up for her, just like no one would be waiting up for Kelly. He marveled at how he and Bobby seem to know who would have no one waiting up. It was as if they possessed a kind of primordial predatory sixth sense.

A crow swooped close to Mitch's head, landing on one of the waterlogged deer's antlers. Had he paid attention in literature class, he'd have taken it for the same eerie sign that Kelly did.

"Creepy," she whispered looking up at the bird, putting her feet firm on the river bottom. She did her best to steady herself as the water swept around her, threatening to knock her small form off balance. The water no different than this world, tossing her this way and that.

She leaned her head back, smoothing her hair down once more. Mitch was sure this moment, her there right in front of him nearly naked, wet haired in the moonlight, was the closest he'd ever come to being in a movie.

"I don't have to tell you Bobby itn't exactly what you'd call *Daddy material*," he heard himself say.

It was not at all how he wanted to respond. No, in a perfect world, he'd confess his love for her, tell her they could run off together, go down to a courthouse in South Carolina, get hitched, then he'd take care of her. He'd tell her they'd take care of each other for the rest of their lives. There'd be no more Bobby Olsens or cousins in nut houses with illegitimate infants. Somehow, he'd make sure they had a good life. A pretty life, free from those ugly things.

"Oh, you got that right," she laughed a hateful cackle he wouldn't have thought her capable of. "Won't matter. That baby don't need a daddy. That baby needs what every baby in this fuckin' country needs—money. An' once his mama an' daddy find out what their little Bobby's gone an' done, they'll pay out big just to keep people from ever knowin'. Yeah, that money's gonna give that baby a chance."

"At what?" Mitch asked.

She stared at him as if this was supposed to be obvious. He immediately felt stupid and inadequate. There were no two feelings he loathed more. He cut his eyes at her. She had not come along at all because she liked him. No, though still inebriated, he saw it clear that he could have been there or not. He was inconsequential. She'd have gotten in the car with just Bobby. He was her mark. Mitch was a bystander. His whole life he'd been just that.

"That baby'll get a chance at havin' somethin'. That baby gets that money, Anita might get a nice house. Never know, if that baby's real lucky, there'll be enough for a house an' college. Anita an' them can get the hell out a Lee County that's for sure."

As soon as she said it, it was blatantly obvious. The night had blanketed Mitch in an amnesia. He'd forgotten that Bobby was from another world entirely, a world that could give a baby a life while Mitch himself was one rung above Kelly on the ladder of have and have nots. He was on the white side of that rung, but there all the same. If the paternity test proved the baby was not Bobby's, the baby would be no better off. His family had nothing to give.

The more seconds that passed, Mitch saw that there'd be no clear winner in the situation. To be made to take the paternity test, charges would have to be brought against Bobby. Would his friend rat him out, drag him along, telling anyone who'd listen that he had not been alone in showing Anita the repercussions that came from being part of their behind-the-gym entourage? Would he too then be forced to take a test? He could not say, and it got all over him that after all their years together, he couldn't. He felt given the same situation, he'd never tell on Bobby. So many times, he'd never told.

He made his way for the shore as Kelly continued her swim. A loud splash so loud he thought the deer had dislodged and fallen in made him whip around. There she was—Kelly flailing, hands in the air as she struggled, bobbed up then went under. A misstep on a piece of glass, maybe a sink hole or a leg cramp?

Hurrying out to her, he reached down in the water at the last place he'd seen her. Several times he repeated this with no result. At last, he felt a shoulder, pulling her up. She spit water, hacking and coughing in his face. Clinging to him for all she was worth. Their eyes locked. At first hers held a tender thank you, yet as she looked further into his, her pupils widened with panic.

His hands gripped both her shoulders as she kicked at him. He dunked her down, again and again. After the first two or three times, his hands acted on their own, as if speaking a language he was not privy to. A language void of words. Ones like *guilt* or *rape* or *paternity*.

Sooner than he expected, she slipped from his grasp down, under the current. He stood tall, muscles taut, the water swirling around him as if he'd always been a fixture there. And he had—him and his kind. The Mitchum Cobb's and the Bobby Olsen's who presided over every small southern town carrying on traditions long lauded below their blessed Mason-Dixon line. Traditions that had no room for girls like Kelly or Anita or babies wanting chances.

The crow cawed, alighting from the deer's antler, as Mitchum watched to ensure that Kelly did not reemerge. He kept his sights half on the river and half on that black bird in the air worried it might swoop him. The same bird would later circle back, bearing witness as Mitchum wandered up onto the bank, slipped on his clothes. It would stand watch on a branch as he hazily made his way over to his stump and sat against it in a stupor til sleep again assuaged him.

It would caw every few minutes, letting its presence be known as the other boy, a boy the crow had not seen yet that evening, hurried down, from the parking lot, to shake the sleeping one.

"Mitchum! Mitchum, wake up! God damn!" The boy shouted.

It was to no avail. He stood looking down at the pile of clothes, the pair of black and white Converse. He ran to the river's edge, raised a hand over his eyes, searching.

The winged spectator, would indeed be the only one to see that boy, run down into the water, wrestle with something in the brush as it was being dragged by the current along the bank. He emerged with it—the body of the pretty girl. Circling, and swooping, the bird came dangerously close to the boy as he studied the bank, spotted what was needed then dug away at an old drainage filter half covered with roots. Once he'd made enough room, he shoved the girl's body inside, being sure to include her clothes and shoes alongside her. Stuffing it all in so unnaturally as if she and her belongings were an inconvenient bag of garbage. He then carefully covered the filter just as he'd found it.

At last, seeing that he was to have no peace there that night, that no one was to have any peace there any night, the crow alighted. He trusted his instincts and wings to take him to a quieter nesting place, leaving the two boys behind. One still obliviously poised against the stump. The other resting on the bank, brushing dirt from his clothes, wiping the sweat from his forehead with his shirt, contemplating the best version of what all had transpired, letting confabulation work its way.

ACKNOWLEDGMENTS

A big thank you to to my editor, Michael Dolan of Winding Road Stories, who when I queried him with one not quite up to snuff, asked "What else are you working on right now?" That just so happened to be the beginning of *Temperatures*. I so appreciate that he greatly believed in my work. His supportive editorship helped me to push through.

Special thanks to:

Author Elaina Battista-Parsons (@Bravelrene77) for her friendship, enthusiasm, encouragement, and support.

Author Heather Levy (@heatherllevy) and her ongoing inspiration, friendship, writerly support and pre-read enthusiasm.

Author Alexander Nader (@AlexNaderWrites) for all his time given to reading it and his great suggestions.

Brett Burk, beta reader extraordinaire, an avid reader and friend who also lent time he didn't really have to help me catch some of the last errors and offer insights.

Major props to so many other writers/readers whose work has spurred me on or who've dispensed constructive advice to me over the years. (S.A. Cosby, Sam Reed, Anthony Gedell, Doug Stuber and many more, if you follow me on Twitter, you'll undoubtedly meet some of them there).

And of course, last but not at all least, a big thanks to my husband, Chad, who has never let up on loving me, cheering me on and supporting me in my life and work since we met. There are no adequate words to be able to express how much it means that he's never turned away from "us" even when the first rung of the ladder broke (he'll know exactly what that means).

ABOUT THE AUTHOR

"The South becomes an encapsulated version of the core of the complication of what we are."

Imani Perry author of *South to America: A Journey Below the Mason-Dixon to Understand the Soul of a Nation*

Suzanne Crain Miller was born, raised and still resides in the Carolinas. Her writing is heavily influenced by having grown up in the south with all its many paradoxes.

Temperatures is her 8th book.

Follow her Twitter: @TattooedDaughtr

Follow her on Instagram: @Tattooeddaughter

Subscribe to her blog: Tattooeddaughter.wordpress.com

CPSIA information can be obtained
at www.ICGtesting.com
Printed in the USA
JSHW022302200523
41779JS00010B/154